Pleasure
SEEKERS

Pleasure SEEKERS

Rochelle Alers

sepia™

PLEASURE SEEKERS

A Sepia Novel

ISBN-13: 978-0-373-83036-7
ISBN-10:   0-373-83036-X

www.kimanipress.com

Printed in U.S.A.

Dedicated to my editor—Glenda Howard

CHAPTER 1

The pool room at the Four Seasons

"Tell me what's wrong with this picture, girlfriend? I'm a young, educated, professional black woman living with a man who says I'm everything he wants in a woman, yet he refuses to commit."

"Alana Gardner, we're celebrating your birthday dinner, and I don't want to spend the next couple of hours listening to you bitch and moan about Calvin McNair."

The glow from a votive candle turned Faye Ogden into a figure of shimmering gold when she leaned over the table. The flickering flame flattered the burnished undertones in her tawny-brown face and highlighted the gold in her eyes, and the short texturized hair dyed an attractive blond color.

"What's wrong is that you've allowed a trifling ass, no-account Prince wannabe to shack up with you while he waits for his big break. Damn, girl, that parasite will hang around until he decides he wants out, then he'll go off and marry someone half his age and live happily ever after. You know what Oprah says, 'Show him the door!'"

"That's easier said than done, Faye."

"Whose name is on the lease? Yours or Calvin's?"

"Mine, of course."

"Then it should be easy for you to get rid of him, Lana."

Shaking her head in disbelief, Faye stared at Alana. Her best friend was tall, full-figured and drop-dead beautiful, but the talented magazine editor had always sought attention from the wrong people. Her live-in lover may have been what Alana wanted, but Calvin couldn't or wouldn't *ever* offer her what she needed most for emotional stability.

Shaking her head, black curly hair moving sensuously over her shoulders, Alana folded her arms under her breasts. "I can't."

"You can't? Or you don't want to?"

Alana picked up her wineglass and took a deep swallow. "Why are you being a bitch tonight?" Her dark, slanting eyes narrowed.

"You think I'm a bitch because I tell you what you don't want to hear? Grow up, Alana. You turned thirty-three last week, and the dog you call your man didn't even have the decency to come home."

"He was rehearsing at the studio."

"And you believe *that?*"

"Why shouldn't I? I love and trust Calvin."

"You house him, feed him, wash his clothes, then spread your legs whenever he wants a free *fuck!*" She'd whispered the expletive. "And he couldn't give up strumming a guitar for a few hours to celebrate your birthday with you? I'm not being judgmental, Lana. I've been there. I divorced a man who cheated on me because he didn't even try to hide his indiscretions. I loved him, too, but not more than I love *myself*. You're going to have to make your mind up whether you love Calvin more than you love Alana."

"Are you sure you haven't been eavesdropping on my therapy sessions?" Alana's eyelids fluttered as she blinked back tears.

Faye smiled. "Quite certain. You're my sister-girl, Lana, and I want to see you happy."

Sniffling, Alana blotted her eyes with a cocktail napkin. "Are you happy, Faye?"

There was a pulse beat of silence before Faye said quietly, "Yes, I am."

"I don't know how you do it."

"Do what?"

"Abstain."

"I don't miss what I don't have." Looking up, Faye caught the eye of their waiter. "I'm going to order a bottle of champagne."

Alana's full lips parted in a smile, exhibiting teeth she'd spent a small fortune straightening and whitening. "What are we celebrating?"

"Your birthday *and* our friendship."

"I'll drink to that."

CHAPTER 2

Enid had heard enough, and signaled her waiter. "Please let Alain know I'd like a word with him."

"Yes, Ms. Richards."

The maître d' approached Enid Richards's table. "Yes, madam?"

Enid beckoned him closer. "Alain, tell me what the two women sitting behind me look like." Her voice was low and mysterious.

"They are very beautiful, madam."

Enid smiled, realizing her internal radar was as sharp as ever.

She reached into her purse, took out a small monogrammed silver case and removed two business cards and a pen. She scrawled *Please call me—E* on the pale blue vellum.

Handing them to Alain, she said, "Please enclose my cards when they're given their check."

Eavesdropping on Alana and Faye's conversation and a second cocktail helped ease Enid's annoyance with the figures in the binder in front of her.

A cell phone rang at a nearby table, and Enid stared at

the man who'd neglected to turn off the ringer. The Four Seasons' hard-and-fast rule of No Cell Phones was strictly enforced. After the first infraction it wasn't unusual that subsequent reservations were denied a patron because the distraction impinged on the restaurant's reputation of dining in a peaceful atmosphere.

Her glance strayed from the table, and she sat up straighter, all of her senses on full alert as she watched a tall, impeccably dressed black man approach her table.

She inhaled the tantalizing scent of Marcus Hampton's specially blended cologne as he leaned over and kissed her cheek. Enid met his direct stare, an unconscious smile softening her mouth.

"Sorry about being late," he apologized. "I would've called, but their policy about no cell phones…" His words trailed off when he saw the inviting look in Enid's eyes. "Perhaps," Marcus continued, "the next meeting should be at your place."

Enid patted the leather seat. "Please sit down, Marcus. Would you like a cocktail before we order dinner?"

Marcus wanted to tell Enid he needed more than a drink. He needed her. "Yes." He gave his drink order to the waiter.

Enid noticed the frown line between Marcus's large gold eyes. It wasn't often she saw him scowl and it bothered her because the expression marred his near-perfect face.

Obsessed with beauty and perfection, she'd found herself momentarily mute four years before when first introduced to Laurence Marcus Hampton at an art auction in Sag Harbor, Long Island; they'd exchanged business cards. A month had passed before Marcus called and invited her to another fund-raising event with him.

She'd accepted his invitation, and over the next three months they slipped into a relationship that was socially beneficial for both of them.

Then everything changed when they left a snowy New York City to spend a week on a private island in the Caribbean, sleeping late, drinking potent tropical concoctions and endlessly making love. Marcus was the first man who'd shared her bed, Enid realized, whose libido surpassed hers. The fact that at fifty-six she was twenty-two years his senior was of no consequence once they merged business *and* pleasure.

Enid picked up a menu and handed it to Marcus. "Order for me, please." Marcus's black eyebrows in an equally dark face lifted.

Enid smiled, knowing she'd shocked him with the request because she never permitted anyone to make a decision for her. But tonight was the exception. Her earlier frustration had diminished within seconds of her eavesdropping on the conversation in the other booth.

She stared surreptitiously at her dining partner. Marcus was the epitome of tall, dark and handsome. His slender proportioned physique, angular sable-brown face with chiseled cheekbones, strong nose and firm mouth afforded him fashion-model status. His large, deep-set, gold-flecked eyes were his face's most noticeable feature. Their color, so incongruent to his dark complexion, glowed with a light that mesmerized her.

She smiled. L. Marcus Hampton was her lover and business partner. He controlled her in bed and she controlled him out of bed. It had become a win-win combination.

CHAPTER 3

Marcus's face relaxed as he studied the entrées. During the time he had come to know Enid Richards intimately he'd never presumed to make a decision for her. In bed he neither conferred, debated nor compromised.

"Rack of lamb and steamed asparagus."

Enid pressed her back to the banquette. "Excellent choice. What are you having?"

"Couscous and a salad."

"Are you back on your vegetarian diet?"

"Only until the end of the month. I'm alternating two weeks on, two weeks off red meat."

When she reached over and covered Marcus's hand, she felt his fingers tense before relaxing under her light touch. "What's wrong?"

Marcus met her direct gaze. "Nothing. Let's eat, then have our meeting so I can go home and finish grading papers."

He knew he hadn't been truthful. There were a lot of things wrong with their relationship. Whenever Enid summoned, he came running, responding to her like Pavlov's dog to his master's bell.

He'd tired of playing the game she played better than

any woman he'd ever known. She ran Pleasure Seekers with the dogged determination of a CEO of a Fortune 500 company; however, along the way, Marcus felt as if he'd become one of her clients. The only difference was, she paid him for his services, not the reverse.

Enid sat up straighter, her eyes narrowing. "To save time we can discuss business while we eat."

"It's your meeting."

She went completely still. Something *was* bothering him, and he had just lied to her. If they'd met at her office or in her home she would've pressed the issue, but not here.

Her delicate jaw hardened. "Well, I compared April figures to March, and profits are down. We picked up two very wealthy clients last month, and you predicted business would increase."

Marcus reached for the binder, flipping pages. "We've already discussed this, Enid. Did you read the activity schedule? The overall number of contact hours is down ten percent. They've been on the decline for the past six months."

Enid stared at the monthly percentages. "They're always off between Thanksgiving and Valentine's Day, but pick up again in the spring." Her gaze shifted to Marcus's impassive expression. "Tell me, if you were a client of Pleasure Seekers, who would you like?"

Marcus took a sip from his cocktail, savoring the blend of scotch and vermouth on his tongue before the liquor slid down the back of his throat. A hint of a smile played at the corners of his mouth. The bartender at the Four Seasons made the best Rob Roy in Manhattan.

"None of your ladies."

"Why not?"

Marcus leaned closer, the fabric of his suit jacket grazing her arm. "Because they're not my type."

"Would a woman your hue be more your type?" Smiling, she rubbed her thumb over the back of his hand.

He returned her smile. "Yes. But you're the only exception, Enid."

She flashed an attractive moue, bringing his gaze to linger on her rose-colored lips. "I've never denied being black."

Now his hand covered hers. "But you don't advertise it, either."

"Would I have gotten this far if I'd hung a sign around my neck advertising my race?"

He continued to stare at her mouth. "No."

Do you know that you look a little like Lena Horne? Enid lost count of the number of times she'd been compared to the legendary singer/actress. She acknowledged their physical similarities, but there were also differences—hair and eye color.

She had inherited her looks from her father—a white man she never knew, a man who'd seduced her teenage mother, gotten her pregnant, then moved his family out of Jefferson Parish when he'd been told he was to become the father of a mixed-race child.

Janetta Richards died within hours of delivering Enid,

so she never met her mother. And she would've become a ward of the state of Louisiana if Darcie Richards hadn't come to claim her grandchild.

But Darcie's attempt to obtain legal custody of Enid was challenged by a social worker who felt Darcie unfit to raise a child. She had become the subject of an ongoing police investigation over rumors that her rooming-house business was a front for other illegal activity.

Darcie called one of her customers—a judge, and a week later Riva Enid Richards slept in a third-floor bedroom of the large white house in Storyville under the watchful eye of a live-in wet nurse.

The judge's intervention was repaid with barter. Darcie offered him lifetime privileges at her place of business: the pick of any of her girls. Unfortunately his copious sexual appetite and an aphrodisiac purported to enhance and sustain sexual desire proved a fatal combination. A week following his signing documents giving Darcie Richards legal guardianship of her granddaughter, he died from a massive coronary.

Enid smiled as she sipped her martini. It felt ironic that after retiring from a successful law practice, she'd started up a business similar to her grandmother's.

Both offered women to men for a price.

However, there was a difference.

Darcie Richards had sold sex.

Enid Richards sold companionship.

CHAPTER 4

They're not my type.

Taking furtive sips of her martini, she pondered Marcus's statement.

The women who worked for her escort service weren't *his* type, but her clients, staggeringly wealthy men from all races and nationalities who demanded long-legged, slim-hipped, large-breasted blondes and redheads. Months ago Marcus had suggested she hire social companions of color, but she'd resisted, not wanting to upset the status quo.

Now the contact hours were down, the company's profits were also down and she knew she had to act quickly to counter the slide.

"What are you hatching in that beautiful head of yours?" Marcus whispered in her ear.

"I've been thinking about your suggestion."

"Which one?"

"I've decided to take your advice and diversify."

"What brought on this epiphany?"

Enid smiled mysteriously and told him about the conversation she'd overheard before he arrived.

Marcus traced the rim of his glass with a forefinger. "I know someone who would be perfect for Pleasure Seekers."

"Who?"

"Ilene Fairchild."

"The supermodel? Tall, thin, with waist-length hair extensions. To say she's stunning is an understatement. Is she available for an interview?"

Marcus took his time answering, smoldering over Enid's "sudden interest" in adding black women to her stable of pale-skinned beauties. After the third month in a decline of contact hours he'd suggested she include women of color, but she'd only agreed to think about it, and it had taken six months and a steady decrease in profits for her to *think* about it.

"Probably not for another week. She's in Vegas shooting a music video."

"Have her get in touch with me." Enid's voice was soft *and* firm.

"I'll see what I can do." He decided he would talk to Ilene and feel her out before having her contact Enid.

Ilene was only one of a number of beautiful women he'd met since becoming financial adviser to three hip-hop record-producer cousins, young men he'd grown up with in Westchester County.

The trio had made inroads into the music industry while he'd buried his head in accounting manuals. Their lives had taken different directions, but a chance encounter at a Mount Vernon block party had brought them together again.

Vincent, Derrick and Anthony Warren had amassed a small fortune, lived large, but had neglected to pay taxes on their earnings. They came to him with letters from the IRS with amounts owing over seven figures. He filed five years of back taxes for them while negotiating for lower interest rates and penalties.

The Warrens gave him A-list access to video shoots, studio rehearsals, concerts, backstage, launch and after-parties, all of which he politely declined.

He taught accounting and business courses at a New Rochelle community college, partnered in Pleasure Seekers and now managed the finances of three record producers. Enid was aware of the first two ventures, the latter, he kept secret for now. His entrée into the world of rap and hip-hop gave him the one advantage he needed to become Enid Richards's equal partner—in and out of bed.

CHAPTER 5

The waiter placed a small leather binder on the table in front of Faye. She glanced at the bill, and then reached for her handbag.

Alana picked up one of the business cards in the binder. "What's this?" The pale blue vellum was high-quality paper. She noted the engraved initials P.S., INC. and a telephone number with a Manhattan area code before she turned it over.

"Is someone playing a game?"

Faye read the message on the reverse side. "It sounds interesting."

"I'm going to ask the waiter who gave these to him."

Faye waved her hand. "Forget it, Lana." She dropped one card into her handbag. "It's not the first time someone has passed me their business card anonymously."

Alana's waxed eyebrows lifted. "Really? I always dine out when I interview people for my magazine column, but I've never been the recipient of an anonymous introduction. What do you do with them?"

"I hold on to them for at least a month, then I have my

assistant call the number. It usually takes about a minute to discern whether it's business or personal."

"How many times has it been business?"

Faye slipped a credit card into the binder. "Only once. It didn't start out that way. After I told my secret admirer that I was in advertising, he admitted to starting up a new company and needing someone to assist with a marketing campaign."

Resting an elbow on the table, Alana cupped her chin in her hand. Her dark eyes sparkled. She always loved listening to Faye talk about the quirky people she met as an account executive.

"Was that an excuse to get you into bed?"

"I'll never know. I got his account without sleeping with him."

"Was he a brother?"

"No."

"White?" Faye nodded. "Would you have slept with him?"

Faye rolled her eyes at her friend. "Hell, no. The day I resort to sleeping with a man to land an account is the day I change careers."

"Then why did he give you his card?"

There were times when Faye found it hard to accept Alana's naiveté. "He was curious, Lana. He'd never dated a black woman, and going out with me under the guise that it was business related made it all right in his book."

"So, you never dated him?"

"No. Whenever we met it was strictly business." She held the other card close to her nose. "A woman wrote this. The perfume smells familiar."

"Oh, shit! Don't tell me we're being hit on by a woman," Alana whispered, frowning.

"Not necessarily." Faye stared directly at Alana. "I'm going to call Mr. or Miss E and find out what they're selling."

"I'm not feeling the name P.S., Inc. It sounds a little kinky to me."

"It could be a new magazine."

Snatching the card from Faye's fingertips, Alana tore it into tiny pieces and dropped them onto her dessert plate like confetti. "Whatever."

Faye signed the credit card receipt then glanced at her watch. They'd been at the Four Seasons for more than two hours. "I don't know about you, girlfriend, but I overindulged on champagne tonight. I'm taking a cab home. I'll drop you off on the way."

"You don't have to do that," Alana protested. "Why should you ride crosstown with me when we're already on the east side?" Her apartment overlooked Central Park and Faye's the East River.

"I don't mind."

Alana shrugged a shoulder. "Okay. Suit yourself." Gathering her handbag off the leather seat, she pushed to her feet and adjusted the hem of her dress. The black knit fabric hugged every curve of her full, shapely body. "I'll take care of the taxi."

Following suit, Faye slipped her arms into her jacket. Smiling, she drawled, "Whatever."

Both women walked out of the restaurant as a pair of blue-gray eyes watched intently.

CHAPTER 6

Faye flagged down a taxi within minutes of walking out of the restaurant. "Go through the park at Sixty-fifth, then head north to Ninety-second Street," she told the driver. The directions were barely out of her mouth when the cabbie took off with a burst of speed.

"Damn," Alana whispered, holding on to the edge of the seat. "We're not in *that* much of a hurry to get home." It was apparent the driver heard her because he slowed down considerably.

When the taxi stopped across the street from Alana's building she leaned over and kissed Faye's cheek, while pushing a bill into her hand. "Thanks for dinner."

Faye smiled at her. "Anytime."

The driver got out and opened the door for Alana; he stared as she strutted across the street in a pair of pumps that added three inches to her statuesque figure. Her one hundred eighty-five pounds, evenly distributed over a five-foot-nine-inch frame competed with her face and thick raven-black hair for attention.

Faye had met Alana two years before during Fashion Week. The two women had bonded quickly. Alana had covered the event as the American-based lifestyles editor for *British Vogue.*

Alana had become her sister, confidante and, at times, her conscience. She was artistic, generous, honest, unpretentious, and there wasn't anything Faye wouldn't do for Alana Gardner.

"Where to, miss?" the cabbie asked Faye after Alana disappeared into her building.

"Ninety-fourth and First." She braced herself as he accelerated recklessly into the flow of traffic, sped northward, then reversed direction and drove back to the east side in record time.

Faye paid the fare on the meter, along with a generous tip, smiling at her building's doorman as he opened the rear car door for her. She exited the cab with an audible sigh of relief. She had survived another wild New York City taxi ride.

The doorman touched the shiny brim of his maroon hat. "Good evening, Miss Ogden."

She nodded at the elderly black man who always had a friendly smile and warm greeting for the building's tenants. "Good evening, Mr. Bennett."

CHAPTER 7

Faye walked into the richly appointed lobby of the prewar high-rise apartment building and removed the day's mail from her mailbox.

Everything would have been close to perfect if not for her brother's incarceration. Craig Jr., or CJ as he was affectionately called, had been found guilty of raping a married woman who purportedly had slept with a number of men in their Queens neighborhood.

CJ's conviction coincided with her divorce, so Faye had to grieve twice—for the loss of her brother's freedom and a union she'd gone into believing it would last forever.

The incident had caused a rift in her family. Craig Sr. had insisted on retaining the legal services of a friend to defend his son; within days of the arraignment the defense attorney accepted a plea rather than go to trial.

Against the vehement wishes of Faye and her mother, Craig Sr. convinced his son to accept a sentence of five to eight years in prison in lieu of a possible fifteen to twenty if found guilty by a jury. Another downside of the plea was CJ had to serve five years before he was eligible for a parole hearing. He had just completed his second year.

Faye stopped talking to her father or visiting the house where she'd grown up in the Springfield Gardens, Queens, neighborhood. She only called her mother when she knew Craig Sr. wouldn't be there.

The last time she'd shared dinner with Shirley Ogden, she informed her mother that she'd begun an exhaustive search for an attorney willing to appeal the case. What she did not tell her mother was that she'd found one, but his fees were exorbitant. She'd completed the application to secure a loan against the equity in her cooperative apartment, but it still wasn't enough to cover his fee; her long-term goal to use her property as collateral once she set up her own advertising agency for black-owned businesses had become very, very long-term.

The doors opened and she stepped into the car, pushing the button for the fourteenth floor. The elevator rose quickly, silently, and soon the ride ended.

Faye made her way down the carpeted hallway to her apartment, unlocking the door and walking into a spacious entryway that opened out to a sunken living room with a panoramic view of the East River and Long Island City.

She'd accepted the one-bedroom, one-and-a-half-bath co-op as a divorce settlement in lieu of alimony, and it had soon become her sanctuary—a place where she shut out the sounds of the city.

The overstuffed club chair with a matching footstool in an alcove off the living room was where she read, composed copy, watched television, listened to the radio and meditated.

At home she spent more time in the den than she did in bed, although there'd been a time when she'd spent entire weekends in the king-size bed with her oral surgeon ex-husband making love and being loved.

A wry smile twisted her mouth as she placed her keys and handbag on the small table next to the chair, her gaze lingering on a family photograph.

Kicking off her heels, Faye sat down, raised her feet onto the footstool, closed her eyes, covered her face with her hands and willed her mind blank. Her hands came down quickly as she opened her eyes. The scent from the anonymous card lingered on her fingertips.

A knowing smile softened her features. She was familiar with the fragrance because her firm had designed an aggressive holiday marketing campaign last year for the classic perfume.

She reached into her handbag for the card. The delicate loops in the letter E and the navy blue ink confirmed that a woman had written the message.

And there was only one way to decipher the cryptic message from Mr. or Ms. E.

This task she would not give to her assistant.

She would place the call herself.

Tomorrow.

Lowering her feet and pushing off the chair, Faye made her way into her bedroom and adjoining bath. She lit half a dozen lavender-scented candles on a table, turned on the water in the tub, removed a jar of bath salts off a built-in shelf and poured a generous amount under the running water. The lavender fragrance filled the air as she stripped off her clothes, leaving them on a padded bench in the corner.

Faye then went through her nightly ritual of cleansing the makeup from her face and brushing her teeth before she settled into the lukewarm water for a leisurely soak.

When she climbed out of the bathtub forty-five minutes later, she was completely relaxed, her mind free of everything that had gone on in her life for that day. She blotted the moisture from her body with a thick velour towel, then walked into the bedroom and crawled into bed.

The cool air coming through the vents of the air conditioner whispered over her naked body, raising goose bumps on her flesh, but Faye didn't notice it. She had fallen asleep.

CHAPTER 8

Leaning back in her chair in the sun-filled office, Faye stared out the window. The sounds coming ten stories above Third Avenue were still audible. She'd spent the past couple of hours revising copy for a family-style restaurant chain whose executives wanted an inviting hometown theme for their upcoming Thanksgiving and Christmas holiday sales pitch.

Swiveling, she faced her desk, her gaze lingering on the legal pad. She'd listed more than two dozen words, crossing out some and circling others. The ones that remained were: *small town, Main Street, winding roads,* family members that ranged from great-grandmother to an infant. The idea came to life in her head when she decided to include a young soldier in desert fatigues who surprises everyone when he walks into the restaurant to share Thanksgiving dinner with his extended family, while meeting his infant son for the first time. The camera would zoom in on his wife's face as tears of joy fill her eyes. She hands him his son as the music swells.

Picking up a pencil, Faye scribbled: background music—jazz, R&B or gospel. Singer: soulful voice. She was partial to "I'll Be There," off the Dave Koz CD *The Dance*. Massaging her forehead with her fingertips, she put the words together like puzzle pieces, adding and deleting sentences and phrases until they flowed like the lyrics of the sensual love song.

The soft buzzing of the intercom broke into her concentration. She pushed a button, activating the speaker feature. "Yes?"

"Do you want me to make any calls for you before I leave? I'm going out with the others to celebrate Monica's engagement."

"No, Gina. I'm good here."

"Do you want your calls to go directly to voice mail?"

"No, I'll take them. Have fun."

"Thanks, Faye."

She pressed the button again. Picking up the pale blue business card she'd tucked under the telephone, she dialed the number. The call was answered on the second ring.

"Good afternoon, P.S., Inc. This is Astrid. How may I direct your call?"

Faye lifted her eyebrows. The woman who'd answered the telephone had a beautifully modulated voice. "I'd like to speak with either Mr. or Miss E."

"That would be Ms. Enid Richards."

She was right about the perfume. "May I speak with Ms. Richards?"

"I'm sorry, but Ms. Richards is on an overseas call at the moment. Is it possible for her to call you back?"

"Yes," Faye said, before she could change her mind.

Closing her eyes, she gave Astrid her name and cell-phone number.

"Thank you, Ms. Ogden. Ms. Richards will return your call."

Faye hung up, leaned back in her chair and studied the items in the office that had become her second home. There were no diplomas on the walls or family photos on her desk and credenza. She had established the practice of keeping her private life just that—very, very private. No one at Bentley, Pope and Oliviera knew of her divorce until she updated her personnel file, and her brother's dilemma was something she refused to discuss with anyone.

She'd decorated her office with bamboo shoots in colorful ceramic pots, framed prints of the firm's award-winning marketing campaigns and a watercolor she'd purchased from a Harlem street vendor.

A headhunter, retained by the executives at BP&O had courted her for several months before agreeing to her salary demands, and her association with the prestigious advertising agency had been beneficial to her and to them. They won a Clio the year she signed with them, and they'd picked up another three since that time.

Faye knew why she'd been given a corner office, a higher commission than her counterparts and her choice of accounts. She was responsible for all marketing programs targeted at the African-American consumer. She'd become so proficient at what she did that she now wanted to open her own agency.

Her cell phone rang twice. Reaching for it, she pressed the Talk button. "Ms. Ogden."

"Ms. Ogden, please hold for Ms. Richards." Faye doodled on the pad as she waited for the mysterious Enid Richards.

"Ms. Ogden. This is Enid Richards. How may I assist you?"

Faye's eyebrows lifted before a slow smile parted her lips. The mature-sounding voice coming through the earpiece had a distinctive southern drawl. She'd also noticed that Enid said *assist*, not help.

"That's what I should be asking you, Ms. Richards. Someone at the Four Seasons gave me your business card last night."

"I was that someone, Ms. Ogden. I'd like to meet with you to discuss a business arrangement."

Faye's smile faded as she sat up straighter. "What type of business?"

"That is something I will not discuss over the telephone."

"If that's the case, then I'm going to hang—"

"Please don't," Enid said quickly, cutting Faye off. "I can assure you that what I'd like to propose to you is legal. It is an arrangement that will prove advantageously beneficial to you *and* my company."

Enid Richards's evasiveness should've set off mental warning bells, but Faye found herself intrigued with the velvety timbre of the woman's voice.

"When and where do you want to meet?" she asked.

"I'll leave that up to you, Ms. Ogden."

She glanced at the planner on her desk. She hadn't scheduled any meetings for the afternoon or evening. "Tonight at six, Café de Artistes." She knew she hadn't given Ms. Richards much notice, but if she were truly sincere then they would meet at her convenience.

"I'll make the reservation in my name," Enid said quickly. There came another pause. "Thank you, Ms. Ogden."

Faye wanted to tell her thanking her was a little premature, but said, "You're welcome, Ms. Richards."

CHAPTER 9

Enid arrived at Café des Artistes at five-thirty and requested a table giving her a view of anyone coming through the door.

She'd always thought the artsy eating place naughty *and* boisterous. A place not to conduct business, but to have fun. The murals of frolicking nymphs painted in 1934 by Howard Chandler Christy added to the joie de vivre of the venerable upper west side restaurant frequented by notable theater and media personalities.

Ignoring the goblet of sparkling water on the table in front of her, Enid's eyes widened as she watched the woman heading toward her table.

Faye Ogden was petite with a full lush body that did not have one straight line. The short blond curls hugging her head like a cap matched her eyebrows, the color flattering and brightening her light brown face and eyes.

Enid's penetrating gaze moved from Faye's head to her feet in one sweeping glance. Tasteful makeup, pearl studs in her ears and a matching strand around her graceful neck, a tailored black linen gabardine single-buttoned jacket and slim matching skirt ending at her knees, and a pair of black leather sling straps that bore the same designer label of a few in her own closet. She had tiny feet, slim ankles and curvy calves. Faye Ogden was perfectly exquisite.

Pushing back her chair, Enid came to her feet and extended a hand. "Thank you for coming, Ms. Ogden. I'm Enid."

Faye shook her hand, finding the grip firm and confident. Why, she thought, was Enid thanking her when she'd been the one to set up the meeting? It was apparent that the tall, slender ash blond–haired woman was either overconfident or presumptuous.

"Please call me Faye."

Enid smiled as she waited for Faye to sit before she sat down again. "Then Faye it is. Would you like to order a cocktail?"

"No, thank you."

Enid gestured to a bottle of mineral water. "Will you share the water with me?"

A hint of a smile softened Faye's mouth. "Yes."

With a slight lifting of one pale eyebrow, Enid caught their waiter's attention. She touched her goblet with a finger as he approached the table. The waiter turned over Faye's glass and filled it, then retreated, standing a comfortable distance away.

"Would you like to discuss business over dinner, or would you prefer we finish eating?" Enid asked.

"Over dinner is okay with me," Faye replied.

Enid pretended interest in the menu as she took surreptitious glances through her lashes at the woman she hoped to sign to Pleasure Seekers. She did not think of Faye

Ogden as classically beautiful, but her flawless complexion, coloring and compact curvy body would make her a
standout among the blondes and redheads who worked
for her escort service.

Faye found everything about Enid Richards intriguing.
It was hard to pin down her age, but the saying that
"black don't crack," certainly applied to Ms. Richards.
And despite her fair coloring, pale hair color and
European features, she knew the owner of P.S., Inc., was
a sister-girl. In fact, Enid resembled a great-aunt who'd
moved from Georgia to California, and once there elected
to pass for white.

Working in advertising gave Faye another advantage.
She was able to identify products without seeing their
labels, and Enid was a walking advertisement for understated elegance: gold Cartier watch, Mikimoto pearl
earrings and necklace, Armani suit, Prada shoes and
handbag. She loved Armani, but found the cut too slim
for her generous hips. Therefore, Donna Karan had
become one of her favorite designers.

She glanced at the menu and decided to order a salad. Her
head came up and she found herself looking into a pair of
large, deep-set blue-gray eyes. She thought of Alana's statement that they were being hit on by a woman but quickly
dismissed it. Enid wasn't staring at her the way men did.

"What are you looking for?" she asked, deciding direct-
ness was always better than being evasive—especially
with a woman. "Or should I ask, what are you selling?"

Enid went completely still. Whenever she interviewed a prospective social companion for Pleasure Seekers, she always took charge of the discussion. This was the first time she'd found herself on the defensive and she realized immediately she had to adopt a different attitude when interacting with a woman of color.

"Let's order, then we'll talk," she suggested. There was no way she would permit Faye Ogden to control *her* meeting.

CHAPTER 10

Faye gave the waiter her order, then sat staring at Enid. Her former curiosity had become annoyance. She didn't have many pet peeves, but evasiveness was one.

"Why did you give me your card?"

Enid ran a hand over the back of her neck, massaging the muscles under the blunt-cut, white-gold waves ending several inches above her shoulders. Her tension had returned despite a full body massage earlier that morning.

Lowering her hand, she focused on Faye's mouth outlined in gold-orange lipstick. The younger woman had no idea how appealing she would be to her clients.

"I'd like you to work for P.S., Inc.," Enid said, deciding it was time to be direct with Faye.

Faye blinked once. "I already have a job."

"Where do you work?"

"I'm in advertising."

"Does it pay well?"

"Well enough," she said, refusing to disclose how much she earned.

"Six figures well?" Enid held up a hand. "You don't have to answer that one."

Faye leaned closer. "What is P.S., Inc.?"

"Pleasure Seekers is an escort service."

"Are you asking me to become a prostitute?" She stared at the woman with the sultry voice and cool blue-gray eyes.

"No," Enid said softly. "I told you what I propose is legal. Besides, if I were running a prostitution venture I'd never hire you. I'd consider you *too* old and much *too* intelligent. Men pay hookers for their bodies not their brains."

"Should I take that as a compliment?"

"Yes, you should."

"Well, I don't consider thirty-two old, even for a prostitute. What are you selling, if not sex?"

A small smile of enchantment touched Enid's lips. "Social companionship, my dear. My clients are men, extremely wealthy men who are willing to spend thousands of dollars an hour, day or even a week for my social companions."

"That's it?"

"Why? Do you want more?"

"No. I…I just don't understand."

"There's not much to understand, Faye. It all comes down to supply and demand. I would never ask that you give up your career or day job to work for Pleasure Seekers. You can begin with weekends or one or two nights a week."

"Why me?"

Picking up her glass, Enid took a sip of water, her gaze meeting the gold-flecked one over the rim. "I overheard the conversation between you and your friend last night at the Four Seasons and—"

"You were eavesdropping on a private conversation?"

"Only after I heard your voices."

"What about our voices?"

"I knew you were black women."

"What's the saying? It takes one to know one, Ms. Richards," Faye countered, her eyes glittering like polished citrines.

The skin around Enid's eyes crinkled as she smiled. "Touché, Ms. Ogden. How did you know?"

"You look a lot like my grandmother's sister."

There was something about Faye Ogden that piqued Enid's curiosity. "Is she passing?"

Faye nodded. "Are you?" she asked, knowing she'd surprised Enid when her expressive eyebrows lifted.

"No. If they don't ask, I don't tell." Reaching into her handbag, she took out two envelopes and placed them on the table next to Faye's place setting.

"I'm hosting a party in Soho this weekend. I'd like you and your friend to consider attending."

"Why?"

"I'd like a little diversity."

Shaking her head, Faye stared at the famous murals. "You *need* diversity." Her gaze swung back to Enid. Pleasure Seekers needed women of color and she needed money for CJ's appeal.

"You're right, Faye. I do need diversity. I'd like you to come to the soiree because it will give you the opportunity to meet my clients and the other social companions who work for P.S. And I'd like you to consider the possibility that you can earn upward to five thousand dollars a day as one of my exotic jewels."

"How much would I get?"

"Forty percent."

Faye sat up straighter, an expression of satisfaction shimmering in her eyes. Pleasure Seekers needed black women and she needed money—a lot of money.

"Make it fifty and I'll think about it."

A powerful relief filled Enid as she extended her right hand, and she wasn't disappointed when Faye took it. She knew she was in no position to negotiate a difference of ten percent. It was either fifty or nothing.

"Everyone who signs with Pleasure Seekers receives a thousand-dollar tax-free signing bonus. For everyone you refer and we sign, you'll get an additional thousand-dollar bonus.

"You'll have to attend an orientation session where you'll be apprised of what is expected from you as a social companion. There are also documents that will require your signature."

"What kind of documents?"

"Tax and bank information. Payments will be processed through electronic deposits, and at the end of the year you will receive a ten ninety-nine for your gross earnings. Your bonuses, of course, will be tax free."

Faye felt a newfound respect for Enid. She had what she'd overheard young kids say, that *she had her shit wrapped mad tight*. There were other questions she wanted to ask her, but decided to wait for the party and orientation.

Their entrées arrived and Enid and Faye ate while discussing local and international news, films and the scandal involving a senator's wife. Someone had uncovered evidence that as a college student she'd played major roles in several hard-core porn films.

Enid touched the corners of her mouth with her napkin. "All she has to do is admit to the accusation, then go on with her life."

"Do you think it'll be that easy for her?" Faye questioned.

"It will if she tells the truth. No one respects a liar."

Faye agreed with Enid. Once she had confronted her ex-husband about his discretions, he didn't lie to her. His admission diffused her rage, and made it easier for her to face reality and move on with her life.

Now her reality was that she needed money for her brother's appeal, and Enid had come to her with an offer she couldn't refuse.

She would work for Pleasure Seekers long enough to earn what she needed to pay the attorney to overturn her brother's rape conviction, then she'd focus on setting up her own advertising agency.

Her mouth curved into an unconscious smile. She couldn't wait to call Alana and tell her about Enid Richards.

CHAPTER 11

"Lanie, baby. Wake up! I've got good news for you."

"What?" she mumbled.

"I made it, baby. I'm going to Europe with the band."

Rolling over, Alana sat up, blinking against the light coming from the lamp on Calvin's side of the bed. "What?" she repeated, suddenly wide awake.

She stared into Calvin McNair's dark eyes before her gaze inched lower. She loved his firm lips, dreaded shoulder-length hair and goatee. She had fallen in love with the talented bassist on sight when she'd gone to a Greenwich Village jazz club with Faye.

She'd returned to the club the following weekend—alone, unable to believe her luck when Calvin approached her table and introduced himself. A week later he moved into her apartment.

They were compatible in and out of bed, but Calvin refused to discuss what she wanted most: marriage. She wanted marriage and he fame.

"What did you say about going to Europe?" Her pounding heart slammed against her ribs.

Cradling Alana's face between his palms, Calvin

brushed a kiss over her parted lips as her warmth and scent swept over him like a sensual fog. He loved her, her passion and her generosity, but not as much as he loved his music.

"Jimmy's out and I'm in. Tony caught him smoking crank and fired him on the spot. I'll be leaving with the band Saturday morning."

"Saturday?" The word came out in a strangled whisper. "This Saturday?" Calvin smiled, nodding. Alana struggled to control the hysteria making it difficult for her to draw a normal breath.

A callused finger touched her lower lip. "Yes, Lanie."

Tears filled Alana's eyes. "You can't...you can't just drop this on me."

Pulling her closer, Calvin pressed a kiss over her eyelids. "We've talked about this, baby. I told you I was waiting for my big break, and now that it's come I have to take advantage of it."

"Like you've taken advantage of me."

"How have I taken advantage of you, Lanie?"

"Faye says while I house and feed you, you get free use of my body."

"That dyke bitch better stay the hell out of our business or..." His words trailed off.

"She's not a dyke, Calvin. And she's my best friend."

"I'm sorry I called her a dyke."

He hadn't wanted to apologize, but the two women were friends long before he shacked up with Alana, and he didn't want to say anything that would jeopardize his relationship with her.

She crawled onto his lap like a small child, her arms circling his neck. "How long will you be gone?"

"Six months?"

Alana stared at him as if he'd taken leave of his senses. "You're going to spend six months in Europe?"

"No, baby. We're touring Europe, Africa and Asia."

Her eyes filled again. "No, Calvin," she sobbed, shaking her head. "You can't leave me for six months."

"I *have* to go, baby. I've waited all of my life for this moment."

"But what about *me?*"

Calvin hid his disgust behind an expression of indifference. Alana was so incredibly beautiful and sexy that she could have another man in her bed before he darkened her door. But her beauty and intelligence was minimized by a draining neediness that always set his teeth on edge.

If he forgot to tell her that he loved her she would sulk and pout until he did, and it hadn't taken him long to learn to play her game. If he was asleep when she left in the morning he made certain to call her and tell her or leave a message on her voice mail that he loved and missed her.

"What do you want, Lanie? Do you not want me to go?"

Alana pressed a kiss against his warm throat. "I would never try to stop you from following your dream."

Combing his fingers through her mussed curls, Calvin kissed the fragrant strands. "What's the matter, baby?" he whispered in her hair.

A tumble of confused emotions beset Alana as she struggled to control them. A man she loved was asking her what she wanted and she was too afraid to open her mouth and say what lay in her heart, had lain in her heart for years.

Years and thousands of dollars spent on therapy sessions hadn't prepared her for this moment, even though she had rehearsed it over and over since she'd invited Calvin into her life and into her bed.

"I want to be Mrs. Calvin McNair."

CHAPTER 12

Calvin stared at Alana. "You want *me* to marry you?"

"No, Calvin. I want *us* to get married."

"Where is all of this coming from?"

She rested a hand over her heart. "From here. I want a commitment from you."

"I am committed to you."

"Committed enough to marry me?"

There was a pulse beat of silence. "Yes, Lanie. I am committed enough to marry you, but not now."

The heavy lashes that shadowed Alana's cheeks flew up. Stunned, Calvin's admission had rendered her mute. "When?" she whispered, recovering her voice.

"When I come back we'll announce our engagement."

A frown creased her smooth forehead. "Why wait? Why can't we get engaged now?"

"No, Lanie," Calvin countered, shaking his head. "I want to do it right—the ring, on bended knee with the traditional will-you-marry-me scenario. I also want to save enough money so we can buy a house in the suburbs with a good school system. I don't want our children to go to New York City public schools."

His words did not register on Alana's troubled senses. She didn't want to wait six months. She wanted *now* because she didn't want her life to parallel her mother's, who'd lived with her common-law husband for twenty-three years and borne him three children. The liaison ended after he married another woman—a much younger woman whom he'd gotten pregnant. Melanie Gardner's battle with depression had been exacerbated because none of her children claimed Carlos Moore's last name.

"We both went to public schools and we did all right," she argued quietly.

Calvin ran a finger down the length of her nose. "I don't want them to do all right. I want them to excel."

"How long do you want to be engaged?"

"Probably no more than a couple of years." He held up a hand when Alana's jaw dropped. "I didn't want to say anything before, but there's a possibility that we might be signed to a record label. If that happens, then we can marry next year."

Alana's smile was dazzling. "Oh, Calvin," she crooned against his parted lips. She pressed her breasts to his chest. "Now, show your baby how much you love her."

She caught the hem of Calvin's T-shirt and pulled it up and over his head at the same time he eased the thin straps of a lace-trimmed tank top off her shoulders, exposing her breasts to his heated gaze.

Lowering his head, he lifted one breast and suckled it. Alana's breathing deepened quickly. His mouth emitted a popping sound as he pulled back, watching her nipple swell like a plump berry.

Sliding his hand under the elastic waistband of her pajama pants, he searched between her thighs, finding her wet and pulsing. He massaged the engorged flesh above her vagina, smiling when her juices melted over his hand, then removed his hand and slowly peeled away her pajamas.

Calvin hadn't been faithful to Alana because he didn't believe in monogamy. Alana represented stability, something that had always been missing in his life, something no other woman had offered him. She wanted to play house, and he would grant her her wish. He would marry her, give her a couple of kids but he would always live his life by his own rules.

Alana's mouth was as busy as her hands. She kissed every inch of her lover's face. She undressed him, pushed him down to the mattress, her gaze fusing with his, and straddled his thighs.

The muscles under Calvin's arms rippled sensuously as he reached over and removed a condom from the drawer of the bedside table. He'd never allowed his promiscuity to overshadow the risks involved in unprotected sex. He wasn't ready to father children when he was barely able to support himself, and the possibility of contracting an STD was not an option.

Alana took the foil packet, tore it open with her teeth, inserting the latex into her mouth. Using her mouth, with the skill of a trained courtesan, she slipped the condom down his erection. Her lips closed on the throbbing flesh, eliciting a deep groan from Calvin.

Throwing an arm over his face, he moaned as her tongue lathed the length of his engorged flesh. "That's it, baby. Do it, do it!" he crooned between clenched teeth. "Yes, yes, yes!" he hissed over and over as she quickened her motions.

Alana smiled at the man writhing and bucking beneath her, the tendons in his neck bulging as he struggled not to climax. She'd always let Calvin believe he was in control whenever they made love, but she knew otherwise. Her body was a weapon she used to her best advantage, offered and withheld at will.

Increasing the pressure to the underside of his penis, she pressed her face against his testicles, taking them gently into her mouth and deriving the reaction she sought when Calvin bellowed as if branded by heated steel.

Seconds later, Alana found herself on her back and Calvin inside her. Wrapping her arms around his neck, her legs around his waist, she gave herself up to the waves of ecstasy taking her beyond the reality that she would go through the next six months of her life without the man she loved.

Calvin and Alana climaxed simultaneously, soaring to awesome, shuddering ecstasy. They lay together, waiting for their heartbeats to return to a normal rate. As if on cue, both sighed in pleasant exhaustion before succumbing to the sated sleep reserved for lovers.

CHAPTER 13

A soft knock on the door caught Faye's attention, and she looked up at the woman standing in her office doorway.

She'd been assigned to mentor intern Jessica Adelson, purportedly the niece of a BP&O vice president, but the leggy, perpetually tanned, twenty-something, size-two blonde had let it slip that she wasn't John Reynolds's niece but his mistress.

"Yes, Jessica?"

"Do you think we can get together for lunch today?"

"Why?"

"We need to talk."

"What have we been doing this past month if not talk?"

Leaning against the door, Jessica crossed her bare legs at the ankle and ran a hand through her long, blond hair. "I'm still not feeling you whenever you do your sales pitch *thang*. I want more involvement with your accounts, and I want to try my hand at writing copy."

Faye's hands tightened on the arms of her chair. She wanted to leap across the room and snatch the woman baldheaded, but the tactless, bigoted tramp wasn't worth her being charged with assault.

"Jessica, don't ever come into my office again unless I invite you. And, if you want something, have John put it in writing to me. Better yet, I'll call him and tell him myself." Reaching for the receiver, she punched in his extension, and then activated the speakerphone feature.

"Wendy, this is Faye. I'd like to speak to John." She glared at Jessica, whose eyes were now as large as silver dollars.

"What's up, Faye?" came a deep, resonant voice.

"Jessica's in my office, demanding that I permit her more involvement with my accounts. The last time I checked the table of organization, I reported to you, not your *niece*."

"Tell her I want to see her—*now!*"

Faye smiled. "She heard you, John, you're on speaker."

Red blotches dotted Jessica's cheeks. "Bitch," she whispered under her breath.

Pressing a button to end the call, Faye pushed back her chair and stood up. "I'm not going to be another bitch, so I suggest you leave while you can."

"You'll pay for this," Jessica threatened.

"Close the door on your way out."

Turning on her heel, Jessica slammed the door as Faye dropped into her chair and closed her eyes. Fury choked her, making it almost impossible to breathe.

She opened her eyes. "I've worked here too long," she muttered. She'd given Bentley, Pope and Oliviera five years of her life, five invaluable years that gave her what she needed to strike out on her own. But what good was experience without start-up capital?

The soft chiming of her private line stopped Faye from

sinking into a morass of self-pity. She picked up the receiver after the second ring. "Ms. Ogden."

"Hey, girlfriend."

"Hey yourself, Lana."

"I want you to be the first one to know that I'll be changing my name."

"Calvin proposed?"

Alana giggled like a little girl. "Yes, he did!"

Faye felt Alana's joy as surely as if it were her own. "Congratulations, Lana. When's the big day?"

"Not for a while. Calvin is touring Europe and Asia with his band for the next six months, and when he comes back to the U.S. we'll officially announce our engagement."

"Why put off announcing your engagement, Lana?"

"Because I want the ring *and* Calvin at the same time. There's no rush for the wedding date because we want to save enough money to buy a house."

"I know how you can earn some extra money."

Faye told Alana about her meeting with the owner of Pleasure Seekers and the invitation to a Saturday-night gathering. "Come with me, Lana, and check it out. We have nothing to lose."

"It sounds a little kinky, Faye."

"I'm not concerned about kinky, Lana. That's something we can control."

"Are you thinking about signing up?"

"I'm leaning toward it," she answered, deciding on honesty. "I need money for my brother's legal fees and to follow my dream."

"And I need money for a house *and* a wedding," Alana drawled.

Leaning back in her chair, an expression of satisfaction shimmering in her eyes, Faye nodded. "I hear you, girlfriend."

"Count me in. What kind of party is it?"

Faye read the engraved invitation. "Cocktails at seven, dinner at eight, black-tie optional."

"Nice," Alana drawled.

"I'll pick you up at six-thirty."

"I'll be downstairs."

"And Lana?"

"Yes, Faye?"

"I'm happy for you and Calvin. Really happy."

"Stop or you'll have me crying and soupin' snot."

"On that note I'm going to hang up. Love you, girlfriend."

"Love you back, girlfriend."

Faye ended the call, her mood ebullient. Her confrontation with Jessica forgotten, she returned to tweaking the copy she was scheduled to present later that afternoon.

CHAPTER 14

Enid sat at a beveled-glass table, uncapped a fountain pen and opened a leather journal to a blank page. The practice of writing down her daily activities had begun more than thirty years ago. The first day she walked into the lecture hall at Tulane Law School her life had changed dramatically, and she'd felt compelled to record it.

She'd entered law school with a concentration in criminal law, but within months of passing the bar one of her former professors asked that she come work for him. His modest law practice covered everything from adoption to capital murder and Enid found her niche after she won a generous settlement for a client in a high-profile divorce case. She stayed on for eight years before moving to Palm Beach, Florida, joining a firm specializing in divorces. She became a partner and earned the sobriquet "the female Raoul Felder."

Her courtroom success came from her observations of the gaudy young women who'd worked for her grand-mother, for it was in the courtroom that she became one of Darcie's girls, using her eyes, voice and body to seduce defendants, plaintiffs, lawyers and judges alike. She'd remembered sitting on the staircase, peering through the newel posts, watching practiced, coy glances, pouting mouths and sensual body language as they entertained their "clients" before escorting them up the staircase to the second-floor bedrooms.

The first time her grandmother caught her out of her room after dark Enid couldn't sit down for several days. A quick study, Enid learned to retreat to her third-floor sanctuary whenever she heard footfalls on the staircase. As she grew older, her snooping escalated. She'd forgotten the number of times she'd listened outside the doors to the sound of men and women moaning, grunting and screaming in what resembled "speaking in tongues," and she fell in love with a fellow student during her first year in college, a man who made her moan, groan and speak in tongues.

Smiling, she wrote the date: *May 20—Everything is in place for tomorrow night's gathering. Joaquin Braithwaite and his staff decorated the glassed-in rooftop garden with a dazzling display of light and flora that rivals Tavern on the Green. He erected bamboo poles, draping them with yards of white organza over a table with seating for thirty. The chairs are also draped in organza and tied back with navy blue satin ribbon.*

Dozens of votive candles in glass holders in towering wrought-iron candelabra will be lit before sunset. Vases of white tulips, roses, hyacinth, calla lilies, peonies and mums delivered this afternoon were positioned around the perimeter of the roof. Large colorful pillows are there for those who wish to relax after dinner.

When I sat under the gauzy fabric I felt as if I were in a seraglio. And that's the effect I want my clients to experience.

I'll be introducing my new exotic jewels, Faye Odgen and Alana Gardner, and I'm certain the reaction from my regular companions will be one of stunned surprise.

The caterer and his staff are scheduled to arrive tomorrow at four, the band at six-thirty. I must remind myself to give Astrid a little something extra for pulling everything together for me. I don't know what I'd do without her.

As she closed her journal, the intercom buzzed softly.

She pressed a button. "Yes, Astrid."

"Mr. Hampton is on line one."

"Thank you." She picked up the receiver. "Hello, Marcus."

"I have Ilene's head shot and résumé," he said without returning her greeting.

Choosing to ignore his social faux pas, Enid said, "Did you tell her to come?"

"No. I thought you'd want to meet with her first."

"There's not enough time. I know she's beautiful, but I do want to see her résumé."

"Let me see if I can get a messenger service to deliver it to you before five."

Enid stared at the Asian-inspired ivory figurines lining the fireplace mantel in her expansive office. A mysterious smile parted her lips. "Why don't you bring it to my place. I'll cook dinner," she added quickly. She knew the semester had ended for Marcus and he never taught summer-school courses.

There was a slight pause before he asked, "What's on the menu?"

Her smile widened. "That depends on what you want."

"Shrimp or oyster and sausage file gumbo. I went off my vegetarian diet today."

"You would," Enid teased. "Hang up so I can call the market and order what I need. What time should I expect you?"

"Is seven too early?"

She glanced at the desk clock. It was three-ten. She had enough time to prepare Marcus's favorite New Orleans Creole dish before his arrival. "No."

"Then I'll see you at seven."

"Later, Marcus."

His rich laugh came through the earpiece. "Later, beautiful."

She hung up and locked the journal in a cabinet. It had been almost three weeks since she'd invited Marcus to her Battery Park town house apartment. The only time they'd been apart that long was when she'd returned to New Orleans to bury her grandmother and settle her estate.

A shiver of uneasiness snaked its way up Enid's spine. Something had changed between them, and intuitively she felt as if he was hiding something from her. She'd begun imagining that he was involved with another woman—a younger woman.

Although she had married briefly and had had several affairs, in him she'd found her soul mate—someone whose desire for a fulfilling sex life matched an insatiable quest for business success.

Well, tonight she'd cook for her lover *and* offer him a dessert not found on any restaurant's menu.

She buzzed Astrid. "Tell Henry to bring the car around, then call Maximilian's and let them know I need a delivery asap." She gave her assistant the ingredients she needed for the gumbo.

Minutes later, she walked out of her office, rode the elevator to the street level and settled into the back seat of her town car.

CHAPTER 15

Marcus parked his car in a twenty-four-hour indoor garage a few blocks from Enid's town house and strode along sidewalks that were crowded with people taking advantage of the unseasonably warm spring weather. A tall, muscular man dressed in black leather bumped into him, and he tightened his grip on a decorative shopping bag.

He didn't break stride or offer an apology, remembering his mother's warning never to make eye contact or speak to anyone whenever he informed her as a teenager that he and his friends were going to hang out in the city.

He'd grown up in New Rochelle, a northern suburb of New York City, the only child of an accountant father and math-teacher mother. The family joke was that he was born counting on his fingers and toes.

Marcus didn't know if he'd inherited the special gene that made math easy for him, but he took full advantage of the skill which enabled him to decipher complicated mathematical equations in his head. He earned an accounting degree from New York University School of Business, graduating summa cum laude, and a subsequent MBA from Wharton.

He had no siblings, so he competed with himself, missing his goal to have his first million by age thirty by four years. That accomplished, he set another—five million by forty. As an equal partner in Pleasure Seekers and with an accounting client list that included record producers, video directors and his first hip-hop performer, he knew he'd realize that objective before his thirty-seventh birthday.

Marcus turned down the quiet tree-lined street with 19th century town houses and brownstones. The events of September 11 had changed the tony Battery Park neighborhood when many abandoned their historical houses until the air was declared safe enough for their return.

Enid had lived with him in his Pelham condominium for six weeks, and once she informed him that she was going back home he experienced a loss of companionship for the first time in his life. Their living together had offered him a glimpse of what it would be like to be married to her.

He rang the bell to the sand-colored three-story building, identifying himself after Enid's sultry voice came through the intercom. When she lived with him he'd given her a key to his condo, yet she hadn't reciprocated and he loathed asking her for one.

Marcus walked up the staircase to the second floor instead of taking the elevator, and as soon as he stepped onto the landing the door to Enid's duplex opened. A quick smile crinkled the skin around his eyes when he stared at the woman who, when not at Pleasure Seekers, was a chameleon.

Enid closed the distance between them, put her arms around his neck, took off his baseball cap, pulled his head down and kissed him with a hunger that belied her outward calm. "I've missed you," she whispered against his parted lips.

Marcus's free hand cradled her waist, his fingers splayed over the band of exposed flesh under her skimpy tank top. "I've missed you, too," he whispered into the fragrant hair tickling his nose. "What did you cook?"

"Gumbo with lagniappe."

Marcus kissed the end of her nose. "Which means?"

"It's an old Creole word for *something extra.*" She reached for his arm. "Let's eat, because the shrimp get tough once they're reheated."

"Something for you."

Enid peered into the bag he handed her. There were two bottles of her favorite white wine and a large envelope with Ilene's head shot and résumé. "Thank you, darling."

"I'll be with you as soon as I wash my hands."

Marcus walked into a bathroom off the living room. The sunny yellow and lime-green furnishings were inviting, the complete opposite of the bathrooms in the Soho loft. Enid had decorated her business space in Asian-inspired minimalist furnishings, while her home radiated the warmth and sensuality of the French Quarter. Most of the furniture, a mix of Regency and French Country styles, had come from her grandmother's house, including an antique French painted chest and eighteenth-century French clock with a subtle banjo shape that had been appraised at mid–six figures.

If Enid ever decided to sell her share of Pleasure Seekers she'd still be a very wealthy woman. She owned the town house and charged exorbitant rental fees to the first-floor tenants for the prime location.

Marcus dried his hands, then climbed the winding staircase, which led into Enid's gourmet kitchen where the intoxicating smell of piquant spices from the gumbo lingered in the air. Slowing his approach, he stared at Enid standing barefoot in the enclosed rooftop terrace.

He loved seeing her this way, bare feet and body-hugging tank top and jeans. She was sexier than women half her age. Once he'd discovered she was old enough to be his mother, it was too late. He'd fallen in love with her beauty, intelligence, passion and ambition.

She'd told him that she'd married well and handled her own divorce that left her with a sizable settlement. She'd moved from Palm Beach, Florida, to New York and set up her own law firm; ninety percent of her cases were divorces.

CHAPTER 16

"May I pour the wine?" he asked.

She smiled. "Please."

Marcus and Enid ate in silence, enjoying the food, wine and the moment. The sun had set, taking with it the heat of the day, while millions of stars lit up the nighttime sky. The city was settling down momentarily before gearing up for a night of endless frivolity.

Marcus emptied the remains of the wine into Enid's glass. The lighted votives on the wrought iron table cast a warm glow over her scrubbed face, which even without makeup, was ravishing. And it wasn't for the first time that he wondered why he was drawn to an older woman.

"I don't know how you do it, darling."

"Do what, Marcus?" Her voice was lower, sultry. Whenever she drank, the timbre of her voice deepened.

"Prepare just enough for one meal."

"I don't know," she said, shrugging a bare shoulder. "I suppose it comes from not wanting to eat leftovers."

"You can always throw it out."

A scowl distorted her balanced features. "I'd never throw away food. That's sinful."

Resting his arms on the table, Marcus leaned forward and smiled. "Sinful?"

Enid's frown deepened. "Do you think I'm not familiar with the word?" Not waiting for his reply, she said, "I grew up with nuns reminding me every day of my life that I was born in sin and that I had to fight against the evil forces that were determined to keep me from the kingdom of heaven because my mother had been a whore and my grandmother owned and operated a whorehouse. It didn't matter how much she donated to the church. I was still tainted.

"I said my daily devotions, went to confession and prayed for strength not to succumb to the weaknesses of the flesh. I was told that vanity was sinful, so I grew up believing I was hideous until I went to college. Attending a black college gave me the confidence I needed to become a proud black woman. The girls liked me because I didn't deny I was one of them, while boys who preferred white women could pursue me openly without the threat of being lynched because I was as close to white as they would ever have. So, please don't talk to me about right and wrong."

Marcus's benign expression didn't change. "It doesn't bother you that you offer women to men for a price?" It had taken him two years before he'd morally accepted Pleasure Seekers' raison d'être. He'd invested in the business because he knew it would make him a millionaire even though it went against his strict Baptist upbringing.

Lowering her gaze, Enid stared at Marcus through her lashes. "No. Once I understood the concept of free will I was able to absolve myself of guilt."

"Do you ever experience guilt about sleeping with me without benefit of marriage?"

She made an attractive moue. "Never. You, darling?"

"Sometimes." His answer appeared to surprise her as her delicate jaw dropped.

"Why?" The word came out in a whisper.

"Because I've been involved with you longer than I've been with any other woman in my life. I'm totally committed to you and our business venture, but there are times when I want permanence."

"You think getting married would make you feel more secure about us, our future?"

"At times I do."

"It's either yes or no, Marcus."

He hid his annoyance behind an expression of indifference. Marcus wanted to tell Enid yes, but to admit insecurity meant weakness. And there was no way he would give her that advantage. "No."

Enid sighed. She did not want to get into a dialogue with Marcus about love and marriage. She loved him, but not enough to marry. She'd married once, and had no intention of repeating the act.

Reaching for the envelope Marcus had brought with him, she opened the clasp and took out a glossy black-and-white head shot. The dark face with the slanting catlike eyes was mesmerizing.

Enid met Marcus's direct stare. "Do you think she'll fit in? I've heard she has a reputation for being difficult to work with."

"That's going to be up to you to make her fit in. Her modeling career is over and she's squandered her savings. She'll do whatever you'll tell her because the last thing she wants to lose is her Chelsea co-op,"

"I'll watch her closely tomorrow night." She dabbed the corners of her mouth with a cloth napkin. "Are you ready for dessert?"

His former annoyance forgotten, Marcus smiled. "Yes."

Pushing back her chair, Enid came to her feet. Marcus followed suit. He rounded the table and pulled her into a close embrace, his hands cupping her hips.

"Thank you for dinner. It was delicious, as usual."

Resting her head on his chest, Enid counted the steady beats of his heart as she inhaled his natural scent that blended perfectly with his cologne's subtle fragrance.

"Don't thank me yet."

Marcus rested his chin on the top of her head. "When can I thank you?"

Easing back, Enid tried making out his expression in the glow of the flickering candles. "After dessert." She threaded her fingers through his. "Come."

CHAPTER 17

Marcus followed Enid down the staircase and into her bedroom where soft music played constantly. Tonight he did not mind the classical station once he recognized *Boléro*, Ravel's hypnotically sensual composition that always reminded him of a man and woman making love, the haunting melody ending in a crescendo akin to climaxing.

A lamp on a corner table provided barely enough illumination to make out the four-poster iron bed draped in mosquito netting embroidered with tiny yellow butterflies.

They began their ritual: he took off his running shoes and socks, then removed her tank top; she removed his T-shirt. He removed her jeans, his gaze fused to her high breasts with the rose-tipped nipples before moving lower to a flat belly, slim hips and long, slender legs. He made a motion to slide her bikini panties down her hips but she stopped him, pushing his hand away.

Enid took her time unsnapping the waistband of his jeans, then unzipped him so slowly that if not for the music, they would've heard the sound of the zipper's teeth. An audible gasp escaped her parted lips once she realized Marcus wasn't wearing briefs.

"I decided to go commando," he said close to her ear. "I wanted everything to hang loose."

Slipping her hand into his jeans, Enid squeezed his penis, the flesh hardening quickly against her palm. Marcus's fingers curled around her wrist, pulling her hand away.

"Slow down, baby, before you make me pop."

Enid rubbed her breasts against his smooth, muscled chest. "I don't want to wait."

Pushing his jeans down his hips, Marcus stepped out of them. His mouth twisted as he sneered. "Wait, Enid? You're a fine one to talk. How do you think I feel having to wait three weeks to fuck you? It's not as if you can use the excuse that you're on your period." She'd admitted to him that she'd had a hysterectomy after a Pap smear confirmed precancerous cells six months after her marriage to the president of a major insurance company.

"I've had things on my mind, darling."

His fingers tightened around her upper arms. "So have I. But that hasn't stopped me from wanting to make love to you."

Tilting her chin in a gesture of defiance, Enid met his angry stare. "Well, you have me *now*."

"Yes—I—do."

Marcus's voice was void of emotion, and that unnerved her more than his thunderous expression. His hands moved down to the waistband of her panties, and in one strong motion he tore them in half. She stared numbly at the scraps of silk lying at her feet.

Her right hand came up, but she found her wrist imprisoned between fingers that tightened into manacles. This Marcus Hampton was a stranger, a man she did not know.

Her temper rose quickly. "Do it!" she taunted as high color suffused her face.

Marcus picked her up, swept back the netting and placed her on the cool sheets, his body covering hers. There was no tenderness in his kiss as his mouth ravished hers. His hands were everywhere—in her hair, on her breasts. Holding her wrists captive, he slid down the length of the large bed and buried his face between her thighs. His tongue searched for the opening and plunged in and out over and over until he felt the spasms seize her body, hold her captive, then release her to start all over again.

"No!" Enid screamed, biting down on her lower lip, loving and hating Marcus at the same time. She loved the sensations he evoked whenever he put his tongue into her vagina, but hated him because it made her helpless against his sensual assault on her mind *and* body. She wanted to release the desire that swirled like a twister moving over the earth, disintegrating everything in its path. Then, without warning, he pulled back.

Moving out from under him, she reversed their positions. It was her turn to punish Marcus the way he'd tortured her. She kissed him, tasting herself on his lips and tongue, easing her way down his body. Everything about her lover was clean and masculine.

He bellowed as her mouth closed on his engorged penis, sucking gently until she took as much of him as she could without gagging. Her tongue worked its magic, he rising off the mattress at the same time as unintelligible, guttural sounds drowned out the music coming from the speakers concealed in an armoire in the adjoining sitting room. Enid licked, stroked and suckled, bringing Marcus close to ejaculation twice before changing tempo.

She gasped in surprise when he sat up and forcibly extracted her mouth from his throbbing flesh. Supporting his back against the headboard, Marcus pulled her down to straddle his lap. Lifting her with one hand, he guided her until he was fully sheathed inside her.

He set the rhythm, Enid following. Her respiration quickened as she closed her eyes and moaned softly.

It was no longer a battle of wills, a competition for dominance or control. They were male and female, man and woman, lovers whose love was deep, boundless and infinite.

Marcus cupped Enid's hips in his hands, squeezing and pulling her closer as electricity arced through the nether regions of his body. He lowered his head and fastened his mouth to the side of her neck.

"Don't mark me," she screamed, but it was too late. Marcus's teeth caught the tender skin at the base of her throat as he smothered a growl. She felt him explode inside her, and within seconds her body vibrated with liquid fire as she melted all over him. The pulsing went on and on until she collapsed against his moist body, her breath coming in long, surrendering moans.

Her lips, still quivering with a lingering passion, brushed his. "I love you."

Marcus did not respond to her declaration of love. The

only time Enid told him that she loved him was in the throes of passion. When, he wondered, would she ever tell him that she loved him out of bed?

He held Enid until his heart settled back to a normal rhythm, then he eased her down to the mattress. Resting an arm over her waist, he pulled her closer.

"Thank you for dessert," he crooned against the nape of her neck.

Enid smiled. "How would you like dessert every night next week?"

Marcus went completely still. "Why the change of heart, darling? Wasn't it you that said you can't put up with a man for more than two consecutive nights?"

"Don't forget I lived with you for six weeks following nine-eleven."

"That's because you didn't want to stay here. Would you want me to live with you for six weeks?"

Shifting, she turned to face him. "Why don't we try it?"

He stared at her thoroughly kissed mouth. "Try what?"

"Living together. You don't work the summers, so we can stay here during the week and go to your place on the weekends."

Marcus gave Enid a long, penetrating stare. "Are you trying to fuck with my head?"

She placed her fingertips over his mouth. "No, darling. And please don't curse at me."

"Don't tell me what to say, Enid. I'm not your son."

"And I don't want to be your mother, Marcus. At least not one who would sleep with her son."

The seconds ticked off as they stared at each other in what was certain to become an impasse.

"Okay," Marcus conceded. "We'll live together this summer." Lowering his head, he kissed her fragrant hair. "I don't want to fight with you, baby."

"Nor I you," she countered softly.

"Sweetheart?"

"Yes, darling."

"I love you."

Enid pressed her face to his chest rather than let him see the tears welling up in her eyes. He loved her and she loved him. But what were they going to do with their love?

She lay in bed with Marcus until he fell asleep. Then she left the bed and showered before returning to the kitchen to clean up the remains of dinner. The evidence of Marcus's lovemaking was stamped on her body like a tattoo. The dress she planned to wear to Saturday's soiree would have to be replaced with one that covered her throat.

Her expression brightened when she thought of one she'd bought in Hong Kong. It would be the perfect outfit in which to welcome her exotic jewels.

CHAPTER 18

"Ladies, how are you this fine evening?" crooned the tall blond man dressed entirely in black and wearing an earpiece in his left ear. He stood outside the entrance to the Soho loft.

Faye smiled, handing him the invitations as he signaled for another man standing inside the building's lobby to open the door.

Alana flashed the solidly built black man with a shaved head and goatee her winning smile. "Thank you." Her sultry voice had dropped an octave.

His impassive expression did not change. "The elevator will be down in a minute."

The doors to the elevator chimed open and another man, also in the somber color, motioned to them. As he reached out to hold the door, Faye saw a bulge of a firearm under his left arm. "Please come in, ladies."

She exchanged a knowing glance with Alana as they walked into the elevator. The men in black were obviously bodyguards. The doors closed, the car rising quietly, swiftly, and seconds later the doors opened again, and they stepped into a glass-enclosed penthouse garden.

* * *

As Enid watched Faye Ogden and her friend walk confidently into the penthouse, a knowing smile parted her
lips. At the same time, conversations stopped, heads
turned, necks craned and gazes were trained on the two
newcomers.

Faye Ogden was exquisite in a sheer gunmetal-gray
sheath dress lined in black silk with shimmering floral
beaded designs from neckline to hem; the flattering
garment ended at her knee. Her tiny feet were encased in
a pair black silk sling-strap heels with narrow ties encircling her slender ankles. Eye makeup in inky-dark shades
made her gold eyes look dramatic, mysterious.

Enid's gaze shifted to the lush, exotic-looking woman
who'd come with Faye. Shiny curls fell to her bare shoulders, and a black crepe de chine strapless dress drew one's
attention immediately before a generous slit displayed an
expanse of long bare legs in a pair of black satin Chanel
ballet stilettos.

Holding the skirt of her midnight-blue cheongsam, Enid
crossed the floor to greet them. "Thank you for coming,"
she smiled, extending her hand to Faye.

"This is my friend, Alana Gardner. Alana, Enid Richards."

"Please come have something to drink before I introduce you to the others."

Alana stared at the tall, slender woman with ash-blond
hair, cool blue-gray deep-set eyes and perfectly symmet-
rical features. A light tan added color to what would've
been a normally pale face.

"I don't think the other ladies are too happy about us being here," Alana said perceptively. Her gaze shifted from Enid to the exquisitely dressed blond, brunette and red-haired women impaling the newcomers with hostile glares.

"That is not your problem," Enid said with a polite smile. She waved a manicured hand. "Please come with me."

Alana and Faye followed Enid to the bar where identical twin bartenders mixed, poured and stirred cocktails. They were bronzed, buffed and natural blonds; their perfect bodies displayed to their best advantage in black tank tops and tailored slacks.

Faye hadn't believed Enid could improve on perfection, but she had. Her moonlit hair, brushed off her face and pinned at the nape of her neck, was the perfect complement to the Asian-style dress with side slits that exposed a glorious expanse of leg whenever she took a step. The dark blue Alexandra Neel sandals cost more than some earned in a week.

Enid smiled at a distinguished silver-haired man as he stared openly at Alana, his startled gaze fixed on the swell of satin brown flesh spilling over the revealing décolletage.

"Jonathan, I'd like you to meet to Faye Ogden and Alana Gardner. Ladies, Jonathan Hamilton."

Both women recognized the name immediately. The Hamiltons were an old-moneyed family who'd made their fortune setting up department stores.

"I'm charmed, Mr. Hamilton." Alana smiled, extending her hand in a limp gesture denoting helplessness.

Jonathan held Alana's hand, then tucked it into the

bend of his elbow. "May I get you something to drink?" Alana's towering height eclipsed his by a full head.

"Why, aren't you darling."

Since when did you talk with a Southern drawl? Faye longed to ask Alana.

Her friend had spent the morning in tears after seeing Calvin off and Faye thought she was going to have to attend the Pleasure Seekers party alone until Alana called her back, asking, "Where the party at?"

She smiled at one of the wannabe Baywatch bartenders. "I'd like a gin martini, please."

"What kind of gin?"

She gave him a blank stare.

"Give her a Beefeater's. Make it extra dry and very dirty," ordered a soft male voice behind her.

Faye turned to stare up at a tall, middle-aged man with close-cropped silver hair and intense gray eyes. Not handsome, but very attractive. The tailored lines of the dark suit on his slender body had not come off a rack. She smiled at him, bringing his gaze to linger on her mouth.

"What will you have, Mr. Houghton?" asked the other twin.

"I'll have what the lady's drinking."

Faye lowered her lashes in a demure gesture. "Thank you, Mr. Houghton."

He angled his head and smiled, the expression softening his rugged features. "It's Bart."

Faye extended her right hand. "Faye."

He held her fingers, bringing them to his mouth and dropping a kiss on her knuckles. He waited until she looked up at him before releasing her hand. "Does Faye have a last name?"

"Ogden."

"Faye Ogden," he said thoughtfully, as if memorizing her name.

The twins gave Bart and Faye their cocktails; they touched glasses. Faye felt the heat from Bart's gaze burn her face as he stared openly at her. She knew he was intrigued by her, but wanted to tell him he was too old for her, and more important, he wasn't her type.

As she took a sip of her martini, the iciness slid down the back of her throat then exploded in a ball of fire in her chest. She blew out her breath.

"Whoa. That's potent."

Bart sipped his martini, nodding. "It is a little strong. Would you like them to make you another one?"

Faye shook her head. "No. I'll nurse it for the rest of the evening." She gave him a too-bright smile. "It was a pleasure meeting you, Bart. Please excuse me. I'm going to circulate."

The last thing she wanted to do was give Bart Houghton the impression she was interested in him, because she wasn't. In fact, if the truth were told, she wasn't interested in any of the men in attendance, doubting if any were under forty. She drifted over to where a quintet played softly while the waitstaff circulated with trays of champagne, caviar and sushi.

"Lovely," crooned a rotund man with a wet-look comb-over hairdo when she passed him and the statuesque redhead clinging to his arm.

Peering over her shoulder, she winked at him. "Thank you."

Enid stood next to Marcus, her gaze shifting between Alana and Faye. It hadn't taken her long to analyze the two women. Alana was outgoing and flirtatious, Faye sedate and definitely more complex. However, both women played the game well. They were courteous and gracious.

She knew without talking to Bartholomew Houghton that he was drawn to Faye Ogden. Bart had been one of several clients whose contract hours had dropped appreciably.

Enid had also noticed that her regular companions glared at the two black women. Usually very competitive with one another, there was no doubt they would join forces to alienate her exotic jewels.

"Where's Ilene?" she asked Marcus *sotto voce.*

"She'll be here." Marcus took a sip of chilled champagne. "She probably wants to make a diva-style entrance."

Enid's eyes narrowed. "She *is* here."

For the second time that night, the guests fell silent as Ilene Fairchild strutted out of the elevator like she was on a Paris runway, waist-length braided extensions sweeping over her rounded bottom sheathed in a skintight dress ending six inches above the knee.

Ilene spied Marcus and headed toward him. "Darling,"

she crooned. At six foot two in her heels, her head was level with his.

Marcus held the ex-model at arm's length before she could kiss him. "I'm glad you could make it, Ilene. You were supposed to be here at seven." He hadn't bothered to mask his annoyance.

She waved a hand. "Whatever. I'm not even an hour late."

Enid raised her eyebrows as she listened to the interchange between her lover and the model. If her clients hadn't been gawking at the young woman, she would've had her escorted out of the building.

An attaché with the French consulate approached Ilene and lapsed into rapid French.

She replied in the same language, the words flowing fluidly from her lips. "*Oui, monsieur,* I would love a glass of champagne," she crooned, switching back to English.

Enid looked at Marcus, who lifted his shoulders under his tuxedo jacket before she went in search of her party planner. The cocktail hour was winding down and it was time they sat down to eat.

Bart approached her as she headed toward the elevator. "May I have a minute of your time?"

She offered the real estate developer an enchanting smile. "Of course, darling."

"What are the odds of me sitting next to Faye Ogden?"

"Very good."

"Thank you, Enid." Bart angled his head and lowered his voice. "I'm hosting a party out East next weekend to celebrate the promotion of one of our African-American executives to a senior position, and I'd like to book the three women of color."

Nothing in Enid's expression indicated the smugness she felt because her exotic jewels had hit the jackpot. "Call Astrid Monday and she'll set up whatever you need."

"Thank you again, Enid."

She gave him her most beguiling smile. "You're welcome, Bart."

CHAPTER 19

There days later, Alana, Faye and Ilene were summoned by Astrid Marti to return to the Soho loft for an orientation session. They were seated in plush chairs at a black Asian-inspired lacquered table in a second-floor office instead of the penthouse garden. A tray cradling bottles of sparkling water and goblets were provided for their liquid refreshment.

Enid entered the office, her expression impassive, and closed the door behind her. Saturday evening she'd smiled, chatted and had become the perfect hostess. But today it was only business, as evidenced in her choice of attire and hairstyle. She wore a black linen pantsuit with a brightly colored scarf tied at her throat; her hair was pinned up in a French twist.

"Good evening, ladies," she said with a hint of a Southern drawl. "I thank you for being prompt." Her gaze lingered briefly on Ilene before she joined them at the table. "I've taken the liberty of ordering a light repast, but first I'm going to give you an overview of Pleasure Seekers, then I'll answer any questions."

She paused, staring at each woman. "I've established

Pleasure Seekers to offer social companionship to a select group of men. All of my clients have been scrupulously screened, and it doesn't matter if someone is CEO, entertainer, athlete, politician or a Middle Eastern prince, all go through the same background-check process.

"You all are adults, so I'm not going to play big mama. My business is run on discretion, discretion for the clients and discretion as to their social companions. And you will be paid quite well *not* to talk about who you see, where you go and what you do. I must caution you about sleeping with your clients. It always spells trouble. I will not tolerate any form of pornography or drug use. I cannot stress enough that I am *not* running a brothel."

"What happens if it just happens?" Ilene asked. "I mean, the sleeping together," she added.

"How old are you, Ilene?" Enid knew her age because she'd gleaned the data from the back of her head shot.

"Thirty."

"At thirty, it just doesn't *just* happen," she countered, glaring at her. "Do not, I repeat, do not ever attempt to see a client without going through P.S., Inc. A single infraction will result in immediate dismissal. What you earn depends upon how often you choose to work. Most companions begin working weekends. I charge my clients a thousand an hour, with a two-hour minimum. There will be times when you can earn upward of five thousand a day. You'll be paid fifty instead of my usual forty/sixty percent split." Her gaze narrowed. "Please keep this information among yourselves."

Faye and Alana exchanged sidelong glances. It was apparent P.S., Inc.'s women of color were worth more to Enid Richards than their Caucasian counterparts.

Ilene raised her hand again. "If you're charging a thousand an hour and if we work all day, wouldn't that calculate into at least a ten-thousand-dollar split?"

A hint of a smile touched Enid's lips and crinkled the skin around her eyes. "No woman is worth ten thousand dollars a day." Her expression changed like quicksilver, her gaze narrowing as the nostrils in her straight nose flared slightly. "I've established a ceiling of five thousand a day, but if you, Miss Fairchild, can think of a reason why you'd be worth more, then I'd like you to let me and these other exotic jewels in on your secret."

Ilene stared down at the table as she bit down on her lower lip. The gesture showed deep dimples in her smooth dark brown cheeks. Ilene Fairchild's face competed with her slim beautifully proportioned body for one's attention. Small, round and with doll-like features, her face was stunning with or without makeup. Her lips, whether pouting or parted in a dimpled smile, had become her signature trademark.

"How are we paid?" Alana asked, her question diffusing what could've become an uncomfortable situation for Ilene.

Lacing her fingers together, Enid raised her coiffed head slightly. "All payments will be processed as electronic transfers. I'm going to need your banking information.

After you eat, Astrid will give you a questionnaire that will give me an idea of your personality, a signed release so I can conduct a background check on each of you and you'll be asked to leave a urine sample for a drug test."

Ilene raised a hand yet again. "Why would you want to check us out?"

Enid's delicate jaw tightened. There was something about Ilene she did *not* like; she found her crude *and* gauche. "I need to know if you've ever been arrested or convicted of a felony or whether you're taking drugs. I can't afford to set up a client with a woman who has a rap sheet as long as his arm. Let me know now if you're unable to pass the background check or drug test."

There came a moment of silence before Enid and the others let out an audible breath. She smiled for the first time since walking into the room.

"Good. Never *ever* accept money from a client. He may give you a gift, but not cash. You are social companions, not hookers."

"Do we have the option of refusing a client?" It was Faye's turn to ask a question.

"Are you asking if you can refuse before you go out with him the first time?" Enid asked.

Faye nodded. "Yes."

Enid shook her head. "No, Faye. But, on the other hand, after the first time, you'll have the option of not going out with him again."

She knew Faye was uneasy about Bartholomew Houghton. Although seated together, Enid knew Bart hadn't tried coming on to Faye. She'd noticed them talking quietly and several times Faye had laughed at something he'd said.

She lifted an eyebrow as she continued to stare at Faye. Perhaps Miss Ogden found herself drawn to Bart when she didn't want to be.

"The day I call you for your first assignment you will receive a thousand-dollar tax-free signing bonus."

"You're going to tax our earnings?" Ilene asked with an incredulous look on her pretty face.

Enid smiled at Ilene. "I pay taxes on mine, so why should you be exempt?" Now she was certain the calorie-challenged model foreshadowed trouble, yet she planned to sign Ilene because the French attaché and a Japanese financier had both asked for her.

"Speaking of taxes," Enid continued, "remember to keep receipts for your clothes, makeup, hair, nails and transportation for write-offs."

A knock on the door garnered everyone's attention. A young woman with a spiral-curl hairdo stuck her head through the slight opening. "I'm sorry to interrupt, but the food is here."

Enid nodded at Astrid. "Give us another five minutes." The door closed again. "I hope all of you are available this weekend. A client has requested your presence at his Southampton estate Saturday afternoon. He just promoted an African-American executive to a senior position and would like to have some professional women of color in attendance. You will be picked up separately and driven out to Long Island. At no time are you to let on that you know one another."

Alana smiled at Enid. "I'm available." She had a lot of time now that Calvin was in Europe.

"I'm also available," Faye said.

Ilene waved a hand. "I can make it." She needed money, like, yesterday. She was nearly three months behind on the maintenance for her Chelsea co-op.

Enid pressed her palms together. "Wonderful. As soon as I receive confirmation on your background information Astrid will contact you."

Pleasure Seekers' payroll listed six employees. Astrid Marti, her booking-agent executive assistant and a private investigator were integral to the company's ongoing success. Victor Payton, a retired FBI special agent with links to police departments, the Bureau and the IRS more than earned his annual six-figure fee.

Astrid had proven herself invaluable because of her fluency in English, Spanish, French, Portuguese and German. The daughter of a Haitian mother and Dominican father, she'd come to the United States on a student visa as a language major. After graduation she worked with the United Nations as an interpreter; she'd found herself a victim of workplace sexual harassment and contacted someone at the Haitian consulate, who'd referred her to Enid. Instead of bringing a suit against a man with diplomatic immunity, Enid hired Astrid as an executive assistant for Pleasure Seekers.

Bartholomew Houghton hadn't blinked when Astrid

quoted a fee for the services of Faye Ogden, Alana Gardner and Ilene Fairchild. The three women were different—in looks and temperament, their potential earning power incalculable to men where the asking price for companionship was infinite.

"Are there any more questions?" Enid asked.

The three young women shook their heads.

Lowering her gaze, Enid stared at them through her lashes. It was a look of supreme satisfaction; a look she usually gave a man whenever she set out to seduce him, and a look she'd learned and studied from the young women who'd worked for Darcie Richards; the coy glance of an experienced courtesan who'd never had to use her body to get what she wanted from a man or a woman.

Pushing back her chair, she rose to her feet. "Thank you, ladies." Enid walked out of the room, leaving the subtle scent of a classic perfume in her wake.

Within seconds of her departure the door opened and a man and woman entered, pushing a serving cart filled with cellophane-covered trays. Reaching for a bottle of water, Faye twisted off the cap and filled a goblet with mineral water. She didn't want to acknowledge that she'd just committed to becoming an escort to wealthy men who thought nothing of spending thousands to have her entertain him with her presence.

It sounded almost too good to be true, but if what Enid Richards professed to be true was, in fact, true, then there was no doubt she would be able to earn enough money by the end of the summer to retain the best appeal attorney in the Northeast.

"What do you think?" Alana whispered close to her ear.

"It sounds good," Faye whispered back.

Alana leaned closer, her shoulder touching Faye's. "Do you really believe we don't have to sleep with these men?"

"It doesn't matter because I don't plan to sleep with any of them," she said through clenched teeth.

Alana filled her glass with bottled water, her thoughts going into overdrive. If she saved the money she earned working for P.S., Inc., then she and Calvin could marry as soon as he returned from Europe. She had three weeks' vacation leave coming to her, and instead of spending that time with her mother or working on the book she'd been writing for the past two years she would work as a social companion. There was no doubt she would earn enough to buy the house in the suburbs Calvin wanted. A knowing smile parted her lips. She'd just turned thirty-three and she was about to realize her dreams.

CHAPTER 20

Ilene hadn't done it in a very long time, but today she prayed her urine wouldn't show traces of the cocaine she'd snorted three weeks ago.

She'd dabbled in recreational drugs for half her life and cocaine had become her drug of choice because she could either snort or smoke it, and it kept her thin. The times she smoked marijuana she couldn't stop eating, and the result was that she'd lost a major modeling assignment because she couldn't fit into the designer's creations.

A few models Ilene knew were into heroin, injecting themselves between their toes, under the soles of their feet, or in their pubic area, but Ilene was too vain to mar her body with needle marks or even a minute tattoo.

Her body and her face were her greatest assets, and although her modeling career was winding down, she'd diversified and begun a new one in music videos. She planned to dance, strut and shake her behind until she found a man with enough money to indulge all her fantasies.

Tossing a profusion of freshly braided human-hair extensions, hair that had cost her more than she could afford to pay for at this time, over her shoulders, Ilene smiled at

Alana, then Faye. When she'd entered the penthouse Saturday night and saw the two black women, she'd viewed them as her competitors until she felt the overt hostility from the preening blondes and redheads.

"Miss Fairchild."

Ilene turned and stared at Astrid. "Yes?"

"I'll test you first, then Miss Ogden and Miss Gardner. Please come with me."

Please, Lord, help me, Ilene prayed again as she stood up and followed Astrid to a bathroom where she was handed a plastic cup with her name printed on an affixed label.

"Don't tell me you're going to watch me piss?"

Astrid's solemn expression did not change. "Yes, I am."

"Enjoy the view," she mumbled, unbuttoning the waistband of her fitted jeans and sliding them down her hips.

As a model, modesty wasn't in her repertoire. Her gaze locked with Astrid's as she eased her thong panty below her knees, squatted over the commode and urinated into the cup while Astrid slipped on a pair of latex gloves. She half filled the cup and left it on a low table beside a vase of fresh flowers.

"How soon will I know?" Ilene asked, adjusting her clothes and washing her hands in the black marble sink.

"When you get the phone call," Astrid said noncommittally. "Please let Miss Ogden know that I'm ready for her."

Enid made her way through her office and into a space that had become an office within an office and her inner sanctum; she sat down on one of two facing deep-cushioned maroon tapestry club chairs, rested her feet on a matching footstool and waited for Astrid to bring her the scores from the personality profiles and drug-test results.

Floor-to-ceiling glass walls brought the outdoors in regardless of the hour; the gurgling sounds from a Zen fountain, lighted scented candles and the distinctive sound of Gregorian chanting coming from concealed speakers provided the perfect environment for total relaxation.

Enid closed her eyes and inhaled a lungful of air, held it, then exhaled slowly as she opened her eyes. Lengthening shadows came through the glass with the waning daylight. It would be dusk in a matter of minutes, her favorite time of day, a time when she loved to sit on her rooftop terrace and watch the neighborhood settle down from the frenetic daytime bustle to the leisurely nighttime hours.

She glanced down at her watch. She'd promised Marcus she'd be home before ten because they'd planned to walk over to the South Street Seaport for a late dinner. Under another set of circumstances she would've left following the orientation, but tonight was the exception. Waiting until the following day to go over the outcome of Faye's, Ilene's and Alana's drug tests and personality profiles was not an option for Enid.

Sitting up straighter, all of her senses on full alert, Enid stared at her assistant as she entered the room cradling three folders to her chest. The glossy curls framed a dark-skinned, youthful face that would've belied her actual age of twenty-eight if it hadn't been for Astrid's full, womanly figure.

"Let me know now if what's in those folders is going to make me upset."

"Quite the opposite." Astrid smiled, handing her boss the data she'd collected from P.S., Inc.'s latest social companions.

Enid gestured to the facing chair. "Please sit down and tell me the good news."

"All passed the drug test," Astrid began, smiling. Enid had directed her to order testing kits from a company in the Midwest rather than send the urine samples to a local laboratory. The kits were more expensive than lab fees, but the advantage was that the wait time for results was instantaneous.

"I'll begin with Ilene Fairchild," the booker continued. "She's single, thirty, speaks fluent French and began modeling at the age of fifteen. She was born Ella Williams in Gulfport, Mississippi, but legally changed her name for professional purposes. Ilene lived in Belgium and France for thirteen years before returning to the States two years ago."

"What about her education?" Enid asked.

"She never attended high school, but has a GED." Astrid paused. "I don't know if this is going to present a problem ..." Her words trailed off.

"What kind of problem?"

Astrid heard the slight edge that had crept into Enid's voice. It wasn't often that she saw the owner of Pleasure Seekers lose her composure, and when she did, it usually did not bode well for the person who'd upset her.

"She only checked off Caucasian in the racial-preference category."

Enid lifted an eyebrow. "Why do you see that as a problem?"

Astrid paused again. "I believe it would limit her earning potential."

"What did she indicate as a reason for signing on as an escort?"

"She wants a husband."

"I don't see her wanting to date white men as a problem," Enid said. "I don't know if Ilene is aware of it, but she's more European socially oriented than American. And since she is a former supermodel, most men, regardless of race, would want to be seen with her. What is a problem is her wanting to use P.S., Inc. as a dating service, because most of our clients are already married. What about Alana and Faye?"

"Both indicated they're signing on to make money."

Good for them, Enid mused. If Faye and Alana were motivated by money, then it stood to reason that they were willing to work—and often.

Biting back a smile, Enid nodded. "What else, Astrid?"

"Alana's racial choices are African and Caribbean American, Hispanic and Middle Eastern. Faye's preferences are African and Caribbean American, followed by Hispanic, Native American and, lastly, Caucasian."

Enid listened intently as her assistant revealed what she'd gleaned from the three personality profiles. "Fax everything to Victor and label it Rush." She handed the folders back to Astrid.

A soft exhalation of breath from Enid followed Astrid's

departure. She didn't know why, but she felt as if she'd been holding her breath since the night she'd met Marcus at the Four Seasons to discuss the decline in their company's profits.

Rising to her feet, she walked into her office and sat down at the glass table. Reaching for a Montblanc fountain pen, she unscrewed the cap. The writing instrument, a Christmas gift from one of her clients, was one of only seventy-five of a limited edition produced two years before. It took her nearly three months to write with a pen whose price tag astounded her. She would've sold it and donated the money to her favorite charity if it hadn't been engraved with her name.

Unconsciously her brow furrowed as navy blue ink flowed over the pale blue blank page. *May 24—I will know within hours whether Alana, Ilene and Faye will become P.S., Inc.'s latest social companions.*

Enid paused, the solid gold nib poised over the page as the delicate chiming of the telephone shattered her concentration. Marcus's name and cell phone number showed in the display. She pushed a button for the speaker.

"Are you calling to cancel dinner?" A deep husky laugh greeted her query.

"No. But there's going to be a change of plans."

Enid sat up straighter. Marcus knew she didn't like surprises. "What is it?"

"I've decided to cook for you."

Her pulse quickened as a rush of color suffused her face. Marcus had only cooked for her twice before, and both times when she hadn't been feeling well. She'd thought of herself as very good cook, but his culinary skills were exceptional.

"What are we celebrating?"

"We're not celebrating anything. And please take me off the speaker."

Enid deactivated the telephone feature, then picked up the receiver. "There's no one here with me."

"That may be true, but walls do have ears."

A slight frown furrowed her smooth forehead. "What do you want to tell me that's for my ears only?"

"I love you."

Enid's frown vanished, replaced by an easy smile. "And I love you, too, Marcus."

"Hurry down, baby."

"Where are you?"

"Downstairs. I told Henry that I was taking you home."

Her eyebrows lifted. "You've dismissed my driver and offered to cook for me. What other surprises do you have in store for me tonight?"

He laughed, the sensual sound sending a shiver up her spine. "I'm certain I'll think of a few more before we get home."

It was on a rare occasion that Marcus Hampton showed Enid another side of his staid personality. It was only when they were on vacation together, away from his students, clients and their business that he was totally relaxed.

"I'll be down in five minutes."

Enid capped the pen and placed it and the journal into

a black lacquered box covered with Chinese characters for love, peace, prosperity and good luck. She locked the box and pen in the drawer of an antique side table.

She was looking forward to her dinner rendezvous with Marcus. He'd moved some of his clothes and personal items into her apartment on Saturday, and when she awoke to find him in bed beside her Sunday morning, it wasn't to panic, as she'd anticipated, but to a gentle peace she hadn't thought possible.

Marcus loved her and she loved him, but where would their love for each other lead them?

CHAPTER 21

Faye cradled a cordless phone between her chin and shoulder as she filled an overnight bag with clothes for several days.

"I'm sorry, Mama, but it's too late for me to change my plans for the weekend."

"Can't you give up one day to spend with your family?"

"No, Mama."

"You already work five days a week. Shouldn't that be enough for your boss?"

Faye rolled her eyes even though Shirley Ogden couldn't see her. "This is not about my boss."

"Then who is it about?"

"No one you know."

It took all of Faye's self-control not to scream at her mother. Shirley was talking about family get-togethers when she had to focus on getting through the weekend wherein she'd become a social companion to a middle-aged white man who was willing to spend thousands for her to entertain him.

"There will be so many other folks at the cookout that you won't have to speak to your daddy if you don't want to," Shirley continued in the whining tone Faye detested.

"This client is very important."

"How can a client be more important than your family, Faye Anne Ogden?"

And she hated when her mother called her Faye Anne. "Right now, *this* one is."

Faye wanted to tell Shirley that Bart Houghton was Sugar Daddy, Big Willie and Daddy Warbucks all rolled into one. She'd researched Bartholomew Houghton on the Internet and was astounded by the number of articles written about his company. And to her the real estate developer represented a means to an end—lots of money.

"Is your client a boyfriend?"

"I'm going to pretend you didn't say that." She hadn't done it at twenty-two, and now at thirty-two Faye didn't feel that she had to report to her mother about who she saw or slept with.

"What am I going to tell everyone when you don't show up?"

"Tell them I've committed to a working holiday weekend and that I'll see them for the Fourth."

"When am *I* going to see you?"

Faye smiled for the first time since answering the call. "Why don't you come into the city on Friday and spend the weekend with me. We can check into a nice hotel, order room service and shop until we drop."

"I thought you were trying to save money for CJ's appeal."

"I am. But I believe I can afford to treat my mother to a little R&R."

There was a pause on the other end of the line. "That's all right, baby," Shirley crooned softly. "You don't have to. Besides, I have to check with your father to see if he has planned—"

"Stop it, Mama!" Faye shouted, cutting her off. "You know you don't have to check with anyone. Call me before your train gets in to Penn Station and I'll meet you by the information booth," she continued, her tone softening considerably. "I'm going to have to hang up because I don't want to keep my driver waiting. Give everyone my love, and I'll see you Friday."

"Okay, baby. I love you."

"Love you back, Mama."

Pressing a button, Faye ended the connection. If she'd known she was going to get into it with her mother she never would've answered the telephone. She needed to be in control for what she was about to embark upon.

Astrid had called her cell phone Thursday morning to let her know she'd been contracted to work for P.S., Inc. The signing bonus and an additional thousand were deposited into her checking account because Alana Gardner had been hired as well. The booking agent wasted few words when she told her that Bartholomew Houghton wanted her to spend the three-day Memorial Day weekend at his Southampton estate, and that Mr. Houghton would arrange for her return to Manhattan early Tuesday morning.

Astrid had quoted a figure for what she would make for the weekend that rendered her mute long after she'd hung up. Faye was aware of those who won millions on the turn of a card, roll of the dice or with the purchase of a single lottery ticket; but those were games of chance that anyone could win or lose. However, she was a guaranteed winner as long as she worked as a social companion for P.S., Inc.

Glancing at the clock on the bedside table, Faye realized she had less than fifteen minutes before the driver arrived to take her to Southampton. She rechecked her bag, zipped it and placed it in the entryway with the garment bag containing her clothes for Tuesday.

Retreating to her bedroom, she removed a short black silk robe that covered a peach-colored swimsuit; she slipped into a pair of black stretch cropped pants, pulled a white cotton and silk–blend tank top over her head, tying the sleeves to a matching cardigan around her shoulders as she pushed her feet into a pair of black-and-white pinstriped high-heel mules; she peered into a full-length free-standing mirror in the corner of her bedroom. Smiling at her reflection, she squared her shoulders.

Faye Anne Ogden was ready for Bartholomew Houghton and her first assignment as a social companion.

Bartholomew Houghton's chauffeur stood on the sidewalk next to a gleaming black Maybach. He became suddenly alert when he spied a woman matching his boss's description. Striding forward, he reached for her weekender and garment bag. Inclining his head, he gave her a polite smile, his gleaming white teeth a startling contrast against his deeply tanned olive skin.

"Miss Ogden, I am Giuseppe, and I promise to make your ride to Southampton a most comfortable one."

Faye was charmed by the man's accent and his modest confidence. She returned his smile, bringing his gaze to linger briefly on her mouth. "Thank you."

Giuseppe shifted the garment bag to his left arm, bent slightly and opened the rear door of the luxury limousine. He waited until Faye was seated, closed the door, then stored her luggage in the trunk. Minutes later, he pulled away from the curb, maneuvering down streets leading to the Triborough Bridge and Long Island.

Faye settled back against the white napa leather seat that was soft and supple as velvet. She touched the natural-stained wood trim on the doors. The gorgeous black lacquer against the white leather created an art deco mood.

Bentley, Pope and Oliviera handled the Maybach account. The three-ton 57S in which she was a passenger was touted as a super-sedan that delivered luxury and performance combined at the highest level. It was advertised to be impressive and not imposing like the Rolls-Royce Phantom, and even though it didn't catch the eye the way a pricey car should, the ad agency's sales pitch was that people rich enough to own the Maybach didn't always want to look rich.

She stared out a side window, her curiosity piqued. Exactly who was Bartholomew Houghton, president and

CEO of the Dunn-Houghton Group, a man whose private life was shrouded in mystery, a man who'd sent his personal car and chauffeur to bring her to his Southampton estate, a man who'd paid an escort service thousands of dollars for her to entertain him?

The Dunn-Houghton Group, known in the business world as DHG, was still privately owned. There had been talk of it going public ten years before, but the rumors proved unfounded. There was also talk that the CEO of DHG controlled more land than any private developer in America, and though low-key, his real estate projects eclipsed Donald Trump's. And unlike Trump, Bart almost never granted interviews and was highly secretive about his operations.

Letting out a barely audible sigh, she closed her eyes and her mind. She had at least an hour to bring her fragile emotions under control. She didn't want to think about her mother's accusation, her brother's plight or what she was about to embark upon.

When she opened her eyes again she'd left the towering buildings, rumbling subways and pedestrian traffic of the city behind for the pastoral tranquility of the suburbs.

Road signs indicating unfamiliar hamlets and villages dotting Long Island's south shore gave way to Patchogue, Quogue, Shinnecock and finally Southampton.

Giuseppe maneuvered onto a local road, passing farm stands, vineyards and acres of farmland. Faye sat up straighter when she stared at the sprawling properties of the rich, famous and upwardly mobile. Her eyes widened when out of nowhere a large gray-and-white-trimmed three-story house with connecting outbuildings appeared as if she'd conjured it up. It was built on a rise that over-looked the Atlantic Ocean.

A large white tent was erected at the rear, providing shade for those, most dressed in white, who sat at tables, stood around in groups of two or three or danced to the tunes spun by a disc jockey.

Giuseppe turned off the engine and came around to assist her. "I'll see that your bags are taken inside."

Faye nodded. "Thank you."

Glancing around, she recognized Bartholomew Houghton; his back to her, he was engaged in conversa-tion with a woman clinging possessively to his arm. A lone swimmer swam laps in an Olympic-size swimming pool while a bikini-clad nymph floated facedown on an inflated hammock.

Bart's face was darker than it had been the week before, and it was apparent he had taken advantage of the warm weather. The richness of his sun-brown skin was offset by the pristine whiteness of a loose-fitting linen shirt and matching slacks. A pair of tan sandals complemented his stylish dressed-down look.

She saw Alana gazing adoringly into the eyes of a tall, black man whose well-toned body should've graced the cover of a bodybuilding magazine, while Ilene danced with an elderly man who couldn't take his gaze off her. Enid's exotic jewels, as she'd called them, were earning their commissions.

Closing the distance between her and her host/client, Faye said softly, "Mr. Houghton?"

Bart turned slowly when he recognized the dulcet feminine voice, unaware that he'd been waiting a week to come face-to-face with Faye Ogden again. And what he saw made the wait more than worthwhile.

He turned back to the woman beside him. "Please excuse me, Judith, but I must see to my guest."

He forcibly removed the hand resting on his forearm, welcoming the intrusion because he suspected his neighbor's wife had been coming on to him. Even if he'd been desperate to bed a woman, he never would sleep with another man's wife.

CHAPTER 22

Reaching for Faye's right hand, Bart brought it to his lips and pressed a kiss on her fingers, his gaze never straying from her face. Her eyes, sans the smoky hues of eye shadow, shimmered with gold warmth. However, it was her mouth, full and temptingly curved, and with a hint of gloss, that held his rapt attention.

"Welcome to Southampton. I'm so glad you could make it. I also trust you had a pleasant ride."

Faye felt a slight shiver snake its way up her arm. It wasn't from Bart holding her hand but from the way he was staring at her. She'd been on the receiving end of that type of stare enough to recognize lust.

He reminds me of someone I've seen before, she thought, mentally running through images of men she'd encountered. *Anderson Cooper.* His classical features were more refined than the TV journalist, but their resemblance was remarkable.

A hint of a smile softened her mouth. "Thank you for inviting me, and, yes, the ride was wonderful."

Gently squeezing her fingers and tucking them into the bend of his elbow, Bart returned her smile. "Would you like something to drink before I make the introductions?"

"No, thank you." She'd had a bottle of imported mineral water from the Maybach's built-in bar.

She stood with Bart as he introduced her to his Southampton neighbors and the members of DHG's executive staff. As cautioned by Enid, Alana and Ilene pretended not to know her.

With the introductions behind them, she studied her host. He still held her hand, his touch cool and protective without being possessive. Bartholomew Houghton looked nothing like the men to whom she'd find herself attracted. And even if he'd been black he still was too old for her.

The music lowered and the DJ's crooning voice came through the powerful speakers around the tent. "Ladies and gents, I'm going to take it down a notch and spin a few old school jams from back in the day. Come on, people, everyone up and dancing."

The classic number-one hit, Force MD's "Tender Love" filled the air and Bart wrapped his arms around Faye's waist, his fingers splayed over her back, she chuckling softly as he sang off-key along with the vocals.

Lowering his head, he pressed his mouth to her ear. "What's so funny?"

She laughed again. "The only thing I'm going to say is that you dance much better than you sing."

Pulling back, gray eyes filled with amusement, he angled his head. "Are you saying that if I had to sing for a living I'd starve to death?"

"I don't know about starving, but there's no doubt you'd go hungry unless someone took pity on you."

Bart pulled Faye closer, twirling her around and around in an intricate dance step. "Would you take pity on me and give me a morsel to keep me from starving?"

There came a moment of silence as she tried concentrating on following his fancy footwork. "Of course I would," she said in a breathless whisper.

She was fighting for breath, not so much from dancing but from the contours of the lean, hard masculine body pressed intimately against hers, and the clean, metallic scent of the cologne that complemented Bart's natural scent. There was something about him had evoked strange sensations she didn't want to acknowledge.

I don't know how you do it.

Alana's declaration invaded her unsettling thoughts. Her best friend could not understand how she could go months, and as of late, more than a year without sleeping with a man. And as she danced with the man who was her client, a man under whose roof she would reside for three nights, a man who'd paid P.S., Inc. thousands for her companionship, she realized he had unknowingly forced her to question her decision to remain celibate.

Dancing with Bart reminded her that she was a woman who'd been alone for far too long, a woman who'd known of the strong passion within her but had chosen to ignore it.

"Do you mind if I cut in, Mr. H.?"

Bart recognized the voice of the urban planner in whose honor he was hosting the event. Hakim Wheeler was young, brilliant and ambitious, much more ambitious than Bart had been at his age. A Penn State and Columbia School of Business graduate, Hakim was on the fast track to become a key player in the cutthroat world of real estate and investment banking.

With great reluctance, Bart introduced Hakim to Faye and relinquished his hold on her. Under another set of circumstances he would've refused the other man's request. However, he could afford to share Faye because over the next two days he would have her all to himself.

Faye found herself in Hakim Wheeler's embrace. She stared up at him through her lashes, and thought him too beautiful for a man. Exemplifying tall, dark and handsome, his close-cropped haircut afforded him a conservative look, and his smooth mahogany-brown skin, large dark eyes, square jaw, firm mouth, high cheekbones, straight teeth and strong nose were evidence that he'd inherited his parents' best features.

Hakim studied Faye for a long moment. "Are you new at DHG, because I don't remember seeing you around?"

She smiled up at him. "That's because I don't work at DHG."

Hakim's expression did not change with her disclosure. *Nice voice, and very nice face.* Faye Ogden's skin, hair color and eyes reminded him of the Stevie Wonder hit "Golden Lady."

"How do you know Mr. H.?"

"We're friends."

"Boyfriend?" he asked with a slight lifting of his eyebrows.

Faye returned his intent stare. "No. We are friends, Hakim. What do you do at DHG?" she asked without taking a breath, deftly shifting the topic from her to him.

"I'm an urban planner."

"What do you plan?"

Hakim gave her a wide grin, his upper lip flattening against the ridge of his teeth. "I can't say."

It was Faye's turn to lift her eyebrows. "Can't or won't?"

Hakim glanced over Faye's head, encountering Bart's intent stare. He'd worked closely with Bartholomew Houghton for the past three years and had come to admire and sometimes fear the man with the mercurial moods who ran his company like a despot.

When Bart made introductions, there was something in the possessive way he'd held the hand tucked into the bend of his arm that indicated Faye was special. How special he didn't know. Faye said they were friends, while Bart's body language suggested otherwise.

His gaze returned to the face of the woman in his arms. "I can't. DHG employees are bound by a confidentiality agreement not to discuss business outside the office."

"Does that pledge extend to an employee's family?"

He nodded. "Yes, it does."

Hakim's disclosure about the confidentiality agreement told Faye more than she needed to know about her client. It was apparent he was a control freak.

The musical selection ended and Faye dropped her arms. "Thank you for the dance, Hakim."

He winked at her. "Thank *you*. Can you spare a few minutes later?"

"Sure."

She felt the heat of his gaze on her retreating back as she made her way over to a bar where the bartender mixed drinks with a theatrical flourish. She was flattered that Hakim was interested in her, but the truth was that she hadn't come to Southampton to flirt with the sexiest brother she'd encountered in a very long time.

She'd come to work.

CHAPTER 23

"What can I get you?"

Faye forced herself not to stare at the tattoos covering the bartender's forearms. His body art was a collage of black Asian characters with colorful fire-breathing dragons.

"Two Beefeater martinis, extra dry and very dirty."

"Two dirty beefs coming up," Deacon Jeffries repeated. Minutes later he placed the cocktails on the bar.

Faye smiled at him. "Thank you." She picked up the glasses, walked over to Bart and extended one. "May I offer you one Beefeater martini, very dry and very dirty?"

Bart took the glass, his fingers brushing against hers. "Thank you, Faye."

"You're welcome, Mr. Houghton." She dropped her eyes before his steady gaze and took a sip of the cool liquid. It was perfect.

A slight frown dotted Bart's forehead. "I thought we'd established last week that you would call me Bart and I'd address you as Faye." His reprimand was as soft as sterile cotton.

Her expression did not change with the slight rebuke.

"What image do you want *us* to present to your guests? Are we business associates or are we friends?" she whispered.

Bart took a deep swallow of his martini, welcoming the iciness followed by the heat spreading throughout his chest. He'd underestimated Faye Ogden. When they'd sat together over dinner he'd found her intelligent and at times very witty. But now there was something in her tone and body language that indicated defensiveness.

"Friends, Faye."

Holding his gaze, she said in a quiet voice, "I know I'm here on business, and that is what it will remain, because I've made it a practice never to crawl into bed with a man after only one encounter." Rising on tiptoe, she leaned in closer. "Maybe it will never happen."

If she'd sought to shock Bart, then she did when he recoiled as if she'd slapped him. She'd misunderstood his intentions for hiring her.

His eyes darkened like angry storm clouds. Reaching out with his free hand, he led her over to an area of the garden where they wouldn't be overheard by the others. "You're right, Faye, because I didn't *pay* P.S., Inc. because I want to sleep with you."

Pay. The three-letter word reminded Faye why she was in Southampton and not in Queens with her own family. She'd become a paid escort for Pleasure Seekers.

"Then I take that to mean that I'm here for your new vice president."

Seconds ticked off as Bart stared down at the woman

who made him feel things he didn't want to feel. Shaking his head slowly, he said, "No. You're here for *me*."

The seconds ticked off as they stared at each other. Faye had her answer. "Thank you for your honesty."

"Let *me* clear up something before we go any further," Bart said in an eerily quiet tone. "You'll be spending the next two days with me because I'm paying you for companionship." A half smile softened the sharp angles in his face. "Yes, I know you may find that hard to believe, but that's it. I have no hidden agenda. And before you ask whether I'm gay or impotent, the answer is no to both." He winked at her, then put the glass to his mouth and drained it. "Please excuse me, but another one of my guests has just arrived."

Faye didn't move even after Bart disappeared from her line of vision. "Damn!" she spat out between clenched teeth. Her ego had overridden her common sense. Why, she thought, was she so programmed into believing men were attracted to her because they wanted to sleep with her?

But she knew the answer the instant the thought formed in her mind. Every man she'd ever dated eventually wanted the same thing: sex. It had been that way with her first lover, the men that followed and with her husband. Norman admitted he'd married her because he couldn't get enough of her; but he also couldn't get enough of Kendra, Lisa, Cherie and others too numerous to name.

She took another sip of her drink, recalling what Enid had said during the orientation: *I'm going to caution you against sleeping with your clients. It usually spells trouble.*

If Enid's social companions were warned not to sleep with their clients, then there was no doubt the clients were given the same warning.

Faye had to remember she was a companion not a hooker. She'd made a serious *faux pas* when broaching the subject of sleeping with Bart Houghton. However, she had the rest of the weekend to put things right between her and her client.

What she also had to remember was that Pleasure Seekers was a business, and as a contract worker she had to conduct herself like a businesswoman.

She'd come to Southampton as an actress in a role, a role in which she intended to give an award-winning performance.

Her gaze shifted to Alana and Ilene. The two were laughing and dancing, enjoying themselves while she agonized over minutiae. All she had to do was be pleasant and polite for the next two days, and come Tuesday morning she would go back to all that was familiar and predictable.

CHAPTER 24

Bart half listened to his chief financial officer ramble on incessantly about a golf game, his attention was focused on Faye Ogden.

He watched her set her martini on the bar. What he'd suspected the night he sat next to her at Enid Richards's dinner party was confirmed. She wasn't much of a drinker.

Faye had intrigued him the first time he saw her, and she continued to intrigue him. Dressed for the evening, he'd found her beautiful, sensual, alluring. Dressed casually, she was still beautiful but radiated an aura that said look but don't touch.

And he wanted to touch her. His touching did not translate into making love because that would ruin his fantasy, vivid images that swept over him when he least expected.

What Bart had found shocking was that he hadn't indulged in capricious daydreams about the opposite sex since puberty. Then his fantasies weren't about black girls but a well-endowed redhead at his prep school. When he wasn't dreaming about Hannah, it was a nubile Hollywood starlet.

He wasn't certain whether he was undergoing a midlife

crisis, but if he was, he wanted it to continue until he discovered what it was about Faye Ogden that had him so preoccupied with her.

"Nice party, Bart."

He shifted his gaze, nodding and acknowledging the head of DHG's banking division. "Thanks, Jeff."

It was the first time he'd hosted a gathering at his Long Island vacation retreat. He always planned holiday parties for the employees of the Dunn-Houghton Group at upscale Manhattan restaurants, but no one, other than the six who made up his executive team, had ever been inside his Olympic Towers penthouse with panoramic views of the East River, and the many bridges connecting Manhattan with the other boroughs.

He hadn't taken his company public, but that hadn't stopped business analysts from following DHG's successful ventures or failed deals.

His private life was shrouded in mystery, the way he preferred it. A distant cousin had become his date for an occasional soiree, but now that was about to change. He planned to take Faye Ogden to the Cayman Islands for the wedding of the daughter of a former college buddy.

CHAPTER 25

Alana couldn't pull her gaze away from the brilliance of the perfect Lucinda cut diamond solitaire on the finger of a young woman clutching her fiancé's hand. A wave of envy swept over her, as she realized she wanted to be the one wearing the ring while sharing adoring gazes with Calvin.

The day, which had begun so delightfully with the limousine ride to Southampton, had suddenly soured. She'd spent the afternoon eating, drinking and floating on an inflated raft in a heated Olympic-size pool before playing a vigorous game of tennis with a man who reminded her of her favorite dessert, Duncan Hines double-chocolate devil's food cake. The brother literally and figuratively looked good enough to eat. Lowell Knight was single, lived alone and wasn't a baby daddy. He would've been perfect if she wasn't committed to Calvin, who had promised to call her as soon as he recovered from jet lag. She'd been to England enough times to know that it didn't take eight days to get over jet lag.

Her light playful mood had vanished, replaced by a headache and a dark mood that would linger for days unless she sought relief from an over-the-counter medication. And, despite the number of people gathered under the large tent, their voices raised in laughter, and the frivolity that accompanied a relaxed outdoor social gathering, she felt completely alone, abandoned by the one man who claimed the same initials as the first man who'd walked out of her life when she needed him most. Her father: Carlos Moore.

Reaching for her large leather purse, Alana searched its cavernous depths until she found her cell phone. She punched in the numbers for her voice mail, then the access code. Biting down on her lower lip, she willed the tears pricking the backs of her eyelids not to fall when the familiar voice telling her there were "no messages" came through the earpiece.

Scrolling through the directory, she depressed another button for her therapist's number. "This is Alana Gardner," she whispered into the tiny microphone. "I would like to come in Tuesday at six. Please ring me back Tuesday morning to confirm." She ended the call and dropped the tiny phone into her bag.

"Are you all right, Lana?"

She turned to find Faye staring at her. "Sure," she said much too quickly.

Faye sat down next to Alana, studying her closely. She knew there was something wrong with her friend, but decided it was not the time or place to question her. They'd come to Long Island to have fun and make lots of money while doing it.

Alana forced a smile. "What's up with you and Hakim? I hope you got his number."

"No, I didn't."

"What!"

Faye winked at her. "I gave him mine."

Alana returned the wink despite her throbbing temples. "Now, that's my girl."

Faye had told Hakim she wouldn't be able to go out with him until after Labor Day because she was working on a special project. What she didn't tell him was that the project was working as an escort.

"After Bart introduced you two, I saw you hanging on to Lowell Knight."

Alana massaged her temples with her fingertips. "It was all for show."

"Nice performance."

"It's not like that anymore, Faye. I'm totally committed to Calvin. "

But is Calvin totally committed to you? Faye wanted to ask.

"What time are you leaving?" Alana asked. The party was winding down and the crowd was beginning to thin out with the onset of dusk.

"I'm not."

Alana stared, tongue-tied. "You're spending the night?"

Faye's body stiffened in shock. Her best friend's query was layered with an accusatory tone that set her teeth on edge. "Yes."

Alana leaned closer. "What the hell are you doing,

Faye?" she whispered. "Just because Bartholomew Houghton waves some paper in your face, you're ready to drop your panties and—"

"Stop it, Lana, and get your mind out of the gutter." Faye's voice was low and filled with a seething rage she found hard to control. "You should know me better than that. The man wants me to spend the weekend with him, and sleeping together doesn't figure into the equation.

"In case you've forgotten why I decided to sign on with P.S., Inc., let me refresh your memory. I need money for my brother's appeal—a lot of money, because most lawyers see rapists and pedophiles as bottom-feeders in the criminal-justice food chain. Even murderers command more respect. So if Bartholomew Houghton wants me to spend a month with him, then I'll do it. And if it means lying on my back to get the last dollar, then I'll do that too."

Alana studied the bright pink polish on her toes rather than meet Faye's angry gaze. She *had* forgotten about Craig Ogden Jr. because despite the turmoil going on in the Ogden household Faye always appeared so well adjusted. The only time she saw her lose her composure was after Faye received a letter from her brother informing her that he'd spent a week in the Auburn Correctional Facility hospital recovering from a beating that prison officials documented as an accident at the maximum-security penitentiary.

"I don't know why I keep forgetting about your brother." Her head came up. "I'm sorry."

Faye saw the tears filling Alana's eyes. "Damn, Alana,"

she whispered. "You'd cry if you stepped on an ant. There's no need to apologize. Please dry it up, Lana, before we both start bawling."

"Do you have anything for a headache? My head is pounding."

"No, but I'll ask Bart if he has some in the house."

Alana closed her eyes, willing the pain to go away. When she opened them again it was to see Lowell Knight sitting in the chair Faye had vacated, his dark gaze fixed on her face.

"What's the matter, beautiful?"

She closed her eyes again. "I have a mother of a headache."

Shifting his chair behind hers, Lowell rested his hands on her shoulders. "Relax," he crooned as he gently massaged her shoulders and neck. "You've got knots everywhere."

Alana lost herself in the warmth and sensual smell of the body pressed inches from her own, and the strength of the fingers moving sensuously over the nape of her neck. She let down her guard, and for a few minutes she fantasized that it was Calvin's hands on her bared flesh.

However, reality surfaced when Faye returned with a bottle of water and a tiny paper cup containing two aspirins.

CHAPTER 26

Alana spent the drive from Southampton to Manhattan with her eyes closed and her head in Lowell Knight's lap. The pounding in her temples had subsided but it was the warmth of the hard thigh under her cheek, the gentle touch of fingertips messaging her temples and the gliding motion from the limo's smooth suspension that eased her tension headache.

"Come home with me tonight," Lowell whispered close to her ear, even though he doubted the driver could hear him on the other side of the closed partition.

"I can't."

"It's not as if you have someone waiting for you at home."

Alana opened her eyes, and sat up, scooting over on the leather seat to put some distance between herself and the handsome architect. She'd confided to Lowell that she was engaged and that her musician fiancé was currently touring with his band.

She glared at him. "I come home with you and we do what?"

Lowell smiled, displaying deep dimples in sable-brown

sculpted cheeks. His steady midnight gaze was filled with amusement. "It's not what you think, Alana."

Some of the stiffness left her body. "What is it I'm thinking, Lowell? That because my fiancé is out of the country, I'd crawl into bed with you?"

Shaking his head, Lowell moved over and pulled her to his side. He rested his chin on the top of her head, her curly hair tickling his nose. "Are you this distrustful of every man you meet?"

Alana trusted Calvin, yet that hadn't been the case with the other men she'd been involved with. There was something about Calvin that told her *he was the one* she wanted to spend the rest of her life with; *he was the one* whose babies she wanted to have.

"Not every man."

An inexplicable look of withdrawal came over Lowell's face. He liked Alana Gardner—a lot. She was beautiful, smart and claimed a sense of humor he found refreshing. She was candid, something he'd found missing in some of the women he knew, and that included his ex-wife, and, despite her affianced status he saw a sadness in Alana she attempted to conceal behind a too bright smile and witty quips.

"I share a brownstone in Fort Greene with my brother and his family. If you don't feel comfortable staying with me, then you can sleep in a guest bedroom in my brother's apartment. We're going to have a block party tomorrow afternoon, so I'd like to invite you to come as my guest."

Tilting her chin, Alana stared up into the obsidian gaze

of the man with sculpted features reminiscent of a carved African mask, and just for an instant regretted her involvement with Calvin. However, the moment passed as quickly as it'd come.

"I'd love to accept, but I'm expecting an overseas telephone call from my fiancé."

It felt good to refer to Calvin as her fiancé instead of her boyfriend, partner or live-in companion. But on the other hand she wouldn't have to tell anyone she was engaged if she'd been wearing a ring.

If Lowell was let down by her declination, he did not show it. "Perhaps I can call you at the magazine and we can either meet for lunch or dinner. I will leave that up to you."

She lowered her gaze. "I can't, Lowell, because I don't want to give you the impression that anything could possibly happen between us." Glancing up, she met his penetrating gaze again, smiling. "Where were you a couple of years ago when I was trolling clubs looking for a together brother?"

Lowell's mouth took on an unpleasant twist. "Even if you were unattached two years ago I doubt we would've met."

"Why?"

"Because I was going through a divorce, and I've never trolled clubs. I'm not looking to get married again—at least not for a few years. I thought we could see each other as friends."

Pushing against his chest, Alana straightened. "It wouldn't work," she said softly, "because there may come a time when we may want more than friendship."

"And what would that be, Alana?"

"Sex, Lowell. I've never been unfaithful to Calvin."

Lowell's expression was tight with exasperation. He never had to try this hard to convince a woman—any woman—to go out with him, but Alana Gardner was testing his patience. "Is that why you're pining over your globe-trotting musician boyfriend, because he's promised you marriage?"

Alana's temper exploded. "Who the hell do you think you are to fix your mouth and say something like that to me?"

A sardonic smile parting his lips, Lowell said, "Lowell Russell Knight."

Rage made it difficult for Alana to draw a normal breath. Within seconds Lowell had become her father and every man who'd done every woman in the world wrong. They were all egotistical bastards who, like spoiled little boys, wanted what they wanted, and when they couldn't get their way they either pouted, sulked or went on the defensive.

"Fuck you, Mr. Lowell Russell Knight!" she hissed.

Lowell studied Alana thoughtfully for a moment before he slid over and stared out the side window, swallowing the acrimonious words poised on the tip of his tongue. He was still in the same position, unseeing eyes staring at landmarks he knew like the back of his hand when the driver maneuvered westward along One Hundred and Twenty-fifth Street, then turned in a southwesterly direction onto Frederick Douglass Boulevard to Central Park West.

He sat up straighter when the chauffer stopped in front of a canopy building facing the park. He opened the rear door and stepped out onto the sidewalk, smiling when

Alana slid over and placed her hand in his. Hand in hand he escorted her under the dark red canopy as a doorman in matching maroon livery surreptitiously averted his gaze.

Leaning down, Lowell pressed a kiss to Alana's cheek. "It would've been good, Alana."

She gave him a long, penetrating look. "It's too bad we'll never know."

"You're wrong, because one of these days you're going to regret your decision not to become friends."

Lowell's prediction was layered with an arrogance that sickened her. "Goodbye and good luck, Lowell."

Not waiting for a response, she turned and walked into the lobby, stopping at a wall of mailboxes to retrieve her mail. Flipping through the stack, she looked for a letter or postcard with a London postmark.

Her heart sank. There was nothing from Calvin. Tears blurred her vision as she made her way over to the bank of elevators. By the time she exited the car on the eleventh floor her brain was in tumult, and a war of emotions within her raged uncontrollably.

She opened the door to her apartment, dropping her handbag and keys on the table in the entryway. She didn't remember undressing, taking a shower or crawling into bed—alone.

What she did remember when she awoke four hours later and peered at the display on her telephone was that Calvin still hadn't called. Then she did something she'd promised herself she wouldn't do. She dialed the number to his cell phone.

Her heart pumping a runaway rhythm, her palms moist, a knot forming in her stomach, Alana counted off two rings. She quickly changed her mind, pressing the button to disconnect the call. Her movements were mechanical as she replaced the receiver in the cradle, turned off the bedside lamp, lay down and pulled the sheet up over her head as she'd done as a child whenever she heard her parents arguing.

She'd reverted to a time in her life when she'd pretended she was a princess and all she had to do was make a wish and her prince would come and rescue her.

She would give Calvin McNair another week. If he didn't call her, then she would call him.

CHAPTER 27

The music stopped and the catering staff finished loading their van when the large orange ball of the sun dropped below the horizon, leaving streaks of red in the darkening sky.

Faye lay on a cushioned chaise, eyes closed, listening to the sounds of fading automobile engines and the lulling, relaxing surge of the incoming tide. She'd swum laps in the pool, joined in a vigorous game of water volleyball, washed off the chlorine in a freestanding shower in the pool house then joined the other partygoers for a leisurely sumptuous buffet, followed by dancing nonstop to music spanning decades.

She loathed moving. If the nighttime temperatures didn't drop too much, she would be content to spend the night where she lay.

Faye must have dozed off, because something jolted her awake. Within seconds her flesh pebbled. It wasn't from the cool breeze blowing off the water.

"Would you like a pillow and blanket?"

Her gaze met and held Bart's in the remaining daylight. "No, thank you."

Hunkering down beside her, he angled his head. "Would you like to go inside?"

Rising slightly, she patted the cushion on a nearby chaise. "I'm not ready to turn in. But I would like company." She knew her request shocked him because he went completely still for several seconds then complied, folding his lanky frame down to a nearby matching lounge chair.

Staring up at the spray of stars littering the darkening sky, Bart was able to identify a few visible constellations in the late-spring heavens. He pretended interest in the stars instead of the woman lying less than six inches away. Lights surrounding the house and property were coming on with the encroaching nightfall while everything about Faye Ogden engulfed him in a diaphanous spell, her feminine essence holding him captive.

He closed his eyes, still seeing the play of gold on her satiny skin, her slanting light brown eyes, high, exotic cheekbones, temptingly sensual outline of full lips and her sexy body.

"Did you hire Hakim and Lowell for their looks or for their brains?" Faye said, her query breaking the comfortable silence.

Bart opened his eyes, sat up, blinking in bewilderment. "What did you say?"

Faye's eyebrows lifted as she struggled not to laugh. "I said, did you hire your black vice presidents because they meet the criteria of tall, dark and hand—"

"Stop it, Faye," he countered softly, interrupting her. "Do you actually believe I'm that shallow?"

"I don't know, Bart. You tell me."

He noticed a smile tugging at the corners of her mouth. It was apparent she was teasing him. Teasing or not, he wondered if Faye was interested in Hakim, because there no doubt the extremely talented urban planner was interested in her. And it wasn't the first time someone had mentioned Lowell's and Hakim's striking good looks.

Bart lay down again. "It's just a coincidence that they happen to be the total package."

"How many people work for you?"

"They don't work for me, Faye. They're employed by DHG."

The seconds ticked off as a swollen silence escalated between the two strangers. And despite Faye's disclosure to Hakim that she and Bart were friends, the fact remained that they didn't know enough about each other to claim that designation.

Her expression stilled and grew serious. "Are you always so literal, or is this your subtle way of telling me to mind my business?"

Bart laced his fingers together and positioned them under his head. "I would never do that." There came another lengthy pause. "What is it you want to know about me?"

Turning over to face him, Faye rested her head on a folded arm. Why hadn't she noticed the deep timbre of Bart's voice before? A deep, soft voice filled with a power that defied one not to question or challenge his authority.

"You can begin by telling me a little about Bartholomew Houghton."

He smiled. If he hadn't endeavored to keep out of the spotlight, he knew Faye wouldn't have asked him to talk about himself.

"There's not much to tell."

"Then tell me whatever you're willing to disclose."

Bart shifted on his chaise, staring directly at her. "I'm fifty, widowed and have no children. I was born upstate about thirty miles west of Albany. I grew up dirt poor. My father did odd jobs to keep a roof over our heads, and my mother worked in a dress factory and a local diner on weekends to put food on the table. The year I turned twelve, everything changed. Dad was hired as caretaker for the Rhinebeck Academy. We moved out of a rented trailer and into a three-bedroom house in the Hudson Valley. Dad took the position because he had steady work, a decent place to live and his sons were offered a tuition-free prep-school education."

"Which means you were given the advantage of a privileged education," Faye said, smiling.

Bart returned her smile, the expression deepening the lines around his extraordinary eyes. "Yes." There was no modesty in the single word. "I was able to read Chaucer in Old English years before my public-school counterpart. The first day I walked into class and the instructors called me Master Houghton made me aware that if I studied harder than the other kids, I'd eventually overcome the stigma of being the *janitor's kid*."

Without warning, he sobered. "And it wasn't until years later that I realized that many of my classmates weren't enrolled in Rhinebeck because they had above-average intelligence, but because their wealthy parents sought to conceal their academic and behavioral weaknesses."

Faye tried making out Bart's expression in the shadowy light. "Do you think you'd be who you now are if you hadn't gone to an elite private school?"

He shook his head. "No. Attending Rhinebeck gave me access to those with financial and political clout I never would've met no matter how hard I studied or worked."

"Did you work hard, Bart?"

He chuckled. "I'm still working hard. But that's going to change in ten years."

"What's going to happen in ten years?"

"I'm going into semiretirement."

"Don't tell me you're going to become an amateur golfer." Much to her surprise, Bart laughed heartily, the deep rumbling sound coming from his chest.

"How did you know?"

She sat up and swung her legs over the chaise. "I think I read a survey somewhere about what men want to do once they retire, and the number-one choice is golf."

Following her movements, Bart sat up and reached over to grasp her fingers. "What would you like to do in ten years?"

Faye felt the power in his slender hands, and the energy of his touch radiating up her arm. How many times, she wondered, had he sealed a deal with a mere handshake?

She was alone with an extremely wealthy man who hadn't bothered to hide his attraction for her while she continued to agonize about whether her becoming a paid social companion was morally correct.

"Faye?"

Bart calling her name brought her out of her reverie. Flashing a plastic smile, she stared up at him through her lashes. "I would like to follow your example."

His gaze fixed on her mouth, he angled his head. "How?"

"I want to run my own marketing firm."

"Do you have the startup capital?"

She shook her head. "Not yet. That's why I'm working for P.S., Inc." She'd told him a half truth. She needed *his* money for her brother's appeal.

Bart was hard pressed not to laugh aloud. Faye Ogden had just walked into a trap of her own choosing. "I believe I can help you out."

"How?"

"I want you to work exclusively for me. It will always be weekends, although there could be an occasional weekday evening. I've been invited to a wedding in the Cayman Islands in two weeks and I'd like you to accompany me."

Faye was certain Bart could feel the runaway beating of the pulse in her wrists. His request for her to become his personal social companion was the solution to all of her problems.

"When are *we* leaving?"

Bart stared at Faye as if he was photographing her with his eyes. Her remarkable face fascinated him. "Do you have a valid passport?" She nodded. "We'll lift off Friday evening around seven. Giuseppe will pick you up at five at your home. Will that present a problem for you?"

Faye felt a rush of excitement. Bartholomew Houghton would give her entrée into a world where she was expected to be ready to jet off to a foreign country or island at a moment's notice. "No, it won't."

An expression of satisfaction filled Bart's gaze. "I'll contact Enid next week and give her all the particulars." Tightening his grip on her delicate fingers, he rose to his feet, pulling Faye up with him. "Let me show you to your room, because as tempting as it may appear, sleeping outdoors is risky even in Southampton."

Leaning against Bart to keep her balance, Faye slipped her feet into her shoes. He cupped her elbow as he led her off the patio through a set of French doors and into a two-story great room with two stone-facing fireplaces.

"Would you like to go golfing with me early tomorrow morning?"

Her eyes narrowed. "How early is early?"

"Five." Faye stopped suddenly, causing Bart to bump into her. Tightening his grip on her arm, he steadied her. She gave him a look that spoke volumes. "You can say no without giving me an eye roll."

Unconsciously her brow furrowed. "What?"

"You did that thing with your eyes—"

"Are you trying to say that I…I rolled my eyes?" Faye sputtered, interrupting him.

He nodded. "Yeah, that." Much to Bart's surprise, Faye threw back her head, baring her throat, and laughed, the husky sound sending a shiver through his body. She even had a sexy laugh. His mercurial mood changed quickly as his dark eyebrows slanted in a frown. "What's so funny?"

Faye moved closer, a breast brushing his arm. "It's called *rolling one's eyes*." She made a distinctive sound with her mouth. "And that's *sucking one's teeth*. Both gestures are viewed as defiance and disrespect. If my eyes said anything, it was *you've got to be kidding*."

Bart flashed an irresistibly devastating grin before he leaned over and kissed her forehead. "You don't have to get up and go with me. I should be back before nine."

"What have you planned for Sunday and Monday?" Her query had come out in a breathless whisper.

"I didn't plan for anything. But if you want to go some-where, then let me know." He'd declined an invitation for a Sunday-evening dinner cruise with an award-winning movie director because he wanted to use the time to become better acquainted with Faye. "And if there's anything you need please let me know. I'll have Giuseppe go to town and get it for you."

Faye shook her head. "Thanks for offering, but I don't think I'll need anything."

"I want you to feel at home this weekend. I've informed Mrs. Llewellyn and Jamie that they're to see to your needs."

"I told you that I don't need anything, Bart."

He winked at her. "I'm telling you this in case you change your mind."

Bart had come to depend on Mrs. Llewellyn to keep his residences running smoothly. The dependable live-in housekeeper divided her time between Manhattan and Long Island during the summer months, while her grandson, a full-time student at the Long Island University Southampton campus, lived year-round at the house.

He slipped his arm around Faye's waist and led her across the cavernous space and up a staircase to her suite of rooms. It'd been months since he'd requested a social companion from P.S., Inc. Those he'd chosen in the past were usually pretty; however, they were superficial, one-dimensional and a few downright silly.

However, he knew it would be different with Faye Ogden. Not only was she intelligent and articulate, but also very feminine. It was the first time he'd introduced a companion to his employees, and in two weeks it would become the first time he would travel out of the country with one.

He'd never been one to take risks with women, but this time he hoped that he'd hit the jackpot.

CHAPTER 28

A table lamp cast a soft glow in the sitting room as Enid shifted on the daybed and rested her head on Marcus's shoulder. A soft sigh escaped her parted lips as she sought a more comfortable position.

Marcus trailed his fingertips over her bare shoulder. "Why are you so jumpy?"

"I was just wondering how my exotic jewels performed today."

He smiled. "I suppose it really doesn't matter, because you'll get paid no matter how well they perform."

Enid moved again, pushing her buttocks against his groin. "It's not all about money, Marcus."

His mouth replaced his fingers. "You're wrong, Enid. That's all it's ever been from day one when you came up with the concept of establishing an escort service."

"Anyone who goes into business is always concerned with the bottom line. But it goes deeper than that, darling."

Marcus's hand moved to her hair. "What are you talking about?"

"It's about being successful. It's—"

"You *are* successful," Marcus insisted, interrupting her.

"You were a very successful attorney and P.S., Inc. is a very successful escort service. What more do you want?"

"I need five million dollars."

Without warning, Marcus sat up, bringing Enid up with him. He stared at her, baffled. "What are you talking about?"

"Remember when I had you set up that annuity for me?"

"Yes. But what does that have to do with you and five million dollars?"

Pulling her knees to her chest, Enid wrapped her arms around her legs. "I want to set up an endowment for a new charity."

"What!"

She shook her head and thick flaxen waves fell over her forehead. "Don't, Marcus."

Moving off the daybed, Marcus sat on the cool wood floor and pulled Enid down to his lap. His arms tightened around her waist. "Please don't be that way. What charity are you talking about?"

"Habitat for Humanity."

Pressing his mouth to her damp hair, Marcus closed his eyes. Just when he thought he understood who Enid Richards was, she changed before his eyes, leaving him confused and off balance. Enid was a wealthy woman— a very intelligent wealthy woman—who controlled every phase of her life *and* her finances.

She was conservative when it came to investing her money and generous when contributing to her favorite causes. She'd admitted to him that she'd drawn up a will that included leaving the bulk of her estate to the United Negro College Fund and the St. Jude Children's Research Hospital.

"What brought this on, darling?"

Enid turned and faced Marcus, straddling him, her love for him evident in her gaze. "The destruction left by Hurricane Katrina. When I saw televised footage of the area where I'd lived and gone to school, I felt as if someone had stabbed me."

Cradling her head between his hands, Marcus kissed her forehead. He'd forgotten his lover was a native Louisianan. "What do you want me to do, darling?"

Enid buried her face against the side of his neck. "I need you to liquidate a few investments, then work up a projection based on our average summer contact hours."

"Okay. I'll see what I can come up with." He hesitated. "May I suggest something?" Easing back, she nodded. "Why don't you host a fund-raiser before the end of the summer? You definitely know enough people with deep pockets who'd be willing to contribute to a very worthy cause."

Throwing back her head, Enid laughed, the sensual sound sweeping over Marcus like a soft warm breeze. "You are remarkable."

His smile matched hers. "Why, thank you, darling. I think I can help you out with a few well-heeled contributors."

Enid kissed his smiling mouth. "Who are they?"

Tightening his arms around her body, he whispered, "I can't tell you." He planned to ask the record producer cousins and some of their high-profile hip-hop recording artists to come to Enid's latest philanthropic project.

"You know I don't like it when you keep secrets from me," she chided. There was a hint of censure in her voice.

Bracing one hand on the floor, Marcus came to his feet, bringing Enid up with him. He hadn't bothered to shave and the stubble of an emerging beard made his dark skin appear almost blue-black.

He dropped his arms. "I'm never going to tell you everything about me, Enid. And I don't want to know everything about you. That would spoil the fantasy."

A rush of color stained her face. "You think what we have, what we share with each other, is fantasy?"

"Some of it is."

It wasn't often Enid found herself at a loss for words, but this was one of those times. "I see."

"No, you don't see," he countered. "Age difference aside, what we have is a very unconventional relationship. We're business partners *and* lovers."

"Need I remind you that we were lovers before we became business partners?"

"That's true. But the instant we became business partners we should've stopped sleeping with each other, but we didn't."

"That's because I don't want to stop sleeping with you."

"I feel the same, but how long do you think we can continue like this? Maintaining separate residences, setting up appointments to see each other. Now I live with you during the week, and you come to live with me on weekends." He paused. "I grew up in a very stable environment that makes me conservative and somewhat parochial. I don't do well with change or instability. I suppose that's why I became an accountant. Numbers are submissive and they don't lie." Leaning over, he kissed the end of her nose. "I'm like a column of numbers, darling. You can use your head or a calculator to add me up, and the result will always be the same."

There was a Marcus Hampton Enid loved and there was a Marcus Hampton that tested her. At the moment he'd become the latter. "You're lecturing me and that always annoys me."

"No, Enid. I'm being truthful." He glanced at his watch. "I don't know about you, but I'm ready to eat. If we're still going to walk across the Brooklyn Bridge to Andrés Bistro we should leave now."

Rising on tiptoe, she pressed her lips to his in a caressing motion that left him breathing heavily. "All I have to do is put on some running shoes and comb my hair."

"I'll wait for you downstairs." Marcus walked out of the sitting room, into the bedroom and over to the night table on his side of the bed. Opening the drawer, he took out a small leather case with his credit cards and driver's license, then counted out several bills from a sizable stack, pushing them into a zippered pocket of his track-suit pants.

He left the duplex, taking the staircase to the street level. The quiet tree-lined street was teeming with couples strolling leisurely, while dog walkers stopped to chat as their dogs communicated in their own canine way.

Marcus loved warm weather, the pulsing nonstop

rhythm so inherent to Manhattan and Enid Richards, but not necessarily in that order.

He hadn't been waiting that long when Enid joined him, her pale hair concealed under a New York Mets baseball cap. She wore a lightweight sweatshirt over a tank top and a pair of faded jeans.

She was beautiful.

And she was his.

CHAPTER 29

Faye uncrossed her legs, picked up the remote and turned off one of the TV screens installed in the back of the Maybach's headrests.

"Will you please stop fidgeting, Faye?"

Faye turned and stared at Bart; he looked nothing like the casually dressed man with whom she'd spent the past two days. This morning he wore a crisp white shirt with his initials embroidered on the left French cuff and a dark gray silk tie. He'd draped one dark gray, faint pin-striped–covered leg over the opposite knee and had put on a pair of reading glasses to read a report nestled between the covers of a leather binder.

"I'm not fidgeting," Faye countered, not bothering to hide her frustration. She told Bart that she *had* to return to Manhattan in time for a breakfast meeting to present a marketing campaign for a classic Italian luxury automobile. How could she be at her office at eight-thirty when it was seven-thirty and she still was in Southampton?

Removing his glasses, Bart slipped the collapsible eyewear into a slender metal case, giving Faye a sidelong glance. He closed the portfolio, his gaze caressing her lightly made-up face before it moved lower to her feet, encased in a pair of navy blue ostrich-skin pumps.

"You've crossed and uncrossed your legs at least five times."

She gave him an incredulous stare. "Crossing my legs bothers you when the television doesn't?"

Leaning back against the white leather seat, Bart closed his eyes for several seconds. "The images on the screen aren't half as distracting as your legs." He smiled, his expression softening. "I would've asked you to turn off the TV if it *had* annoyed me." He reached for the remote and pressed a button. The familiar face of a *Good Morning America* anchor appeared on the screen once again.

Faye stared out the side window as she mentally ran through her proposed sales pitch. The weekend that had begun with trepidation for her had been nothing short of perfection. The suite she'd been assigned in the farmhouse's guest wing was reminiscent of those in the best hotels. Tables cradling cobalt-blue vases filled with fresh white roses and tulips filled the space with a soft floral fragrance. A utility kitchen was tucked away next to a dining area and living room with Federal-era antiques, a spacious bedroom and adjoining bath, all decorated with differing shades of blues and white: a sea of blue floral carpet, indigo-and-white patchwork quilts, Wedgwood blue-and-white fabrics covering tables and armchairs and matching footstools. A full-tester bed, covered with a sheer creamy fabric with a faint diamond pattern, had beckoned her to stay in bed long beyond her usual rising time.

She'd finally left the bed, made her way to the bathroom and spent the next three-quarters of an hour in the garden bathtub, relaxing amid the warm waters of the Jacuzzi.

By the time she walked into the kitchen she'd forgotten about her brother's imprisonment and that she'd agreed to become an exclusive social companion for Bartholomew Houghton.

Bart turned out to be the perfect host. He'd returned from his golf outing in time to join her for breakfast of huevos rancheros, a melon salad with yogurt-honey dressing and almond-currant scones while they read the Sunday *Times*. They'd discussed the articles when they took a leisurely walk along the beach. The remainder of the afternoon was spent swimming laps in the pool and napping on the patio; they ate dinner outdoors with the setting sun as backdrop.

True to his word, Bart hadn't tried to get her to sleep with him. His interaction with her had become that of friend. They were able to talk about everything: sports, movies, books and even politics.

Monday was a repeat of Sunday until rain forced them indoors. After dinner, Bart popped a large bowl of microwave popcorn while she sorted through hundreds of DVDs for a movie she hadn't seen. All of the titles were alphabetized, but there was a separate section for Best Picture Oscar winners. When she selected Clint Eastwood's *Unforgiven*, Bart teased her, saying he thought she would've chosen a chick flick.

"This is as far as we go."

Faye sat up straighter. The car had stopped and Giuseppe had gotten out and opened the rear door for her. Reaching for her handbag, she offered the driver her hand. Sitting in an open field off a narrow road sat a helicopter with the DHL Group logo emblazoned on its side. She wasn't given time to acknowledge that her ride back to Manhattan would not be by road but by air, when Bart reached for her hand and led her toward the helicopter.

She glanced up at his impassive face. "What about my luggage?"

"Giuseppe will bring it later. He told me that you live in a building with a doorman, so he'll leave them with whoever is on duty."

She nodded and made her way up the steps and into the aircraft, Bart following. She sat down and buckled herself in. Bart sat beside her as the pilot shut and locked the door. Closing her eyes, she clasped her hands together and mumbled a silent prayer. She didn't like flying but knew it was the fastest and most efficient mode of transportation.

Bart buckled his seat belt, then draped his suit jacket over his lap. Reaching over, he placed his left hand over Faye's clasped hands. "Is this your first copter ride?"

"Yes," she said, not opening her eyes.

He squeezed her fisted hands. "The first time is a little scary, but you'll get used to it."

Faye opened her eyes. The gold orbs glistened from unshed moisture. "Do you always travel between the city and Southampton by helicopter?"

Bart smiled at Faye as if she were a small child. He'd

found her mature beyond her years, her knowledge of different subjects astounding, yet she reacted to her first helicopter ride like a frightened child.

Leaning over, he pressed a kiss to her temple. "Yes."

It was the last word they exchanged as the pilot started the engine and the aircraft rose off the ground, tilting slightly to the right until they were airborne.

Faye glanced at her watch at the same time the pilot put the copter down at the heliport on Thirty-fourth Street and the East River. It was exactly eight o'clock. A bright smile curved her mouth when she met Bart's amused stare.

He winked at her. "You thought you were going to be late, didn't you?"

A rush of heat burned her cheeks. "Yes, I did."

He winked at her again. "You're going to have to learn to trust me, Faye."

She met his gray-eyed stare, recognizing determination and confidence in his stoic expression. He was right. She had to trust him if she hoped to make enough money for her brother's appeal.

"I know."

Their gazes held until the pilot opened the door and lowered the steps. Bart alighted, then turned and assisted Faye. He pushed his arms into his suit jacket and tucked the leather case under one arm. His free hand cradled the small of her back as he led her over to where a driver and car awaited their arrival.

The black-suited man opened the rear door. "Good morning, Mr. H."

Bart inclined his head. "Good morning, Kevin." Faye got into the town car and he moved in beside her. "Where do you want me to drop you?"

Faye gave him the address to the building housing the offices of Bentley, Pope and Oliviera, then settled back to enjoy the short ride uptown.

The chauffeur drove quickly, expertly, and ten minutes later maneuvered in front of the thirty-two-story office building on Third Avenue. Kevin came around to open the rear door. Bart alighted, then Faye.

Tilting her head and extending her hand, Faye gave Bart a warm smile. "Thank you for a wonderful weekend."

He inclined his head and ignored her hand. Taking a step, he brushed a light kiss over her parted lips. "Thank you for being you," he whispered near her ear.

He stepped back and watched as Faye made her way toward the entrance of the towering office building. He was still in the same spot after she'd disappeared from his line of vision. It was another full minute before he ducked his head and got back into the limo, the solid door closing behind him.

Reaching into his shirt pocket, he took out his half glasses, placed them on the bridge of his nose and opened the leather case to review the report that had been faxed to him earlier that morning.

All thoughts of Faye Ogden vanished as he slipped into the mind-set of CEO of the Dunn-Houghton Group.

CHAPTER 30

"I think it's time BP&O use marketing tools designed to mainstream hip-hop." A lifting of eyebrows, dropped jaws, and gasps followed Faye's opening statement. "Hip-hop mogul Sean 'P. Diddy' Combs's Sean John fashion label is touted as the urban Ralph Lauren, while brands like Rocawear, Phat Farm, FUBU, Ecko and Enyce urban apparel has steadily gobbled up the market share from the big three menswear brands of the 1990s—Polo Ralph Lauren, Tommy Hilfiger and Nautica. With sales of eight billion last year, urban apparel is considered the fastest-growing category in the 58-billion-dollar menswear industry. We—"

"What does this have to do with selling cars?" A senior executive responsible for the Maybach account interjected.

Faye narrowed her eyes. "If you don't interrupt I'd tell you how it's related to selling cars." She'd already used up two of the fifteen minutes allotted her.

"Hip-hop has expanded beyond its young black and Latino audience to reach a broader demographic," she continued smoothly. "In many ways the auto industry is just catching up with the rest of corporate America, because hip-hop brand endorsements date back to the early 1980s with running shoes and soft drinks. Now, here we are twenty years later still pondering if rap is a fad. *We* have to say no, it's not a fad, because it's the leader in terms of influencing today's culture.

"No car has benefited more from hip-hop culture than the Escalade SUV. It may be partly because the Cadillac has long been a coveted brand among African-Americans. How many of you have seen MTV's *Pimp My Ride?*" Surprisingly, half a dozen hands went up. Faye smiled. "The show's host, Xzibit, has referred to the Cadillac as 'the king of cars.'"

She placed a large photograph of a sleek black roadster on an easel. "The same can be said for Italy's Andino. When first introduced in 1948 the response was lukewarm. However, sales have risen steadily over the past five decades. But now with a new design and a 469-horsepower supercharged V–8, the manufacturer can market it to a young and very hip consumer. The engine enables it to hit sixty miles per hour in less than five seconds, and a new six-speed automatic transmission lets the driver change gears manually with a tap of the gearshift lever. Another innovative feature is adaptive headlamps that pivot in conjunction with the car's steering wheel to illuminate the road around curves."

Faye took a breath. She could tell by the rapt expressions that she had everyone's attention. "Chrysler got rapper 50 Cent to debut their 300 C in his rap video and sales exploded. I'm certain Andino can achieve similar success if they debut their LXR–V in a similar video."

John Reynolds stopped scribbling notes on a legal pad. "Isn't the one-hundred-thousand-dollar price tag a little steep for this gangsta-image generation?"

"Do you own a Rolls or Learjet, John?" Her words were layered with a sweetness that disguised her sarcasm.

"No. Why?"

"I can name several hip-hop artists and rappers who do." She frowned slightly. "I will never stand before you and propose to market a product to a particular population who can't afford to buy that product. And to answer your question, John—The price tag is not too steep for any African-American who wants to own an Andino LXR–V. Contrary to popular belief, *we* buy whatever we want and can afford."

Faye sat down, chest heaving and runaway heartbeat pounding in her ears. BP&O had hired her because she had her finger on the pulse of the black consumer, yet something wouldn't allow her boss to trust her completely. Had she not proven herself over the past five years?

She looked at John staring back at her, seeing something in his expression that hadn't been there before. He was upset because she'd taken him to task in front of his superiors. Well, she never would've verbally spanked him if he hadn't challenged her in an open meeting.

Her gaze shifted to the notes on the pad in front of her. When Bart Houghton had asked her what she wanted to do ten years from now she'd told him she wanted to run her own marketing firm. As soon as she finished her presentation, the one she'd wanted to use for her own company, she realized there was no way she would remain with BP&O for another ten years. Now she doubted whether she would stay beyond the end of the year.

Bart had asked her to work exclusively for him, and she said she would. Unknowingly, he had become her genie and fairy godfather, the one man who would grant most of her wishes.

She smiled at John Reynolds before her gaze shifted to Jessica Adelson. There was no doubt his *niece* had insisted she attend the presentation. Faye wanted to tell the attractive middle-aged advertising vice president that it always spelled disaster when a man permitted a woman to lead him around by the *head* between his legs.

CHAPTER 31

There hours later Faye's mind was still a jumble of emotions ranging from anger and resentment, to disappointment, when John Reynolds knocked on the door to her office, walked in and closed the door. She'd worked closely enough with John to know that whenever he closed the door he didn't want whatever he had to say to her to go beyond the boundary of their respective offices.

Slightly built and always impeccably dressed, the forty-nine-year-old senior vice president had recently celebrated his twenty-fifth wedding anniversary, married off his twin daughters and acquired a mistress. His expression was a mask of stone.

As John took the chair in front of her desk, Faye could see him struggling not to lose his temper. "You crossed the line, Faye."

Her light gold eyebrows flickered. "You believe I crossed the line because I spoke the truth?"

"I'll not tolerate your disrespect."

Faye refused to back down. "You talk about disrespect when you were insulting and condescending when you referred to my people as gangsta." She spat out the last word. "But I will give you credit for knowing the vernacular. In case you haven't noticed, not all of us are thugs."

His lips thinned into a hard line. "I didn't mean to imply that, and you know it."

"The campaign will *work*, John," she said, her voice soft and purposefully seductive, "only because it's been proven. Top General Motors executives heightened the Cadillac's luxury truck's hip-hop success when they produced five thousand units of the Cadillac Escalade ESV Platinum Edition, which boasts twenty-inch wheels and two flip-down DVD screens. GM has also raised its visibility at events that attract high-profile black celebrities. They've sponsored King of the Bling contests in which participants showcase their Escalades and Hummers. We could get Andino to do something similar with the LXR–V."

John ran a hand over his thinning salt-and-pepper hair. "It sounds good, but we've decided to pass on your proposal, unless you have something else for us consider."

Faye wanted to tell him about her backup plan, but his rejection to her first presentation made her decide to save the idea for her own company. She shot him a long, penetrating stare. "I'm sorry to disappoint you, but I don't have anything else."

"If that's the case, then I'm going to give the Andino account to Zack and Jessica. Perhaps together they can come up with something a little different."

Faye froze. They were going to give *her* account to two clueless interns! "So, you're not going to target the

African-American consumer?" John nodded. She fixed her gaze on the door. "I guess I win some and lose some."

"Don't think of it as a loss. You're very good at what you do."

"Don't try and placate me, John. I know what I can do. That's why you hired me and that's why you pay me the big bucks."

He pushed to his feet, smiling. "I can't argue with that."

Faye sat in the same position long after John left her office and closed the door behind him. The minutes ticked off until the telephone rang. She glanced at the instrument. It was her private line.

The display showed a private number. Waiting for the third ring, she answered the call. "Ms. Ogden."

"What's up, girlfriend?"

Faye smiled for the first time in hours. She needed to get out of the office and talk to someone she could trust. "Are you free for lunch, Lana?"

"I can't, Faye," Alana moaned. "I've scheduled an interview for noon, and I still haven't left my apartment. How does tomorrow look for you?"

"I'm free for the rest of the week."

"Why don't we go back to that tiny Italian restaurant that has that delicious lobster and mango salad and red pepper pâté?"

Faye penciled Alana's name into her planner for the next day. "You're on."

"I called to find out how your weekend went."

"I'll tell you tomorrow, Lana."

"Just tell me whether it was good or bad."

"It was wonderful."

"Dang, Faye. Now I can't wait to hear the sordid details."

"I'm sorry to disappoint you, but there was nothing sordid about spending the weekend with you-know-who."

"I still want you to tell me everything. I'll meet you tomorrow at twelve-thirty."

"I'll see you there."

"Love you, girlfriend."

"Love you back," Faye said with their usual parting greeting. She ended the call smiling, feeling better than she had since walking out of BP&O's conference room. Alana could always lift her dark mood.

CHAPTER 32

"Good morning, Mr. H."

Bart smiled at the man who'd opened the door to the four-story salmon-colored building on the tree-lined block, four blocks south of Forty-second Street between Madison and Lexington Avenues. A black granite plaque with gold letters identified the address housing the offices of the Dunn-Houghton Group.

"Good morning, Mr. Washington." Thomas Washington was one of the four-member security staff that manned the building 24/7.

Six years before, DHG purchased all the properties along the north side of the street, renovated and refurbished the dozen brownstones and town houses, then sold all but one at prices yielding enormous profits. Bart had relocated DHG from a towering office building on East Fifty-second Street to the quiet, bucolic street in a neighborhood that was within walking distance of Madison Avenue's upscale trendy boutiques.

Although DHG employed a chef for its staff of forty, there were times when the employees sought out the many ethnic restaurants in the Murray Hill and Kips Bay neighborhoods.

The town house office had become a source of pride for Bart; as a trained architect it'd been years since he'd designed a structure. Anyone viewing the building's un-adorned exterior would be hard pressed to imagine the Art Deco–inspired first floor with marble floors with an inlaid pattern and indoor garden–inspired atrium rising to the height of the building. There was no reception area because all visitors were announced by security and escorted to whomever they were scheduled to meet.

A formal dining room, industrial kitchen, health spa with sauna, swimming pool, handball and basketballs courts, and male and female locker rooms took up the entire first floor. Support-staff offices with a formal conference room occupied the second, senior staff and a smaller conference room the third and Bart's office, private bathroom and a Japanese-theme garden solarium claimed the fourth.

He entered the elevator and inserted a key into the panel. Only he, his executive assistant and security had access to his private space. The doors opened and he stepped out to the carpeted area where Mrs. Urquhart guarded his office like a Secret Service agent assigned to the commander-in-chief.

"Good morning, boss."

Bart glared at Geraldine Urquhart. At seventy-three, she was the oldest employee on the payroll, a necessary holdover from his deceased father-in-law's tenure.

Grinning broadly, Geraldine waved a bejeweled hand. A longtime widow, she still wore her wedding ring. "I know. Don't call you boss."

Leaning over her desk, Bart gave her what he hoped was his most intimidating glare. "If you know, then why do you do it?"

She patted her short, shimmering-white coiffed hair. "Because I know you won't fire me."

Straightening, he shook his head. "One of these days I *am* going to fire you," he promised.

She lifted her eyebrows. "No, you're not, Bartholomew. Not when I'm the keeper of all your secrets."

"Not all of them," he whispered. "Please come in. I need you to make several calls for me." Bart waited for her to pick up her steno pad and pencil, come around the desk and walk into his office, he following and closing the door.

Geraldine Urquhart was only partially right. She knew about the woman whom he'd paid for sexual favors since becoming a widower, but nothing of his discreet assignations with Enid's social companions.

Bart waited for Geraldine to sit on a contemporary oyster-white upholstered club chair in front of the floor-to-ceiling windows, he sitting in a Louis Quinze–style armchair; he placed the portfolio on a low mahogany table that held a telephone and bonsai plant.

"I want you to call Madame Fontaine and set up an account for Ms. Faye Ogden. Let Madame know that Ms. Ogden's gratuity is to be waived." He hesitated as Mrs. Urquhart wrote down his dictation in shorthand symbols only she could transcribe.

"I also want you to call Felicia and tell her that I'll see her Friday at six."

Geraldine's cornflower-blue gaze narrowed. "Is there anything else, Bartholomew?"

"Call Mr. Matamora's secretary at the Japanese consulate and confirm my attendance at his dinner party tonight. Whomever you speak to, please stress to them that I'm allergic to raw fish. And call the florist and have them deliver flowers to the Matamoras' Fifth Avenue residence at least an hour before my arrival."

"Why kind of flowers?"

"I prefer orchids."

"What if they don't have orchids in stock?"

"My second choice is lilies."

"What color?"

"White. If they don't have any white, then pale pink."

"Do you want to give me a third choice?"

Bart massaged his forehead with his fingertips. "Why are you giving me a hard time this morning?"

"In case you've forgotten, the last time I ordered flowers and they were the wrong color you raised your voice to me. I worked with Edmund Dunn for fifty years, and he never once raised his voice to me."

Slowly lowering his hand, Bart stared at the elderly woman whom he felt was the glue that held the company together. Edmund Dunn had hired her fresh out of secretarial school, and in the ensuing forty years Geraldine quickly became his eyes, ears and confidante; and she'd become Bart's confidante following Edmund's unexpected death from a massive coronary three years ago.

"But I apologized to you, Mrs. Urquhart. Do you also

want me to do penance?" Not only had he apologized, but he had given her a generous year-end bonus *and* paid all of the expenses for her trip to the West Coast to visit her grandchildren.

Mrs. Urquhart, sitting up straighter, managed to look contrite. "Penance isn't necessary, Bartholomew. I just don't want you to raise your voice at me again or so help me I'll walk out of here and never look back."

Bart stood up, slipped out of his suit jacket and placed it over the back of the chair. "One of these days I'm going to call your bluff, Geraldine." He knew he'd gotten her attention when a rush of color stained her cheeks. It wasn't often he called the older woman by her given name. Moving over to the elegant Louis Quinze–style desk, he sat down.

"What do I have today?" He relied on his assistant to keep track of his meetings and projects.

Lids lowered, Mrs. Urquhart stared at the silver-haired man she'd come to love like a son. She'd watched him mature from a young architect who'd caught the eye of the boss's daughter, to an astute businessman, and now real estate mogul.

The love between Bartholomew and Deidre Dunn reminded her of what she'd shared with her precious Ivan, who'd died much too young, leaving her with two small sons. However, when Deidre died there were no sons or daughters to remind Bartholomew of the woman who in death still hadn't relinquished her claim on him.

She flipped several pages in the pad. "You have a luncheon with Assemblyman Collins."

"What time and where are we meeting?"

"It's scheduled for twelve-thirty at the Terrace. The cuisine is French."

Bart smiled. "Good. I like French cuisine. What's next?"

"You have an appointment with your ophthalmologist at four."

He didn't expect the meeting with the assemblyman to go beyond three o'clock, which meant he would have time to return to the upper west side to see his eye doctor before he returned home to prepare for the Matamoras' dinner party.

He glanced at the gold timepiece Edmund Dunn had given him the day Dunn Management Sales Group became the Dunn-Houghton Group, Inc. So many things had changed since that day. *He'd* changed so much since that day.

"Please let Hakim and Lowell know that I want to see them at nine-thirty to go over the Hamilton prospectus before I meet with Assemblyman Collins."

The politician had insisted a percentage of the sixty units, with studio apartments starting at three hundred thousand dollars, be set aside for low-income families. Assemblyman Collins had refused to meet with Hakim Wheeler, warning the urban planner that he'd exploit his political influence among his constituents if the CEO of DHG did not come to Harlem to discuss what had become an impasse.

However, Bart was prepared to compromise. He would set aside fifteen units for low-income, ten units for low- to middle-income and the remaining thirty-five for middle- and upper-income families.

"Anything else, boss?"

A hint of a smile played at the corners of his firm mouth. "No, Mrs. Urquhart. That'll be all for now."

Bart waited for the elegant, petite woman to leave his office; he picked up one of three telephones nestled on the corner of the desk. He pressed a button, activating the speed dial feature.

"Good morning, P.S., Inc. This is Astrid. How may I direct your call?"

"Astrid, this is Bart Houghton. Is Enid available?"

"Yes, Mr. Houghton. I'll let her know you're on the line."

Bart had to wait less than ten seconds before he heard the soft, dulcet feminine voice. "Good morning, Bart. How are you?" she drawled.

"I'm well, Enid."

"What can I do for you?"

"I'd like to secure the services of Faye Ogden for the summer season." A loud gasp followed his request. He frowned. "Are you saying this would present a problem for you?"

"Not at all," Enid countered quickly. "It's just that this is the first time any client has requested exclusivity for one of my companions."

His frown was replaced by a knowing smile. "That's because Ms. Ogden is unlike any of your other companions."

"You're right, Bart. She is my most exquisite exotic jewel."

"I'll give you whatever you want for her."

"Astrid will contact you before the end of the week to set up a price that should work well for both of us. From now on you won't have to go through P.S., Inc. to set up appointments with Faye. Astrid will call her and let her know of this new agreement."

"Thanks, Enid."

"You're welcome. By the way, has she agreed to see you exclusively?"

"Yes."

"Good for you."

Good for me.

But was it good for him to become involved with Faye? Despite his wealth and very active social life, he had become an emotional cripple, unable to have a normal relationship with a woman because he refused to let go of his dead wife.

CHAPTER 33

"Who are you going out with tonight?"

Ilene adjusted the lights on her makeup mirror to reflect a nighttime effect, ignoring the query from the figure sprawled across her bed. A flick of a sable brush coated with cinnamon eye shadow over her brow bones accentuated the velvety darkness of her slanting eyes.

She selected a sponge applicator, dipped it into a shocking magenta eye shadow and dabbed the color over the crease of her eyelids. Leaning back on the vanity chair, a smile of supreme satisfaction parted her full lips. She hadn't lost her touch.

Always a quick study, Ilene had watched makeup artists transform her face from an adolescent gamine into a sensual sophisticate, where the arrogant slant of her chiseled cheekbones blended with the tilt of her eyes. There was just enough gold in her brown eyes to give them the appearance of tortoiseshell. Her nose was short, barely the length of the tip of her little finger. It was her mouth and dimpled smile that most people remembered, men in particular.

One Frenchman had whispered in her ear that

whenever he saw her photograph he fantasized about doing naughty things with his girlfriend. His confession empowered her as much as her strutting down a runway with spectators and photographers applauding and capturing her every move.

"Come on, Ilene. Don't be a bitch. Where are you going?"

Ilene caught the reflection of a profusion of shoulder-length curly hair when the attractive young black woman sat up and folded her legs into a yoga position.

Swiveling on the stool, she stared at Yazmin Symington's flushed café au lait complexion and dilated pupils.

"Go home, Yaz, and sleep it off. You're high."

"Who are you to tell me what to do?" Yazmin's usually soft Georgia drawl had taken on a hard edge.

"I don't think I should have to explain why I want you to leave my place."

"Well, *I* want an explanation."

Oh, no, the coked-out be-yotch didn't go there with me, Ilene thought before she counted to five, praying not to lose her temper.

"I'm not going to explain myself, not when you're like this."

Yazmin waved her arms above her head. "Don't get up on your high horse, Ilene, because you've seen me like *this* plenty of times before."

Ilene stood up and a black silk kimono-style wrap opened to reveal a swell of small, firm breasts above a red lace demi-bra. "Get the hell out!"

A lopsided grin found its way across Yazmin's face as

she swung her legs over the side of the bed. "I'm going. But there's no need for you to go ghetto on me."

Ilene's temper flared. "You'll know ghetto when my size tens stomp a mud hole in *yo crackhead ass.*" She'd stressed the last three words. It'd become an ongoing struggle not to revert to a "ghetto ho," but her neighbor had forced her to go there.

Yazmin came from a family of prominent African-American doctors: her grandfather, father, mother and brothers. The plans her family made for her to join their lucrative suburban Atlanta practice were thwarted when the pressure to succeed had become too much and Yazmin dropped out of medical school in her third year, citing mental and physical exhaustion. She'd begun smoking weed, and when that didn't do the trick for her she escalated to pills and, on occasion, crack-cocaine.

Ilene dabbled in smoking or inhaling cocaine, but no one had ever witnessed her using the drug. After all, she had an image to protect. Something she said must have penetrated the transplanted Georgian's drug-induced haze, when Yazmin stumbled out of the bedroom. The sound of a slamming door echoed throughout the apartment.

Ilene refused to let her neighbor ruin her evening, because her life was back on track. She'd paid all her bills, and had some money left over. And she would earn even more tonight when she met a client at Morimoto. The trendy Japanese restaurant was only three blocks away from her co-op.

She finished applying her makeup, then brushed her

hair weave until it shimmered with dark brown and gold highlights. She'd spent hours in the salon earlier that morning taking out the braids and replacing them with tracks of human hair ending halfway down her back. The stylist had touched up her roots until they were bone straight before she sewed in hair that cost as much as Ilene's co-op maintenance. She thought the straight hair a better investment because she didn't have to visit the salon every two weeks to have her braids retightened. After all, she was supermodel Ilene Fairchild, and she couldn't be seen in public with a ratty do.

Walking over to a closet, she slipped a three-tiered black ruffled skirt in silk chiffon off a padded hanger, stepped into it and buttoned the waistband. Peering closely into the full-length mirror on the door, she smiled. The outline of her thong panties and thighs were visible through the delicate fabric. It was just enough to garner the attention she needed. Reaching for a raw-silk blouse in magenta, she buttoned the body-hugging garment with a mandarin collar. Maximo Callucci was still her favorite designer. One season he'd designed an entire line for her body's proportions.

Ilene pushed her bare feet into a pair of black quilted suede mules with a wedge heel. She reached for a small matching purse with a silk cord strap and a black cashmere shawl. She strutted across the bedroom as if she were on a Milan runway and flicked a wall switch, leaving only a bedside lamp lit. Even when she was home alone she worked at perfecting her trademark walk.

She was determined never to allow her celebrity persona

to slip. The year she'd turned fifteen, modeling had changed her life. Her agent changed her name from Ella Williams to Ilene Fairchild, and before her sixteenth birthday she'd become the darling of Parisian couture houses, and the following year the ward of a man old enough to be her father.

CHAPTER 34

Ilene stopped at the host station. "Ilene Fairchild. I'm here for the Nakanogo party."

The maître d' checked the list of reservations, nodding. He beckoned to one of the hostesses. "Please escort Miss Fairfield to Mr. Nakanogo's table."

Ilene removed her shawl, tossed it over her arm and followed the woman. This was her first time inside Morimoto and she was totally impressed with its cool, clean, white-on-white look. The setting was a sparkling wonderland for the glitterati sipping exotic cocktails, laughing, talking quietly and enjoying what had been touted as the best sushi in the city.

When a woman pointed at Ilene, heads turned in her direction. A cast member of a popular TV reality show stopped tapping his cell phone long enough to give her a mock salute.

Ilene flashed her dimpled smile. *Oh, hell yeah. I've still got it!* She didn't care what the fashion critics said; she wasn't too old, she still grabbed the public's attention, and because her face had graced the covers of the world's most prestigious fashion magazines, she would always be acknowledged as a supermodel.

Christie Brinkley was still doing television commercials and print ads, and she was over fifty. Just look at her girl Tyra Banks. She'd started a second career with her own reality show that segued into a talk show. The icing on the cake had been when she took her last walk down the runway as a Victoria's Secret model. Tyra had proven there was life after modeling, and that had inspired Ilene to exploit her very bankable face and body in music videos. She knew she didn't have the temperament to do television; but she wanted to keep her name and face in the spotlight until she met a man willing to give her the lifestyle she'd had when she lived in Europe.

Anthony Nakanogo saw her, and stood up, the other men at the table following his lead. He ran a hand down the length of his four-hundred-dollar silk tie before bowing to her.

Ilene closed the distance between them, resting her palms on the lapels of his exquisitely tailored suit jacket. She pressed her cheek to his smooth one and affected an air kiss.

"Konban wa."

"Good evening, Ilene," Anthony replied in flawless English. Holding her at arm's length, his eyes sent her a private message. *"Ogenki desu ka?"*

Ilene looked at him through artificial lashes fused to her own. *"Hai, genki desu."*

Anthony smiled. "Your Japanese is still very good."

"That's all I remember," she admitted. She'd spent three months in Tokyo and she'd learned enough basic Japanese to exchange polite greetings and order food. Her love affair with sushi had begun the first time she tasted the raw-fish delicacy, and during her stay she'd become a vegetarian, eating only fish and vegetables. As long as she'd lived in Japan there hadn't been a need for her to monitor everything she put into her mouth.

The international banker turned to the others at his table. "Ladies, gentlemen, Miss Fairchild will be joining us this evening." He introduced her to the four men and three women, all of whom seemed surprised that a world-famous supermodel would join them for dinner. She recognized Rohit Sarkar. The handsome actor who was one of Bollywood's leading men. His dining partner was his latest costar, a twenty-something British actress with three ex-husbands. Ilene nodded and gave each her celebrated smile as Anthony seated her. The man to her left was her client's Japanese-American partner, Preston Fuwa. Although all of the men wore wedding rings, none were there with their wives.

Ilene found herself completely charmed with the sixty-year-old grandfather from whom she would earn two thousand dollars for sharing dinner with him and his friends. She ate sparingly, sampling tofu and noodles with shiro, miso, wasabi and sudachi—her favorite was the Morimoto sashimi, terrine-like cubes made from layers of hamachi, smoked salmon, barbecued eel and seared toro—while the men dined on copious amounts of Kobe-style beef and lamb carpaccio dressed with Japanese green onions, grated ginger and garlic oil as countless bottles of saki and champagne were consumed by everyone but her.

Dinner was interrupted several times when well-known personalities and a few wannabes stopped by the table to offer greetings to Anthony and Rohit. Once the word got out that Ilene Fairchild was dining with India's answer to America's Brad Pitt, a steady stream of men and women sauntered by to glance in their direction.

Anthony and Preston were honored that Masaharu Morimoto, a Nobu alumnus familiar to viewers of Iron Chef, came over to greet them. They spoke Japanese too quickly for Ilene to follow their conversation. She managed to charm the famous chef when she greeted him in his native tongue, and blushed furiously when Anthony translated for Morimoto, saying she was even more beautiful in person. With her straight hair, parted in the middle, framing her small, round face, Ilene was more than aware of her effect not only on men, but also on the women gawking at her.

It wasn't quite eleven-thirty when Anthony settled the bill, informing the others at the table he'd be back as soon as he saw Ilene safely home. They stood on Fifteenth Street and Tenth Avenue, waiting for a passing taxi.

"I'd like to see you again," he said in a quiet voice.

Ilene successfully kept her expression impassive. "That can be arranged."

"I will call for you for this weekend."

Her gaze narrowed as if she was deep in thought. "I have to check my planner, but I *think* I'll be available," she lied. There was no way she wouldn't be available for the banker unless another client proposed a better offer.

Reaching into the breast pocket of his jacket, the elegant man with salt-and-pepper hair pulled out a small flat velvet case. "Perhaps this will help you make up your mind." He handed her the case before he signaled for a taxi.

Ilene barely had time to react, when she found herself seated in the back seat of a cab. Anthony handed the driver a large bill, telling him that if he got the lady home safely he could keep the change.

The bearded cabbie turned and looked at Ilene with half-hooded lids. "Where you go, lady?" She gave him her address and he stared at her as if she'd spoken a language he didn't understand. The well-dressed Asian man had given him a hundred dollars to drive three blocks! "Hang on!"

He flipped the meter and took off like a rocket. Two minutes later Ilene stepped out of the taxi and walked to the entrance of her building. The doorman who'd been lounging on a chair in the vestibule got up and opened the door, giving her a lecherous grin.

"Good evening, Miss Fairchild."

"Good evening," she mumbled, not meeting his gaze. She felt the heat of his gaze on her bare legs as she walked toward the elevator; she entered and pressed the button for the fourth floor.

Ilene managed to quell her curiosity long enough to uncover what Anthony Nakanogo had given her until she undressed, cleansed the makeup from her face, braided her hair in a single plait and showered.

Clad in a short pale yellow silk nightgown and matching bikini panties, she sat in the middle of her bed and opened the case. She was unable to suppress a soft gasp of surprise. Her client had just made up her mind whether she would see him again. He'd given her a necklace of alternating black and white Tahitian and South Seas cultured pearls separated by spacers of coruscating diamonds in eighteen-carat white gold. She estimated the pearls to be at least fifteen millimeters.

His gift was exquisite understated elegance. She would wear the pearls when she saw him again. Ilene returned the necklace to its case and placed it in a drawer of the bedside table.

She turned off the table lamp, then pulled the sheet up over her body, smiling. She had the perfect outfit to showcase Nakanogo's gift.

CHAPTER 35

A feeling of relief swept over Faye as she told Alana about her marketing campaign that had been rejected.

Alana swallowed a mouthful of iced tea, her eyes widening. "But didn't you offer them your backup pitch? You know you never create a marketing strategy without putting together an alternative proposal."

Faye stabbed at her salad greens with such force that the bowl almost tipped over. "I was so pissed that I never presented it."

"If you'd presented it you probably wouldn't have lost the account."

"I don't know why, but something tells me that I lost that account even before I opened my mouth. And the fact that John gave it to his so-called niece and another dumb-ass intern who couldn't find his way out of a paper bag with the directions written inside confirms my suspicions."

"You think your boss gave the account to two interns because of internal pressure?"

"It's not what I believe, Lana. It's what I know."

"What are you going to do with your alternate pitch?"

"I'm keeping it for myself. I wanted to present a

timeline, beginning with the postwar model. I'd show a Tuskegee Airman in uniform standing beside the 1948 model, then move forward from the fifties to present day. Each frame would feature a black man, woman or family wearing the corresponding fashion for the decade. The last would show a young woman and man in urban wear lounging against the LXR–V. The soundtrack would reflect the music of black artists beginning with Ella Fitzgerald and Nat Cole to today's hip-hop."

Slumping against the back of her chair, Alana shook her head. "That is one fantastic campaign! Your boss is a fool, girlfriend."

"It doesn't matter anymore, Lana. I'm leaving."

"When?" Alana was barely able to control her gasp of surprise.

"I'm not sure. But I know I don't want to give them another year."

"Do you have something else lined up?"

"No."

"But…but how are you going to support yourself? I know you're not getting alimony from your ex-husband." She gave her a questioning look. "What's going on, Faye?"

"I'm going to be available to Bartholomew Houghton every weekend this summer."

More frightened than shocked, Alana placed a hand over her mouth. "No, no, no. You can't."

"And why can't I?"

"Girl, you're going to get in over your head." Alana reached over and grasped her hand. "Something told me the man wanted you the night we went to Enid's dinner party, and I knew for certain when I saw him watching you this past weekend. It could be he's come down with a serious case of jungle fever, or maybe he's always had a thing for black women."

Faye pulled her hand from Alana's loose grip. "If that's the case then why didn't he pick you or Ilene Fairchild?"

"It could be he likes blondes," Alana said glibly.

Faye rolled her eyes at her. "Cut the B.S., Lana. At the end of the summer I'll have earned enough to pay a lawyer his fee to take my brother's appeal, and hope-fully by the end of the year I'll be able to think about setting up my own company. I plan to use the equity in my co-op as a cushion until I sign up enough accounts to support my business without taking out an addi-tional loan."

Alana sobered and her expression grew serious. "How much do you need for your brother's appeal?"

"At least one-fifty as an initial retainer. Rooney Turner is one of the best appeal attorneys in the country, right up there with Alan Dershowitz. After his staff sorts through the evidence the fee could double or triple."

"Dam-n-n-n, Faye. All in all it could cost you half a mill. I followed the Claus von Bulow trial, where Dersho-witz was able to get his wealthy client's murder convic-tion overturned, but damn!"

"Turner is known as a bloodhound in legal circles because if there's the slightest hint that all the evidence doesn't add up, he goes in for the kill. He's good, Alana.

He said that after he reverses CJ's conviction he's going to sue the state. I told him I'm not concerned about suing anyone, I just want my brother exonerated so he can get on with his life.

"Now, back to Bart Houghton," Faye said, "It's only business, Lana."

"How long do you think it'll remain business, Faye? From what I've heard, he's rich as Croesus. And for a white man he's not too bad on the eyes. I kinda like his George Clooney circa–E.R. haircut."

Faye wanted to confess that she liked Bart's eyes and mouth, which wasn't too thin yet firm enough to be masculine. "What are you doing this weekend?" she asked, deftly changing the topic.

"I don't have anything planned. What about you?"

"My mother's coming in on Friday, and we're going to have a mother–daughter weekend."

Tucking a curl behind her ear, Alana stared out the plate-glass window. "If I don't hear from Enid, I'm going upstate to visit my mother. She wanted me to come up this past weekend, but I told her that I had to catch up on some work."

"How's she doing?"

Alana lifted a shoulder. "I suppose she's doing okay. I can never tell by her voice because she always sounds the same. Taylor and his wife stopped by last week to check on her and found that she hadn't gone out or changed her clothes in a couple of days. Sophia gave her a bath and cleaned the house while my brother went to the supermarket to restock the pantry and refrigerator. Last year Taylor talked about putting on an addition to his house, and have Mama live with him."

"What stopped him?"

Alana shook her head. "I don't think Sophia wants her mother-in-law living that close to her. I can't stand that selfish bitch, but I put up with her because she's my brother's wife and my niece's mother."

"But your mother is so quiet." Unlike mine who has an opinion for everything, Faye added silently. "If I hadn't committed to spending the weekend with my mother I'd go up with you."

"What about the following weekend?"

"I can't." Faye told her about the trip to the Grand Cayman Islands.

"It sounds as if you're going to have a lot of fun this summer." There was a hint of wistfulness in Alana's statement.

"Don't forget, I'm going to be working," Faye reminded Alana. "I intend to use up most of my vacation before I hand in my resignation."

"How much vacation time have you accrued?" Alana asked.

"Forty-two days. Starting this week I'm taking off Fridays and Mondays. I've put in for three weeks in July and another three in August."

"Won't that alert HR that you're up to something?"

"Frankly, my dear, I don't give a damn what they think." Picking up her tea, Alana took a sip. "The folks at

BP&O are going to have a shit hemorrhage when you hand in your resignation."

A smile of pure satisfaction softened Faye's mouth. "There's an expression that says, 'You never miss your water until your well runs dry, and you'll never miss your baby until she says goodbye.'"

"Hel-lo," Alana intoned, touching her glass to Faye's.

Faye held up her glass of tea in a mock solute. "I'll drink to that. Tell me about your interview with Coco Chanel's personal assistant."

Alana told her about her meeting with an elderly woman who'd met the famous French designer as a young girl and eventually became her maid, then personal assistant. What was to be a one-hour lunch stretched into two as Faye was enchanted by Alana's story that covered the Great War, Depression, the Nazi occupation of France, Madame Chanel's love affair with a Nazi officer, her exile to Switzerland and her eventual comeback in 1954 that restored her to the first ranks of haute couture.

Faye returned to her office, closed and locked the door; she did not open it again until it was time for her to leave for the day.

CHAPTER 36

Faye stood at the Long Island railroad's information booth, waiting for her mother. It was 3:10 p.m., and the electronic board confirmed the train from Saint Albans was in the station.

She'd called Shirley the night before, asking her to come into Manhattan earlier than they'd originally planned because she was taking the day off. Within minutes of hanging up she had another call, this one on her cell phone. Astrid Marti had called to let her know that the agreement wherein a client *must* go through P.S., Inc. to contact a companion was no longer in effect because of Bartholomew Houghton's exclusivity arrangement.

Her second call of the night came from Bart. He'd confirmed the time she would be picked up the following Friday, and asked that she not bring an outfit for the wedding because he planned to buy her whatever she needed once they arrived on the island.

A flicker of apprehension had coursed through her when she realized she would travel out of the country with a man who wasn't her lover or husband, but her anxiety was short-lived. She had to stay focused. At no time could she afford to forget that Bart was her client.

"Faye Anne."

Turning, she saw her mother standing less than a foot away. She'd come up behind her. Moving closer, Faye reached for Shirley's overnight bag and kissed her cheek.

There was no doubt Shirley and Faye were mother and daughter. At fifty-five, Shirley's stylishly cut short curly sandy-brown hair was liberally streaked with silver, and her gold-brown face claimed a few laugh lines around a pair of light brown eyes that sparkled like polished citrines. She'd worked briefly as a pattern cutter in the garment district before opting for marriage and becoming a stay-at-home mother.

"Mama, you look so beautiful." Shirley had chosen to wear a tailored pantsuit in a becoming peach shade with a pair of low-heel black patent-leather pumps.

"So do you, even if you are too thin."

Faye lifted an eyebrow at her mother. "It's the dress, Mama." The ice-blue sheath dress had artfully concealed her curves.

Shirley wrapped an arm around her daughter's waist. "You *are* thinner."

Faye rolled her eyes upward. Shirley was like a dog with a bone. "I always lose a few pounds with the warm weather because I'm eating more salads."

"How much do you weigh now?"

"I don't know, Mama."

She hadn't bothered to hide her annoyance at being

interrogated about her weight loss because she'd made a concerted effort to lose ten pounds. She hadn't changed her eating habits but had begun walking during her lunch hour three times a week.

"What hotel did you choose?"

A secretive smile softened Faye's lips. "I'm not saying because I want to surprise you."

Shirley looped her arm through Faye's. "You know I don't like surprises."

"This is one surprise I know you're going to like."

"Ladies, the gentleman at the bar would like you to have these." The bartender set down two glasses, one a manhattan and the other a cosmopolitan.

Faye stared at a young black man sitting at the bar in the Bull and Bear who nodded in acknowledgment, but before she could signal her thanks he'd turned back to the older man on his right.

Turning her attention to her mother, who sat across from her with a smug expression on her face, Faye shook her head in amazement. "Were you flirting with that man?" Shirley reached for the cosmo, successfully avoiding her daughter's accusatory stare. "Were you, Mama?" she asked again.

Shirley took a sip of the cool pale pink cocktail. "I can't believe this little thing is so good." She waved a manicured hand. "Don't act so put out, Faye Anne. He kept looking this way and all I did was smile and wave."

"We came here to have predinner drinks, Mama, not flirt."

"How am I going to get grandchildren if I don't look out for you, Faye Anne? Besides, he looks like a successful young man, given the cut of his suit."

Faye had noticed the man when she and her mother sat down at a table in the popular bar on the ground floor of the Waldorf-Astoria. But it hadn't crossed her mind to flirt with him or, for that fact, with any other man.

"You'll never get grandchildren if you feel it's your duty to pick up men for me," she said between clenched teeth.

Unperturbed, Shirley took another swallow of her drink. "You've been single for more than two years, and not once have I heard you talk about having a special friend."

"I have a friend." The pronouncement was out before Faye could censor herself.

Shirley's hand halted in midair. "Is he special, Faye Anne?"

She picked up the manhattan and took a deep swallow, welcoming the cold, then the heat, spreading throughout her chest. "No. He's just a friend."

"Do you think he'll become more than a friend?" Shirley whispered, intrigued.

Faye met the gaze of the woman she loved beyond description. She hadn't always done what her mother wanted her to, but Shirley was always there to support her whenever she failed or faltered. Shirley's *wait until you become a mother then you'll understand what I'm talking about* was a constant reminder that she wasn't a mother. She and Norman had talked about starting a family after three years, but their marriage had barely survived the two-year mark.

"I doubt it, Mama."

"Why?"

"Because I don't want more," she said truthfully.

How could she tell Shirley that her friend was a client, a man who paid her to entertain him? In some cultures she would be seen as a courtesan or geisha, but Enid Richards legitimized and made her business morally correct by referring to them as social companions. Although cautioned not to sleep with their clients, Faye wondered if Enid was naïve, or had she chosen to ignore that her clients and social companions were adults who could or would do anything as long as it was consensual.

Shirley patted her daughter's hand. "Don't you want to get married again?"

Faye gave her mother a long, penetrating look, knowing what she would look like in twenty years. Despite having been out of the workforce for more than three decades, the older woman was as stylish as any contemporary working counterpart.

"Yes, I do. I miss the companionship of living with someone."

"What about the intimacy, baby?"

Faye nodded, smiling. Leave it to Shirley Ogden to go straight to the jugular. "That's what I miss most."

Leaning over, Shirley pressed a kiss to Faye's cheek. "Finish your drink before I'm so drunk that you'll have to call someone to carry me out of here."

"Would you mind having dinner in our room tonight?"

"Of course not, dear. In fact, I was going to suggest that."

She knew she'd shocked Shirley when they'd gotten into a taxi outside Pennsylvania Station and directed the driver to take them to the Waldorf-Astoria Hotel. Faye had selected the elegant hotel as much for its historical significance as for its Art Deco lobby, beautifully furnished rooms and impeccable service.

Faye finished her manhattan and signed the bill. Rising, she made her way over to the bar. Resting a hand on the shoulder of the man who'd paid her second round of drinks, she thanked him for his generosity. And before he could ask her her name, she walked out of the Bull and Bear, Shirley several steps behind her.

Quickening her pace, Shirley caught up with Faye and looped an arm around her waist. "You're going to have to help your mama because I'm slightly tipsy."

Faye smiled at the petite woman. "You only had two drinks."

"My limit is one nowadays."

"You need to get out more. You and Daddy used to party quite a bit."

Shirley sobered quickly. "We used to do a lot of things together. Everything changed when that whore accused CJ of rape and assault. How could he rape someone who opened her legs for every man in the neighborhood?"

"Please let's not talk about that now, Mama. I wanted you to spend the weekend with me so that we can have a good time."

Shirley took a deep breath. "You're right, baby."

Faye didn't want to talk about her brother. Even though

he'd confessed to sleeping with the married mother of three who'd made it a practice to trade her body for food or drugs, he'd vehemently denied raping or beating her.

CJ had made mistakes in the past because he hadn't always made the best choices, but Faye knew her brother was no rapist.

She walked into the Waldorf's lobby and gasped inaudibly. Bartholomew Houghton had approached a statuesque redhead who apparently had been waiting for him. Dressed in a Chanel dinner suit, the slender woman appeared to be in her early forties. He offered his arm, and as she took it he glanced up and met Faye's gaze.

Faye stared wordlessly at him, her heart pounding a runaway rhythm as he stared back with complete surprise freezing his features. There was a silent moment of recognition and acknowledgment in the gray orbs before he looked away.

Never breaking stride, Faye led her mother to a bank of elevators that would take them to their suite. She didn't recognize the woman with Bart as one of the companions who'd attended the P.S., Inc. dinner party, nor was she at his Southampton gathering.

She knew Bart was as shocked at seeing her as she was, but why, she asked herself as she entered the elevator, was she so flustered just because she'd seen him with another woman?

Shirley pushed the button for their floor while questions assaulted Faye like invisible missiles. Why would it matter who he saw when he was only her client? Why when he'd said they were friends? And why when he'd said there wasn't even the remotest possibility that they would ever sleep together?

Girl, you're going to get in over your head. Why, she mused, did Alana's predictions always bring her back to reality?

The doors opened at their floor and she exited the elevator. Within minutes of her inserting the key card in the slot, pushing open the door to their expansive suite and kicking off her shoes, she'd forgotten about Bartholo-mew Houghton and the very attractive woman clinging possessively to his arm.

CHAPTER 37

Bart withdrew from Felicia Mathis's moist body; he sat up, swung his legs over the side of the bed, headed for the bathroom and closed the door. He slipped the condom off his flaccid penis, tied a knot in the latex sheath, placed it into a self-stick envelope on the vanity, then sealed it. It was a ritual he'd established the first time he'd ever paid a woman for sex. Call it paranoia but he didn't want to leave behind any evidence of his sexual encounters.

Sliding back a glass door, he stepped into the shower stall and turned on the water. He hadn't begun to wash the smell of sex and Felicia's perfume from his body when the door opened and she joined him.

He grasped her upper arms. "What are you doing?"

Tilting her head, she smiled up at him through her lashes. "What does it look like, darling? I've decided to share your shower."

Bart's fingers tightened on her pale flesh. "No, Felicia."

"Don't you want me to wash your back?" Her smoky voice had dropped an octave.

"I want you to get out of the shower." He gave her a lethal glare. "Now, Felicia."

They'd showered together in the past, but he didn't want her tonight. He'd come to the hotel for one purpose: to slake his sexual frustrations. And if Felicia wanted more then she'd struck out, because seconds before ejaculating he realized he didn't want the woman moaning and writhing beneath him to have alabaster skin, dark auburn hair or blue eyes but burnished-gold brown skin and eyes. For one brief moment he'd fantasized making love with Faye Ogden.

Felicia left the shower stall, reaching for a terry-cloth robe from a stack on a low table. She was a call girl not a psychologist. Men paid her the big bucks to take care of their sexual needs, not to try and get inside their heads.

This was a Bart Houghton she hadn't seen before. They'd been sleeping together for years, and this was the first time she thought of him as a john. She'd lost count of the number of men she'd slept with for money; Bart was only one of the half-dozen wealthy men who paid her handsomely to give them sexual pleasure who didn't make her feel as if she were performing a service.

With Bart it was never slam bam, thank you, ma'am. There was always foreplay and after-play that temporarily held her demons at bay, demons that wouldn't permit her to feel something other than loathing whenever she slept with a man.

Felicia returned to the bedroom, lay across the bed and closed her eyes. Bart couldn't exist in her world, nor would she ever become a part of his. The problem was, she liked Bartholomew Houghton—a lot. He was affectionate, generous, virile and, unlike many of her middle-aged and elderly clients, he didn't need artificial gadgets to achieve an erection.

She was still in the same position when Bart leaned down and kissed her forehead.

"I'll call you."

She opened her eyes and met his steady gaze. He'd showered and put on his clothes. "Okay."

It was their usual parting exchange. Felicia knew it would be a while before he contacted her again. There was a time in the past when they'd slept together several times a week, and occasions when they wouldn't see each other for months. However, whenever he called she rearranged her schedule to accommodate him.

And like every man who'd come into her life he was only good for one thing: money.

CHAPTER 38

Giuseppe held an umbrella over Faye as she handed him her single piece of luggage. He opened the rear door to the Maybach, waiting until she was seated before he closed it. He stored her bag in the trunk, came around the sedan and slipped behind the wheel; he closed the partition behind him before maneuvering away from the curb in one smooth motion.

Faye settled herself onto the back seat of the car next to Bart. She was more than ready for sunshine, palm trees and the clear blue-green ocean because it'd been raining steadily for the past three days.

Smiling, she met Bart's gaze. Was there uncertainty in the gray eyes, or had she just imagined it? Was he uncomfortable because she'd seen him with another woman? A woman who could've been a friend, relative, or even a business client?

He was dressed for traveling: jeans, running shoes and a pale blue Polo Tee. She'd chosen Seven jeans and her favorite Ralph Lauren navy blazer and a matching T-shirt. Leaning to her left, she kissed his cheek. He went completely still before relaxing. She knew she'd surprised him with the show of affection, but she'd made a promise to herself that she was going to enjoy her Cayman Islands weekend.

"How are you, Bart?"

His expression changed to one of faint amusement. "I'm better now that I've seen you."

He'd been bombarded with one crisis after another: a West Coast construction company was beset with union problems, a loans officer in his L.A.–based banking division had been arrested because of an altercation with the police at a DWI checkpoint, and the Harlem assemblyman was pressuring him to increase the number of low-income units in his new development from fifteen to twenty.

A flash of humor parted Faye's lips with Bart's back-handed compliment. "I take it your day didn't go too well?"

Resting his arm over the back of her seat, Bart turned to face Faye. "Would I offend you if I said it was a bitch?"

She shook her head. "No."

"How was your day?"

"Wonderful."

"What made yours wonderful?"

"I woke up my usual time but decided to stay in bed until hunger pangs got the best of me. I was *feenin'* for a down-home country breakfast, so I made scrambled eggs, bacon, sausage links, grits and homemade biscuits, sat in front of the television and watched everything from *The View* to Oprah."

His dark eyebrows shot up. "You cook?"

Faye managed to look insulted. "Of course I cook. Who do you think feeds me?"

"I was under the belief that career women only know how to make reservations."

Seeing the amusement in his eyes, Faye laughed. "Now, that's a sexist statement if I ever heard one."

His arm slipped lower to rest over her shoulders. "How many nights a week do you turn into a master chef?"

"Only one, *dah-ling*" she said in her best southern drawl.

"You cook one out of seven days?" he asked incredulously.

"Yes. I cook enough on Sundays for an entire week. I put everything into microwavable containers and reheat them when I get home."

"Will you cook for me?"

Faye rolled her eyes at him. "No! You have a cook."

"I cooked for you."

"You put a steak on the grill that Mrs. Llewellyn had already marinated."

Bart refused to relent. "I still cooked it."

"I haven't cooked for a man since I ended..." Her words trailed off.

"Since you ended your marriage," he said intuitively, completing her statement. Turning her head to stare out the side window, she nodded. "You don't have to cook for me if you don't want to."

Faye looked at him again, and for a long moment Bart studied her with a curious intensity. She knew more about him than he did her. But he intended to use the weekend to penetrate the fragile shell she'd erected to keep him at a comfortable distance.

The beginnings of a smile tipped the corners of his mouth, bringing Faye's gaze to linger there. She didn't know why, but she liked staring at his firm, sensual lips, lips that had touched hers briefly in a parting kiss. A gentle, comforting kiss that was anything but sexual.

"You know you got me for assuming you didn't cook." Faye winked at him. "It serves you right for being so opinionated."

"I apologize."

She inclined her head. "Apology accepted."

Bart curbed the urge to run his fingertips along the column of her neck. Her skin was soft as velvet, her natural feminine scent clean and sweet. She'd been *feenin'* for food, and he was *feenin'* for Faye Ogden. "You should've told me you weren't going to work today because I would've arranged for us to fly down earlier this afternoon."

Unconsciously her brow furrowed. "When you called to confirm our departure time, I was under the impression it couldn't be changed."

"I could've changed it with a phone call."

"I suppose I should let you know that I'm not going to work Fridays and Mondays during June, July and August."

He removed his arm and opened a small compartment next to the built-in bar. He took out a BlackBerry and activated the calendar feature. His thumbs moved with lightning speed as he entered her name on every Monday and Friday for June, July and August.

"Are you able to take more time?"

"How much more?"

"A couple of weeks."

Faye studied his distinctive profile. "I'm also taking vacation the first three weeks of July and August." She watched as he entered this information. "What have you planned?"

Bart palmed the cell phone. "How would you like to hang out in Europe with me?"

The shock of what he was offering hit Faye full force. He'd asked whether she'd go to Europe with him as casually as asking the time. "What countries in Europe?"

"It's your choice."

"How many choices do I get?" Much to her surprise, Bart showed no reaction to her query.

"As many as you want."

"France."

He nodded. "Paris, Cannes and Monaco."

Her smile was dazzling. "That'll do."

His smile matched hers. "Have you ever been to Ibiza?"

"No."

"Would you like to visit Venice and la Riviera di Ponente?"

"Yes and yes."

Bart reached for Faye again, pulling her to his side. "I want to show you a good time." Resting his chin on the top of her head, he closed his eyes. "We're going to have fun, Faye."

Relaxing completely, Faye leaned into her client's lean upper body. He planned to take her to the French, Spanish and Italian Rivieras. Things were happening so quickly that she found it hard to distinguish between fantasy and reality.

"Did you eat dinner?" Bart asked after a comfortable silence.

"No."

He smiled, tightening his hold on her shoulders. "We'll eat once we're airborne."

"Which airport are we flying out of?"

"Newark."

It was Friday, rush-hour traffic was a circus, and they were scheduled to lift off at seven. "Do you think we'll make it in time?"

"The pilot will wait." Faye sat up, but Bart pulled her back to lean against him. "We're not taking a commercial carrier."

She didn't know why, but Faye suddenly felt gauche. CEOs of billion-dollar companies did not stand in line with the masses to fly first-class on commercial carriers. They either owned or rented private jets.

CHAPTER 39

Alana told the doorman her name. He checked his list then opened a stained-glass door. She made her way into Hoops, a new Harlem sports bar/club owned by a quartet of basketball players and a hip-hop record producer. She was met by the babble of voices and the driving beat of music from powerful speakers. The interior decor was a mix of East, West and Art Deco with neon lights and sculptures, stained-glass windows and steel-framed chairs with deep plush cushions. Pale blue votives flickered from every flat surface.

Couples crowded the dance floor, gyrating to the infectious rhythms, while others stood in line for a buffet dinner from which sumptuous aromas tantalized olfactory nerves. People gathered at the spacious bar were two deep. More than half the tables, with seating for eight, were occupied.

Astrid had called her midweek to inform her that she was to attend a private party at Hoops hosted by the partners to celebrate the NBA's post-season playoffs.

She hadn't met Derrick Warren, one of the cofounders of Bawdy Records, at the P.S., Inc. dinner party, and when she asked Astrid where Mr. Warren had gotten her name the booker responded, saying, "Someone associated with Mr. Warren recommended you attend the soiree."

Alana didn't know who that someone was, but she was grateful for the referral. Becoming a partygoer at Hoops would serve a threefold purpose: she would earn several thousand in commissions, permit her entrée to a coterie of upwardly mobile young African-American men and women and give her more material for the book she'd been writing for years.

She'd begun a Jackie Collins–style novel, complete with the ubiquitous celebrity and scheming wannabe characters set in exotic locales spanning the globe; but she hadn't picked up the manuscript in weeks because of writer's block. She'd come up with reason after reason why she wasn't writing but none were valid. The fact was, she had more time for herself now that she was alone, but if she were truly honest, she would have to admit the underlying reason was Calvin McNair.

It was three weeks and he still hadn't called her; after a heart-searching session with her therapist she decided not to call him. Calvin had programmed her cell-phone number, her direct line at the magazine and even her mother's number into his cell phone before he'd left for Europe. The only thing she knew was that he'd better have a good excuse for not calling; otherwise she'd put a *cussin'* on him that he'd never forget.

The lighting inside the club was dim but not so dim she couldn't see where she was going as she followed a hostess across a space crowded with young, beautiful people dressed in the ubiquitous New York City black. She'd also elected to wear black: a pair of stretch pants with a cuffed hem, a Lycra off-the shoulder top that hugged her ample 38D bosom like a second skin, and a pair of high-heel sling-back sandals. She'd stopped at Jade Nails after work for a manicure and spa therapy pedicure.

The blood-red color on her toes, fingernails and lush lips was certain to attract the attention she sought, along with the flyaway hairstyle with its profusion of curls that moved whenever she turned her head. She'd utilized Faye's technique for making her dark eyes appear more mysterious by adding smoky-gray and soft black eye shadows. When she saw the results in the mirror, Alana was more than pleased with her new look; there was something about her eye makeup that reminded her of the late-actress/R&B performer Aaliyah.

A tall figure stepped in front of Alana and she would've lost her footing if a large hand hadn't reached out to steady her. A swoosh of air escaped her parted lips when she found herself imprisoned against a body hard as steel.

"I'm sorry."

"Watch it there, sugah."

Alana raised her head to see the face of the man whose fingers were manacles around her upper arm. When she did look up it was into the smiling face of a high-scoring point guard for a Midwest basketball team she couldn't remember.

Kris Dennison felt as if he'd been poleaxed when he felt

the bountiful curves pressed intimately to his body. The woman in his arms was exotic, beyond beautiful with curly black hair, red-brown coloring, slanting dark eyes and a lush, kissable full mouth.

"*Wassup,* sugah?" he asked, smiling.

Staring up at him through her lashes, Alana affected a sensual grin. "You, playa." She stood close to six feet in her heels, and he towered over her by a full head. The ballplayer had to stand at least six-nine or perhaps six-ten.

"Who you here wit, sugah?" he asked, deep voice rumbling in a broad chest under a black silk tee and jacket.

You're good-looking, talented and make millions of dollars a year yet you can't talk worth a damn, Alana thought. "I'm a guest of Mr. Warren's," she said with a tight smile.

"Now, if you unhand the lady, Kris, I'll make a proper introduction."

Derrick Warren knew it impolite to stare, yet he couldn't pull his gaze away from Alana Gardner's face. Marcus Hampton had described Alana, but his friend and financial consultant hadn't done the lady justice. She was drop-dead gorgeous.

Derrick kissed her cheek. Not only did she look good, but she smelled good, too. "I'd like to offer you a very special welcome to Hoops."

Alana, assuming the man greeting her was Derrick Warren, pressed her cheek to his. "Thank you, Derrick."

There was something about his permanently furrowed forehead and the loose skin around his eyes that made him look like a shar-pei; but what he lacked in the face department he more than made up for in his demeanor and style of dress. The brother was wearing the hell out of his Armani suit. The wool jacket was draped over his broad shoulders in the same manner as European men wore theirs.

Smiling, Derrick cradled Alana's hand in the bend of his elbow. "Kris, this lovely lady is Alana Gardner. Alana, Kristofer Dennison."

Alana gave the point guard a polite smile. "It's nice meeting you, Kris."

"I'm sorry to drag Alana away," Derrick said, apologizing to Kris, "but there are a few people I'd like her to meet."

"Is she coming on the July Fourth boat ride?" Kris called out as Derrick turned to lead Alana away.

Derrick stopped and stared at Alana as her lids slipped down over her eyes. "Are you available on that day?"

Alana raised her gaze to find Derrick watching her. She knew she was flirting with him but didn't much care. She was alone *and* lonely. "Do you want me to be available?"

"Yes, I do." There was no emotion in his reply or on his face. Alana nodded, and Derrick nodded to Kris. "Yes, she is."

The smile that lit up Kris's handsome face was as bright as Christmas lights. "Later, Alana."

She smiled over her shoulder at him. "Later, Kris."

Tightening his hold on the hand in the bend of his arm, Derrick led Alana over to a table on a raised platform in a secluded corner. He seated her, then sat down opposite her. The flickering light from a votive cast long and short shadows over his face.

A waiter appeared out of nowhere. "Is there anything I can get for you, Mr. Warren?"

Derrick smiled at the woman sharing his table. "Would you like some champagne?"

"Yes, thank you."

"Cristal, Moët or Dom Perignon?"

"Dom Perignon." She was flattered that she'd been given a choice. Usually men offered her whatever they drank.

"A bottle of Dom Perignon for the lady, and I'll have my usual. Also, tell Hilda to put together a little something for me and my guest."

Waiting until the waiter left to place his order, Derrick directed his full attention to Alana Gardner. "So, what do you do, Alana?"

Tilting her chin, she smiled at the record producer. What Derrick Warren didn't know was that he would be perfect for her column. "I'm a magazine editor."

"What magazine?"

"*British Vogue.* I'm the American Lifestyles editor."

"You interview people?" She nodded. "Who have you interviewed lately?"

"I just completed one with a ninety-four-year-old French-Jewish woman who'd been Coco Chanel's assistant. Madame Chartres escaped Paris within days of the Nazi occupation and lived in London for forty years before coming to the States to live with a distant cousin."

Alana told Derrick about some of the other celebrities

and personalities she'd interviewed, stopping when a waiter arrived with bottles of chilled Perignon and Cristal, and another with a platter of assorted hors d'oeuvres.

A minute later, place settings and flutes filled with the bubbling wine were set out on the table. Derrick picked up his flute, extending it to Alana. "Here's to the most intelligent and beautiful blind date I've ever had."

Smiling, she picked up her flute. "Thank you, Derrick." She touched his glass to hers. "Here's to friendship."

He paused, his flute inches from his mouth, as his soulful gaze moved with agonizing slowness over her face. Marcus had set him up with Alana Gardner not because he couldn't get a woman but because Alana was different from those who came on to him wanting either money, fame or bragging rights that they'd slept with one of today's fastest-rising music producers. It didn't matter that he'd paid P.S., Inc. thousands for Alana's company. He'd been willing to pay six figures because she provided the perfect cover for his sexual proclivity. No one knew, and that included his family, other than Marcus Hampton, that he was gay. He couldn't afford to come out of the closet as some actors were doing, because homosexuality was looked upon as a scourge in the hip-hop community. Whom he slept with would remain his secret.

Derrick didn't know if Alana had a boyfriend and really didn't give a damn. The fact that she was working as an escort meant she was available.

"To friendship," he repeated.

* * *

Derrick had offered his car and driver to see her home, and Alana waited for the doorman to open the rear door of the dark blue Bentley.

She'd spent four hours at Hoops, drinking champagne and spreading tiny spoonfuls of beluga caviar onto wafer-thin triangles of toast. Derrick ate most of the smoked oysters, clams on the half shell and mussels. When she asked him to dance with her, he'd politely declined, saying he didn't dance. But that didn't stop Alana from dancing with the ballplayers who stopped by the table to exchange pleasantries with the club owner.

She realized she was more than slightly tipsy from the champagne and exhausted from dancing, but she'd do it all again in a heartbeat because it brought her one step closer to her goal of saving enough money to have a mega-wedding *and* her dream house in the suburbs.

CHAPTER 40

Faye woke up to incessant knocking. She sat up, disoriented; then she realized that she wasn't in her own bed and that brilliant sunlight came through shuttered windows. Smiling, she remembered where she was.

She'd felt like Alice in Wonderland the moment she boarded the Boeing Business Jet. The aircraft, large enough to accommodate eighteen passengers, had two full bedrooms, two and a half baths and nearly a thousand square feet of living space. Within minutes of takeoff they were served a sumptuous dinner of veal scallopini with lemon-parsley sauce, penne a la vodka, celeriac salad and white wine.

Bart had suggested they rest during the flight, and both retreated to their bedrooms, where she'd fallen asleep. The jet touched down at the Owen Roberts International Airport, where they were whisked through Customs and escorted to an area where a driver awaited their arrival. The scent of saltwater and blooming flowers flowed through the automobile's open windows during the drive to a private villa overlooking the ocean where the wedding and reception were to be held on the beach at sunset.

She slipped out of bed. "I'm coming." Reaching for a peach-colored silk wrap at the foot of the bed, she pushed her arms into the generous sleeves. Walking on bare feet, she crossed the room and opened the door. Bart stood there in a pair of walking shorts, T-shirt and a pair of sandals, smiling at her behind the lenses of a pair of sunglasses.

"I thought you would have been up by now." There was a teasing quality in his voice.

"What time is it?"

Bart glanced at his watch. "It is exactly five-fifteen."

"Five…fifteen," Faye repeated, sputtering. "We're on vacation and you wake me up at five freakin' fifteen in the morning!"

Crossing his arms over his chest, he angled his head. "Has anyone ever told you that you look very sexy early in the morning?"

Faye glanced down at her chest. She hadn't bothered to close her wrap and there was no doubt he was talking about the lacy décolletage that was anything but modest. She closed the robe, tying the sash around her waist.

A slight frown creased Bart's forehead when his gaze traveled downward. "What size shoe do you wear?"

She wiggled her bare toes. "Five. Why?"

"Will you be able to find women's shoes in your size?"

Faye's expression registered disbelief. "Yes, Bartholomew."

He flushed under his light tan. Her calling him by his full name was no doubt a reprimand. "How would I know, Faye? I'm not in the habit of buying shoes for a woman."

Faye felt properly chastised. She had no right to assume that he shopped for women. "I'm sorry—"

"There's no need to apologize," he said, cutting her off. "I've arranged for us to eat breakfast at six. At seven we'll be given a full body massage, facial, manicure and pedicure. We'll leave around eleven to go shopping. After that you're on your own until the wedding. Let me know now if this meets with your approval...or whether there is something else you want or need?"

Heat found its way up Faye's chest to her cheeks. Bartholomew Houghton had just verbally spanked her. "Your plans sound wonderful."

Lowering his arms, Bart glared at Faye behind the dark lenses. There were times when he wanted to raise his voice to her, this being one, and there were many more times when he wanted to kiss her. Not a mere brushing of the lips, but a kiss that would make her swoon.

"I will see you on the veranda at six." Turning on his heel, he walked away.

"Aye, aye, boss," Faye called out to his retreating back, then pulled in a quick breath when he turned around, closed the distance between them and stood over her like an avenging angel.

"Is that how you see me, Faye? You think of me as your boss?"

She'd argued enough with Norman not to be intimidated by any man—and that included Bartholomew Houghton. "Why shouldn't I? After all, you're paying me to entertain you."

"Wrong! I'm paying you to keep me company. Women I pay to *entertain* me I sleep with. So let's not confuse one with the other."

Folding her hands on her hips, Faye lifted her chin in a defiant gesture. "I'll be ready at six." Stepping back, she closed the door, shutting out his thunderous expression.

She took off the wrap and flung it on a rattan chair. "The arrogant son of a bitch," she mumbled as she headed for the bathroom. Bart sought to ease his conscience by making what he did morally correct when in fact he was no different from any man who paid a woman to spend time with him. They weren't sleeping together, but the fact remained, she never would've dated Bart if Enid Richards hadn't brought them together.

After a breakfast of sliced fruit, poached eggs, a fluffy croissant and rich Jamaica coffee, Faye lay on a table enjoying the expert ministrations of a full body massage and hydrating European facial. She opened her eyes to meet Bart's amused gaze as he lay nude on a matching table; a towel covered his hips.

"Feeling better?"

She smiled at him. "Yes, thank you."

He lifted his eyebrows. "You have to let me know when it's your time of the month so I'll know to keep my distance."

She stared wordlessly at him. Her mouth opened and closed several times before she said, "You're basing what I say to you on hormones?"

Bart winced when the masseuse kneaded a knot in his

shoulder. The slender man had fingers like steel. "What other reason can you give for snapping at me? When are you due to get your period?"

"That's none of your business," she hissed between clenched teeth. Faye couldn't believe he was asking her something so personal, and in front of two strangers.

"That's where you're wrong, Faye. Whenever we're together everything about you is my business."

There he was again, subtly reminding her that she was a bought woman. "Next week," she said reluctantly.

"I thought so," he said, closing his eyes.

Faye didn't want to tell Bart that whenever she experienced PMS she sometimes went into bitch mode. She closed her eyes as her masseuse's hands worked their magic.

She lost track of time and when she finally opened her eyes it was to stare at the man asleep on a table less than a foot away, a man who'd become the answer to all her prayers and dreams.

CHAPTER 41

Faye knocked on the door to the adjoining suite. The door opened. Bart stood there in a pale gray linen suit, matching shirt open at the throat and a pair of black slip-ons. He'd elected not to tuck the hem of his shirt into his waistband. His look was casually chic.

Shifting, she presented him with her back. "I need your help." She'd managed to zip her dress halfway.

Bart couldn't move. Faye was a vision of ethereal femininity. She'd spent two hours in a boutique trying on countless garments before she finally selected an A-line slip dress in lime-green chiffon with a lavender underskirt. The garment was perfect for her petite figure.

It took only twenty minutes for her to choose a Louis Vuitton wedge sandal in a soft pearl hue. He'd surprised himself when he'd sat patiently watching her model dresses and shoes for his approval because accompanying his late wife had not been an option. Deidre had claimed she always wanted to surprise him, and most times she did.

Deidre Dunn-Houghton had been a pretty, young woman who'd inherited her frumpy taste from her maternal grandmother. The older woman had assumed responsibility of raising the child after Deidre's mother's downward spiral into a world of alcohol and pills that eventually took her life when she was injured in a horrific automobile accident. Unfortunately Deidre suffered the same fate as her mother when she swallowed a bottle of sleeping pills after her fourth miscarriage in eleven years of marriage.

Bart blinked once. Everything about Faye had snared him into a sensual maze from which he did not want to escape. The play of light in her gold-flecked eyes was mesmerizing, the glistening sheen of her satiny-brown skin hypnotic, and the curves of her body sent his libido into overdrive whenever she fixed him with her sensual stare. Everything about her seduced his senses because she had a way of staring at him that made him feel as if he were the only man in the world.

Faye peered at him over her shoulder. "Will you please zip me up?"

Bart prayed she hadn't felt his trembling fingers when he completed the task. "You're…" His words trailed off when a bell echoed throughout the villa. Lowering his head, he kissed the nape of her neck. "Don't move."

Faye smiled. He sounded so mysterious. "What is it?"

"Give me a minute, and I'll be right back."

Bart walked out of the bedroom and through a narrow hallway to the space doubling as a living room. He opened the door; a young dark-skinned man stood on the veranda.

"Bartholomew Houghton?"

He nodded. "Yes."

The man handed him a cloth-covered flat case. "This is for you." Reaching into his shirt pocket, he removed a pen and receipt. "I need your signature."

Bart scrawled his name on the receipt. He reached into the pocket of his slacks and handed the messenger a tip. "Thank you."

The messenger nodded. "Thank *you,* sir."

Bart closed the door and returned to the bedroom. Faye sat on a chair, legs crossed, one sandal-shod foot tapping rhythmically on the floor.

He winked at her. "I thought I told you not to move."

Faye gave him a saucy grin. "Your minute was up."

He beckoned to her. "Come here."

She moved gracefully off the chair, the hem of her dress flowing fluidly around her shoes. She appeared taller, more willowy with the four-inch lacquered wedge heels. He handed her the case.

"What's this?"

"Open it, Faye."

She complied, her hands shaking noticeably when she saw what lay on a bed of white satin. An amethyst briolette suspended from a necklace of beaded peridot was the perfect complement for her dress. The case also held a pair of peridot briolette earrings.

"They're beautiful." She stared up at Bart. "When did you get these?" She slipped the wires into her pieced lobes.

He took the necklace and fastened it around her neck. The amethyst briolette lay between her breasts. "I called a jeweler and told him what you were wearing."

"You have impeccable taste."

"I know," he whispered without a hint of modesty. He extended his hand. "It's time we head over to the festivities."

The weather and the setting were perfect for a beachfront wedding. Hundreds of yards of gauze secured to bamboo poles billowed in a gentle ocean breeze. Lighted candles under chimneys formed a path upon which the bridal party would proceed to the beach. Eight tables, with seating for four, were set up under the makeshift tent.

"Are you a friend of the bride or groom?" Faye asked Bart as they neared the wedding site.

"The bride's father and I were college roommates."

"Which college did you attend?"

"I did my undergraduate work at Yale, and I got a graduate degree from Columbia."

"What were your majors?"

"Architecture at Yale, and business management at Columbia. Where did you go?"

"I went to Pace College for marketing and finance, then on to NYU for an MBA."

Squeezing her fingers gently, Bart smiled and nodded. "Nice."

Real nice, Faye thought sourly. So nice that the company she'd given her blood, sweat and now tears to for five years had given her account to two knuckleheaded interns—one who was sleeping with Faye's boss, and the other who was the son of a vice president. Talk about nepotism and preferential treatment.

Bart let go of her hand and looped an arm around her waist. "Is there anything else you want to know about me?"

Tilting her head, Faye smiled up at him. "Is there anything lurid in your past that I could use to sell to a tabloid?"

Throwing back his head, Bart laughed. "I'm sorry to disappoint you, beautiful, but I'm no A-list movie or rock star. In fact, on a scale of one to ten, ten being shocking and scandalous, I'd come in about a two."

"You like being that inconspicuous?"

"I prefer it. Once your face is that recognizable your life changes so dramatically that you can never go back to do what is considered ordinary. When actors or performers really hit it big, they preen on the red carpet while their adorning fans scream for their attention. Then when they decide they want anonymity and a photographer puts a camera in their face, they're threatening lawsuit because of an invasion of privacy. Once you whore for the public there's no turning back."

Bartholomew Houghton managed to keep a low profile, but Faye wondered how much her life would change now that she'd become his companion. And there was no doubt a mixed-race couple was certain to drawn some attention.

Leaning into Bart's length, she made herself a promise. She was going to enjoy her role as social companion to one of the world's richest men until he decided it was over, or she did. And she was realistic and mature enough to know that it would eventually come to an end.

A tall woman in a becoming pale pink suit approached

them. "Bart, I'm so glad you could make it." She threw her arms around his neck and kissed him flush on the mouth. "Gary told me you sent back your response indicating you were coming, but he also expected you to call."

Releasing Faye, Bart reached up and extracted his ex-roommate's sister's arms from his neck. "It's nice seeing you again, Abbey. We'll talk later, but first let me introduce you to my guest." The woman stared at Faye as if she'd just materialized. "Faye, this is Abigail Grogan, the bride's aunt. Abbey, Faye Ogden."

Abbey's bright blue eyes narrowed as she shot Faye a suspicious look. "I thought you were bringing your cousin."

Bart frowned. "She couldn't make it. Abbey, you're forgetting your manners," he chastised softly.

A flush spread over Abbey's face. "I'm sorry, Bart." She nodded to Faye. "Nice meeting you, Faye. Is it all right if I call you Faye?" she asked facetiously.

"Of course you may, Abigail."

Abbey checked her watch. "We're going to be starting in less than half an hour. The wedding planner will show you to your table. I'm sorry to rush off, but I have to see if my niece needs my assistance."

A woman wearing a headset came toward them as Abbey scurried away. "May I have your name so I can direct you to your table?"

"B. Houghton and guest," Bart said, reaching for Faye's hand.

The woman checked off their names on a list attached to a clipboard. "Please follow me."

Faye noticed several women whispering behind their hands as she passed their table. A slight smile curved her mouth when she heard one of them say, "Vera Wang." It was apparent they'd recognized her dress's designer. The garment was simple and elegant, the colors reminding her of green and lavender jade.

Bart and Faye where shown to a table several feet from the bridal table. He seated Faye, leaning over and inhaling the subtle fragrance of cologne on her bared flesh. His gaze lingered on her profile.

"Can I get you something from the bar?"

Tilting her chin, Faye met his gaze. "I'd like a soft drink, please."

He noticed waiters were coming around with trays of champagne and finger foods. "I'll bring you something to eat."

"Thank you."

As Bart made his way toward the bar, he stopped a waitress and asked her to serve the woman with the short blond hair. He pointed to the table where Faye sat.

The waitress's mouth dropped open. "Is...is she Eva, the...the girl who won *America's Next Top Model?*" When Bart gave her a puzzled look, she said, "I saw the television show when I was in New York."

Bart had no idea what the woman was talking about. He rarely watched prime-time TV shows. Public television, CNN and networks devoted to business and finance were the exceptions. Newspapers were his preferred medium of information.

"No, she's not *that* Eva."

The waitress smiled. "But she is as beautiful as Eva." Her voice was filled with awe.

Bart had to agree with her. Faye wasn't the Eva this woman was stammering about, but she definitely was beautiful. He'd enjoyed watching her try on clothes and surprising her with the necklace and earrings.

It'd been a long time since he was given the opportunity to spoil a woman. The first and only one had been his wife. He had no living relatives other than his cousin, who'd moved to Utah to marry a Mormon.

His personal net worth was staggering, he had no heirs to whom he would leave his fortune, and he wanted to enjoy what was left of his life; with Faye as companion he was certain he'd never be bored.

When he received Enid's invitation for her spring soiree, his first inclination was to decline, then he changed his mind. The moment he saw Faye Ogden's legs, feet and finally her face he knew he'd made the right decision to attend. Unknowingly, the petite woman with the blond hair, gold eyes and sassy attitude had changed him.

CHAPTER 42

Garrett "Gary" Grogan led his daughter, stunning in a Carolina Herrera wedding gown, over a flower-strewn path to where her groom, wedding party, three dozen guests and string quartet had gathered on the beach in bare feet. The rays of the setting sun, the calming sound of the incoming tide and the harmonic melody of the wedding march completed the surreal setting.

Faye couldn't stop the flood of tears filling her eyes and trickling down her cheeks. She wasn't certain whether they were tears of joy or tears of regret; joy for the young couple repeating vows that would bind them and their lives together or regret for her own short-lived marriage.

Bart took a quick glance at Faye. His held his breath for several seconds before releasing it. She was crying. For the first time since meeting her she appeared fragile, vulnerable. Gathering her in his arms, he kissed her cheeks, tasting salt on his tongue.

"I'm sorry," she mumbled, as a fresh wave of tears flowed. Faye buried her face against Bart's chest.

Bart patted her back. "It's all right, baby."

Faye took delight in the warmth and smell of the man

holding her to his heart. He reminded her of what she'd missed, had been missing since her divorce; she missed being held, missed making love, loving and being loved.

Reaching inside his jacket, Bart removed a handkerchief. He dabbed her tears, taking care not to smudge her eye makeup. Anchoring a hand under Faye's chin, he raised her face. Moisture had spiked her lashes and turned her eyes into shimmering orbs of burnished gold. Smiling, she lowered her lashes demurely and he was lost, and enchanted by a delicate femininity that in no way detracted from the strength he'd come to admire.

"I cry at weddings."

Cradling her face between his hands, his lips slowly descended to touch hers, her mouth sweet and warm under his. "And I cry at funerals."

"Somehow I can't imagine you crying," she whispered.

He kissed her again. "Why?"

Faye couldn't respond, not with his mouth making her feel things she didn't want to feel. It was not easy to remain in control with him so close, with his kisses sending her pulse spinning.

"Why?" he asked again between soft, nibbling kisses over her lower lip.

"Because..." She never got to complete her statement, because the sound of applause captured her attention. Zarcarias and Helena Grogan-Crane were now husband and wife.

"We'll continue this later," Bart promised.

Everyone on the beach waited for the wedding party

to sit at the bridal table before they returned to their assigned seating.

It wasn't until hours later, when Faye and Bart were alone, that they were able to talk without someone eaves-dropping on their conversation. They lay on a blanket on the beach, facing each other.

The wedding and reception that had begun at sunset went on for hours. The music from the string quartet gave way to a local calypso band with steel pans that had the entire wedding party and their guests up on their feet until they retired to their respective tables to dine on a sumptuous feast of Caribbean-inspired dishes.

A renowned caterer and his staff had prepared platters of lobster, crab, conch, fork-tender filet mignon, jerk pork and chicken, along with side dishes of fried plantain, rice with pigeon peas and the ubiquitous crudités with exotic vegetable dips. The distinctive spices in the dishes were the perfect complement for the potent rum punch and finest vintage champagnes. And for the first time in a very long time Faye overindulged.

When it came time for the limbo, she lifted her dress above her knees and shimmied under the length of bamboo. She and a male cousin of the groom were crowned limbo king and queen. She'd felt Bart's gaze on her the entire time the young man danced with her when they celebrated their victory.

She'd lost count of the men who'd asked her to dance, but once she found herself in Bart's arms he refused to relinquish her. After a while the other men stopped asking. What they didn't understand was that she wasn't there for them, but for Bartholomew Houghton. He was paying *her* for companionship.

The bride and groom had retreated to their honeymoon bungalow half a mile from the resort, while their guests continued to drink and dance until the clock signaled the beginning of a new day. Soon after, Faye told Bart she wanted to leave because she was beginning to feel the effects of the rum punch. They'd walked back to their villa, changed into T-shirts and shorts before walking down to the beach.

Splaying a hand over Faye's back, Bart massaged her bare skin under the cotton fabric. "How's your head?"

She smiled. "It stopped spinning."

"How many drinks did you have?"

"I took a few sips of champagne and had a couple of glasses of rum punch."

His fingertips caressed the length of her spine. "The punch was like Hawaiian Punch."

Faye smiled again. "Yeah, right. Hawaiian Punch with a little extra."

Shifting on the blanket, Bart nuzzled the side of Faye's neck. "How did you meet Enid Richards?" She told him about Enid eavesdropping on her conversation with her best friend at the Four Seasons, and their subsequent meeting.

"I'm glad she did," he mumbled, placing tiny kisses along the column of her neck. "I'm glad you signed on with her, glad I decided to come to her soiree and ecstatic because I have you all to myself."

I am not your chattel. Faye swallowed the words poised on the tip of her tongue.

She *had* to learn to play the game in order to win the ultimate prize: a half million dollars. Bart had given Enid a million dollars for her services for the summer, a sum to be paid out in amounts that would not raise a flag with the IRS.

Moving closer, she placed her leg over his. "Me, too."

"Me, too, what?"

"I'm glad that I met you, that I'm with you." Why, Faye thought, did she sound so sincere? When had she become such an accomplished actress?

The fingers of Bart's left hand feathered over the nape of her neck. "Show me how much you want to be with me."

For the first time since she'd come face-to-face with the man holding her to his length, Faye took the lead. Instinctively, her body arched toward him as she closed her eyes and kissed Bart, kissed him with a passion she'd withheld from every man since ending her marriage.

His fingers circling her neck, tongue slipping between her parted lips and the growing erection he was unable to conceal quickened her pulse and sent waves of excitement coursing throughout her body. Aroused, Faye pressed closer.

Bart, deepening the kiss, reversed their position until she lay between his legs. The motion elicited an unbidden pulsing between her thighs that made breathing difficult.

Bart reversed their position again; this time he lay between Faye's legs, and went completely still, unable to move because he couldn't move. If he did, it would be to break his promise not to make love to Faye. He was enthralled by her smell, the satiny feel of her skin, the sweetness of her mouth.

I lied, Bart's inner voice taunted. He'd lied to Faye and to himself. He'd told her that he wouldn't sleep with her when that was exactly what he wanted to do.

He'd accomplished and accumulated more than he'd ever dreamed of achieving, but he wanted more.

And the more was Faye Ogden.

CHAPTER 43

A smile replaced Enid's frown the moment she detected the scent of the familiar cologne. She didn't have to turn around to know who'd come up behind her, although the gallery was a bustle of activity with the caterer and his staff setting up a bar and several tables with platters of finger foods.

"What do you think of this one, darling?" She pointed to a matted black-and-white photograph of a Japanese woman holding her toddler daughter.

"It's nice, but I never figured you for cute."

She'd asked Marcus to meet her at the Madison Avenue art gallery. The owner of the gallery, a P.S., Inc. client and former celebrated photographer in his own right, had opened the gallery an hour early for his elite customers to view a collection of black-and-white prints Peter Janus had taken during a year-long stint in Asia. Art critics were now comparing the up-and-coming photographer's work to that of Ansel Adams. She owned several Janus photographs, and when she had them appraised, she found that her investment had increased appreciably.

Enid moved closer to Marcus, looping her arm through his. "What's wrong with cute?"

Lowering his head, he pressed his mouth to her ear. "Didn't you say you don't like photographs or paintings with children?"

Tilting her chin, she met his honey-gold gaze. They'd been living together for almost a month, and she had to admit the experience was most enjoyable. However, it hadn't been that way with her ex-husband. She'd married the insurance executive, eighteen years her senior, not because she'd been in love with him but because he'd helped her attain a social plateau she'd always dreamed about. She would've been content to give her twice-married older husband an heir, but fate intervened on her behalf. What she hadn't told her husband was that she didn't like nor want children.

"They are scene stealers, darling."

"Scene stealers or you don't like children?"

"Both," she admitted. Enid had been forthcoming with Marcus early on in their relationship when the one time they'd made love and he hadn't used a condom she told him that she couldn't get pregnant because of a surgical procedure, and even if she could, she didn't want children.

Enid glanced at the catalog, taking note of the price. The print was reasonable, compared to one of the others she'd selected. "Despite the child, there is something I like about the photo," she admitted.

"If you like this one, then you should see two others." The gallery owner had overhead her.

Pulling her arm from Marcus's, Enid turned to find Stephen Jacobsen standing a few feet away. Tall, slender, with a pockmarked face, Stephen had affected a short blond beard to conceal the aftermath of adolescent acne that had continued well into his twenties and thirties. His lament was, "Where the hell was Proactiv when I was a teenager?"

"Which ones, Stephen?" Enid asked.

"Six and ten. Six is a photo of the grandparents, and ten the little girl's great-grandparents. You can hang them to form a triptych."

Enid and Marcus moved over to view the photos. The great-grandparents wore traditional Japanese garb, and the grandparents a mix of Japanese and Western, while the young mother and child were resplendent in what Enid recognized as Dior and Ralph Lauren.

"How much for the three?"

Stephen angled his head as he mentally tallied the price of the three photographs. Enid was one of his best customers, so he decided to offer her a discount. He quoted a price, his expression registering anticipation. The figure was high, but not so high that Ms. Richards wouldn't at least consider it.

"Take ten percent off and I'll take it," Enid said smoothly.

"But I've already discounted ten percent."

"What do you think, darling?" she asked Marcus.

Marcus had watched the interchange between his lover and the gallery owner with what appeared to be bored indifference. He was hard pressed not to laugh. Enid had played this game so well that he knew she didn't actually need his opinion.

"Thirty-six fifty does appear to be a little steep for three photographs," he drawled, sighing as if totally bored.

A flush stole its way up Stephen's neck to his flaxen hairline. "I've already taken nine hundred off the catalog price."

"Nine hundred is nothing when I'm willing to pay ten thousand for the one with the Kyoto teahouse."

Stephen had to admire Enid Richards. Not only was she exquisite, but she was a shark when it came to business. She wanted something the gallery owner had, and he wanted something she had.

"I'll give you the four of them for ten but..."

Enid's pale eyebrows lifted. "What do you want, Stephen?"

"I want you to arrange for me to photograph Ilene Fairchild."

A knowing smile touched Enid's lips. Stephen was as sly as a fox. "I can ask whether she'd be willing to sit for you, but I believe you're going to have to deal with her agent who still handles her modeling jobs."

"I don't want to deal with her agent."

"What do you plan to do with her photos?" Marcus asked, deciding it was time he became involved in the discussion. After all, he was responsible for Ilene becoming a social companion for Pleasure Seekers.

"I'd like to exhibit them here at the gallery."

"Do you plan to sell them?" Enid questioned.

Stephen nodded. "I will if Ilene signs a release."

"What's her take?" Marcus asked.

Stephen shrugged a shoulder under his black silk and wool jacket. "Fifty."

Enid and Marcus exchanged a glance. "Give her sixty," Marcus said, "and I'll talk to her. I know a way we can get around her agent."

Grinning broadly, Stephen offered Marcus his hand. "Deal."

Enid wanted to throw her arms around Marcus's neck and kiss him. There was no way she or her partner would permit the gallery owner to exploit their social companion. "I'll draw up the agreement and you can have your attorney look it over before Ilene agrees to sign your release." Without warning, she'd gone into legal mode.

"No problem, Enid." Stephen wasn't going to argue with her when there was the possibility that he would photograph one of the most beautiful faces to ever grace the cover of a fashion magazine.

Opening her purse, Enid took out her checkbook and business card. "Please have them delivered to my office." Sitting at a small table, she made out the check to the gallery.

Bowing elegantly, Stephen took the check. He beckoned to Marina, his assistant. He gave the woman the check and business card. "Please place Sold stickers on numbers six, ten, eighteen and thirty-two."

Reaching for an envelope in the pocket of her slacks, Marina put the check and card inside and wrote down the numbers of the prints on the front. It would be another forty minutes before Jacobsen Galleries opened for the Janus showing, and seven of forty photographs in the exhibit were already sold.

Enid offered her hand to Stephen. "Thank you. It's always a pleasure doing business with you."

He took the proffered hand, kissing her fingers. "Aren't you going to stay and have some champagne?"

Easing her hand from his gentle grip, Enid smiled at him from under her lashes. "I'm sorry, Stephen, but not this time. Marcus and I have an engagement at Lincoln Center in less than an hour."

Stephen inclined his head to Enid, then Marcus. "Anytime you want a private showing, please call me or Marina."

Looping an arm around Enid's waist, Marcus led her to the entrance. One of the employees opened the door, but before they exited, a man and woman entered. He felt Enid stiffen before she relaxed against his arm. Bartholomew Houghton had come to the private showing with Faye Ogden on his arm.

Initially, Marcus had thought the man much too old for Faye, but after seeing them together he realized they were a striking couple. Both were fashionably dressed, quite tanned and, from the way they were smiling, obviously got along well. The two couples exchanged polite nods as they passed one another.

Verbal acknowledgment between clients and social companions was not an option because P.S., Inc.'s ongoing success was based on the utmost discretion.

Marcus escorted Enid to where their driver waited to take them across town for a concert at Lincoln Center. "Your exotic jewel looks wonderful."

Enid nodded. "She looks happy."

His fingers tightened on her waist. "Don't tell me you're matchmaking, darling."

"You know I'd never advocate a companion falling in love with a client. That would be bad for business."

"Do you ever stop thinking about business?" he teased.

"Of course I do," Enid countered.

"When is that, Enid?"

There came a prolonged pause before she said, "Whenever you make love to me."

Marcus smiled. "I rest my case, Counselor."

CHAPTER 44

Ilene straddled a chair with a delicate stainless-steel frame, a profusion of sea foam–green silk flowing around the ties encircling her slender ankles in a pair of matching stilettos; she lifted her hair off her shoulders and stared directly into the photographer's lens, forcing a smile. She'd learned quickly to give her clients her undivided attention. After all, that was what she was being paid very well to do.

"Lift your chin a little to your right, Ilene," Stephen Jacobsen crooned as he got off three more frames in quick succession. "That's it, baby."

He lowered his camera but couldn't pull his gaze away from the woman on the chair. Although he'd found Ilene Fairchild a little thin for his personal taste, as an artist he appreciated the perfect dimensions of her slender body. Besides, his camera would add the extra pounds that would make her spectacular looking in print.

"Would you mind joining me for dinner?"

Ilene wanted to say no, not because she was exhausted, and not because she wanted to go home and get a few hours of sleep before heading to the airport for a flight to a private island in the Caribbean. Working as a social companion was like being on a runaway train. She'd been working nonstop, every night with a different man from a different country.

She'd likened modeling to a roller-coaster ride, up, down, around and around, speeding up, slowing until it came to a complete stop. But times had changed, because she was no longer on every designer's wish list to model their creations. That aside, she had yet to be relegated to over-the-hill or has-been status. If Stephen Jacobsen had asked to photograph her, then her supermodel standing was still bankable.

Stephen's photographs were first exhibited at a Greenwich Village gallery at the tender age of twenty-two, and over the next two decades art critics compared his genius to that of Richard Avedon and Diane Arbus. Then without warning, forty-two-year-old Stephen packed away his cameras and lenses and opened his own gallery, becoming a preeminent collector of black-and-white photos.

Ilene flashed her dimpled smile. "I can stay for an hour."

"Why the rush, beautiful?"

Rising to her feet, she shook her head, the fall of hair settling around her shoulders. "I have to go home, pack and grab a few hours of sleep before I head out early tomorrow morning. I have a 7:00 a.m. flight out of Kennedy."

Stephen set his camera on a nearby table and closed the distance between them. He stared at the catlike eyes staring back at him. He hadn't lied when he called her beautiful because she was. Ilene Fairchild was more than beautiful—her face was perfect.

"I have something that will make you feel good, Ilene."
A hint of a smile tilted the corners of his mouth upward.
Reaching into a pocket of his jeans, he took out a tiny
bottle filled with a white powder. "It will make you forget
about sleeping."

Ilene's impassive expression didn't change. She knew
Stephen was talking about snorting coke. "I don't do
drugs, Stephen," she lied smoothly.

He traced the contour of her cheek with his free hand.
"That's not what I heard." His voice had taken on a
crooning quality, his gaze inching from her mouth to the
soft swell of flesh rising and falling above a demibra.

Ilene did not drop her gaze. "Whoever said that was a
liar."

"Come on, baby. Try it."

Her delicate jaw tightened. "No. And even if I wanted
to I can't. Enid Richards conducts random drug testing,
and if I come up dirty then I'm out of a job."

Stephen's hand dropped. "You believe working for
Enid is a job?"

Bending over, Ilene untied the satin ties around her
ankles and stepped out of the stilettos. "It pays the bills,
Stephen." Then she took off the dress, leaving it on the
chair. Clad only in a bra and thong panties, she reached
for her jeans and tank top.

"I'll pay your bills."

"That's not enough," she said, zipping her jeans at the
same time she pushed her bare feet into zebra-print mules.

"What more would you want?"

Ilene pulled the T-shirt over her head, flipped her hair, then reached for a hobo purse that had been a gift from her Nigerian client. "Marriage, Stephen. I want to settle down, become a wife and a mother."

"You want to ruin *that* body with stretch marks?"

"It's not about my body anymore, Stephen. It's all about me, what I want for me and my future. I want someone to love me for me, and not because I have a marketable face and body. I want financial security so that I don't have to fill up on tuna when I want caviar. And I want to grow old with someone who I know will be there for me in sickness and in health, in the good *and* the bad times. Am I asking for too much?"

"No, Ilene, you're not. It's just that I can't give you what you want."

Ilene brushed a kiss over his bearded cheek. "That's okay, lovey," she said in her best Cockney accent. "I hope this means we can still do business together."

Stephen nodded. "Of course."

He returned the tiny bottle to his pocket, crossed his arms over his chest and watched Ilene Fairchild strut out of his loft as if she were wearing a Valentino gown instead of a pair of faded hip-hugging jeans and a tank top.

CHAPTER 45

Ilene lay on a blanket on the fine white sand on Pine Cay under the fronds of a palm tree, eyes closed. She'd left New York earlier that morning on a commercial jet. She'd been content to deal with the crowds waiting to get on the 757 aircraft because of her first-class standing. After landing at Miami International she was met by a man holding up a sign with her name who'd escorted her to a charter flight to Grand Turk. From there she'd boarded a catamaran for the private island of Pine Cay.

She was scheduled to spend a week in the Turks and Caicos as a guest of a trio of businessmen who were purported to be members of a larger group who controlled the White House irrespective of the president's party affiliation. Astrid had informed her that her hosts were celebrating the success of a film they'd financed that had grossed more than half a billion in box-office receipts in less than three months. The action sci-fi flick was estimated to surpass *Titanic,* the all-time, top-grossing American movie.

Ilene could care less how much the movie backers made. Their success had become her success. She would earn a cool forty thousand for an all-expenses-paid vacation to a private island hideaway that was a virtual Garden of Eden. Pine Cay's peaceful atmosphere was preserved because of a no-automobile rule. The normal mode of locomotion was either by bicycle, golf cart or on foot. She planned to take a tour of the eight-hundred-acre island at another time. Right now all she wanted to do was relax.

"Don't you think you would be more comfortable in your room?"

Ilene opened her eyes to find a woman standing over her, recognizing her as the hotel owner's daughter. A profusion of black curly hair framed a rosewood-brown, heart-shaped face.

"Thanks for asking, but I'm good here."

"If you need anything, anything at all, I'm here for you."

"Thank you again."

Ilene wanted to ask the woman, whose name tag identified her as Amelia, why would she make herself available to fetch for hotel guests when there was a full staff made up of a bell captain, concierge, kitchen, housekeeping and maintenance personnel.

Amelia smiled, nodding. "You're most welcome, Miss Fairchild."

Ilene closed her eyes, not opening them again until someone shook her gently. "Miss Fairchild. Dinner will be served within half an hour." It was Amelia, again hovering above her.

Rousing from what had become the best sleep she'd had in ages, Ilene stood up and headed toward the plantation house–style hotel and her room. Private bungalows, several hundred feet from the hotel and occupied by those hosting the week-long festivities, were ablaze with light in the encroaching darkness.

Three-quarters of an hour later, Ilene made her way down to the beach in a flowered bikini with a matching sarong. She'd braided her hair into a single plait that fell down her ramrod-straight spine. She was more than fifteen minutes late, but her tardiness was carefully orchestrated to make for a more dramatic entrance. She recognized the faces of several Hollywood power brokers but not their names until she was formally introduced to them.

Again, as with all of her former clients, none had come with their wives. How, she thought, was she to find a husband if her clients were already married? What she refused to be was a kept woman—again.

Like the diva she believed she'd become, Ilene handed out air kisses like a monarch acknowledging her adoring subjects. She was seated next to Demetrious Reyniak, the son of an immigrant Armenian businessman who'd made a small fortune in the commodities market. Demetrious had become a very wealthy man in his own right when he bought government leases to drill for oil in the Gulf of Mexico. A waif-thin actress with oversize fake breasts that made her look as if she would fall on her face at a moment's notice clung to Demetrious's arm as if he were her lifeline. And from the way his right hand caressed her bare back and hips, it was obvious they were more than acquainted with each other.

But, for Ilene it was different. She'd come to Pine Cay to enjoy herself and not to sleep with any of the fifteen men in attendance. More than half were close to sixty, all were married and, even if they hadn't been married, none were her type. She'd lived with a man much older than her at one time in her life; however, the arrangement had proven beneficial to the seventeen-year-old girl from the Mississippi Delta who up until that time had existed in a world of poverty from which, at her tender age, there was no escape.

She recognized an A-list heartthrob actor who'd come to the island with his partner, a very pretty young man who doubled as his manservant. A director who was touted by *Variety* as the next Spielberg was accompanied by one of his daughters. Why the man wanted to expose his adolescent daughter to an environment where depravity was certain to be the rule rather than the exception was beyond Ilene.

It wasn't until hours later, after platters of jumbo prawns with accompanying piquant dipping sauces, and broiled and fried fish, fresh and roasted vegetables, and tropical fruits indigenous to the region were consumed and washed down with libations from an open bar that Ilene discovered the girl wasn't the daughter but the latest in a string of young girls who were paid to sleep with the director.

Dessert was served in two bowls: one filled with cocaine and the other with colorfully wrapped condoms. A small silver plate, a tiny silver spoon and a straw were also placed on the table in front of each dinner guest.

Less than twenty-four hours before, Ilene had turned

down Stephen Jacobsen's invitation to indulge, but something made her throw caution to the wind to top off a sumptuous meal with a high she couldn't get from marijuana or alcohol. After all, she was on a private island with people who had as much, maybe even more, to lose if the word leaked out that they were snorting cocaine.

She inhaled the white powder and within seconds she was somewhere else, sailing high above the ocean, high enough to touch the clouds. The setting sun had turned the sky into a kaleidoscope of the most awesome colors in the spectrum.

Music blared from hidden speakers and Demetrious eased her up to dance with him. She found herself in his arms, his hands undoing the clasp on her suit top, and she was unable to stop him. The top fell to the sand, followed by her sarong, and finally her bikini bottom. When she opened her eyes it was to find everyone naked and gyrating to the driving rhythms that made her want to whirl faster and faster like the dervishes she'd seen in Greece.

It didn't matter that she was kissed on the mouth, breasts and groped between the legs. All she knew was that it felt good and that she didn't want it to stop. Laughing uncontrollably, she stumbled and fell backward, the soft sand cushioning her fall. Ilene closed her eyes, smiling when she felt something warm and rough between her thighs. It wasn't someone's hot breath but the profusion of hair on her belly that prompted her to see who lay between her legs. It was Amelia.

Her dark eyes sparkled in the remaining daylight. "Come with me to my room," she said in British-accented English.

Ilene was too high to protest. Rising from the sand, she followed Amelia around the side of the hotel to a door that led directly into her private suite.

They shared a shower, splashing water on each other like children. Their playing stopped when they took time to dry the other, then hand in hand they made their way to a king-size bed. Ilene couldn't remember the last time she'd slept with a woman, but when Amelia made love to her it was if the other women never existed. Her mouth and hands worked their magic and for the first time in a very long time Ilene experienced multiple orgasms.

Hours later they made love again; this time it was Ilene's turn to bring Amelia to climax before they fell asleep, limbs entwined and in each other's arms.

CHAPTER 46

Alana sat in her therapist's office staring at the potted plants lining the bookcase. She'd already used twenty minutes of her fifty-minute session, and other than greeting the woman, she hadn't been able to say anything.

"I had a disturbing dream last night."

"What was it about, Alana?"

She looked at the woman dressed in a conservative navy blue suit, white blouse and functional black pumps. She'd been coming to Dr. Marilyn Novak for three years, and the psychoanalyst affected the same hairstyle and always wore a conservative suit and white blouse. Her piercing light blue eyes were the only color in an otherwise unnaturally pale face. Summer or winter, her complexion retained the same pallor.

A chill shook Alana as she closed her eyes. "I was running through a tunnel looking for Calvin."

"Did you know he was inside the tunnel?"

Alana opened her eyes. She shook her head. "No. I just assumed he was on the other side because he told me to wait there for him."

Dr. Novak paused. "Did you find him, Alana?"

"No. I came out the other side, but I couldn't find him."

"What did you do?"

"I walked around for a while, then went back the way I'd come."

"What was on the other side of the tunnel? Who did you see?" the psychologist asked.

Alana's brows drew together in an agonized expression. "I really don't know. I suppose there were people, but I didn't pay much attention to them."

"Was it dark or light on the other side?"

"It was light and warm. The sun was shining because I noticed the difference in temperature as soon as I left the tunnel."

"How long has it been since you've spoken to Calvin?"

"Six weeks."

"You decided not to call him?"

"Yes."

"Why, Alana?"

"Because he promised he would call me."

Dr. Novak leaned forward. "What are you going to do if he doesn't call?"

Crossing her arms under her breasts, Alana bit down on her lower lip. "I don't know."

"You're going to have to decide whether you want to continue this relationship. And if you choose to end it then you're going to have to be the one to contact Calvin to let him know, otherwise you're going to spend the next five months in an indeterminate state wherein you're not going to be able to move forward."

"What if I do call him, and he gives me the excuse that he's been too busy to call? What do I say?"

"I can't tell you what to say, Alana. But what I want is for you to be aware that your fiancé will not be the same person who lived with you before he left the States."

Alana nodded. "That's what frightens me."

"Why?"

"Because that's what happened before my father walked out on us."

"Don't you mean on your mother?"

"No, Dr. Novak. Not only did he desert his common-law wife, but also his children. It didn't matter that we were adults—he still walked out of our lives. Several months before Daddy left I knew something was wrong because he'd stopped talking to my mother. It was like he was hiding something, and in the end we found out that he'd been sneaking around with another woman whom he'd gotten pregnant. So, when a man stops talking I interpret that to mean he's hiding something."

Alana clamped her jaw tight and stared at the therapist, silently daring her to challenge her. There were times when Calvin failed to come home after a gig that she told herself that he was with another woman, but something wouldn't permit her to believe it unless she had absolute proof. Now she wasn't so certain.

Six weeks was a long time, long enough for her to gather enough strength to leave him before he walked out on her. She refused to mirror her mother's life, where she'd give a man her love, her body and bear his children while he didn't think enough of her to give her or his children his name.

The session ended as it had begun—in silence. Alana told Dr. Novak she would call her if she needed her again.

Faye stood in Alana's kitchen tearing lettuce leaves. She walked over to the refrigerator and opened the door. "What do you want me to put in the salad?"

Alana glanced over her shoulder. "Olives, chickpeas, Bermuda onion, thinly sliced cucumber and grape tomatoes. Check that avocado on the countertop. I felt it yesterday and it still wasn't soft." She placed two lean strip steaks in a baking pan. "Do you think we're going to need something else besides the steak and salad?"

"What were you thinking about?"

"How about a loaded baked potato?"

"With butter, sour cream, bacon, cheese and chives!" they said in unison.

"Bring them out, bring them out, girlfriend," Faye crooned.

She'd suggested a girls' night in either at her apartment or Alana's, and Alana had offered hers because she wanted to clean out her refrigerator before she went upstate for the weekend to visit her mother.

"Are you sure you don't want me to hang out with you this weekend? It's been a while since I've seen your mother."

"I thought you were seeing Bart on the weekends."

"Not this weekend. He's leaving for Hong Kong in the morning."

"I'm surprised he didn't take you with him."

"He's going on business."

Alana pierced two baking potatoes with a fork before putting them into the microwave. "Does he ever talk to you about his business?"

Faye shook her head. "No."

"What do you talk about? No, let me rephrase that. What do you do when you're together?"

Reaching into a drawer under a counter, Faye took out a sharp knife. "What do you mean?"

"Are you sleeping with him?"

"No, Lana. He's made it very clear that we will not sleep together."

"Would you if he changed his mind?"

"No. You keep forgetting that I'm in this for the money."

"So am I," Alana concurred, "but there're times when I'm as horny as a mink in heat that I want to slap the hell out of Enid Richards for her smug-ass rule about not sleeping with a client."

"She can afford to be smug because her boy toy is probably screwing her brains out every night."

"No!" Alana gasped. "You really think she's sleeping with what's-his-name..." She snapped her fingers. "Marcus..."

"Hampton," Faye supplied. "Yes."

"Why would you say that?"

Faye told Alana about running into Enid and Marcus at the art gallery. "Bart and I were coming in when they were leaving. Judging from their body language, they're definitely a couple."

"Ain't that nothin'," Alana drawled. "Big Mama's got it goin' on if she can hold on to something *that* fine. How old do you think she is, Faye?"

"It's hard to tell. She could be anywhere between forty and fifty."

"Do you think she's been overhauled?"

"I dunno, Lana. But you have to give her credit because you can't make a silk purse out of a sow's ear. There's no doubt Enid Richards will be stunning at fifty, sixty and into her seventies."

The topic segued from Enid to Alana's clients, Faye laughing hysterically when Alana related how they invariably saw her breasts as a pillow.

It was Alana's turn to laugh when Faye told her about the snobby women who paid Madame Fontaine a small fortune to make them look the same as they did when they entered the overpriced, upscale day spa.

They talked, cooked, ate, cleaned up the kitchen, then took a taxi to Faye's apartment where she packed a bag for the weekend. They made it to Grand Central Station in time to make the train scheduled to stop in New Paltz. Their girlfriends' night wouldn't be a night but a weekend.

CHAPTER 47

Alana unlocked the front door to the house where she'd grown up. The blaring sound of a radio and the familiar smell of chocolate indicated she'd come home. "I'm willing to bet that Mom's baking cookies."

"What I don't need is your mother's cookies after that sinfully loaded baked potato," Faye said as she stepped into a parlor that harkened back to another era, with flower-sprigged upholstered overstuffed love seats and armchairs, crocheted doilies, rag rugs and fringe-trimmed lampshades.

"You know if you don't eat one she's going to spend the entire weekend sulking."

"Okay, Lana. I'll eat one. Just one," she hissed.

Alana rolled her eyes at Faye as she brushed past her and headed for the kitchen. "I don't know why you're dieting. I've never seen you this thin. Is it because Bart likes his woman with no ass?"

"Wrong. I'm not Bart's woman, and even if I lose fifty pounds I'd still be *bootylicious*." Faye smacked her hip for effect.

Alana sucked her teeth loudly. "*Pul-leese,* Faye. This is

your girl you're talking to. The man shells out big bucks for you to go to Madame Fontaine and you say you're not his woman. You're deluding yourself, girlfriend."

Faye caught her friend's arm, stopping her. "Please, Lana. Promise me we won't talk about Bartholomew Houghton, Enid Richards and her boy toy, or anything that remotely resembles P.S., Inc. for the rest of the weekend."

Talking about her relationship with Bart made it seem real, normal, when it was just the opposite. She would earn half a million dollars to provide him with companionship, something he could get from any woman. She'd tried rationalizing that as a P.S., Inc. social companion she was nothing more than eye candy, an inanimate object who'd made herself available to a wealthy man for his own prevarications.

Alana exhaled audibly. "Okay." She continued along the narrow hallway leading to the kitchen. "Mom, we're here!" she called out, hoping not to startle Melanie Gardner.

Melanie, who sang along with an old Whitney Houston hit at the top of her lungs, went completely still when she saw her daughter and her friend standing in the entrance to the kitchen. She placed a cookie sheet on a trivet, took off her oven mitts and extended her arms.

"Good gracious! What a wonderful surprise. Why didn't you tell me you were coming, Alana? And isn't it nice that you brought Faye with you."

A wave of momentary panic raced through Alana as she walked into the kitchen and hugged her mother. It was apparent Melanie hadn't taken her medication. "I told you yesterday that I was coming."

Melanie smiled. "I must have forgotten."

Alana's initial fear was offset by the fact that the older woman had at least bathed herself. Or, she wondered, had Sophia come by and assisted her?

She stared down at a woman who'd dedicated her young life to a man who didn't deserve her trust and loyalty. Alana didn't hate her father, because it was too hard to erase the twenty-one years, twenty-one very happy years Carlos Moore had been in her life. But she would never forgive him for what he did to her mother. Her brothers were more understanding, but she refused to see him, talk to him, and in no way did she want to meet her ten-year-old half sister.

Alana turned off the radio. "Did you take your pills today?"

A slight frown creased Melanie's forehead. She'd recently celebrated her sixty-third birthday but looked years older. The grooves bracketing her generous mouth appeared deeper, and there were lines around her eyes that hadn't been there before. Her chestnut-brown skin, stretched over sharp cheekbones, had the fragility of rice paper. Thick curly hair, hair that Alana had inherited, was braided in two salt-and-pepper plaits that reached midway down her frail back.

"I don't remember."

Faye watched the tender reunion between Alana and Melanie, and for the first time she felt a pang of guilt. She was the one who'd been bemoaning and crying about her brother, when Alana had to worry about a parent plagued with mental-health issues.

When, she thought, had she become so narcissistic? Even if she wasn't able to have her brother's conviction overturned, he only had another three years before he had to face a parole board. Meanwhile, Melanie Gardner's mental state held her in a prison from which there would be no parole or vindication.

Walking over to Melanie, she kissed her cheek. "I'm going to wash my hands and take those cookies off the sheet and let them cool on a rack."

Melanie smiled. "Thank you. No one wants to eat mushy cookies."

Alana steered her mother over to a stool at the cooking island. "Sit down, Mom, and relax. Faye and I will finish baking the cookies and cleaning up the kitchen."

"I don't feel like sitting," Melanie said, protesting. "I'm going upstairs to lie down."

"You feel all right, Mom?"

She managed a tired smile. "I'm good, Alana. I'm just a little tired. I was going upstairs anyway after I finished the last batch."

Alana kissed her forehead. "Go, Mom. I'll look in on you later."

As soon as Melanie left the kitchen, she picked up the telephone and dialed her brother's number. "Sophia, this is Alana. May I please speak to Taylor? Yes, I know it's late, but I *have* to talk to him."

Her sister-in-law could be such a bitch at times. Rolling her eyes and shaking her head, she waited for Taylor to come to the phone as she watched Faye gently lift the oatmeal chocolate-chip raisin cookies off the sheet and place them on a wire rack to cool.

Faye had lost some weight, but the results were fabulous—not that she'd been overweight to begin with. Her hips were slimmer, belly flatter, her clear complexion radiating good health. And despite her protests, Alana knew Faye's relationship with Bartholomew Houghton was comfortable and stress free.

It was not that she hadn't enjoyed her own clients, especially Derrick Warren. The record producer was the consummate gentleman. Soft spoken with impeccable manners, he always gave her his undivided attention and never tried coming on to her as some of the other men attempted to do despite the rule that clients and social companions were not to sleep together. He would've been the perfect man *if* he hadn't paid her to be with him.

After all, Alana mused, *I'm not like the other women who used the most ingenious stunts in an attempt to garner his attention. One had even gone so far as to sit down in a skirt that barely covered her snatch and spread her legs to offer a view of what was left of her pubic hair cut into a heart-shaped design. The ho was definitely shameless!*

"Don't you know what time it is, Alana?" Taylor Gardner's deep voice boomed through the earpiece.

"I'm well aware of the hour, Taylor. I'm calling about our mother."

"What about her?" His tone had softened considerably.

"Do you check to see whether she's taking her medication every day?"

"Dammit, Alana, you woke me up to talk about pills?" Her temper flared. "Just answer my question!"

"I'm not going to tell you shit! If you're *that* concerned about Mom, then you should give up your view of Central Park and move back to the boonies." It took several seconds, after listening to the incessant sound of the dial tone, for Alana to realize that her brother had hung up on her. "My brother just hung up on me. He's never done that before."

She replaced the receiver on its cradle, trying to come up with a good reason why her eldest brother was so hostile. She expected hostility from Sophia, but not Taylor. "One of these days I'm going to forget my home training and give my sister-in-law the beatdown of her life," she mumbled under her breath.

There were a few occasions when she'd overheard Sophia complaining about Melanie, claiming her mother-in-law either should be confined to a mental hospital or a skilled nursing facility. Whatever Taylor had said to his wife angered her because Sophia had stormed out of the house and spent the next hour on the porch.

"I'm going to hire a nurse to come in every day to check on my mother."

"Isn't she eligible for a home-health aide?" Faye asked.

"I won't know until I check with her caseworker. Even if her Medicare doesn't cover the costs, I'll pay it."

"Have you thought about having your mother live with you, Lana?"

"Yes, but I know it wouldn't work. Mom would never

leave New Paltz. She loves this house because it's her only tie to her past when she was truly happy with her so-called husband and children. Daddy wouldn't marry her, so I suppose giving her the house free and clear absolved him of some of his guilt."

Alana paused, watching as Faye dropped cookie dough onto a baking sheet. She called Melanie at least three times a week, but whenever she came to New Paltz to see her mother she found it more and more difficult to come to grips with her mental impairment. The fact remained that Melanie Gardner was not getting better; in fact, she was thinner now than she'd been two months before.

She knew she had to reach a decision about her mother's medical care before the end of the summer.

CHAPTER 48

Faye began the first day of her three-week vacation with a brisk walk along First Avenue. She'd walked farther than planned, but on the return thirty-block trip she stopped at a Starbucks for a cup of coffee with a double shot of espresso. The caffeine gave her an extra boost of energy, and she looked forward to the next three weeks with the anticipation of a child going on vacation.

She'd enjoyed her weekend in New Paltz, and the difference in Melanie's behavior was startling after she'd taken her medication. She was alert, spry and exhibited a wicked sense of humor that kept everyone in stitches. Sophia appeared unusually attentive to her husband's mother, but Faye suspected the display was more for Alana's approval than genuine affection. It was apparent the sisters-in-law weren't fond of each other.

The chiming of the telephone greeted Faye as she opened the door to her apartment. She picked up the cordless instrument from a table in the spacious entryway.

"Hello."

"Thank goodness I got you!" said a breathless female voice.

"Gina?" Faye wondered why her assistant was calling her at home when she knew she was on vacation.

"Faye, listen, and don't say anything until I'm finished."

"Where are you?" she asked, ignoring Gina.

"I'm in the conference room."

"Why?"

"Please, Faye. I could lose my job for calling you."

"Okay."

"John and Stuart are in your office going over your accounts. I heard someone say that they want to give one or two of your clients to Jessica and Zachary. Apparently the executives at Andino are in seventh heaven over the marketing campaign those two assholes put together for the LXR-V. I'm sure you've seen the new GM commercial with the *Then. Now. Always.* pitch comparing the old to the new."

"Yes, I have." The commercial had a catchy theme contrasting sock hop to hip-hop, AM to XM radio.

"They stole your hip-hop idea and passed it off as their own, Faye. Now they're strutting around here like their shit don't stink."

"And because of their success with Andino, they wait for me to go on vacation then help themselves to my accounts."

"They're clueless, Faye," Gina whispered angrily. "Do they really think they can do what you do?"

Faye's brain was in tumult, strange and disquieting thoughts racing out of control. As an African-American she was hired to tap into the psyche of the African-American consumer, and her success had become Bentley,

Pope & Oliviera's success. However, it was apparent she'd outlived her usefulness at the advertising firm.

What if, she mused, she hadn't planned to leave at the end of the year? What if she hadn't had another source of income? Sitting on a chair beside the table, she closed her eyes, hoping to bring her inner turmoil under control.

"It's all right, Gina," she lied with deceptive calmness. "It doesn't matter."

"Are you shittin' me, Faye?"

When she opened her eyes they were filled with tears. "No, I'm not. I really don't care."

"But you can't say that."

"Yes, I can." There was only the sound of breathing coming through the earpiece. "Gina?"

"Yes, Faye."

"Thanks for the heads-up." Depressing a button, she ended the call.

Faye hated lying to Gina because she *did* care, cared more than anyone could imagine. She'd sacrificed taking vacation for years and curtailed her social life to advance her career. But where had it gotten her? Absolutely nowhere because a pack of jackals had invaded her office to steal what she'd worked so hard to develop.

She stirred uneasily in the chair, trying to pinpoint when her working relationship with John Reynolds had begun to deteriorate, mentally recapping the meetings they'd shared. He'd disagreed with several of her creative ideas yet they'd always managed to compromise. She'd found

John open, perceptive and respectful; that's why she'd found his comment about projecting a gangsta image so repugnant.

As much as Faye didn't want to place blame on any one person, she couldn't stop thinking about Jessica Adelson. Somehow Jessica had convinced John she should become the account executive for the African-American market.

The scheming wench may have won this round, but there was no way she would permit her to win the fight.

Faye dialed the number, praying Mrs. Urquhart would answer her call before she lost her nerve and hung up. Bart had given her a business card with his executive assistant's name and extension at DHG, and also his cell-phone number in the event of an emergency. Bart may not deem her losing her accounts an emergency, but she did.

"Mrs. Urquhart."

Sitting up straighter, Faye tightened her grip on the receiver. The woman's voice was strong, no-nonsense. "Mrs. Urquhart, this is Faye Ogden. May I please speak to Mr. Houghton?"

There came a pause. "Hold on, Miss Ogden. I'll see if Mr. Houghton is available to take your call."

"Faye?"

"Yes," she whispered when hearing his deep voice.

"Are you all right?"

She closed her eyes, holding her breath for several seconds. He was asking whether she was all right when there was the possibility that on returning to work she might not have a job. Her five-year contract had expired in April, and John hadn't broached the subject of renewing it.

"I'm physically all right."

"Then what's going on?"

"I need to see...to talk to you."

"Where are you, baby?"

She opened her eyes. "I'm home."

"Meet me in front of your building in twenty minutes."

A soft click indicated he'd hung up. Faye scrambled off the chair and headed for the bathroom. She had to shower and change her clothes before reuniting with a man she unknowingly had come to depend on.

CHAPTER 49

Astrid knocked softly on the door to Enid's office. Waiting until Enid turned to look at her, she said, "I still can't locate her. I've called her home, cell and nothing." A Belgian diamond dealer had requested Ilene because he wanted her to accompany him aboard his new yacht to tour the Greek Isles before docking at Saint Tropez. Monsieur Caribert expected the cruise to last two weeks.

Enid's eyes narrowed in concentration. Ilene Fairchild was MIA. It was more than a week since she'd purportedly returned from Pine Cay. She knew for certain she'd returned because Demetrious Reyniak had called to thank P.S., Inc. for Ilene. She'd so impressed everyone that she'd come back to the States in one of the partygoers' private jet.

Enid met Astrid's expected gaze. A sixth sense alerted her that Demetrious hadn't told her everything about the Pine Cay bacchanal. "Call Claude Wells and tell him that I need to speak to him."

"Yes, ma'am." Enid barely had time to react to her booker's staid form of address when Astrid's voice came through the telephone's intercom. "Mr. Wells is on line two."

"Thank you, Astrid." Picking up the receiver and

pressing a button, she said cheerfully, "Good afternoon, Claude. How are you?"

"I would be a lot better if you would come and visit me."

"I'd come but only if I'm invited."

She always enjoyed flirting with the transplanted South African. The grandson of a South African who'd owned and operated one of the largest diamond mines on the continent, Claude, repulsed by the system of apartheid, sold the mine and purchased a private island in the Caribbean.

He lived in Jamaica while building the hotel on Pine Cay, fell in love with a local woman and married her when she told him she was carrying his child. Two weeks after the hotel was completed, Claude's wife drowned in a boating accident, leaving him to care for their three-year-old daughter.

"But will you come alone?"

"Now, you know I can't do that."

"Are you still involved with your boy, Enid?"

"How are you using that term, Claude?" At no time could she ever forget white men's insidious reference to black men as *boy*.

"It's not what you think, Enid. I'm only referring to his age."

"Marcus hasn't been a boy in a very long time, Claude. I trust you to remember that."

"I apologize for being tactless."

"Apology accepted."

"What do I owe the honor of this call?"

"I need you to tell me about Ilene Fairchild."

Enid listened intently as Claude told her what she needed to know. Surprisingly, she wasn't shocked or angry. Ilene had simply reverted to type. "Thank you for the information," she said after hearing his explanation. "This is not an empty promise, but I'm going to come to Pine Cay."

"When can I expect you and Marcus?"

"How's December?"

"That's six months from now."

Enid smiled. "I know. And it's after hurricane season."

"If you let me know the date, then I'll save a private bungalow for you."

"I'll let you know before the end of the summer." What she didn't tell Claude was that she was seriously considering marrying Marcus. However, it was her secret, one she would reveal to her unsuspecting lover when the time was right.

She rang off, then buzzed Astrid to come into her office. "Leave a message on Ilene's phones that I want to see her as soon as she returns to the States."

CHAPTER 50

Bart was waiting for Faye when she walked out of her building. He opened the rear door of the Maybach, waited until she was seated, then slipped in beside her. Pressing a button, he closed the security panel between the back seat and the driver.

Shifting, he stared at the woman who tugged at his heart even when he was halfway around the world; he pulled her into his arms, his chin resting on top of her head. She smelled delicious.

He knew his feelings for Faye Ogden had changed when he told Enid that he wanted her for the summer because weekends weren't enough; and his feelings had intensified when he'd given her his private number at DHG and cell-phone number.

Within minutes of the jet lifting off for Hong Kong, he'd been tempted to instruct the pilot to abort the flight. It took all of his resolve not to call Giuseppe and tell him to pick Faye up and bring her to the airport so she could accompany him on his Far East business trip.

Faye leaned into the contours of Bart's body, inhaling the distinctive scent of his aftershave; she drank in the soothing comfort of his nearness like a warm blanket, and she knew what she was feeling, what she was beginning to feel for Bart was something she was unable to fathom or make sense of. What she hadn't wanted to happen had: dependency. It'd begun with financial and progressed to emotional.

"I'm sorry you had to leave work and—"

"No apologies, Faye," Bart said, cutting her off. "I gave you my numbers in case you needed me. You called, so it's apparent you need me." The fingers of his left hand toyed with the wisps of hair over her ear. "Now, tell me why you called me."

Faye told Bart everything, from her failed presentation, subsequent meeting with John Reynolds and the details of Gina's telephone call as Giuseppe maneuvered down FDR Drive.

"I'm usually not suspicious by nature, Bart, but I can't shake the feeling that I'm being set up. My contract with BP&O expired several months ago, so why not let me go? Why would they conspire to dismantle what I've worked so hard to create for them?"

Bart kissed her hair. "They're not dismantling what you created for them."

"If not that, then what the hell are they doing?"

He buried his face in her short hair. "Think of yourself as a company they want to acquire, but you're refusing to sell."

She went completely still. "Are you equating what's happening to me as a hostile takeover?"

"Yes. Do you know your competition?"

"I believe I do."

"Who is he?"

"He's a she." Faye told Bart about Jessica, John Reynolds's so-called niece.

"Don't worry about it, baby," Bart crooned, tugging at her earlobe.

"What?"

"I'll take care of everything."

Pulling out of his comforting embrace, Faye stared at Bart, and as their eyes met she felt a lurch of awareness, a ripple of excitement eddy through her. "What are you going to do?"

"I can't tell you."

"Why can't you?"

He ran his pinkie down the length of her nose to her parted lips. "If I told you, then it wouldn't be a surprise." His mouth replaced his finger, moving over hers in a slow, drugging kiss that stole the breath from her lungs.

Faye found his kiss surprisingly gentle, healing. She gasped audibly when Bart lifted her onto his lap, her arms circling his neck at the same time his lips seared a path from her mouth to the column of her neck, and lower to the pulsing hollow at the base of her throat.

A soft groan escaped her when she felt the growing hardness under her buttocks. Sitting on Bart's lap had turned him on and his erection turned her on.

Cradling her face between his hands, Bart took Faye's mouth again, ravishing it and branding her his possession.

He wanted her, not the little pieces she parceled out like bread crumbs, but all of her.

"Bart," Faye whispered between his frenetic, nibbling kisses that left her mouth on fire.

"I know." His breathing had deepened with the increasing hardness he was helpless to control.

"We can't."

Pressing his forehead to hers, Bart winked at her. "We can, but we won't." *Not here, not now,* he thought.

Faye moved off his lap and stared out the side window. "Where are you taking me?"

"You're coming home with me."

CHAPTER 51

Giuseppe inserted a key into an elevator at a manned underground-parking garage, the door opening smoothly, quietly. Faye walked in, followed by Bart, then the chauffeur. Giuseppe inserted another key into another slot marked PH 1, and the car rose swiftly to the upper floors of the East River Drive high-rise apartment building.

The car came to a stop, the doors opening to reveal an expansive entryway with an exquisite chandelier and black-and-white vinyl checkerboard floor. Chippendale chairs flanking a table with a vase overflowing with fresh flowers and a stately grandfather clock created a reserved stately look.

The driver nodded to Bart. "I'll be in my quarters if you need me."

Bart smiled at his chauffeur. "I won't need you until Thursday."

Faye opened her mouth to ask Bart how was she going to get back home, but he cut her a look that said, *Not now.*

Waiting until the elevator doors closed behind Giuseppe, she asked softly, "What are *you* doing, Bart?"

He'd inserted a key into the penthouse 2 slot. Within

seconds the doors opened to glass walls with panoramic views of the East River and the bridges connecting Manhattan with the Bronx, Queens and Brooklyn.

Reaching for her hand, Bart led her into a foyer with a parquet floor in a herringbone design boardered in rosewood.

"What *we* are going to do is spend the next three weeks together. I'd planned for us to get together tomorrow, but since you called me today we'll start now. You'll spend the night with me. Then we'll decide how you want to celebrate the Fourth of July holiday."

"What about clothes? I didn't pack anything. And as for tomorrow, I promised my mother I would spend it with her. The family's getting together for a cookout."

"Where does she live?"

"Queens."

"Where in Queens?"

"Springfield Gardens."

"You're going to have to give me the address so I can arrange transportation for us."

Faye pulled back, but couldn't escape when Bart tightened his hold on her hand. "Us? You want to come with me?"

"Why not? Are you ashamed to be seen with me because of our age difference?"

"No! It's not that," she said much too quickly.

Faye stared at Bart as if he'd taken leave of his senses. The man had to be completely clueless. She wanted to tell him it wasn't his age, but his race. She'd never dated out of her race, and she wasn't certain how her parents, her father in particular, would react to her dating someone who wasn't black.

"Okay, that settles it. We'll go hang out with your family then come back here."

"And do *what*, Bart?"

"We'll do whatever you want."

"When are we going to Europe?"

"Not until August. Most Europeans go on holiday in August, but by midmonth a lot of the tourists are gone, so we don't have to deal with large crowds."

"I still have to go home and get some clothes."

Pulling Faye to his chest, Bart stared at her, his eyes making love to her face. "Why do you worry about something so inconsequential as clothes?"

"Inconsequential!" she repeated. "I hope you don't expect me to wear the same outfit for several days. Or would you prefer that I romp around butt naked like a wood sprite?"

A lascivious grin spread from his lips to his eyes. "Will you, please?"

"Hell, no!" she spat out before she stuck her tongue out at him.

Bart sobered. "Don't do that, Faye."

"Do what?"

"Offer me your tongue."

"Why?"

His hold tightened around her waist. "Just don't," he warned softly. "Come, I'll give you a tour before I show you to your room. We'll see the first floor later."

Winding her arm around Bart's waist inside his jacket, Faye glanced up at his profile. "What's on the first level?"

"Giuseppe and Mrs. Llewellyn occupy apartments on either side of the kitchen. There is also a living room, formal dining room and a small ballroom. There are pocket doors separating the three rooms that can be opened to expand the space, depending on how many people I want to entertain."

"What's the capacity?"

"It could comfortably accommodate seventy-five."

"Do you do a lot of entertaining?"

"No," he answered truthfully. He hadn't entertained since becoming a widower. And he'd never entertained at the penthouse triplex.

Bart led Faye down a hallway that doubled as his art gallery. The walls were filled with framed paintings, prints and photographs. Before he married Deidre, he wouldn't have recognized a Picasso from a Pollock. But her passion for art was transferred to him whenever he accompanied her to Sotheby's, galleries and museums. Even after nine years he couldn't pass an art gallery without stopping in to see their inventory.

"This floor is off limits to everyone but Mrs. Llewellyn, who'll only come here when I'm not home." His bedroom, adjoining bathroom, sitting room, walk-in closet, in-home office and library took up more than half the space.

Faye realized Bart's very masculine bedroom was twice the size of the average Manhattan studio apartment. In fact, his walk-in closet was larger than her bedroom. Suits hung from racks in corresponding hues of blue, black and brown. Shoes in different styles and colors were lined up like sentinels, while shirts, ties and belts were displayed with the same precision.

Cupping her elbow, Bart steered Faye out of the closet. "Your room is through that door."

He opened a connecting door to a bedroom that was as feminine as his was masculine. Instead of the leather, dark woods, black-and-white-pinstripe duvet, the bed was a French Country sleigh design covered with antique linens, blankets and throws. Sheer delicate lace panels covered the floor-to-ceiling windows taking up two of the four walls. A matching armoire held a large-screen television and the components for a state-of-the-art stereo unit.

"Your clothes are in there," Bart said, pointing to a door.

Faye opened the door to find a walk-in closet similar to Bart's. Skirts, slacks, blouses, jeans, T-shirts, casual and formal dresses and shoes lined racks and shelves. She reached for a tag hanging from a pair of slacks. They were her size.

Crossing his arms over the front of his crisp white shirt, Bart smiled when she turned to face him, her expression mirroring disbelief. "Didn't I tell you not to worry about having something to wear?"

Faye was too shocked to do more than nod. "When did you buy these?" she asked when she'd finally recovered her voice.

"While you were trying on dresses at that boutique in Grand Cayman I told the owner to send me what she thought would look nice on you. She already had your measurements, so that made it easy for her. You'll find underwear and other frilly things in the drawers."

Lowering her gaze, Faye blushed furiously, wondering whether the man who'd paid for her for the summer season had entertained lascivious thoughts when he saw her *frilly things*.

Bart pressed a button on the panel that regulated the recessed lighting and a drawer opened. Light reflected off a tray of black velvet littered with necklaces, bracelets, earrings set with precious and semiprecious stones.

Faye closed her eyes as the significance of what she'd become to Bartholomew Houghton shook her to the core. She'd become a bought woman! He hadn't missed a beat when he set out to seduce her with clothes, jewels and trips abroad, all the while professing that he wouldn't sleep with her.

She opened her eyes. She'd be a fool not to accept what he was offering. Now, with her job in jeopardy, she knew she had to step up her game. *If* Bart had come down with a case of jungle fever, she'd give him what he wanted and then some. In the end, both of them would come out winners.

Moving closer, she kissed his cheek. "Thank you. Everything is exquisite."

Bart didn't move. "I'm glad you like it."

Faye pulled his arms down and threaded her fingers through his. "Is there more to see?"

He squeezed her tiny hand. "Come."

The bedroom opened out to a sitting room with a club

chair and matching ottoman upholstered in pale pink roses with a pinstripe ruffle in a deeper pink. Mahogany tables, Waterford table lamps and a priceless Aubusson rug beckoned her to come and while away the hours without a care. Shelves held books, wireless speakers and a collection of onyx and lapis paperweights.

Faye successfully suppressed a gasp when she walked into a Wedgwood-green bathroom. A garden tub, dressing table, freestanding shower stall and a wall of frosted glass for privacy radiated warmth and spaciousness.

"The drawers under the vanity contain everything you'd need for your face and hair."

Faye walked over to the vanity and pulled out one drawer. It was filled with hair and skin products she'd been given at Madam Fontaine's. Another contained bottles of perfume and body crème in her favorite fragrance. She opened another to find a variety of feminine products.

Straightening, she turned and studied the lean face with the penetrating gray eyes. She saw something in his expression that hadn't been there before—a silent sadness. Was he, she wondered, comparing her to his late wife? And if he was, what were the similarities?

"You've thought of everything."

"I tried to, but if there's something I missed please let me know."

She nodded. "Thank you, Bart."

"Don't thank me, Faye. I just want you to trust me."

She walked over to him. "Why do you keep reminding me of that?"

"And I'll continue to remind you until you come to trust me unconditionally."

Smiling up at the man whom she found more and more difficult to think of as her client, she said, "What's upstairs?"

"Come and I'll show you."

Another flight of stairs led to a solarium and rooftop garden heated and cooled by solar panels. Faye walked over to the tempered-glass walls, awed by the three-hundred-sixty-degree view.

Moving behind her, Bart wrapped both arms around her body. "What are you thinking?"

"How awesome it must be to sit here and watch the snow fall."

"I wouldn't know because I've never done it."

Faye turned in his embrace to face him. "Promise me you'll invite me over for the first snowfall of the winter."

Her passionate plea for a promise was something Bart found hard to resist. Didn't she know? he asked silently. Did she not know the power she wielded over him? He would promise and give her anything just to keep her in his life.

"I promise."

Shrugging out of his suit jacket and throwing it over one shoulder, Bart continued to stare at Faye. He'd called himself fool of fools once he made the decision to have her live with him for the summer, but once the clothes were delivered and put away in the closet he realized he was trying to recapture his past—another time when he looked forward to coming home to find a woman waiting for him. He knew he should've asked Faye if she wanted to live with him, yet his stiff-necked pride wouldn't permit him to give her a choice.

He glanced at his watch. It was after one, and except for a cup of coffee and a slice of wheat toast at six that morning he hadn't eaten anything in hours. "Where would you like to have lunch? We can eat lunch out and have dinner here, or vice versa."

"I'd rather eat lunch out."

"Where do you want to eat?"

"How's your cholesterol?"

"It's under two hundred. Why?"

"When was the last time you ate at the umbrella room?"

Grinning, he shook his head. "Do you eat your frank with the works?"

Faye sucked her teeth. "You eat the frank. I'm going for a hot sausage with mustard, onions and sauerkraut."

Bart wrinkled his patrician nose. "Remind me not to kiss you if you're going for the onions."

"You shouldn't be kissing me anyway."

He sobered, his mood changing like quicksilver. "Why shouldn't I kiss you?"

"Because it could lead to something more serious—intimate."

Staring at her under lowered lids, he took a step. "Would that be a bad thing?"

The very air around her seemed charged with something Faye couldn't explain. She felt the movement of his breathing keeping pace with her own. She wanted to move, run away, but his compelling eyes, masculine magnetism rooted her to the spot.

Her response to him was so potent that she found it difficult to draw a normal breath. Without warning, it hit her. She wanted him! She wanted to lie with a man whose very presence reminded her that she was a woman—a normal woman with a need that had to be assuaged. Alana talked about being horny as a mink in heat, while she'd denied she didn't need to sleep with a man, that it was okay to wake up feverish and shaking from erotic dreams in which her orgasms were remembrances of past encounters.

She shook her head slowly. "No, Bart. It wouldn't be a bad thing."

A hint of a smile softened his mouth as he reached for her hand. "As soon as I change into something more comfortable we'll eat."

Instead of taking the stairs, he led her to a private elevator that serviced only the second and third floors. Faye walked down the winding wrought-iron staircase to the first level while Bart retreated to his bedroom to change.

When she got up that morning, she never would've predicted how dramatically her life would change. First the telephone call from Gina, then her call to Bart, and now her admission that she was ready to sleep with him.

Sitting on a tall stool at the cooking island in the stainless-steel kitchen, she mumbled a silent prayer that she would come through the summer unscathed. It wasn't her body she was concerned with, but her heart.

CHAPTER 52

Derrick Warren was waiting for Alana when she alighted from the Bentley. A warm smile deepened the folds under his eyes. Despite his proclivity for a same-sex relationship there was something about Alana Gardner that made him question his decision not to sleep with a woman.

And it wasn't that he hadn't slept with women in the past, it was just he preferred men. Perhaps, he thought, he wasn't homosexual but bisexual.

She was stunning in white: halter top, slacks and espadrilles. He'd heard someone in his entourage refer to her as the "black Anna Nicole." Derrick agreed with him, but added that Alana was more intelligent, beautiful, natural and exotic than the buxom blonde.

Reaching for her hands, he kissed her fingers. "Welcome, Alana."

A warm breeze coming off the Hudson River stirred wisps of hair around her face. "Thank you, Derrick." Leaning forward, she kissed his cheek.

Cradling her hand in the bend of his elbow, he led her down a sloping hill to a moored yacht crowded with partygoers that had gathered at his White Plains compound earlier that morning for breakfast. He'd planned a leisurely sail down the river to lower Manhattan, before a return trip would culminate with a cookout on the lawn of his recently completed twenty-two-room mansion. Derrick had invited Marcus Hampton, but his financial manager had declined because of a prior commitment.

He escorted Alana up the gangway. "We're ready to sail," he told the boat's captain.

Alana took off her shoes and placed them in an area with the others. The wood on the deck of the yacht was warm and soft as cotton under her bare feet.

"We meet again, sugah" crooned a voice close to her ear.

She turned to find Kris Dennison grinning at her. "Hey, playa," she drawled as if she'd just come from the Deep South.

His hands went to her waist as he pulled her close. "Damn, baby, you get mo' beautiful every time I see ya. I don't care what Derrick says, but you is mine today."

She glanced around his wide shoulders. "Where's your wife, Kris? I don't want no mess."

"Ain't goin' be no mess, sugah. We done wit each other."

Alana gave him a skeptical look. "Since when?"

Kris beckoned to another ballplayer. "Yo, man, tell this lady that me and Maeretha is done."

"They're done," he confirmed.

"Okay, Kris. We'll hang out together."

"What you drinking, sugah?"

"I'll have a mimosa. Champagne and orange juice,"

she explained when he gave her what she considered a *dummy look.*

"Oh. Why didn't you just say that?"

Alana groaned inwardly. It was only one in the afternoon and she knew it was going to be a very long day if she let Kris follow her around like a lost puppy. And there was no way she could lose him on the boat like she could in a club.

She stared at the other passengers and smiled. Young, talented, educated and fashionably dressed in white, they mingled in small groups, laughing and sipping cocktails as if rehearsing to take their place as the next generation of upscale African-Americans.

Kris returned with her flute, his white teeth gleaming in his smooth dark face. Lowering her gaze and smiling up at him through her lashes, she said, "Thank you, Kris."

The point guard recoiled as if a heavyweight boxer had punched him in the gut. Alana Gardner was so damn sexy that he'd just gotten an instant hard-on. Shifting slightly, he attempted to conceal it from her. It was a good thing he'd worn the loose-fitting shirt outside the waistband of his slacks or he would've embarrassed himself in front of her.

He had to have her! And he would have her before the night ended.

CHAPTER 53

"Are you sure you know how to get there?"

Faye had given Bart her parents' address when they'd returned from lunch the day before. They'd walked more than ten blocks to find a hot-dog vendor who hadn't run out of hot sausage. Bart ate two franks to her one sausage before they shared a large salted pretzel. Both downed a bottle of soda, then lamented how good their unhealthy lunch was and offset their guilt with a long walk.

No one recognized the real estate mogul in a pair of jeans, T-shirt, running shoes, baseball cap and sunglasses. Only in Manhattan were the rich and famous able to blend in with the mass of humanity going about their business as if only they existed.

Bart took his eyes off the road for a couple of seconds to glance at his passenger. "Yes, I do. Could it be you want to drive?"

Shifting on her seat, she gave him a Cheshire cat grin. "Can I drive back?"

"I don't know, baby."

"What do you mean, you don't know?"

"This car is like my baby."

Folding her hands on her hips, Faye glared at him. "Didn't you just call *me* baby?"

"Yeah, but that's different."

"How different, Bartholomew?"

He lifted his eyebrows. "What's with the Bartholomew?"

"I'm pissed!"

"Pissed because I won't let you drive my car?"

"Yes."

Folding her arms under her breasts, Faye stared out the windshield. She'd thought because Bart had given Giuseppe the day off he would either get another driver or drive the Maybach himself to Queens. But when they exited the elevator at the garage level and he pulled a tarpaulin off a vintage two-seater, her breath had caught in her throat.

She'd grown up around cars because her father was a mechanic. Craig Ogden knew the specifications on every car ever built. It only took one glance for him to identify the year and model.

"Are you pouting, darling?"

"Yes. And don't call me darling, because I'm not your darling."

Bart accelerated as he entered the Queens Midtown Tunnel. "You could be my darling."

"Forget it, Bart."

He smiled. "Oh, now we're back to Bart. Does that mean I'm back in your good graces?"

"Dream on, mister."

"I never figured you for a spoiled little minx."

"That's because you don't know me."

"You're right. But before summer's end I *will* know you."

"And I you," she countered.

Bart nodded. There was no doubt before the end of summer they would know a great deal more about each other. They'd begun the day before when they'd walked for blocks, holding hands and stopping to window-shop.

They'd returned home and spent several hours in the rooftop solarium reading while listening to an XM station that featured hits from the eighties and nineties. Faye had surprised him when she offered to cook dinner because Mrs. Llewellyn was in Southampton with her grandson. The highlight of the evening wasn't her Caesar salad with pancetta and grilled salmon steaks but his sitting down to eat with her. It wasn't until they sat at the table across from each other that he realized how much he missed sharing a meal with a woman he really liked—liked a lot more than he was able to openly verbalize.

"You can drive home," he said after a lengthy silence.

"Thank you, Bart."

"Yeah, yeah," he grumbled good-naturedly. "Did you tell your folks you were bringing a guest?"

"No. I wanted to surprise them."

"Why?"

"It's been a long time since I've brought a man to meet my parents. And it will be the first time they'll see me with a man who's not black."

Bart gave her another quick glance. "Do you think that's going to bother them?"

"It doesn't matter, Bart, because they know they can't tell me who I should date or not date. But there is something I should tell you."

"What?"

"My father and I have been somewhat estranged."

She told Bart everything, about her brother's arrest, his plea and subsequent incarceration. "I told you that I signed with Pleasure Seekers to earn enough money to start up my own company, but the real reason was to earn enough money to hire an attorney to appeal my brother's case."

"Do you still want to set up your own company?"

"Yes. But that's not my priority."

"Do you have a lawyer willing to handle your brother's appeal?"

"Yes. I sent him a check last week as an initial retainer."

"Who is he and how much does he want?"

Bart listened as Faye told him how much she'd expected to pay for her brother's freedom. The price was exorbitant, but he understood why she was willing pay up to a half million dollars for a loved one.

"Did you check him out thoroughly?"

"Yes. He's the best in the state."

"Our lives aren't that different."

"Why would you say that?" Faye asked.

"Your brother is in jail for a crime he didn't commit, while my brother couldn't keep his ass out of jail."

She was caught off guard by the sudden hardness in Bart's voice. "Where is he now?"

There was a swollen silence before he said, "Dead. Paul

was three years older than me. He was the meanest son of a bitch to walk the earth. There wasn't a day when he wouldn't get into a fight. One day I asked him why he fought so much and he said it was because he hated being poor white trash. He hated my father because he didn't have much education, hated my mother because although better educated she lowered herself to marry him.

"I thought things would change once we were enrolled at Rhinebeck, but it didn't. Paul found the worse kids to hang out with. They smoked dope, cut classes and vandalized homes and cars. The other kids got away with it because their parents paid for what they considered childish pranks, but my folks were barely getting by, so Paul spent many a week in the county jail because they couldn't pay the fines.

"His juvenile infractions escalated to misdemeanors and finally to a felony when he burglarized a sporting goods store, stole several handguns and robbed a local convenience store. He took all of the money in the register before he pistol-whipped the store clerk. He was given a sentence of five to eight for armed robbery and assault and was granted parole after he'd served three years."

Faye felt a shiver snake its way down her spine. "Did he stay out of trouble?"

Bart shook his head. "He couldn't, not when he had a serious drug problem. He'd graduated from weed to heroin. He began snatching purses to support his habit, and when the police came after him he ran onto a pond that wasn't completely frozen over and fell through the ice. By the time a rescue unit got to the scene he'd drowned.

"His death devastated my parents. My dad suffered a heart attack and died a week later. My mother willed herself to death, and within six months she was gone. Neither of them ever got to see me graduate college."

Faye, leaning to her left, rested her head against Bart's shoulder. She felt a shudder as he drew in a sharp breath. It was as if his life was mired with deaths: his brother, father, mother and wife.

She found herself mute, unable to say the words that could or would erase the pain and loss he'd encountered. At that moment she made herself a promise to make the time she would share with Bartholomew Houghton an experience he would remember long after their association ended.

CHAPTER 54

Faye pointed. "It's the last house on the right. Pull up behind my father's Volkswagen," she said as Bart decelerated.

He parked behind a classic shiny yellow Volkswagen Beetle, smiling. It was apparent Craig Ogden also liked old cars. The smell of grilling food was redolent when he opened the door and came around to assist Faye.

"Something smells good."

She sniffed the air. "That smells like Uncle Teddy's barbecue sauce."

"How can you distinguish one sauce from another? I'm willing to bet most people are grilling." Smoke from outdoor grills floated from several backyards along the dead-end street.

"I know Uncle Teddy's marinade when I smell it," she said confidently. "He's a caterer." Faye waited for Bart to take a shopping bag filled with wine from behind her seat, then escorted him around the English Tudor-style house to a spacious backyard.

Craig Ogden, manning a large gas grill, nearly dropped his tongs when he saw his daughter. His dark brown eyes narrowed slightly then crinkled in a smile when she approached, arms outstretched.

Handing the tongs to his sister, he swept Faye up in his arms, kissing her cheek. "Thank you for coming, baby girl."

Biting down on her lower lip, Faye willed the hot tears behind her lids not to fall. "Don't, Daddy." She kissed him above the short, neat salt-and-pepper beard he'd affected the year he'd turned fifty.

"I'm so sorry, baby, for fighting with you," he whispered close to her ear.

"If you start, Daddy, then I'm leaving," she threatened softly.

"Okay." He set her on her feet, holding her at arm's length. "You look beautiful, Faye."

"Thank you." She wore one of the dresses Bart had purchased for her. She'd paired the eggshell-white linen sundress with spaghetti straps and a pleated bodice top tied in the back and leaving the small of her back bare, with a five-strand ruby torsade with diamond spacers. Her earrings were cushion-cut rubies suspended from bezel-set diamonds.

Shirley came out of the house in time to see her husband and daughter embracing. Carrying a tray of marinated spareribs, she straightened her spine as she neared them.

"I'm glad you made it, Faye Anne. Where's your friend?"

Faye turned to find Bart cradling the bag with the bottles of wine to his chest. She walked over to him. "Mama, Daddy, this is my good friend, Bart Houghton. Bart. These are my parents, Shirley and Craig Ogden."

There was a pulse beat of silence before Craig wiped his hand on his apron and extended it to Bart. "Welcome, Bart."

Bart shook the proffered hand. "Thank you." He smiled at Shirley. "Here's a little liquid refreshment, Mrs. Ogden."

"I'll take that," Craig offered, peering into the bag.

Shirley forced a smile. She hadn't expected her daughter to bring a white man to her house, *and* she hadn't expected him to be that much older than her.

"Welcome to our home, Bart." Her voice was shaded in neutral tones.

"Somebody parked a fly-ass ride behind your car, Uncle Craig. You've gots to see it!"

Faye frowned at her young cousin while Shirley shot him a warning look. "Watch your language, Hassan," Shirley cautioned softly.

"Sorry, Aunt Shirl," the teenager apologized. "Uncle Craig, come take a look."

Craig gave Shirley the bag and tongs. "Please look after the grill, baby." He'd always referred to Shirley as "baby" and Faye as "baby girl."

Shirley lifted her eyebrows at her daughter. "Why don't you get Bart comfortable under the tent, and then bring him something to drink. As soon as the others get here we'll be ready to eat. Even though I told you not to bring anything I do want to thank you for the flowers and the filet mignon."

Faye's jaw dropped when she looked at Bart, then her mother. "I didn't send any…" Her words trailed off when she realized why Bart wanted her parents' address. "It was Bart who sent them."

Shirley gave Bart a friendly smile. Earlier that morning a messenger had delivered a box marked Perishable. She'd opened it to find more than twenty pounds of fork-tender filet mignon cut into half-inch slices. Minutes later, there was another delivery of an enormous vase filled with white roses and tulips.

"Thank you."

Bart returned her smile. "It was my pleasure, Mrs. Ogden."

"Please call me Shirley."

Faye and Bart exchanged amused glances. It was apparent her parents had survived the initial shock of seeing them together. She felt he was appropriately dressed for an outdoor gathering: raw silk off-white shirt, navy slacks, and a pair of oxblood slip-ons.

She led him over to a large tent shading several picnic tables and matching benches. He sat down. "What would you like to drink?"

"I'll have a beer."

"Hey, Bart, is that your car?" Craig called out as he returned to the backyard.

Bart stood up. "Yes."

Craig's face lit up like a spotlight. "A 1939 Ford roadster with a three-hundred-five-cubic-inch engine."

"Do you want to look under the hood?"

"Yeah, man." Craig dropped an arm around Bart's shoulders as he led him out from under the tent. "Faye, please bring the man a beer. We've got business to discuss."

"You better not sell it," Faye said in a threatening tone.

Craig and Bart exchanged a glance. "Are you going to let your woman tell you what to do with *your* car?"

Bart shook his head. "Oh, hell no, man."

Craig patted his back. "Good for you. Put your foot down in the beginning and there won't be *no-o-o* trouble."

Shirley waved the tongs in the air like a rapier. "You keep mouthin' off, Craig Ogden, and Bart's going to find himself in more trouble than he can shake a stick at."

"He ain't scared, Shirley." Craig glared at Bart. "Are you scared?"

"No."

"Good. Don't forget to get the beers, baby girl."

Resting her hands on her hips, Faye stared at her mother. "First it was a beer, and now it's beers."

"Go get them, Faye Anne. It's been a long time since I've seen your daddy act a fool. There's no doubt he's glad to see you."

"And it's good to see him, too, *especially* when he's acting a fool."

CHAPTER 55

Alana couldn't wait until her feet were firmly planted on terra firma. Being on the water for more than seven hours, dancing and drinking more than eating had left her feeling off balance.

The luxurious yacht finally docked at the slip below Derrick's house and the passengers began disembarking. They were less boisterous than they'd been when boarding the gleaming vessel.

"Are you all right, Alana?"

She glanced up to find Derrick staring at her. A muscle quivered at his jaw. "I think I'm a little seasick."

"I think you got too much wind and sun." Her face was now the color of henna.

"I'll be all right after I lie down."

Derrick waved to his houseboy. "Take her to the bedroom overlooking the garden."

Kris Dennison watched Alana being led away. "Where's she goin', Derrick?"

"Upstairs to rest. She may have sunstroke."

"I'll look after her."

Derrick put a hand on Kris's arm. "Leave her alone. I don't want no shit to pop off in my house."

"I ain't gonna do nothin' to her, D. You should know me better than that."

"What I do know is that if anything happens to the lady you can forget about playing ball because I'll personally fuck you up myself."

Kristofer Dennison outweighed Derrick Warren by a hundred pounds and stood a full head taller, but there was something about the record producer that was scary. Maybe it had something to do with his lopsided face or the fact that he never raised his voice.

"Why would I want to hurt the next Mrs. Kris Dennison?"

Derrick's eyebrows flickered. "You like her like that?"

"Why do you think I broke up with Maeretha?"

The seconds ticked off as the two men stared at each other. "Okay, Kris. Go take care of her."

Kris caught up to the man responsible for keeping Derrick's household running smoothly. "I'll take her." Bending slightly, he picked Alana up as if she were a small child. Her head fell forward onto his chest, and he smiled.

He carried Alana up the staircase and into a room, closed and locked the door, and deposited her on the bed. Kris sat on the side of the mattress and gathered her in his arms.

"What's the matter, sugah?"

Her eyelids fluttered. "I'm just a little dizzy. I'll be all right if I just lie here for a while."

Combing his fingers through her curls, Kris smiled.

"Relax, sugah. In a few minutes you won't remember anything."

Alana tried opening her eyes but couldn't. They felt as if they were weighted down with stones. Kris hadn't lied. A quarter of an hour later she lay naked as he, equally naked, eased his penis into her vagina.

She felt the weight, the hardness pushing into her body, but was helpless to repel the man making love to her. And somewhere between fantasy and reality she thought it was Calvin. He'd come back and he was making love to her. Arching, she met the heavy thrusts as a moan of ecstasy escaped her lips. A ripple of starving desire spiraled throughout her body and the shudders increased until she was mindless with the passion scalding the blood in her veins.

She opened her mouth to scream but found her voice locked inside her throat by an object that wouldn't let her breath. Thrashing, she pounded the chest of the man who'd just released his passion inside her. Just when she thought her lungs would explode from lack of oxygen she slipped away into nothingness.

CHAPTER 56

Faye stood in the kitchen with her mother and aunts, filling take-out containers with leftovers while the men lingered in the tent talking about everything from cars, sports, politics and the economy.

"Your friend seems to fit in with the rest of the menfolk, Faye Anne."

Shirley glanced at her sister-in-law. "Why shouldn't he? He's just as crazy about cars as your brother."

"He seems rather nice," said another aunt for whom Faye had been named.

"He *is* nice," Shirley insisted.

"But isn't he a little too old for you, Faye Anne?" her namesake asked.

Faye halted putting a serving spoon of potato salad into a section of the plastic container. "Are you asking me if he's too old to make love, Aunt Faye?"

"Faye Anne!" the other women chorused.

She gave them a challenging glare. "Isn't that what you want to know?"

Shirley patted her arm. "You don't have to answer that, Faye Anne."

"But I want to, Mama. Bart and I are friends who happen not to be sleeping together."

Shaking her head, Shirley went back to stacking containers in plastic bags. She handed them to her daughter. "Please take these outside." She glared at the other women. "You heifers can be so tactless at times. Y'all always want to know somebody's business but won't tell your own."

Faye walked out of the kitchen. She wasn't about to get embroiled in a confrontation that occurred every time the women in her family got together. They were as competitive as crabs in a barrel, one vying to outdo the other.

Leaving the house through a side door, she made her way across the backyard and placed the shopping bags on the picnic table. Taking a quick glance at Bart, she saw him deep in conversation with her father and Uncle Teddy. Her younger cousins had retreated to a neighbor's house where hip-hop blared from outdoor speakers.

Craig glanced up and waved to Faye. "Please come here, baby girl."

Pinpoints of heat stung her cheeks. Even after thirty years her father still viewed her as a little girl. Sitting down beside Craig, she rested her arm over his shoulder. "What's up, Daddy?"

"Bart just invited me and your mother to come out to his house on Long Island this weekend."

Faye cut her eyes at Bart. What was he doing? It was one thing to accompany her to a backyard family celebration, and another completely to ingratiate himself into her parents' lives.

"That's nice. I'm sure the two of you will enjoy your-selves."

Craig turned and stared at her. "Won't you be there?"

"Of course she will," Bart said in a dangerously quiet tone. "Faye has agreed to be my hostess for the next three weeks."

Craig rubbed his palms together. "This is going to work out just fine because this is the first summer that I'm going to close the garage on Saturdays."

Faye wrapped her arm around her father's neck. "Good for you. Mama always said you work too hard."

Leaning across the table, Bart offered Craig his hand. "I'll send someone to pick you up early Saturday morning. And if the weather holds, then perhaps we can get in a few holes of golf."

Craig pumped Bart's hand vigorously. "I knew there was something I liked about you the first time I laid eyes on you."

"Does this mean you approve of me dating your daughter?"

"You don't need my approval, because I've never been one to tell my daughter who she should fall in love with or marry." Craig ignored Faye's soft gasp. "The only thing I ask is that you treat her right. If not, then your ass will belong to me." Everyone sitting at the table knew Craig Ogden was not issuing an idle threat.

If it hadn't been for the incessant thumping of a bass coming from the speakers across the street, the sound of chirping crickets along with the measured breathing of those at the picnic table would've been audible. The strained silence stretched on until Faye wanted to scream at her father and Bart to end the unnecessary male posturing. The flames from votives that were lit with the encroaching darkness flickered behind glass chimneys with a rising nighttime breeze.

Bart eased his hand from Craig's grip. "I would never deliberately hurt Faye. Not for anyone or anything."

Before anyone could react to his impassioned declaration Shirley came out of the house with Faye's handbag. "Your cell phone hasn't stopped ringing."

Rising to her feet, Faye reached into her purse for the phone. Alana's name showed in the display. Pressing a button, she put it to her ear. "Yes, Lana?"

"Faye!"

Her heart racing uncontrollably, she moved away so no one would overhear her conversation. Alana was crying hysterically. "Where are you, Lana?"

"I...I'm home." This was followed by another wave of sobbing.

"What's the matter?"

"Please come. Please, please…"

Biting down on her lower lip, Faye struggled to keep her composure. "It's all right. I'll be there as soon as I can."

"Please."

"I'm coming, Lana."

Faye ended the call and walked over to Bart. Leaning down, she said, "We have to go back to the city. My friend needs me."

He met her startled gaze. "Now?"

"Yes, Bart. Now!"

Moving off the bench and reaching into the pocket of his slacks, he took out his car keys. "I'm sorry but we have to leave." He shook hands with each of the men, then, placing a hand in the small of Faye's back, led her to the car. He handed her the keys. "You said you wanted to drive back."

"I can't," she said. She didn't trust herself not to wreck his classic automobile.

Curving a hand around her neck, Bart peered down at Faye. "Are you all right?"

"No. I just got a call from my best friend, and she sounded so upset."

"What's the matter?"

"I don't know, and I won't know until I see her."

Opening the door to the coupe, Bart helped Faye into the vintage roadster. Rounding the car, he got in beside her. "Where does she live?"

She gave him Alana's Central Park West address as he turned the key in the ignition.

The return ride was vastly different from the one to Queens. Bart concentrated on maneuvering in and out of the holiday traffic while Faye sat silently praying Alana was all right, that when she saw her it would just be a false alarm, that it was just Alana Gardner being a drama queen.

CHAPTER 57

Bart parked in front of Alana's apartment building. His right hand gripped Faye's wrist as she attempted to get out of the car. "Do you want me to come in with you?"

"Thank you for offering, but no."

"Are you coming back tonight?"

She met his gaze in the muted light from the dashboard. "I don't know."

He released her hand, shifted on his seat and reached into the pocket of his slacks. He handed her a set of keys. "Take these. The silver key is for the elevator to the first floor. The gold one will take you directly to the second level. I'll leave your name with the doorman so you can get into the building."

Faye placed her hand on his cheek. "Thank you for being you." It was the same thing he'd said to her after their Memorial Day weekend.

His fingers wrapped around her wrist. Bringing her hand to his mouth, he pressed a kiss to her soft palm. "Good luck with your friend." He got out and came around to open the passenger-side door. Extending his hand, he helped Faye out.

Leaning forward, she pressed her parted lips to his, kissing him with a hunger that belied her outward calm. "I'll see you later."

Bart felt her absence even though they stood inches apart. "Later," he whispered as she turned and made her way toward the liveried doorman holding the door for her.

Faye rang the doorbell, listening for movement on the other side. "Alana?"

She heard the distinctive sound of the cylinders as Alana unlocked the door. Stepping into the darkened living room, she took one look at Alana and knew this was not one of those times when her friend was just being over-dramatic. Her eyes were red, swollen, and her hair looked as if she'd been hit by a jolt of electricity.

She hugged Alana. "It's going to be all right."

Dissolving into another crying jag, Alana rested her head on Faye's shoulder and sobbed until she had dry heaves. "It can't be all right, Faye."

Smoothing the flyaway curls, she kissed her cheek. "Why are you in the dark?" The only light coming into the room came from street lamps and the apartment buildings on the other side of the park.

"No, Faye. I don't want the light."

Turning like an automaton, Alana shuffled into the living room, pulling her robe around her in a protective gesture. She sat down on the apricot-hued leather sofa, staring across the meticulously decorated room with unseeing eyes. It'd been a momentous day when she'd taken possession of the spacious one-bedroom apartment with views of Central Park, but now, tonight, it felt like a prison without bars.

She'd called Faye because she couldn't call her mother. Melanie's fear that something horrible would happen to her daughter if she lived in New York City had been manifested. How could she tell Melanie that her only daughter had become a date-rape statistic?

Faye sat in a leather armchair, dropping her handbag onto the carpeted floor. She waited for Alana to open up as to why she'd called her, why she'd been crying. The seconds ticked off to minutes.

"What's the matter, Lana?" she asked, ending the impasse.

There was another moment of swollen silence. "Somebody raped me."

Swallowing an expletive, Faye moved from the chair to the sofa, pulling Alana into a protective embrace. "Did you report it to the police? Go to a hospital?"

"No."

"Don't tell me you took a shower?"

"I took a bath."

"But you washed away evidence."

"It doesn't matter because I don't know who did it."

"It does matter, Lana. A doctor or nurse could've gathered evidence for a rape kit, and then matched it with DNA from the men who were at the party."

"Do you really think they're going to step up and voluntarily offer a DNA sample?"

"They will if they want to prove their innocence."

"And what if they don't? Do you think they want to get caught up in a sex scandal with a woman who's an escort? Have you forgotten that we get paid to entertain men?"

"That's bullshit, Alana. Just because a man offers us money to spend time with him, that doesn't give him the right to take us against our will!"

Alana buried her face in her hands. "I don't know if it was against my will."

"What are you talking about?"

Lowering her hands and clasping her fingers, Alana stared up at the ceiling. "I can't remember anything after I got off the boat. I know I was feeling dizzy, but I thought it was because I'd drunk too much and hadn't eaten enough."

"How much did you drink?"

"I had a couple of mimosas."

"What else?"

"I know I had a White Russian."

"You had at least three drinks over how many hours?"

"We set sail at one, and we were scheduled to return around eight."

"It's not adding up, Lana. I've seen you down a bottle of champagne in three hours and you weren't so drunk that you couldn't remember who you were or what you did. I think someone drugged you."

"No, Faye. That's not possible."

"You don't know. Let me take you to the hospital so they can take a blood test."

"No!"

"Stop blaming yourself for something you had no control over."

"Stop it, Faye! I can't take any more tonight."

"Okay, Alana. The only thing I'm going to say is you have to get tested."

Hot tears rolled down Alana's face. Contracting an STD frightened her more than becoming pregnant. "I know. Will you come with me?"

"Of course I will."

"Will you do me a favor, Faye?"

"Yes. What do you want?"

"Please hang out here with me until I fall asleep."

"What if I spend the night?"

A cynical smile twisted her mouth. "Are you afraid I'm going to do something to myself?"

Faye stared at the lights coming from across the park. "No. You never would've called me if you planned on hurting yourself."

Pulling her legs to her chest, Alana rested her forehead on her knees. "You're right about that." Lowering her legs, she pushed to her feet. "Thanks for being a real friend."

"There's no need to thank me, Lana. You were there for me when I broke up with Norman. And I can recall being a mood-swinging, snot-slinging wretch until you finally told me to snap out of it and get on with my life." She stood up. "This time I'm going to tuck you into bed."

"Where will you sleep?"

"I'll crash on your sofa."

"Don't forget you have a change of clothes on the top

shelf of the linen closet, and you'll find toothbrushes in the vanity drawer."

Faye moved cautiously in the darkened apartment as she followed Alana to her bedroom, waiting until she was in bed, then retraced her steps and retrieved her handbag. Searching its depths, she found her cell phone.

"Hi," she whispered when she heard the familiar masculine voice.

"Hey, baby."

"I'm calling to let you know that I'm going to spend the night."

"You're a good friend, Faye Anne Ogden."

"Don't you dare call me Faye Anne!"

"Why not, baby girl?"

"You're pushing it, Bart."

"Didn't your daddy tell you that I wasn't scared? And speaking of families—your folks are super."

"I suppose I'll keep them."

"You suppose? If you don't want them then I'll ask them to adopt me."

"Good night, Bart. I'll see you tomorrow night."

"Okay. Good night, Faye."

It wasn't until she hung up that she recalled Bart's remark about being adopted into her family. He had no family with whom to celebrate birthdays, weddings or holidays.

Faye realized that in spite of Bartholomew Houghton's vast wealth and opulent lifestyle, he was a private, lonely man.

Why else would he pay a woman to be with him?

CHAPTER 58

Amelia Wells stood in the doorway, watching her lover dress. She'd come to know every inch of the model's body from her slanting eyes, flawless dimpled cheeks, small firm breasts with large nipples, flat belly, slim hips and long shapely legs, to her narrow, high-arched feet. Ilene Fairchild had become an addictive drug from which she did not want to free herself. Her normally warm dark brown eyes grew flat with an unreadable emotion.

"I don't want you to leave."

Ilene halted zipping up a pair of stretch slacks and glanced over her shoulder at the woman with whom she'd shared the most satisfying sex in a very long time.

"You know I can't stay."

Crossing her arms under her ample breasts, Amelia walked into the bedroom. "I know nothing."

"I have to work."

"Why do you need to work, Ilene?"

Her eyes widening, Ilene stared at Amelia as if she'd taken leave of her senses. "Why does anyone work? To pay rent, buy food, clothes and to take care of the extras that make life a little easier," she said, answering Amelia's and her own question.

"I will take care of you."

Flipping her hair over her shoulders, Ilene continued dressing as she slipped her feet into a pair of three-inch sandals. "I'm sorry, Amelia, but I can't let you do that. I've lost count of the number of men who've offered to take care of me, but in the end I always had to take care of myself. Thanks, but no thanks."

Panic like she'd never known before gripped Amelia, making it almost impossible for her to breathe. She didn't want to lose Ilene because she'd fallen in love with her. Ilene had become only one of a string of affairs she'd had since her first encounter at a London-based all-girls boarding school, but at thirty-five she wanted it to be her last.

"What do you want, Ilene?"

Picking up a pair of sunglasses and placing them atop her head, Ilene gave Amelia a long, penetrating stare. "I want financial security for the rest of my life. I want enough money so that I don't have to skin and grin at wrinkled old men to keep a roof over my head. I want enough money for when the time comes, and it's gonna come, when I'm too old to pop my ass in a music video.

"I don't want to be my mother who was forced to spread her legs for the husbands of the women whose houses she cleaned so that he'd throw a few extra dollars her way to feed her children more than corn bread with pot likker. I grew up dirt poor, and I swore on my mother's grave that I wouldn't die dirt poor."

She reached for her oversize designer purse. "I'd appreciate it if you have someone take my bag out to the boat." Turning on her heel, she walked out of the bedroom, leaving Amelia staring at her retreating back.

Ilene opened the door to her Chelsea co-op, wrinkling her nose. She'd turned off the air-conditioning unit and the buildup of heat was smothering. Dropping her bags in the entryway, she kicked off her sandals and made her way into the living/dining area. She turned on the window unit to the maximum-cooling setting, repeating the action on the bedroom unit.

Discarded slacks, blouses and underwear were strewn everywhere. A week before, Amelia had called to tell her that she wanted her to come back to Pine Cay, and that a first-class ticket awaited her at the American Airlines terminal at Kennedy Airport. Ilene hadn't heard from anyone at P.S., Inc. for several days, so she threw whatever she could find in her closet into a bag, called down to the doorman to hail a taxi to take her to the airport.

She'd spent a total of ten days on the private island, touring, eating, sleeping and sharing Amelia's bed. She hadn't wanted to leave Pine Cay, but the prospect of earning thousands as a social companion proved a greater lure.

Picking up the telephone, she heard the familiar sound indicating she had voice mail. She punched in her code, then sat down on the edge of the unmade bed with wide eyes as she listened to Astrid Marti asking her to contact her as soon as she received the message. There were two other messages, one from her brother asking for money to pay back child support, and another from her younger sister who was getting married again—for the fourth time. She deleted all the messages before she dialed the number to Pleasure Seekers.

"Good afternoon, P.S., Inc. This is Astrid. How may I direct your call?"

"Astrid, this is Ilene Fairchild. You left a message asking that I call you."

"Oh, yes, Miss Fairchild. Enid would like you to come to the office at your earliest convenience."

Ilene glanced around her bedroom. She had to clean her apartment before she did anything else, because she found it easier to think without the clutter. "Will Enid be available tomorrow morning?"

There was a slight pause. "In the interest of continued employment with P.S., Inc., you might want to reconsider and come today, Miss Fairchild."

Continued employment. The two words shattered Ilene's composure, causing a momentary wave of panic. They couldn't let her go. Not when she hadn't saved enough for at least five years of maintenance payments for her co-op. She'd depleted her savings when she bought the apartment because she hadn't wanted a mortgage hanging over her head.

"I'll be there in about an hour." This was not the time for her to go into diva mode.

"Enid will be expecting you."

Astrid hung up before Ilene did, and the click followed

by the droning dial tone chilled Ilene to the bone. Propelling herself off the bed, she headed to the bathroom to shower and change before taking the subway several stops downtown to Soho.

CHAPTER 59

Enid moved from behind her desk as Astrid escorted Ilene into her office. She motioned to an armchair. "Please sit down, Miss Fairchild."

Ilene complied, trying to gauge the older woman's mood, but her impassive expression gave nothing away. Enid, as usual, was fashionably dressed in a long-sleeved white silk blouse and pencil skirt that ended at the knee. Her shoes were a pair of Ferragamo pumps.

Enid sat opposite Ilene, silently admiring the model's conservative look. She looked every inch the business-woman, with a black linen pantsuit and matching V-neck silk top. Instead of her usual stilettos, she wore a two-inch leather pump. Her hair, pulled tightly off her face, was fash-ioned into a chignon at the nape of her long, graceful neck.

Crossing her legs at the ankles, Enid affected a cold smile. "Do you have any idea why I asked you to come in to see me?"

"No, I don't." Ilene's voice was soft and even.

"Are you certain, Miss Fairchild?"

Ilene did not drop her gaze as a pair of blue-gray eyes bore into her. After she'd recovered from Astrid's veiled threat, she gave herself a pep talk during the subway ride from Chelsea to Soho. Didn't they know who she was? And in case they forgot, she would have to remind them that she was Ilene Fairchild supermodel extraordinaire. Her name would always be mentioned in the same breath as Gia, Linda Evangelista, Naomi Campbell, Cindy Crawford and Jean Shrimpton.

Ella Williams had worked hard to erase the stigma of being the daughter of a sharecropper daddy and house-maid mama to hit the fashion runways big-time. And the same determination it took to reinvent her returned by the time she walked into the lobby of the loft that housed the offices of P.S., Inc.

Oh, no, you half-white bitch, I'm not about to let you intimidate me. I know you're a sister-girl on the down low, but you just can't stay in the closet because you like dark meat. Marcus Hampton would be perfect for your so-called exotic jewels, but you snagged him for yourself. How long do you think he'll hang around, Miss Richards? How long will it be before he'll want someone younger and kick your pale ass to the curb?

"I'm very certain," she said confidently.

Enid uncrossed her ankles and looped one leg over the opposite knee as she rested her manicured hands on the scrolled arms of her chair. "In case you've forgotten what you were told at your orientation, let me refresh your memory.

"You were warned not to attempt to ever see a client without going through P.S., Inc., because a single infraction will result in immediate dismissal." Enid held up a hand when Ilene opened her mouth in an attempt to either explain or defend herself. "You returned to Pine Cay without going through Pleasure Seekers, Ilene, and because you did I lost thousands of dollars and so did you. And I don't need to tell you that losing money puts me in a very bad mood."

Ilene's rising temper simmered. "How do you know that?"

"I have eyes and ears all over the world, Miss Fairchild. Nothing that has to do with P.S., Inc. gets past me."

"But I went back on my own."

A rush of color darkened Enid's face. "You are a stupid little girl, Ella Williams. Pine Cay *is* my client!"

Ilene wanted to smack Enid in her too-perfect face for calling her that dreadful name—a name that reminded her of who she'd been and what she'd gone through before she reinvented herself.

"You missed the opportunity to take a two-week cruise of the Greek Isles before docking in Saint Tropez with a very wealthy client because apparently you prefer to give away free pussy than get a hundred thousand dollars and the pick of several diamond baubles." She shook her head slowly. "You've come so far and yet you know nothing about how to play the game. And do not lie to me, because I haven't forgotten all the little tales you'll attempt to make up."

Someone had told Enid that she'd been sleeping with Amelia Wells. What did she intend to do with the information? Sell it to the tabloids? It no longer mattered because she was beyond threats or intimidation, and pride wouldn't permit her to give in to Enid's bullying.

"If you're going to fire me, then do it, because I have to go home and clean my apartment."

"I'm not going to fire you, Ilene, because I need you." Ilene gasped softly and Enid successfully bit back a smile. It was apparent her decision had shocked the self-centered young woman. "I'm going to sanction you for two weeks for your infraction. And if you agree, then you *must* make yourself available for Astrid's calls at any time during this time."

Ilene's cheekiness slipped away like a whisper of expelled breath. She'd been given a second chance. Her dimpled smile was slow in coming. "I'll make certain I'm available."

Enid studied Ilene for a long while, annoyed because as a social companion her earning power was limitless. Faye Ogden had hit the jackpot as a favorite of Bartholomew Houghton. Alana Gardner was sought after by entertainers and athletes, whereas Ilene Fairchild was adored by men of every race, men who were young, old, rich or poor.

"Go home and clean your apartment," she said, waving a hand in a gesture of dismissal.

Rising gracefully, Ilene walked out of the office, lips compressed tightly to keep the curses from spewing out and ruining her chance for earning more money. And she planned to make a lot of money before she told Enid Richards exactly what she thought of her.

CHAPTER 60

Faye sat at a bistro table with Alana at their favorite Greenwich Village outdoor café. Earlier that morning they'd waited at a clinic where Alana was interviewed by a certified HIV counselor, then had blood drawn by a physician's assistant.

Alana lifted a goblet of club soda. "I never thought I'd say it, but I toast a negative outcome."

Lifting her own goblet of sparkling water, Faye touched glasses. "Hear, hear." She took a sip of the cool liquid. "It's going to be all right, Lana."

"How can you be so perky when…"

"When what?"

Alana closed her eyes. "I could become a dead woman walking." When she opened her eyes they glistened with tears.

Setting down her glass, Faye reached over and covered Alana's icy-cold fingers. "Please, Lana. I spent the night on your sofa tossing, turning and praying for you. Don't make me question my faith."

Touching her napkin at the corners of her eyes, Alana

managed to smile. "You are the most focused person I've ever met."

"I'm not that focused."

"What are you?"

"I'm determined and stubborn as a mule when I believe in something or someone. That's why it took me so long to come to the conclusion that Norman was cheating on me. I loved him so much that I refused to see his faults."

"Do you still love him, Faye?"

"No. But I still have feelings for him because we did have some wonderful times together."

"Do you ever hear from him?"

Faye shook her head. "No. And it's better that way because I don't want to dredge up what was and what never will be again."

A waiter came and placed their orders on the table. "Can I get you ladies anything else?"

"No, thank you," Alana and Faye chorused. Both had ordered individual pizzas with sun-dried tomatoes and fresh basil.

Alana plucked a sliver of tomato off her pizza and popped it into her mouth, chewing thoughtfully. "I envy you, girlfriend."

"You've got to be kidding me!" The words exploded from Faye's mouth. "You're drop-dead gorgeous, and you have a glamorous job that takes you to Europe several times a year. You get to rub shoulders with and interview the international elite while I'm stuck here fighting with a hungry-looking whore masquerading as an intern out to get my job. I'm sorry, Lana, but I'm not buying that."

"It only looks glamorous. There're times when I feel like vomiting after I've spent hours with people who feel I should be honored to just sit in their presence. Most of them are has-beens and penniless. They'd join the rest of the homeless population living in cardboard boxes if old friends or distant relatives didn't pay their hotel bill. They'd rather live in hotels because it's more prestigious than a co-op or condominium."

"I believe an exception would be Trump Towers."

Alana lifted her glass again. "Touché." She gestured to the profusion of dark red beads hanging over the white T-shirt Faye had tucked into a pair of jeans. "Are those diamond spacers?"

Faye touched the ruby torsade. "Yes."

"Bart Houghton?"

"Yes."

"You like him, don't you?"

"He's nice, Lana."

"I'm not asking if he's nice, Faye. Do you like him?"

What did her friend expect her to say? Yes, she liked Bart. Liked him a lot more than she believed she would come to like him.

"Yes," she said, deciding to be truthful.

Propping an elbow on the table, Alana rested her chin on her hand. "Good for you."

Faye stared across the table, complete surprise on her face. "What are you talking about? The last time we discussed Bart Houghton you warned me about getting in over my head."

"That's because I was jealous."

"How can you be jealous? The man is a *client!*" She'd whispered the last word.

Alana rolled her eyes. "Sometimes you can be so smart, then there're times when you're dumb as dirt." She ignored Faye's audible gasp. "If he's paying for you to spend the summer with him it has nothing to do with you being his social companion. You're his girlfriend and soon-to-become lover."

"We are not sleeping together."

"Not yet."

Faye's nostrils flared with seething rage. "You're trying to bait me, aren't you? You want me to say—"

"I want you happy," Alana spat out, interrupting her. "You deserve someone who'll treat you better than Norman did. You get on my ass about Calvin, but as funky as he is at times he's never fucked another woman in my bed. Oh, you think I didn't know about that?" she asked when Faye's mouth opened. "One night when you'd had too much to drink you told me about the time you came home early from work and found Norman in your bed with one of his patients.

"I don't know anything about your Big Willie, but something tells me that he wouldn't disrespect you like that, because he has enough money to have a different woman every night if that's what he wants." Leaning over the table, she peered closely at her friend. "What's the matter?"

"I can't believe I told you that."

"Well, you did, and it will go no further than this table. Stop playing, Faye. Bart's come down with an incurable case of jungle fever. Give the man some black pus-sy." The word came out like *pooh-say*.

"Stop it, Lana!"

"You'll have him beating his chest, howling and swinging from a chandelier like Tarzan," Lana continued as if Faye hadn't spoken. "You know what they say about 'once you go black you'll never go back.'"

Both women laughed until tears rolled down their cheeks. Whoever said laughter was the cure for everything was a genius. They sobered enough to finish lunch before setting out on a walking tour of the historic neighborhood, heading east until they reached the South Street Seaport.

Alana stared up at the cables spanning the Brooklyn Bridge. "I'm so busy worrying about HIV and other STDs that I hadn't thought that maybe I could be pregnant."

That's why I wanted you to go to the hospital where you could've gotten something that would prevent you from becoming pregnant. Faye thought it when she couldn't say it. Besides, her friend had gone through enough without her verbally beating up on her. And she didn't know what the counselor had told Alana, so she didn't want to undo what he'd done.

"And if you are, Lana? What do you plan to do?"

An expression of serenity softened her eyes and mouth. "If I'm negative, then I'll have it."

"What about Calvin?"

Alana glared at Faye. "Don't mention that sonof-abitch's name!"

"He still hasn't called you?"

"Has he called you, Faye?"

"No."

"There. You have your answer. I don't need him or his bullshit. If I am pregnant, then I'll work as a companion until I start showing. The money I'll earn working for Enid, along with what I've saved, will tide me over for a couple of years. Then I'll hire a nanny to take care of little Faye or little Taj."

Faye couldn't believe what she'd just heard. If pregnant, then Alana wanted to have a child that was the result of rape. What would she tell her son or daughter if they asked about their father?

"Are you serious, Lana?"

"I'm as serious as a heart attack. I've never had anything that belonged totally to me. My brothers used to break the heads off my favorite dolls, my mother devoted her life to a man who didn't love her enough to make her his wife, and the first man in my life transferred the love he should've had for his daughter to another woman young enough to be his daughter.

"So, don't stand there acting so sanctimonious because for the first time in a long time I'm in control, in control of my body, and in control of life. I don't need Calvin to make me feel like a woman, and I don't need Dr. Novak telling me that I must think things through before I make a decision." Alana pressed her hands to her middle. "Growing up, I always wanted the house, the husband and the baby. Well, I'm grown, can't get any more grown, just older. And if I am pregnant, then I'm keeping it. I'm not asking you to support my decision, Faye. I just want you to be happy for me."

There was a long brittle silence until Faye extended her arms. "Come give me a hug, Lana. I'm here for you. I'll always be here for you no matter what you decide." The two women hugged each other, garnering glances from the throngs weaving their way over the cobblestone streets. "I want you to promise to make me godmother to your baby, and if it's a girl Faye can be her middle name."

The tightness in Alana's chest eased, replaced by joy and satisfaction. "I promise."

"I have a three o'clock appointment at Madame Fontaine for a facial and shiatsu massage. Do you want to come with me?"

"And do what? Watch you?"

"No, Lana. You can come as my guest."

Alana's smile was dazzling. "Let's go, girlfriend."

CHAPTER 61

"Bartholomew, John Reynolds is on line three."

Bart picked up the receiver. "Thank you, Mrs. Urquhart." He depressed another button. "Mr. Reynolds—may I call you John?"

"Yes, of course. Mr. Houghton—"

"Bart," he interrupted softly. "Please, call me Bart."

"Okay, Bart. How can I help you?"

"I'd like to set up a meeting with you to discuss a marketing program for a special construction project in Harlem."

"When would you want us to get together?"

Leaning back in his chair and propping his heels on the edge of the desk, Bart stared at a black-and-white photograph of the Brooklyn Bridge. "Sometime next week. However, before we decide on a date and time I want you to be aware that I want a pitch that will target the African-American segment of our city's population."

"We have an award-winning ad exec on our staff who can put a campaign package together that's certain to meet your requirements and approval."

"I like the sound of that. Perhaps he can sit in on the meeting."

"The person I'm referring to is female. Unfortunately, she's going to be on vacation until the end of the month. But, not to hold you up, I can bring someone else in who's just as good."

"What's her name?"

"Which one, Bart?"

"Your award winner."

"Faye Ogden."

"Faye Ogden," Bart repeated, as if hearing her name for the first time. "I'd rather wait for Ms. Ogden. We cannot afford to entrust the marketing of a half-billion-dollar business venture to a summer replacement. Better yet, I thank you for your time—"

"Don't hang up, Mr. Houghton," John said quickly.

"Bart," Bart said softly, correcting him.

"Yes, Bart. Perhaps I can contact Ms. Ogden and have her get in touch with you."

"I thought she was on vacation."

"She is. I don't know whether she's still in town, but I'll leave a message on her voice—"

"There's no need to contact her until she returns." It was Bart's turn to interrupt. "Our projected date of completion is late spring, so we want to begin advertising the specs of available units this fall."

"I can assure you that Ms. Ogden will come up with something that will meet with your approval."

Bart was certain John Reynolds was grinning from ear to ear. "Even though I will not be involved in the ongoing process, the final decision will rest with me and the other members of our executive staff."

He ended the call and lowered his feet. He'd set a plan in motion he was certain would secure Faye's uncertain future at BP&O. Standing, he walked over to the closet to retrieve his jacket. His day had begun with a breakfast meeting that continued through lunch and into the afternoon. He'd had enough and he wanted to go home to see the woman who unknowingly made him reassess all he'd sacrificed to prove his worth to those who no longer mattered.

Faye exited the elevator, stopping short, and gasping in surprise. She hadn't expected Bart to be waiting for her. He smelled of soap and clean laundry. A white T-shirt and jeans were molded to the contours of his slender body. His defined pectorals and biceps were blatant indicators that he worked out regularly. His feet were bare and his damp hair stood up on his head in silvery spikes.

"You frightened me."

Bart reached for the shopping bag she'd cradled to her chest. "The doorman told me you were on your way up," he said by way of explaining his sudden appearance. He kissed her cheek before peering into the plastic bag. "What on earth did you buy?"

"I picked up some fruits and veggies. I noticed there weren't any in the refrigerator."

"That's because we'll be leaving for Southampton tomorrow morning."

"Why didn't you say something, Bart?"

"I would've told you if you'd stayed over last night." Shifting the bag to one arm, he wound the other around her waist as he led her in the direction of the kitchen. "I'll give you a list of what I have planned for us tomorrow." Bart gave Faye a sidelong glance. "What did you do to your face? Your skin looks nice."

"I have you and the esthetician at Madame Fontaine to thank for that. I took my friend with me as a guest."

"How is she?"

"I'm certain she's a lot better after a facial and a hot-stone massage."

His fingers tightened on her waist. "She's lucky to have you as a friend."

"I'm blessed to have Alana as a friend because she doesn't tell me what I want to hear but what I *need* to hear. In other words, she always keeps it real."

Bart felt his stomach muscles contract. It was apparent Faye equated friendship with truth, and unfortunately he hadn't been completely truthful with her. He knew he was falling in love with her. Although he hadn't verbalized what lay in his heart he'd tried demonstrating the depths of his feelings. He'd moved her into his home, made himself available to her at all times and had tried to put in place things that would make her life more comfortable and stress free.

But there was someone from his past he hadn't been able to give up or let go; and until he let her go, he would never be able to move forward to share his future with Faye Ogden.

Bart placed the bag on a countertop next to a double stainless-steel sink. He took out clear plastic bags of seasonal fruits: cherries, white grapes, peaches, pears, blueberries and kiwi. There were vacuum-sealed bags of fresh spinach and herbs. He held up the packaged vegetables.

"What do you want to do with these?"

Faye took charge. "Put them in the fridge's vegetable drawer. I'll put the fruit away after I wash it." Reaching for a large aluminum bowl hanging from a hook over the cooking island, she emptied the fruit into the bowl then washed it with cold water from a retractable nozzle.

She froze when Bart came up behind her and pulled her to rest against his chest, giggling like a little girl when he nuzzled her neck. "What are you doing?"

"I'm trying to see if you smell as good as you look."

"Do I?" she asked, laughing.

"It's a tie." His lips moved down the column of her neck in an agonizing slowness that caused a shudder to ripple through her body. "What's the matter, baby?" Bart crooned as the ripples continued.

Faye's hands curled into tight fists. "Nothing, Bart." Smiling, she closed her eyes.

"Liar," he whispered close to her ear.

"I'm not lying," she whispered back. She was aware *and* Bart was aware than she hadn't told him the truth. His closeness, the hardness of his body, and his mouth moving over her sensitized flesh ignited a heat that threatened to devour her whole.

Turning in his loose embrace, Faye stared up at Bart.

His eyes shimmered like sparks of flint. Although she'd insisted they were just friends, she knew it would be just a matter of time before they'd become lovers. Even Alana had predicted it. *If he's paying for you to spend the summer with him it has nothing to do with you being his social companion. You're his girlfriend and soon-to-become lover.*

She blinked once. "You're right, Bart. I was lying." Her voice was soft, even. She took a step, her legs sandwiched between his spread-eagle ones. "Now it's time for the truth. What do you want?"

Bart was rooted to the spot as he held his breath. Faye was asking what he wanted, what he'd wanted from the first time he saw her at Enid Richards's Soho loft, and like a bumbling adolescent about to embark on his first sexual encounter he couldn't tell the woman in his arms what he wanted.

He'd given Faye everything he thought she'd want while waiting patiently for her to come to him of her own free will. He'd slept with Felicia twice since he'd come to know Faye, and both times he'd felt as if he was cheating on her.

Felicia was a call girl he paid to have sex with him and Faye was a social companion, someone he paid to keep him occupied during his free time, yet he felt like an unfaithful husband—something he'd never been. How had morality crept into the picture when he wasn't legally bound to any woman?

However, he knew the answer to his troubled thoughts before they'd formed in his mind. He was in love with Faye Ogden.

The realization that he'd fallen in love with a woman for the second time in his life left him reeling. He still loved Deidre Dunn, but he was also in love with Faye Anne Ogden.

He blinked as if coming out of a trance. "I want you."

Faye swayed as if buffeted by a strong wind. "How do you want me?"

"I want you in my life—"

"But I'm in your life, Bart," she said, stopping his explanation. "I'll be living with you this summer."

Reaching up, he placed a forefinger over her mouth. "You didn't let me finish," he chastised, smiling. "You're right. You'll be living with me this summer, but I also want you to sleep with me."

"You want to make love to me?"

"I want to make love *with* you, but only after you feel comfortable sleeping with me."

A knot rose in her throat at the same time the rapid beating of her heart slammed against her ribs. This time she heard the soft, drawling voice of Enid Richards in her head: *I must caution you about sleeping with your clients. It always spells trouble.* What she wanted to ask Enid was, would it spell trouble for the clients or for your exotic jewels?

It was she and not Enid who'd found herself ensnared in a world where she found it more and more difficult to distinguish between fantasy and reality; and Bart Houghton had become her fantasy—a man she never would've met or considered dating if it had not been for a business card that had piqued her interest.

But Bart Houghton had also become her reality when
he'd made it possible for her to earn enough money to give
an attorney his retainer to take on her brother's appeal.
And sleeping with Bart would be no different from her encounters with the other men in her past, with the exception that what they'd share was business. She would enjoy
the intimacy, and when it ended she knew she would not
have any regrets.

Rising on tiptoe, she brushed her mouth over his. "Let's
go to bed."

CHAPTER 62

Faye barely had time to catch her breath when Bart swept her up in his arms and carried her out of the kitchen. Tightening her arms around his neck, she buried her face against the column of his neck, enjoying the lingering scent of soap on his skin.

"It's been a long time since I've shared a bed with a man," she confessed.

Bart smiled as he mounted the staircase to the second floor. He hadn't known why she'd waited to share her bed or body with a man, but her admission filled him with a rush of smugness that perhaps she'd been waiting for the right man; and he hoped beyond hope that he was right for her.

"We'll take it slow, baby. And any time you prefer sleeping alone then you must let me know."

Faye, apprehensive about what she was about to embark upon, what she'd agreed to, closed her eyes and mumbled a fervent prayer that she was doing the right thing. And once she opened her legs to Bart things would not and could not remain the same between them. She was realistic and had matured enough to acknowledge that fact.

She counted the steps that took him from the staircase,

down a hallway separating her rooms from his, and ended at thirty-two when he placed her on his bed, his body following hers downward. Reaching over, he took off her shoes.

The wall-to-wall, floor-to-ceiling windows facing the East River provided a sensual backdrop for the sensual joining between two people who, up until two months ago, didn't know the other existed. Streaks of orange crisscrossed the sky as long shadows indicated the approach of dusk. They lay together, their measured breathing coming and going at the same cadence.

Faye turned on her side, facing Bart, one jean-covered leg moving over his. "Aren't you going to draw the shades?" Where the windows in her bedroom were covered with sheer panels of silk, his were fashioned from finely woven mesh shades that lowered with a flick of a wall switch.

His eyes shimmered in the light coming through the windows. "Does the light bother you?"

"Not as much as someone seeing us."

"The only people who can see us are those flying overhead. We're thirty-two stories above the roadway."

Bart's explanation seemed to satisfy Faye because she closed her eyes and snuggled closer to his chest. They lay on the crisp pale gray sheets, sharing each other's body heat, scent, as the sun set and lights came on all over the city.

He rarely drew the shades. Whenever he'd found himself too wound up to sleep, he'd lie in bed and stare out the window. The triplex was high enough not to hear the sound of vehicular traffic along FDR Drive or on the bridges linking Manhattan with the outer boroughs. His home had become his sanctuary, a place where he forgot about business and a place that reminded him of how selfish he'd become because of his reluctance to share his life with a woman.

Bart didn't know what it was about Faye that made her so much different from the other women he'd encountered since becoming a widower. He admired her beauty and her strength; but it was her vulnerability that tugged at his heart the way no woman had been able to do, and that included Deidre.

"Do you plan to sleep in your clothes?" he whispered near her ear.

Faye moaned but didn't stir. She'd dozed off. "I'm too exhausted to move. I didn't get much sleep last night. I usually don't do sofas."

"You don't have to move. I'll undress you."

Bart sat up and unsnapped the waistband to her jeans. Anchoring a hand under her hips, he eased the denim fabric down her hips and legs. Her tee followed. Faye lay on the bed clad only in a sheer café au lait bra and matching panties.

"You're practically naked!"

Faye opened her eyes and tried making out the shadowy face inches from her own. "What are you talking about?"

"I can see through your bra and panties." There was no mistaking the huskiness in Bart's voice.

Rolling over and coming to her knees, she pulled back the top sheet, lay down and pulled it up over her body.

"Are you getting into bed or are you going to ramble on for the rest of the night?"

Moving off the bed, he undressed quickly, leaving his jeans, shirt and boxers on a chair. He slipped under the sheet beside Faye, put a hand on her waist and drew her to him.

Faye went completely still when she felt his erection pressed against her hips. "Bart?"

"What is it?"

"Can you please put your underwear back on?"

"No, I can't, because I always sleep in the nude. Go to sleep, darling. Nothing's going to happen tonight."

He was sure nothing was going to happen, when she wasn't sure how long she could ignore the hardened flesh thrumming against her buttocks as if it had a life of its own.

Sharing a bed with Bart had awakened a response deep within her that reminded her that she was a woman capable of grand passion. Her hand covered the larger one splayed over her belly.

"Good night, Bart."

He chuckled softly. "Good night, baby girl."

CHAPTER 63

Marcus shook his head as he walked into the kitchen after spending the night waging a campaign with Enid for sexual dominance. She'd been insatiable, her ardor surpassing his, and in the end he'd left the bed and slept on the divan on the veranda. Something had to change or they would physically annihilate each other.

Enid sat at the table in the dining area, papers strewn over the table. A silk dressing gown hung open, displaying the rose-colored love bites he'd inflicted on her neck and breasts.

She glanced up, smiling. "June's figures are phenomenal."

Closing the distance between them, Marcus dropped a kiss on her hair. "Good morning, darling. They're good because of Bartholomew Houghton."

Enid offered her lips for his kiss. "Good morning, love. Yes, but let's not forget Faye Ogden."

Marcus moved over to the counter and pressed a button on the coffeemaker. "Yes," he said in a quiet voice, "Miss Ogden."

Leaning against the counter, he stared at the pale hair grazing the neck of the woman he loved without reservation. Their agreement to live together for the summer worked well. They enjoyed a comfortable camaraderie that made him believe being married to Enid would become a positive and lasting union.

Shifting on her chair, Enid turned to stare at her lover. He was breathtakingly virile in a pair of low-rise jeans. The stubble on his chin darkened his face, offsetting his normally urbane appearance. His strangely colored gold eyes reminded her of a cat—not a domesticated feline but a jungle cat.

"Why would you say her name like that, Marcus?"

"Don't tell me you're jealous of Faye Ogden," he teased without smiling.

Enid watched Marcus with a critical squint. "Of course not," she crooned seductively. "Faye Ogden would be no match for you, darling."

Her assessment of Bart Houghton's latest obsession elicited a smile from Marcus. "You are such a supercilious bitch, Enid."

"Isn't that why you love me?"

Lifting one eyebrow, he nodded. "Yes." Sitting down on a stool to wait for the coffee to finish brewing, he stared at the wall clock. "How are you getting along with Ilene Fairchild?"

Marcus usually did not get involved with the booking of clients or social companions, preferring instead to handle the financial component of the business, but Astrid's inability to contact the model had sent Enid into a rage he'd never witnessed during their relationship.

"I sanctioned her for two weeks. I'm not as concerned about Ilene as I am with Alana Gardner."

"What's wrong?"

"Alana refused to go out with Derrick Warren. I'd thought they were getting along well."

"Did she give you a reason why she won't see him?"

Combing her fingers through her hair and holding it off her forehead, Enid gave him a long, penetrating stare. "No."

Swiveling on the stool, Marcus reached for a wall phone, dialed a number, listening for a break in the connection. He counted four rings.

"Hello," said a sleepy-sounding male voice.

"This is Marcus Hampton and I'd like to speak to Derrick Warren."

"He's sleepin'"

"Wake him up!"

"Who's callin'?"

"Mar—cus Hamp—ton." He'd enunciated each syllable. The sweep hand on the wall clock had made four revolutions by the time Derrick came to the phone. "Hey, Mark."

"Hey, man. I need to know what happened between you and Alana Gardner."

"Nothing, Mark. It's all good."

"It can't be all good if she's refusing to see you again."

"I don't know what to tell you. Other than she got too much sun the last time we were together, she seemed okay. I always send her home with my driver, so if anything happened between the time she left my place and made it home, then I have to ask my driver."

"Ask him, then call me back on my cell."

Marcus hung up and checked the coffeemaker. It'd completed its brewing cycle and he reached for two cups with matching saucers. He filled the cups and added a teaspoon of sugar to each. Balancing the cups, he set one down in front of Enid, and then sat down next to her.

His left hand went to her neck, gently kneading the muscles as she sipped her coffee. "You're going to have to stop fighting me in bed, sweetheart."

Enid affected an expression of unadulterated innocence. "What are you talking about?"

"You know exactly what I'm talking about, beautiful."

"I thought you liked it when I'm aggressive."

"I don't mind you being aggressive. What I can't deal with is you trying to control me in bed. We're partners not combatants." He took a swallow of the fresh brew.

Leaning to her right, Enid rested her head on Marcus's shoulder, kissing the warm flesh. "I'm sorry, darling."

He breathed a kiss in her hair. "And I'm sorry I marked you."

A mysterious smile touched her mouth and found its way up to her eyes. "I really don't mind you biting me because every time I see them I get excited all over again."

Marcus chuckled. "You're a freak, Enid."

"I know. And you love this freak, don't you?"

"Of course I do." He traced the outline of her ear with his tongue. "Are you ready to go back to bed?"

Enid flashed an attractive moue. "Now who's a freak?"

Pushing back his chair, he came to his feet. Waiting until she put down her coffee cup, he pulled back her chair and picked her up. "You're the freak and I'm the addict." She pushed the tip of her tongue into his ear, causing him to stumble. "Keep that up and I'll have you on the table."

Enid tightened her hold on his neck and laughed until she found herself on her back, Marcus inside her, and she arching to meet his strong thrusts.

Her passion rose quickly and she forgot everything that existed except the man whose lovemaking never failed to take her to heaven and back with an ecstasy that lingered long after he withdrew from her body.

CHAPTER 64

Bright sunlight came through the walls of glass in the triplex, rush-hour traffic had come to a complete stop along FDR Drive because of a three-car fender bender, barges moved slowly on the East River, their pilots ever aware of the river's dangerous currents, and workers were streaming into office buildings on the last day of the workweek, when Faye woke up.

She was alone in the king-size bed, but when she turned over she realized she wasn't the only one in the room. Bart sat in a club chair reading the *Wall Street Journal*. Resting her head on a folded arm, she stared at the man with whom she'd shared a bed but hadn't made love. Aside from his mussed hair, he looked different, and she realized it was the first time she hadn't seen him clean shaven. This morning he wore a pair of khakis, a black T-shirt and black running shoes.

"So, Sleeping Beauty finally woke up," he drawled with a hint of laughter in his voice. "And she did so without a prince waking her."

Smiling, Faye watched him fold the paper and place it

on a rosewood table next to the chair. "Are you that prince you speak of?"

Rising from the chair and closing the distance between them, Bart sat down on the bed. Leaning over, he pressed a kiss to Faye's forehead. "Do you want me to be your prince?"

Gold and gray eyes regarded each other as the seconds ticked. "Aren't you, Bart?" Faye asked softly.

"I may be a lot of things, but presumptuous I'm not. I would never presume to think or feel for you."

Sitting up and pulling the hem of the sheet over her chest, Faye supported her back against the black leather headboard. "You want to know what I feel for you." The statement came out like a question. Bart inclined his head, his gaze fusing with hers. "I like you," she admitted, deciding it would be best if she was completely honest with him.

"If I hadn't signed on with Pleasure Seekers I never would've given you a passing glance or a second thought. First, because I would've felt that you were too old for me, and second because I've never found myself attracted to white men." His eyes widened. "White people don't have the monopoly on racism and bigotry, and I'm not going to apologize for the way I felt."

"Felt or feel?"

"Felt, Bart. After being with you I'm not going to change my racial preference from black to white, but I do see things differently now. I've always dated black men. Some were good and some not so good. And when I married Dr. Norman Burgess I believed I'd gotten one of the best. The trouble was, women loved Norman and he loved them back.

"I came home one afternoon and found him in my bed with another woman. I left and called him from the street, telling him that I was taking a walk and when I got back he and his whore had better be gone or the bedroom would become a crime scene."

"Did he leave?"

"Yes. The next time he came back it was to get his clothes. We had a quickie divorce and I accepted the apartment in lieu of alimony. Thankfully there were no children, so we had a clean break."

Resting a hand alongside her cheek, Bart closed his eyes. "A man would be a fool to cheat on you."

Faye laughed softly. "You are so good for a woman's ego, Bart Houghton."

He dropped his hand. "I'm not in this to boost your ego."

She met his challenging stare with one of her own. "Now that we're into baring our souls, why don't you tell me why you're truly in this. Why you paid Enid Richards a million dollars for me to jaunt around the world with you. Why you'd rather see me prance around in La Perla lingerie than Victoria's Secret."

Bart's face was a mask of stone. Faye was asking questions, questions he couldn't answer because he didn't have the answers. He knew he'd given her things, material things, but not himself. He'd feared giving her all of Bart because he wasn't prepared for her rejection.

When he'd told Enid he wanted to contract for Faye, it was to assuage his curiosity as to why he'd found himself so drawn to her. He'd thought himself a corporate raider looking to take over a smaller company to make it fit into his larger schematic. However, Faye did not play the game as he'd expected her to play.

She'd signed on with Pleasure Seekers to make money; her desire to set up her own business had taken a back seat to reversing her brother's rape conviction.

"I'm in it because I like you, Faye. Why does there have to be more? Would it make it easier for you if I had an ulterior motive?"

She closed her eyes and chuckled softly. When she opened them she saw Bart staring at her with an expression that registered bewilderment. "You like me," she said in a voice so low he had to strain to hear. "What would you do if you were in love with me?"

Bart wanted to tell her that he would relate to her in the same manner because he *was* in love with her. Moving off the bed, he stood over her, hands pushed deep into the pockets of his slacks. "We're scheduled to lift off from the heliport around one. I suggest you pack enough for four days. I'll see you downstairs for breakfast." Turning on his heel he walked out of the bedroom.

Faye sat staring at the space where Bart had been, berating herself for not enjoying what he'd so freely offered. Most women would've clawed her eyes out to live in a triplex penthouse, wear designer clothes and shoes, and priceless jewelry. She had access to Madame Fontaine, where there was a waiting list and an annual fee of twenty-five thousand for membership, and that did not include the exaggerated rates for their spa packages.

She'd found herself caught up in a world of unlimited luxuries she'd never known and would not have known if it hadn't been for Bartholomew Houghton, a man who claimed he *liked* her. He *liked* her, and she had fallen in love with him.

CHAPTER 65

Ilene sat up in bed, her back supported by several pillows, sipping freshly squeezed orange juice while watching *The View*. "Y'all are a bunch of crazy women," she said to the television screen.

Since Enid had sanctioned her, she'd spent most nights at home. Not used to the inactivity, she stayed up late watching television and woke up even later. Most days she didn't get out of bed until after one. Although she wasn't making any money as a social companion, she also wasn't spending any. Whenever she went out to party with the few people she could still call friends, there were times when she picked up the tab for their food and drinks.

There was a time when money had meant nothing to Ilene. She'd make it and spend it without a care. Whenever her mother, brother or sister called she'd reach for her check-book and send them whatever they'd asked for. After all, they were family, and no matter what, family would always be there when she needed them—or so she'd believed.

When she'd finally returned to the States after a thirteen-year absence, she found her mother living in a homeless shelter instead of the house she claimed she'd bought with the money Ilene had been sending her.

Her sister, the marrying fool she was, picked up men indiscriminately, and had a couple of babies from each. Whenever she bragged that she was the sister of supermodel Ilene Fairchild they proposed marriage, believing they were moving up because of their wife's sister.

Ilene loathed thinking of her brother, who'd become his father's clone. Not only did they look alike, but they also treated their wives and children the same. She didn't know why they found it so difficult to take care of their children. Whenever her brother met a new woman he left his wife. But whenever the relationship soured he moved back. This time her sister-in-law wasn't having it, slapping his lazy ass with a restraining order while suing him for delinquent child support payments.

She was only thirty and at times felt sixty. It was as if she'd lived two lifetimes simultaneously. She'd begun working at fifteen and hadn't stopped. It was time she let someone take care of her, and in return she would play house. She'd cook, clean and give a man what he needed to make him feel like a real *man*. And she wanted a baby, a son or daughter she would raise differently than she'd been raised.

The telephone on the bedside table rang. Leaning over, Ilene peered at the display. It read Unavailable. She waited for another ring, then picked up the cordless instrument.

"Hello."

"Hello, Ilene."

Ilene set down her glass, smiling. The call hadn't come from Astrid Marti, but the person on the other end of the line ran a close second in importance. "Amelia. How are you?"

"I'm well, Ilene. I'm calling you because of what you said before you left."

"What's that?"

"You said you wanted financial security, and I can give it to you."

All of her senses on full alert, Ilene sat up straighter. What was the woman talking about? Amelia had been good to pass the time with, but she would never consider her as a life partner. Ilene Fairchild was bisexual, not a lesbian. But she wouldn't blow Amelia off until she heard what she was offering.

"How, Amelia?"

"I own half the island and the hotel, and I'm willing to give you half my share if you come live with me. I've had my lawyer draw up the papers. He can fax them to you so you can look them over."

Ilene swallowed a laugh when she bit down on her lower lip. Amelia Wells was offering more than any man had—and that included the Belgian industrialist who'd taken her in as his ward the year she turned seventeen.

"How much are you worth?"

"Approximately twenty-two million in American dollars. And don't forget I'm my father's only heir."

"Look, Amelia, it wouldn't work. I want a baby, and you can't give me one."

"Please don't say it won't work until you see the agreement. There is a provision set aside for *our* children."

Ilene grabbed her forehead, unable to believe what Amelia was telling her. "I can't—"

"Don't say anything until you read the agreement. Do you have access to a fax machine?"

"No."

"Give me your address and I'll have a courier deliver the documents to you. Read it, have your lawyer look it over, then call me."

Ilene knew Amelia would call and haunt her unless she agreed to look at what she was proposing. "Okay, Amelia." She gave her the address and rang off.

"Ain't that a bitch," she whispered. A woman was offering her what she hadn't been able to get from a man. She wouldn't write the beautiful island woman off until she saw the agreement.

CHAPTER 66

Faye survived her second helicopter ride without the anxiety she'd experienced the first time she'd boarded the aircraft. She'd spent the ride to Southampton staring out the window at the passing landscape while Bart sent and received e-mail and text messages on his BlackBerry. He worked even when he wasn't at his office.

The pilot set down in an open field at the same time Giuseppe drove up in the Maybach. The driver greeted Bart with a nod and Faye with a warm smile as he opened the rear door.

Bart slipped onto the back seat beside Faye and stored the BlackBerry in a wood-grain compartment. "Don't you need it?" she asked when he draped an arm over the back of her headrest.

He smiled at her. "No. I have a computer at the house, and if someone sends me a message I get it on the Black-Berry and the desktop."

"Are you working or are you on vacation?"

"I think of it as a working vacation. I will be on vacation when we go to Europe. We've been invited to a dinner party given by one of our neighbors tonight. Do you want to go or stay home?"

Faye noticed he'd used the pronouns *we* and *our* instead of *I*. She lifted her shoulders under a soft pink tank top trimmed in lace. "We can go, but if it's bootleg then we'll bounce."

Throwing back his head, Bart laughed loudly. His arm slipped to Faye's shoulders, pulling her close. He could always rely on her to make him laugh. It was a gentle reminder that he should enjoy life and the fruits of his labor.

"I'll take that."

Bart took Faye's overnight bag from Giuseppe's grasp. His free hand went to the small of her back as he led her into the house and up the staircase in the opposite direction from the suite where she'd stayed during her first trip to Southampton. He felt her go stiff against his hand.

"You can stop holding your breath now. Your folks will stay in your room when they come tomorrow and you'll have the one next to mine."

She let out her breath. "Thank you, Bart."

"You're welcome, Faye," he said in a high-pitched feminine voice.

"Keep it up."

"And you'll do what?"

She rolled her eyes at him. "You don't want to know."

They walked into a sun-filled room decorated in shades of blue and white. Faye was drawn to a window seat with recessed lighting. She spun around as she'd done as a little girl. "I love it."

Bart set her bag down next to the closet, turned and extended his arms. "Come here." Faye raced across the space and jumped into his arms. Bart swung her around and around as objects in the room whizzed by in front of her eyes.

"Please stop!"

He continued spinning her around. "What if I don't want to stop? What if I don't want what we have to ever stop?"

Burying her face against the side of his neck, Faye closed her eyes. "It doesn't have to stop, Bart."

He stopped abruptly. "What did you say?" His voice had dropped to a breathless whisper.

Easing back, she saw his startled expression. "I said it doesn't have to stop. Not if you don't want it to."

Bart lowered Faye slowly to her feet, his gaze fusing with hers. He'd waited, dreamed of this moment from the first time he saw Faye, yet he couldn't believe she was ready to come to him of her own accord.

"I don't want it to ever stop."

Faye's hands, resting on his chest, moved down and gathered fabric as she sought the warmth of his flesh under the T-shirt. Her fingers grazed his flat belly, muscles and sinew on his back.

Bart felt her heat, inhaled her scent and he was lost, lost in the delicate femininity of a woman with skin the color of caramelized sugar, a woman with short gold hair that felt like whorls of velvet, a woman with brilliant eyes that sparkled like polished citrines.

Bending slightly, he swept her weightlessly into his arms and carried her through a connecting door to his suite. Taking long strides, he placed her on the bed before closing and locking the doors. He'd wanted to make love with Faye the night before when there was just the two of them in the penthouse, but his employees knew never to enter his private space without permission.

Returning to the bed, he stood over Faye. She looked so delicate, vulnerable. He'd felt her pain when she told him of her failed marriage; he'd also felt her pain and frustration when she related the details of her brother's arrest, incarceration and subsequent break with her father. The men she loved had hurt her—deeply. And he loved her, praying he wouldn't hurt her, too.

He sat down, leaned over and brushed his mouth over hers. He placed tender kisses at the corners of her mouth before increasing the pressure to take full possession of her soft, full lips.

Faye was drugged by Bart's clean and masculine scent, the warmth of his mouth on hers, the invisible pull that made her aware of him as a man, a man she wanted, a man she needed. His hands searched under her top and closed over her breasts, sending tremors of uncontrollable desire throughout her body. A shiver of awareness thrummed between her thighs. She was ready, ready for Bart, ready for whatever the future held for them.

CHAPTER 67

Bart forced himself to go slow when a rush of desire had him close to exploding. He opened a drawer in the table next to the bed and removed a condom, placing it on the pillow beside Faye's head.

Faye glanced at the foil packet. She closed her eyes and let her senses take over as Bart removed her shoes, slacks and top at an agonizingly slow pace that set her teeth on edge. She let out a sigh of relief once he'd relieved her of her bra and panties. It was about to begin.

Bart couldn't pull his gaze away from Faye's nude body as he stripped off his clothes. He was so in awe of her beauty, the perfection of her body that he hadn't realized his hands were trembling uncontrollably until he attempted to put on the latex sheath. He wanted their first time together to be extraordinary; he wanted to bring Faye as much pleasure as he was certain she would offer him.

The side of the mattress dipped when he moved over her and supported his weight on his forearms. Cradling her face between his hands, Bart's gaze searched her face, reaching into her thoughts.

"This is not going to be a hit it and quit it, Faye. I want

you now, I'll want you tomorrow, and every day there-after. And what we're about to share has nothing to do with..." His words trailed off.

"With you being my client," she said, completing his statement.

He nodded. "It's just us, you and me." Desire darkened his eyes as he dipped his head and kissed her with all of the tenderness and passion he could summon from his heart. Her slender arms circled his neck, and Bartholomew Houghton lost himself and his heart to a woman with the power to make him forget his past and move forward to love again—unconditionally.

His rapacious tongue charted a sensual path from her mouth to her scented throat, shoulders and breasts. He lingered at her breasts, suckling until she arched off the bed. Continuing his downward exploration, he planned to taste every inch of her.

She went still, muscles tensing when his breath swept over the soft down covering her mound. Attuned to her every response, he pressed kisses to her inner thighs. What he'd intended to do to her using his mouth would come another time because he wanted Faye to feel comfortable and trust him to bring her ultimate pleasure.

Faye was filled with strange sensations that upset her balance. The hot ache between her legs increased until she felt as if she'd been immersed in an inferno from which there was no escape. Heated blood surged from her head, to her fingertips, and to her toes.

She knew from the uneven rhythm of her breathing, the

runaway beating of her heart, and the soft flutters that had yielded to contractions that she was going to climax.

"Bart!" His name, torn from the back of her throat, faded away to a lingering sigh as her head thrashed on the pillow.

Bart moved up her trembling limbs and positioned himself between her legs. A sensual groan came from deep within his chest as he pushed into her body. Her hot, tight flesh closed around him and within seconds her heat was transferred to him.

Together, they found a rhythm that quickened, slowed, then increased as shivers of giddy desire and ecstasy became explosive currents that shook them from head to toe as they climaxed simultaneously.

Faye looped her arms under Bart's shoulders and held on to him as if her next breath depended on him for her continued existence. Tears of joy leaked beneath her tightly closed eyes as she savored the aftermath of long-forgotten orgasms. She'd missed so much since she'd ended her marriage.

As Bart smiled, the fingers of his right hand traced the curve of Faye's breasts, waist and hips. It was as if he couldn't stop touching and kissing her. Pressing his mouth to her ear he whispered, "You were incredible."

Faye chuckled softly. "You weren't so bad yourself."

Raising his head, he gave her a direct stare. "Does that mean I can expect seconds?"

She wrinkled her short nose. "I'll think about it."

Bart tickled her ribs and she dissolved into a paroxysm of giggles. They rolled around and around on the large bed, their antics coming to an abrupt halt when Faye nearly fell off. Bart caught her upper arm, holding her fast before she hit the floor.

His quick action sobered them both. Pulling her up to sit on his lap, he wrapped his arms around her waist. "I don't know what I'd do if something happened to you."

Bart's passionate admission echoed Faye's thoughts. She rested her head on his chest, her heart filled with a feeling she'd thought she would never experience again. She'd fallen in love with Bart Houghton.

CHAPTER 68

Faye stood on the wraparound porch watching her parents alight from the Maybach. Bart greeted her father with a handshake and her mother with a kiss on the cheek. Wrapping her arms around her body, she expelled a long sigh, astonished at the sense of fulfillment she felt at that moment.

Last night, Bart had called his neighbor, offering his regrets in not attending her dinner party, opting instead to stay at home. Mrs. Llewellyn had prepared a sumptuous dinner of broiled lamb rib chops, green pea fritters with a garlic cream sauce and pasta with Parmesan and Gruyère.

Hand in hand, they'd walked the beach for several miles, retraced their steps, then sat on the sand in silence, watching a magnificent sunset. Her vow to not become intimately involved with her client was shattered the first time they'd made love, and forgotten completely when they made love a second time.

Shirley Ogden spied her daughter as she came off the porch to meet her. "How are you?"

Faye pulled Shirley into a close embrace. "I'm wonderful, Mama. How was the drive?"

"It took a lot longer than I'd expected." She gave Faye a critical look. "There's something different about you."

"What are you talking about?"

"You look different."

"I've decided to let my hair grow out a little," Faye said, running a hand over her hair.

"No, Faye Anne. It's not your hair. It's your face. You're glowing."

"If I'm glowing it's because I'm completely relaxed." She waved a hand. "Look at this place. There's no hustle, bustle or traffic jams. Instead of walking out of my apartment building and getting bombarded with fumes from automobile exhaust, it's the ocean."

Shirley glanced briefly over her shoulder to see her husband and Bart Houghton pantomiming golf swings. Looping her arm through Faye's, she stared at her. "He makes you happy, doesn't he?"

Faye kept her features deceptively composed. "Yes, he does, Mama. Being with Bart makes me very, very happy. Happier than I've been in years."

Shirley clamped her jaw tight and stared over Faye's shoulder. "I want you to be careful, baby girl."

"I don't understand you, Mama. I meet a man who makes me happy and you tell me to be careful."

Shirley met her penetrating gaze. "Just be careful," she repeated in a low tone with Bart and Craig's approach.

Bart hadn't noticed Faye's strained expression when he said, "Faye, please show your mother to her room where she may want to relax or freshen up while Craig and I go into town to pick up a couple of cases of beer."

She flashed a hollow smile. "Sure. Come on, Mama."

Shirley followed Faye into the house, staring up at a two-story great room. "This place would swallow our house."

"I believe it measures about six thousand square feet."

"Why one person needs a house this big astounds me."

Faye led her mother up the staircase. "He's not the only one who lives here. His housekeeper's son stays here year-round."

"That's only two people. I suppose rich people have to do something with their money."

Faye decided it was not the time to try and convince her mother that whatever motivated Bart to purchase a vacation home with enough square footage for a family of six to move around comfortably without bumping into one another wasn't so critical that it should elicit a debate. And she wondered how Shirley would react to his Manhattan address, where his penthouse was made up of the three top floors of the Olympic Towers.

"You and Daddy are in here," she said, walking into the suite. Giuseppe had brought up their overnight bags.

Shirley moved past the utility kitchen and into the living/dining room. "It's beautiful."

"The bathroom is to your left just outside the bedroom. I'll leave you to get settled in while I go down and find out what Mrs. Llewellyn has planned for dinner."

"Who's Mrs. Llewellyn?" Shirley asked.

"She's the cook and also the housekeeper."

Shirley glanced at the watch on her wrist. "What time is dinner?"

Faye looked at her own watch. It was after two. "We'll probably eat around six. Why?"

"That's good, because I want to sit out and relax a while."

"I'll see you downstairs."

Closing the door, Faye walked the length of the hallway, unable to stop thinking about her mother's baseless warning. There was no need for her to be careful because she had no intention of ever letting Bart know the depth of her feelings for him; and if he wanted more, then she would be forced to remind him of their business arrangement: she was a social companion and he was her client.

CHAPTER 69

Enid sat with Astrid, going over a checklist of guests for an upcoming political fund-raiser. She'd sent out invitations to all the clients she knew whose party affiliation matched that of the judge running for reelection.

"Are all of my exotic jewels attending?" she asked Astrid.

The booker scanned the list. "Yes. Alana Gardner replied affirmative, and so did Ilene Fairchild. Bartholomew declined because of a prior engagement but wants Faye Ogden to give the judge his contribution."

Enid smiled. "Good. Please set it up so they go in the same car. And I also want Tricia, Heather and Kristin to arrive together." She paused as Astrid jotted down the instructions in her notebook. "Bettina will travel with Sonya—no, not Sonya. She's a little too temperamental to be with Bettina for more than twenty minutes. Have Sonya go with Lareina."

Lareina was a stunning young Russian woman with a sullen attitude that had men bending over backward to make her laugh. And when she did they were more than willing to shower her with expensive gifts that made her laugh even more because she viewed her middle-aged clients as little boys who craved attention and instant gratification.

Astrid stopped writing and glanced up at Enid. "Is there anything else?"

Enid's left hand went to the back of her neck. The tightness had returned. "I believe that's it," she said as she continued to massage her neck and shoulders.

Waiting until Astrid left her office, she walked into her sanctuary and sat down, lifting her feet to the footstool. The Zen fountain, prerecorded chanting and the lighted candles failed to ease her anxiety.

Although the bottom line for Pleasure Seekers had exceeded her expectations, a sixth sense told Enid that it wasn't going to continue. She'd likened it to Wall Street when the index climbed steadily, then without warning bottomed out, resulting in massive losses for investors.

Ilene's two-week sanction had become one because an African prince had requested the tall, beautiful black woman with the long hair. Prince Mahmoud had given Astrid a gift of an enormous African amethyst pendant framed with two carats of flawless pink diamonds after she'd arranged for Ilene to meet him in Washington, D.C., for a reception at his country's embassy.

A call from Derrick Warren's driver yielded nothing as to Alana's decision not to see Derrick again, and it wasn't Enid's style to cross-examine her social companions. She refused to dwell on it because all of her exotic jewels were working.

CHAPTER 70

Alana sat on the side of the bathtub, unable to pull her gaze away from the wand between her fingers. What she'd suspected for more than a week had been confirmed.

She *was* pregnant! Whomever she'd slept with had picked her most fertile time of the month.

Twin emotions warred within her. She'd always wanted a baby, but not without being married. There was no way she wanted to mirror her mother's life—having babies without the benefit of a husband. But her dilemma was different from Melanie's because her mother knew the father of her children. She didn't.

"Can I do this?" she whispered. Could she bear a child not knowing who'd fathered it? There was no doubt she could afford to raise it alone, but did she really want to become a single mother?

The questions attacked her relentlessly, breaking down the barrier she'd erected after she'd spoken to the HIV counselor who'd called to tell her all her tests had come back negative.

Placing the wand on a table cradling a live fern, she

closed her eyes. *I can do this. I really can do this by myself,* she told herself over and over until she believed she could.

Pushing to her feet, she discarded the results of the pregnancy test and washed her hands. She walked out of the bathroom and into her bedroom, her mind awash with what she wanted and needed to do. She stared at the clock on the bedside table; there was enough time for her to call her gynecologist's office before it closed.

She made an appointment for Monday evening, and as she ended the call a beep came through the earpiece. After glancing at the display, she activated the call-waiting feature.

"What's up, Taylor?" Her brother never called just to say hello or see how she was doing. She supposed she was lucky he called at all.

"Mom had an accident."

"No!" she screamed.

"Don't lose it, Alana. She slipped off the porch and bruised her coccyx."

Alana took deep breaths to slow down her runaway heartbeat. "Did you take her to the doctor?"

"Yes."

"What did he say?"

"She's going to be sore for a while."

"Where the hell was the home health aide, Taylor?" She was paying an agency for round-the-clock nursing care.

"She'd gone into the house to turn off the stove. When she came back she found Mom at the bottom of the stairs. Sophia decided Mom should stay with us until she's better."

Alana wanted to ask her brother why he had to wait

for his mother to fall before his wife would permit her mother-in-law to stay with her. But she knew this was not the time to fight with him about their mother's well-being.

"Call the agency and tell them not to send anyone until I talk to them."

"What do you have in mind, baby sis?"

She closed her eyes. It'd been a long time since either of her brothers had referred to her as their baby sister. She opened her eyes, smiling. "I'm coming up at the end of next week." She would let Taylor know he was going to become an uncle and the plans she'd made for their mother. "I'll talk to you then. And thanks, Taylor, for letting me know about Mom."

There was a beat of silence. "No problem."

Alana ended the call and breathed out through her mouth. She would fix something substantial for breakfast before she went through her closet to find something to wear later that evening.

Astrid had called to say that she, Faye and Ilene would travel together to a fund-raiser in Scarsdale, an affluent community in New York's Westchester County.

CHAPTER 71

Reaching for a tissue, Faye blotted at the moisturizer on her forehead; she repeated the action, the pile of tissues mounting, until her face shimmered. The rich crème, concocted by Madame Fontaine herself and selling at three hundred dollars an ounce, yielded extraordinary results.

Leaning forward on the bench seat to the vanity, she concentrated intently as she made up her face with a sheer foundation that blended perfectly with her skin tone. She applied liner, contrasting shadows and a coat of mascara to her upper and lower lashes. A light dusting of face powder and a coat of magenta-tinged lipstick completed her makeup regimen.

She was scheduled to attend the fund-raiser without Bart because he'd left New York two days before for a business trip and a conference of the American Institute of Architects. He was expected to spend a week in Los Angeles before returning to New York at the end of the following week.

Giuseppe had remained at the penthouse while Mrs. Llewellyn elected to stay on Long Island with her grandson, and Faye decided she would spend the coming week at her own apartment. She'd only come back to the penthouse because Astrid had informed her that a driver would pick her up at the Olympic Towers high-rise.

She thought she would be bored having so much time on her hands, but she'd managed to keep busy cleaning her own apartment and putting together a rough draft for her marketing company.

She'd also written several letters to her brother. Within days of his incarceration, Craig Geoffrey Ogden Jr. had notified officials at the Auburn Correctional Facility that he wouldn't accept telephone calls or visitors. The exception was legal counsel.

This news had devastated the elder Ogdens, who eventually realized their son's shame surpassed his need for family contact. There wasn't a week when Shirley did not get a letter from him. He never asked for anything, only their prayers. Faye was certain her latest letter would lift him from his melancholy, because someone from Rooney Turner's office had informed her that several lawyers at the firm had contacted the Queens County's D.A.'s office on CJ's behalf.

A clock chimed the hour. She was scheduled to meet a driver within fifteen minutes in front of the building. When Astrid called to let her know she would be going to Scarsdale with Alana and Ilene she'd decided to spend the night with her friend.

Ilene moved over on the leather seat when Faye got into the limousine. "You look fabulous!"

Faye gave the supermodel a warm smile. "Thank you. So do you."

Ilene brushed back several strands of hair from her cheek. "*Merci.*"

Leaning around Ilene, Faye smiled at Alana. "Hey, girlfriend."

"Hey, yourself. Ilene's right. You look hot." Alana smiled, her curly hair framing her face in sensual disarray.

It'd taken Faye hours before she decided on a two-piece ensemble with a black silk, off-the-shoulder, long-sleeve blouse with a matching wrap skirt that rode low on her hips; she'd offset the austere color with a cushion-cut candy-pink tourmaline pendant surrounded by diamonds and tourmaline briolette. The magnificent stones were suspended from a chain made of diamond daises.

Ilene reached over and cradled the pendant on her palm. "This looks like a Janet Deleuse creation."

"It is," Faye confirmed. She wouldn't have known the designer's name if it hadn't been stamped on the leather case. It wasn't one of the pieces she'd found in the drawer in the walk-in closet but on the pillow next to hers when she awoke the morning Bart left before dawn to catch a flight to L.A. The attached note read: *Think of me until we're together again.*

She wanted to tell Bart that she could only think of him, that he'd changed her and her world. They'd only made love twice, and she relived the encounters over and over in her dreams and during her waking hours.

"Ladies, please avail yourselves of the bar and refrigerator," the driver announced before he pushed a button and closed the security panel.

Ilene opened the bar, Alana the refrigerator and Faye turned to a radio station blaring a Nelly hit. Ilene uncorked a split of champagne while Faye and Alana opted for water. They were careful not to spill caviar and smoked oysters in tiny tins on their evening wear as the driver maneuvered in a northerly direction.

CHAPTER 72

The fund-raiser was held on the estate of the sister of a state appellate judge up for reelection. The three-acre property was ablaze with lights when the chauffeur assisted Faye, Alana and Ilene from the limousine. The affair was buffet style in a large ballroom with French doors that let the outdoors in. A band of eight played continuously as men in black-tie mingled freely with women in haute couture and priceless gems.

They were greeted by their hostess, and then introduced to the guest of honor. Judge Leighton thanked Faye profusely when she handed him the envelope Bart had given her as a donation for his reelection campaign war chest.

Enid would've been proud of her exotic jewels as they circulated comfortably with the two hundred in attendance, including six other social companions. The women acknowledged one another with imperceptible nods as they charmed the men and garnered hostile stares from the women.

Alana tapped Faye's shoulder. "I don't know about you, but I'm ready to get out of here."

"What time is it?" Faye whispered.

"It's close to midnight."

"Get Ilene and I'll meet you by the car."

Alana leaned in close to Ilene who had enthralled a small group of men, and whispered in her ear. Ilene gave each man a dramatic air kiss then strutted away with her signature walk that left them with their mouths open.

"I ate too much," Alana said when they were seated in the back of the limousine.

"I drank much too much champagne," Ilene admitted.

"I did both," Faye confessed.

Alana slipped off her shoes. "Ilene, Faye's spending the night at my place. You're welcome to join us."

Seemingly surprised by the offer, Ilene said quickly, "Thanks for asking." She grimaced. "I'm sorry, but I'm going to have to take a rain check. I don't have a change of clothes."

"Not to worry," Alana said. "I'll find something in my closet for you." She folded her hands on her hips when Ilene glared at her. "There's no need to look at me like that, Miss Thang. I have a T-shirt and shorts in your size I never got to give my secretary because she went to Trinidad for Carnival, met a man and never came back." Slumping down in the leather seat, she closed her eyes. "I'm going to take a nap. Wake me when we get home."

Alana, Ilene, sans shoes, and Faye, carrying her shoes and overnight bag, entered the elevator, giggling like adolescent girls as the car rose swiftly. They'd all fallen asleep during the return ride to Manhattan.

Their giggles lowered considerably as they made their way down the carpeted hallway. Reaching into her bugle-beaded evening purse, Alana removed a key and unlocked the door to her apartment. Light from a Tiffany-style ceiling fixture cast a soft glow throughout the expansive entry that opened out to a sunken living room.

"This is nice," Ilene crooned as she walked into the living room. "Talk about a room with a view. When I look out the windows in my apartment, all I see are rooftops, while you have Central Park."

Alana placed her shoes in the entryway closet before she joined Ilene in the living room. She lit several candles on the coffee table and another half dozen lining a matching mahogany pedestal table doubling as a credenza.

"I love this apartment," Faye said. "If you ladies will excuse me, I'm going to take a quick shower and change into something more comfortable."

Alana turned and smiled at Ilene. "Let me get you something to sleep in. I hope you don't mind a T-shirt."

"Either it's the T-shirt or y'all have to see me ass naked," Ilene quipped.

"T-shirt alert!" Faye and Alana chorused.

"Faye, why don't you use the bathroom in my room while Ilene uses the one out here," Alana suggested. "Ilene, I'll get you a towel, facecloth and a toothbrush."

Ilene flashed a dimpled smile. "Do you have something I can use to clean the makeup off my face?"

"I do," Faye offered. She opened her bag and took out a cosmetics case filled with tubes, tiny jars and plastic bottles filled with creams and lotions. She handed Ilene a sample bottle of makeup remover. "You can keep it."

Holding the bottle closer to a flickering candle, she read the label. "Who gave you this?"

Faye looked perplexed. "I got it at Madame Fontaine."

"You go to Madame Fontaine?"

"Yes, she does." Alana had answered for Faye. "Compliments of Bartholomew Houghton." She pretended she didn't see Faye roll her eyes at her. "The only reason I got through the front door was because Faye put me down as her guest."

"Is it everything people say it is?" Ilene asked. She'd tried, unsuccessfully, to get past the receptionist at the exclusive spa since she'd returned from Europe but to no avail. Not even her name was enough to permit her access.

"It's a bit overpriced but worth every penny," Faye admitted.

"Madame's twenty-five-thousand-a-year membership fee would pay the maintenance on my co-op for a year and leave me enough for holiday tips for my building's doormen and maintenance staff."

"I hear you," Alana concurred. "But what's twenty-five thousand a year to a billionaire?"

Ilene sucked her teeth loudly. "My advice, Faye, is to get all that you can out of him now, because I lived with a man for eleven years who was a multimillionaire, but in the end I got nada. He gave me whatever I wanted when he was alive, but when he died his heirs tossed me out of his château like I was last week's bathwater."

"How old were you when you went to live with him?" Faye asked.

"I'd just turned seventeen."

Alana's mouth curved into an unconscious smile. She had Ilene Fairchild, a legendary supermodel, standing in the middle of her living room, and she'd always been able to recognize opportunity when it presented itself.

"I'm writing a novel, and I've encountered the mother of all mothers writer's block. Would you mind if I use you as a character in my book? Of course, I'd change your name."

Ilene's dimples deepened like thumbprints in her satiny dark cheeks. "What do you want to know?"

"Anything you're willing to disclose."

"I'll dish after I take a shower and change into something more comfortable."

"Mind if I listen in?" Faye asked Ilene.

"Girl, please. There's nothing I'm going to say that hasn't been said or written about me in the tabloids from New York to Paris to Madrid." Unconsciously her brow furrowed. "I take that back. I do have a few secrets. But, girlfriends, you're in luck tonight, because Ilene Fairchild is about to spill her guts."

CHAPTER 73

Faye lay on the California-king bed with Alana, their backs supported by a mound of pillows against the headboard, while Ilene reclined at the foot of the bed with two pillows cradling her head. The women had showered, changed into loose-fitting clothes and climbed onto the bed like teenage girls at a sleepover.

"Aren't you going to use a tape recorder?" Ilene asked as she shifted into a more relaxed position.

"No," Alana replied. "I don't want to treat this like an interview. I just want you to tell me whatever you want."

Ilene stared at the two women she'd come to think of as girlfriends. She didn't know anything about them, but she was going to reveal things to them she'd never told anyone—and that included her mother and sister.

"I was born Ella Williams in a dusty town in the Mississippi Delta that was so small it barely made the map," she began, lapsing into the dialect she'd worked so hard to eradicate. "My father was a sharecropper and my mama cleaned the houses of white women. I have an older brother and younger sister who, if the truth be told, ain't shit. One day Daddy told us he was going North to get a job in Detroit making cars. He promised to send for us as soon as he saved enough money to buy a house. It never happened. His weekly letters dwindled to once a month for about a year before they stopped altogether.

"Meanwhile, Mama took in laundry to supplement what she earned as a maid. My life changed the year I turned fifteen. I'd stopped growing, my body was no longer flat as a board, and a man Mama did laundry for asked her to photograph me. I found out later that he'd sent my pictures to several New York modeling agencies who wanted to sign me, sight unseen. Sydney Chandler convinced Mama that I should quit school and go into modeling. She signed over guardianship of me to him, and the rest is history."

Faye's eyebrows shot up in surprise. "Your mama entrusted your well-being to a total stranger?"

Ilene stared up at the shadows on the bedroom ceiling. "He wasn't a stranger. Mama had pimped me out to her white lover." She forced all expression from her face when she told Alana and Faye how Sydney became her agent and took her virginity the night of her sixteenth birthday.

Clamping her jaw tight, she closed her eyes. "I hated everything about him—his sweaty palms, his smell, the way he jumped on and off me like an animal in heat. Just when I thought I couldn't take it any longer, a man thirty-five years my senior saved me from Sydney and myself."

"What happened next?" Faye asked quietly after an uncomfortable silence. "How did this man save you?"

Ilene opened her eyes and took a deep breath. "I didn't

know who he was at first, but I'd noticed that he kept turning up at parties and restaurants I'd been invited to. We were formally introduced at a dinner party held at a French diplomat's Paris pied-à-terre. Rene Carpentier was fifty-two, a self-made millionaire and married father of four who was rumored to have a fondness for black women. He admitted that he'd taken a liking to me and was willing to give me anything I wanted if I'd become his mistress."

Alana sat up straighter. "What did you tell him?"

Ilene smiled. "I told him I wanted my freedom. I wanted him to get rid of Sydney Chandler, whom I'd suspected was stealing from me. I later discovered he was taking thirty-five percent of my earnings instead of an agent's usual fifteen or twenty. Rene had one of his representatives make Sydney a deal he couldn't refuse. He signed me over to Rene, and I never heard from him again.

"Rene moved me into a restored château outside Brussels with a full staff to see to all my needs. I was tutored in French, taught table decorum, forms of address for government officials and he taught me how to use my body to bring him and myself maximum pleasure. He never took any of the money I earned from modeling, so I sent it to my mother with instructions that she buy herself a nice house.

"Rene was a very strange man. He claimed he enjoyed making love to me but preferred watching me with other women," Ilene continued, ignoring the soft gasps coming from Faye and Alana. "And I have to confess that I enjoyed being with them, too. They were gentle, affectionate and it was never a contest as to who would come out the winner. And, more importantly, there was never a question of getting pregnant whenever I slept with a woman."

"Do you still sleep with women?" Alana asked.

"I slept with one several weeks back. She was the first one in more than five years." Ilene paused. "I was with Rene for eleven years when he died from a blood clot in his lung. He was sixty-three. His family's executor came to the château and told me that I had to leave because Madame Carpentier was going to use it as her summer residence. I found myself homeless and nearly penniless. I'd sent all my earnings back to the States to my family, so all I was left with was a small fortune in jewelry Rene had given me.

"My modeling assignments had dwindled, and when I saw the new crop of models on the runways, all blond teenagers from Russia or the Eastern European countries, I knew my days were numbered. I sold my jewelry in Paris, paid for a ticket to come back home on one of the last flights on the Concorde and hooked up with a woman in the East Village I'd met in Europe.

"I went to Mississippi to see my mother, and instead of living in a house I found her in a women's shelter. She'd gotten hooked on crack and resorted to selling her body for her habit. When I saw her I didn't recognize her. She had full-blown AIDS and died two months after my return. I buried her, came back to New York, signed up to get my GED and spent every cent I had buying a co-op in Chelsea.

"I found a new agent who got me gigs in music videos, which led to the hookup with P.S., Inc. Believe me, working as a social companion is a lot easier than modeling, and the pay isn't too shabby, either."

"It's real good," Alana admitted, smiling, "but I don't know how much longer I'm going to work."

"Why, Lana?"

"I found out this morning that I'm pregnant."

"Pregnant? Are you sure?"

She nodded. "I'm a week late, and I'm never late. I also took a home pregnancy test and it came out positive. I have an appointment with my gynecologist on Monday."

Ilene sat up and placed a hand on Alana's ankle. "Are you going to keep it? If not then I'll take it."

Alana stared at Ilene as if she'd taken leave of her senses. "I have no intention of carrying a baby to term then give it up for adoption."

Faye hadn't realized how fast her heart was beating when she leaned over and hugged her best friend. "What *are* you going to do?"

CHAPTER 74

Alana returned Faye's hug. Earlier that morning she'd asked herself the same question: What was she going to do? Could she do this? Did she want to end up like her mother, depressed, plagued with episodic breaks in reality, wishing and praying for what'd been and will never be?

"I'm going to do exactly what I told you I'd do the day I got tested. I'm going to become a single mother."

Faye pulled back. "What about Calvin?"

Ilene scooted closer. "Who is Calvin?"

Settling back to her pillows, Alana stared at Faye, then Ilene. "He *was* my live-in boyfriend."

"Was?" Ilene questioned.

"He's in Europe touring with a band."

"How long has he been gone?"

"Two months."

Ilene's mouth formed a perfect O. "Am I to assume that you're not pregnant with your boyfriend's baby?"

"Your assumption is correct."

"Oh, shit," Ilene whispered.

"The fact is, I don't know whose baby it is." Alana was forthcoming when she related the events that led to her being date-raped. "The only thing that bothers me about having this baby is what will I tell my son or daughter when they ask about their father?"

Faye saw the pain in her friend's eyes. "Just tell your son or daughter the truth, Lana. There's no doubt they'll love you even more when you explain that even though they weren't conceived in love, you still wanted them."

"Hey, that's beautiful," Ilene crooned. "You sound like you really have your shit together, Faye."

Faye snorted delicately. "I'm glad you think so. I have a brother in jail on a bogus rape-and-assault conviction, my boss's ho is trying to take my job and I'm practically living with a man whom I find myself liking a little too much to be a client."

Alana gave Faye a sidelong glance. "You slept with him, didn't you? Yeah, you did. Didn't I tell you that you were going to become lovers?"

"Just don't let Enid know, because she'll sanction you like she did me," Ilene warned.

Alana shifted her attention from Faye to Ilene. "Why did she sanction you?"

"I slept with the daughter of the man who owns a private island in the Caribbean."

Alana frowned. "Was the man your client?"

"No. But Enid told me that the island is her client. And please don't ask me to explain that bullshit."

"I doubt if Enid would sanction me," Faye said in a quiet tone. "Bart Houghton paid a cool million to P.S., Inc. for my services for the summer."

Ilene flipped a fat plait over her shoulder. "Dam-n-n-n, Faye! Did he pay the million before or after you gave him some?"

A flash of humor crossed Faye's face. "Before."

"The man's got jungle fever," Alana crooned in a singsong.

"Jungle fever or not, it was the easiest half mil I'll ever make in my life."

Alana sobered. "Was he good, girlfriend? Did you make his eyes roll back in his head?"

"Did you have him speaking in tongues?" Ilene whispered like a coconspirator.

Faye laughed until tears rolled down her face. Reaching for a tissue from a box on the nightstand, she dabbed her eyes. "I thought he was good because it'd been so long since I'd had sex. But I knew better the second time. I have to confess that he turned me out."

"No-o-o!" Ilene and Alana chorused. Faye nodded, laughing at their shocked expressions.

Alana ran her fingers through her hair. "How does his lovemaking compare to Norman's?"

"He's more uninhibited."

"Oh, so there's a little freak in the white man," Alana teased.

"A lot of freak," Faye confirmed.

"Good for you," Ilene complimented. "There's nothing worse than a lover who doesn't know what to do, and you end up having to tell him everything you like."

"I like everything but the back-door action," Alana volunteered.

"I'm with you, Lana. That's where I draw the line."

"No comment," Ilene said smugly.

"No-o-o!" Faye and Alana said in unison.

The three women laughed, holding their sides, as tears rolled down their faces. They'd become teenagers once again, giggling at any and everything.

"I'm thinking of leaving P.S., Inc.," Ilene said once she'd recovered from her laughing fit. The other two sobered quickly.

Faye blew her nose in a tissue. "Why?"

Ilene recounted what Amelia Wells had offered her. As promised, Amelia had the agreement delivered and Ilene had taken it to a lawyer who lived in her building. Amelia had offered to deposit ten million dollars in a bank in her name with an irrevocable clause that stipulated all Ilene had to do was spend three years with Amelia and the money was hers free and clear. She'd also indicated that Ilene would be free to sleep with a man if she wanted a child or elect to be artificially inseminated.

Faye hadn't realized she'd bitten down on her lower lip until she tasted blood. "Damn! What happens if you don't make the three-year goal?"

"I get a million for each year. If I don't complete the third year, then the million will be prorated."

"Do you like her, Ilene?" Faye asked.

"Yes." Her smile told them everything.

"So, are you going to accept her offer?"

Ilene's expression stilled and grew serious. "Yes."

"Is it about the money?" Alana questioned.

"No. My relationships with men have always been filled with bullshit and disappointment. I've been used, abused, cheated and I'd take my own life rather than die in poverty."

Faye and Alana shared a knowing look. Ilene had become the darling of the fashion world at fifteen when she should've been hanging out with her friends at the mall. She'd lost her virginity to a man who had been nothing more than a pimp when he'd used her body and stolen her money. At seventeen she'd become a mistress to a man old enough to be her father, a man who'd introduced her to passion, bisexuality and, in the end, hadn't provided for her future.

Moving down to the foot of the bed, Faye held her arms out to Ilene. "Good luck."

Ilene hugged her back. "Thank you."

Alana repeated the gesture, also wishing her love and happiness.

The fragile bond that had begun hours before tightened until Enid's exotic jewels became girlfriends in every sense of the word.

CHAPTER 75

"I'm sorry to bother you, Alana, but there's a Mr. Warren in the reception area who would like a few moments of your time. If you're busy I can tell him to make an appointment."

Alana, swiveling in her chair, turned to see a summer intern poking her head through the slight opening in the door to her office. She appreciated the interruption because she'd proofread the same article three times in the past hour.

"No," she said much too quickly. "Give me five minutes, and then show him in."

The door closed behind the college student, and Alana stood up, came around her desk and made her way into a restroom across the hall. Why, she wondered, had Derrick come to her office? Had he uncovered why she had turned down his request to see him again? Did he know who'd raped her?

She washed her hands before splashing cold water on her face and patting it dry. Her gynecologist had confirmed her pregnancy, and ruling out any unforeseen complications, she hoped to deliver a healthy son or daughter the following spring.

Alana returned to her office to wait for Derrick. She

stood near the door, watching his approach. A smile softened her mouth. He appeared every inch the successful businessman in a lightweight summer suit in an attractive taupe, stark white custom-made shirt and a silk tie in contrasting colors of ecru and chocolate.

She extended her hands. "To what do I owe this most pleasant surprise?"

Derrick grasped her fingers, squeezing them gently. "I'm sorry to come unannounced, but I did want to surprise you. However, this won't take long."

"Come in, Derrick." Alana waited for him to enter her office, then closed the door. She gestured to a small table with two pull-up chairs in a corner. "Please, sit down."

Derrick pulled out a chair, waited for Alana to sit before he sat down opposite her. She looked different—younger, innocent. Her curly hair was held off her forehead with a black band, her scrubbed face shimmering with a glow that seemed to come from within. Her business attire was a pair of navy blue slacks and a classic white cotton blouse.

"Would you like coffee or tea, Derrick?"

He blinked as if coming out of a trance. He'd forgotten the sound of her beautifully modulated voice. Her voice was only one of many things that had drawn him to Alana Gardner.

"No, thank you. As I said before, I'm not going to take up too much of your time."

Alana clasped her hands in a prayerful gesture. "How can I help you?"

Leaning forward, Derrick met her questioning gaze.

"Why have you turned down my requests to see you? Did something happen on the Fourth?"

"Which question do you want me to answer first?"

A muscle twitched noticeably in his clenched jaw. "Start with the one about the Fourth."

"Why do you think something happened?" she asked, answering his question with one of her own.

He lowered his gaze. "Please answer my question, Alana."

She leaned forward. "Nothing happened, Derrick. I didn't feel too well when I got off the boat, so I went upstairs to lie down."

Derrick's head came up. "You don't remember Kris taking you upstairs?"

There was a pulse beat of silence. "No."

Her answer appeared to satisfy Derrick as he exhaled a breath. "Why won't you see me?"

"I'm pregnant, Derrick."

"You're married?"

"No."

"You're engaged?"

She nodded. "Yes." She hadn't lied because Calvin had promised to marry her.

The folds around Derrick's eyes seemed to shift like slow-moving lava when he wrinkled his nose. "He's a lucky man."

A sad smile touched the corners of her mouth. "I'd like to say that I'm a lucky woman."

"But you're not," Derrick said perceptively. "Lucky, that is."

"I don't want to talk about it."

Reaching across the table, he placed his hand over her clenched fists. "You can't or you don't want to?"

"Both."

Derrick tightened his grip over her knuckles. "Look, Alana, I don't want to get into your business, but if ever you need anything, and I do mean anything, then I want you to call me." He released her hands, reached into his jacket's breast pocket and placed a business card on the table.

Alana picked up the card. It was blank except for two handwritten telephone numbers. "Thank you."

"You're not going to call me."

"Is that a question or a statement, Derrick?"

"Both," he said.

Knowing that the life growing inside her was totally dependent on her for viability gave Alana a sense of strength and comfort she'd never felt at any other time in her life.

"I might need your assistance."

Derrick, with wide eyes, sat up straighter. "Talk to me."

"I want to sell my apartment."

"Where is it?"

"Midnineties and Central Park West."

Derrick whistled. "You're talking about prime real estate."

"I have a neighbor who wants it, but I'm reluctant to sell to him."

"Why?"

"He's offering less than what I actually paid for it."

"What are the specs and how much do you want?"

"I live in a doormanned building with a private health spa and large indoor pool. My apartment has one bedroom, one and a half baths, eat-in kitchen, sunken living room with views of the park, elevated dining area and spacious entryway. There are also plenty of closets."

"What do you want?"

"I'm looking for one point two million, but that's negotiable."

Derrick didn't react to her selling price. He didn't need another property. He'd purchased the house overlooking the Hudson River and owned one-third of the Tribeca loft with his cousins.

"Let me talk to my accountant then I'll let you know," he said, unwilling to commit until he conferred with Marcus Hampton. "Once you unload your apartment where are you moving?"

"I'm going back to New Paltz to live with my mother. She's not well, and hasn't been well for some time."

"What about your fiancé?"

"What about him, Derrick?"

"Is he going to live in New Paltz with you?"

Alana stared at her hands, the fringe of her lashes casting shadows on her high cheekbones. "No, he isn't."

"It's not his baby."

Her gaze came up to rest on Derrick's questioning eyes. "No."

The seconds ticked off as Alana and Derrick sat in silence. The record producer was no longer her client; however, he had ties to P.S., Inc., which meant whatever they discussed would never become fodder for the public or the media.

"Do you want a father for your child?" Derrick asked after a pregnant pause.

"The question should be do I need a father for my baby. The answer is no. Would I like a father for my baby, then the answer would be yes."

Derrick stared at the incredibly beautiful woman whose inner strength had overpowered the glimpses of vulnerability he'd seen during their previous encounters. There was so much he wanted to tell her, but then that would make him weak, vulnerable and put him at risk. He and his cousins were viewed as mavericks in the music industry, challenging the status quo and taking risks others thought were impossible, and all with incredible success. He'd made so much money the first year that he hadn't had time to count it. Once Marcus straightened out their tax problems and monitored their revenues and expenses, the Warrens still were unable to fathom that individually they were multimillionaires, and collectively their net worth approached billionaire status.

He shook his head slowly. "I don't want you to need me, Alana."

"What do you want?"

"I want you to want me," he said in a quiet voice.

Alana looked at Derrick with amused wonder. Did he think she didn't know about his sexual predilection? She'd been around enough men to know when one wanted to sleep with her. And the signals Derrick gave off indicated his interest in her wasn't of a physical nature.

"If I'm going to share my life with a man then I also want him to share my bed. You know and I know that that's not going to happen."

Derrick went completely still as if he'd been impaled by a sharp object. "You know?"

Alana nodded. "I suspected." She waved a hand. "Don't worry, D.," she said, using his hip-hop moniker. "I'll never tell anyone."

"And if you do, then I'll just deny it," he countered.

"It won't happen, Derrick. Friends don't out friends."

An expression of serenity softened his haphazard face. "I'd be honored if you'd permit me to become godfather to your child."

Alana smiled. Her baby was nothing more than a heartbeat and it already had people putting in bids for godmother and father. Faye had asked to be godmother, and now Derrick godfather.

"I'd be honored to have you as my child's godfather."

"Good." Shifting on his chair, Derrick reached into a pocket of his trousers and pushed a small velvet box across the table. "I came here to give you this. When you tire of them you can give them to your son or daughter." Pushing back his chair, he came to his feet, and came around to kiss her cheek. "I'll be in touch about your apartment."

Alana sat staring at the door Derrick had closed behind him, drumming her fingers on the top of the box she knew contained a piece of jewelry.

It was the day after Ilene and Faye had slept over that

she'd decided to sell her apartment and go back home. She needed her mother and her mother needed her.

Ilene Fairchild had become her inspiration to include another character who would give her novel-in-progress the glamour and glitz it'd been lacking.

And with the proceeds from the sale of her property, and the money she'd saved, she could afford to live comfortably until her son or daughter was ready to go to school.

Turning her attention to the gift from Derrick, she raised the top to find a pair of diamond studs. The near-colorless princess-cut diamonds set in platinum rendered her mute. She'd seen a pair of studs with a total weight of two carats, and these were more than twice that weight.

How ironic, she mused. The man who professed to loving her hadn't called her in months, while another who preferred men had offered to take care of her and her unborn child.

When she woke up earlier that morning she never would've predicted how her life would change. And it was changing—every day, with the new life growing inside her.

CHAPTER 76

Bart couldn't wait to return home. He'd missed New York *and* he missed Faye.

Cradling his BlackBerry, he dialed the number to her cell phone, counting off the rings. A smile crinkled the lines around his eyes when he heard her soft greeting.

"Hello, stranger."

"It's only been a week and I've been relegated to stranger status?"

"Where are you, Bart?"

He peered out the side window of the limo. "We landed at Westchester, so I'm in the Bronx. Where are you?"

"I'm home."

"Mine or yours?" he asked.

"Mine."

"How would you like to spend the night with me?"

Her soft laugh came through the earpiece. "What do I get for spending the night with you?"

He chuckled. "We'll start with breakfast in bed."

"It's beginning to sound rather tempting."

"I promise to give you a massage."

"What else?"

"I will wash your back."

"What else, Bart?" Faye crooned seductively.

Vertical lines appeared between his eyes. "What else is there?"

"You think about it on your way here. Bye."

"Don't, Faye!" he shouted as she hung up. A smile replaced his frown. Faye had shown him another side of her mercurial personality. She'd become a tease. He disconnected the call, sat back and stared at the passing landscape as Giuseppe maneuvered smoothly in and out of late-evening traffic as he left the Bronx behind, heading toward Manhattan.

Faye, hearing the familiar ring from the doorman's phone, crossed the living room and picked up the receiver off the wall. "Yes."

"Mr. Houghton is here to see you."

She paused. Whenever Bart came to pick her up he'd always waited downstairs for her. "Please send him up." She hung up, unlocked and opened the door to wait for the man with whom she'd fallen in love despite numerous reasons it would prove disastrous to her emotional equilibrium.

A smile parted her lips when she saw Bart exit the elevator cradling two large grocery bags to his chest. "What on earth did you buy?"

Leaning over, he kissed her forehead. "I brought breakfast, lunch and dinner. I thought I'd spend the weekend with you."

It wasn't until he'd walked into the entryway that she saw

the backpack he'd slung over one shoulder. Faye reached for one of the bags. "Come with me to the kitchen."

Bart took a quick glance at Faye's apartment as he followed her. She hadn't drawn the drapes in the living room. Like his, her apartment overlooked the East River. A seating grouping in the living room reflected her simple, elegant style that was comfortable and inviting. Two facing sofas, upholstered in white on a pale gray area rug, flanked a fireplace, and two easy chairs, one in black, the other in gray, encircled a glass-topped coffee table on a stainless-steel frame. The calming fragrance of dried lavender spilling over in profusion from large earthen crocks in the unlit fireplace wafted throughout the living/dining area. He walked into a large modern kitchen with state-of-the art appliances.

Faye placed her bag on the granite countertop and turned to smile at Bart. "You should've told me that you planned to stay over when you called," she chastised softly.

Bart placed his bag next to the other one, then let his backpack slide to the floor. "I would've told you if you hadn't hung up on me." Taking three steps, he closed the distance between them and took her in his arms. "If it's a problem, we can go to my place."

Moving closer, Faye rested her head on his chest. "It won't be a problem if we don't make love."

"Why should making love become a problem?"

She smiled. "I don't have any condoms."

Bart tightened his hold around her waist and pressed his mouth to her hair. "When are you going to let go and trust me?"

Easing back, Faye stared up at Bart. He looked exhausted. There were new lines around his remarkable eyes. "I do trust you, Bart. And if I didn't I'd go back on the Pill." She reached up and traced the outline of his mouth. "You look tired. Go to bed. I'll put everything away."

He shook his head. "No. I'll help you."

Rising on tiptoe, she brushed a kiss over his mouth. "Go to bed. That's an order."

"Yes, boss," he whispered, kissing her temple, mouth and the column of her neck. "Don't take too long."

Bart released Faye and picked up the backpack. She was right. He was exhausted. Giuseppe had dropped him off at the penthouse, where he'd shaved, showered; he'd lingered to put several changes of clothes into a backpack while his driver called a local gourmet shop for the food items he'd instructed him to order.

He found Faye's bedroom, removed his clothes and pulled back the lightweight quilt on her bed. The scent of her perfume enveloped him as he slipped between the sheets. It was the last thing he remembered before falling into a deep, dreamless sleep.

CHAPTER 77

Faye woke up Saturday literally on the wrong side of the bed. When she'd told Bart to go to bed the night before, he'd gotten in on her side. She couldn't understand how she permitted a man to put his tongue into her mouth yet she didn't want him to put his head on her pillow.

A wry smile twisted her mouth as she shifted slightly and stared at the clock on the night table. She'd slept late. It was almost ten in the morning and rainy weather always made her want to linger in bed beyond her usual waking time.

The hypnotic tapping on the windows, the warmth of the body pressed against hers and the weight of the arm over her waist made her want to spend the morning in bed. But the pressure in her lower belly forced her to reconsider. Grasping Bart's wrist, she lifted his arm and removed it from her waist. He grunted, shifted onto his left side but didn't wake up.

Sitting up and sliding off the mattress, Faye made her way out of the bedroom and down a hallway to the full bathroom. She went through her morning ritual of washing her face and brushing her teeth before sliding back the shower door and stepping into the stall. Plastic bottles of shampoo, conditioner and body wash with labels from Madame Fontaine lined a recessed corner shelf.

Turning knobs and adjusting the water temperature, she stood under the spray of gentle falling water from a large circular showerhead. She'd just reached for a bottle of shampoo when a draft of air pricked her naked body, raising goose bumps. She wasn't given the opportunity to react when the chill was replaced by the heat from Bart's body as he joined her in the stall. Wrapping his arms around her waist, he pulled her back to lean against his chest. She smiled. His moist breath smelled of toothpaste and mouthwash.

"What are you doing?" Faye asked when she recovered her voice.

Smiling and lowering his head, Bart pressed his mouth to the nape of her neck. "I did promise to wash your back."

Faye inhaled sharply as his hands moved down her belly to the area between her legs. "That's not my back," she gasped.

Bart pressed his mouth to the side of her neck, nipping softly. "I know. But it is the second sexiest part of your body."

The softly falling water, the deep crooning voice against her ear and the fingers searching between the folds of her femininity made Faye feel as if she were on the edge of a precipice. She wanted to fall, but the strong arms around her body held her fast.

She closed her eyes, her breathing deepening. "What's the first?"

"The nape of your neck," he whispered, even though there wasn't anyone around to overhear them. "Did you know that Japanese men consider the back of the neck an erogenous zone?"

Forcing air through her parted lips, Faye shook her head. She couldn't think straight. Not when his thumb had worked its magic on her sensitized clitoris, throbbing as if it had a life of its own. Squeezing her knees together, she imprisoned his hand between her thighs.

"Stop," she pleaded. "Please, stop." She'd begged him to stop when she wanted him to go on, to continue to make her feel as if she had taken leave of her senses, had thrown caution to the wind just to feel good.

Bart doubted whether he'd be able to control his rising desire. He'd stood outside the shower stall, watching as she stood under the falling water, the droplets sluicing down her brown skin like diamond dust. He'd hardened instantaneously and he had had to wait until his erection went down. She'd asked him to protect her from an unwanted pregnancy when it was the last thing he wanted to do. He wanted to get her pregnant, wanted to watch her belly swell with their child and he wanted to spend the rest of his life with her as his wife.

It had taken nine years, and a woman with whom he never would've thought of sharing his life made him reconsider marriage and fatherhood. It had been so different with Deidre Dunn. Spoiled, rich and used to getting whatever she wanted, she'd pursued him relentlessly. Once he'd gotten over the fact that she was the boss's daughter, he found himself falling inexorably in love with her. They'd married in what had been called the wedding of the season and settled down to live happily ever after. Their marriage did not survive their twelfth anniversary because Deidre, distraught because of her inability to carry a child to term, had ended her life with an overdose of barbiturates washed down with half a fifth of scotch.

Faye Ogden wasn't Deidre and he wasn't the same Bartholomew Lyndon Houghton he'd been before he walked into Enid's Soho loft that warm May evening what now seemed aeons ago.

Turning her around, his fastened his mouth to hers, inhaling her breath. "Do you really want me to stop, Faye?"

Her firm breasts rose and fell above her rib cage as she sucked in a lungful of air. "No."

Releasing her mouth, Bart stared at her trembling lower lip as the flesh between his legs stirred for the second time that morning, growing larger and harder. Wrapping his arms around Faye's waist, he lifted her off her feet as he fastened his teeth to one nipple, then the other, her soft keening sending shivers up and down his body.

He took several steps, pressing her back against the wall and anchoring her legs around his waist. Bracing his hands against the wall, he eased her down until she lay on the floor, water beating down on their naked bodies, his face between her legs. He did what he'd wanted to do the first time he took her to bed; he made love to her in the most intimate way possible. He didn't make love to Faye; he worshipped her flesh as his tongue moved in and out of her vagina in a measured cadence that had him close to exploding; she smelled and tasted sweet. Everything about her had become an aphrodisiac, an addictive substance of which he didn't believe he would ever tire.

Faye felt as if Bart had launched an all-out assault on her body and her sanity. Her hands went to the head buried between her legs, trying to extract his mouth. His tongue was doing things to her that made her feel helpless as a newborn. Her head thrashed back and forth as screams of pleasure and frustration merged and exploded, contractions shaking her from head to toe.

As the secretions flowing from Faye pooled in Bart's mouth, he was helpless to stem the flow of semen spurting from his penis as he moved up her prone body, thrusting as she writhed against him. He'd wanted to spill his seed inside her and not have it wash down the drain.

Fingers biting into the flesh on her shoulders, he groaned out the last of his passion as the pulsing in his penis eased then stopped altogether. Collapsing heavily on the slender body under him, Bart bit down on his lower lip.

Burying his face against the side of her neck, he waited for his heart to stop its pounding. "Why can't I get enough of you? I don't ever want to let you go."

Faye went completely still. *No!* her inner voice screamed. Bart wasn't playing by the rules. He was now more than a client. It was he who'd reminded her that the women he paid to entertain him he usually slept with. He'd paid her, she was sleeping with him and, instead of remaining her client, he'd become her john.

Her heart felt like a stone in her chest. "Don't, Bart."

Bart came to his feet, turned off the water and pulled Faye up with him. Cradling her face between his hands, he met her tortured gaze. "Don't what? Don't want you or don't love you?" And he did love her, loved her more than any other woman he'd ever met or known in his life.

His admission was dredged from a place where logic and reason could not coexist. However, when it came to Faye Ogden, Bart Houghton was neither logical nor reasonable.

She closed her eyes. "It's not going to work."

"Why wouldn't it work, Faye?"

Faye opened her eyes, meeting his steady, penetrating state. "I've done what I promised myself I wouldn't do with you. It was never my intention to share a bed with you, Bart."

A muscle twitched in his jaw. "Nor mine, but it happened."

"You make it sound so simplistic. That it just happened."

Bart's hands went from her face to her upper arms, holding her in a firm grip. "It just didn't happen, Faye. There's a lot more between us than a social companion and client relationship. And what I want from you goes beyond our arrangement to spend the summer together."

"What exactly do you want from me?" Faye asked.

"Live with me."

"I'm already living with you." Rising on tiptoe, she pressed her mouth to his. "Don't spoil what we have by asking for more than I'm willing to offer at this time."

What I'm willing to offer at this time. Bart nodded. Faye

hadn't rejected him outright, but he knew when to back away, and this was one of those times. He would give Faye the time she wanted and needed to acknowledge that what they had shared superseded their business arrangement.

Lowering his head, he kissed her. "Will you forgive me for putting pressure on you?"

Faye flashed a sensual moue. "I will if you wash my back."

"Isn't that why I came in here in the first place?"

Wrapping her arms around Bart's trim waist, she rested her head on his chest. "I do remember you saying something like that before you distracted me."

"I distracted you? You, my love, distracted me."

"I'm not your love, Bart."

"You think not?" he asked as he reached for a bath sponge and a bottle of body wash. A knowing smile curved the corners of his mouth when Faye turned and presented him with her back. He swore a solemn oath as he squeezed a dollop of thick rich cream on the sponge. He'd loved and lost once in his lifetime, but now that he'd found Faye Ogden he didn't plan to lose her, too.

CHAPTER 78

Ilene followed Astrid into Enid's office, her step light, the sway of her hips more pronounced, arrogant. She smiled, dimples deepening when she saw the look of annoyance—no, it wasn't annoyance but fear—in the penetrating blue-gray eyes.

Enid gestured toward a chair. "Please sit down, Ilene."

The model sat down, crossing her legs at the knees. She looked nothing like she did when she'd been summoned to the loft two weeks ago. Today she favored a pair of white stretch jeans, an off-the-shoulder wraparound silk knit blouse and leopard-print stilettos.

She brushed several strands of the human-hair weave off her forehead. "I asked to see you because I'm leaving P.S., Inc."

Only years of experience as a trial lawyer made it possible for Enid not to visibly react to Ilene Fairchild's disturbing news. "When is your last day?"

"Today is it."

Enid lowered her gaze. There came a beat of silence. "You're not giving me much time."

Ain't that too bad, bitch, Ilene mused, smiling. "I didn't know there was a waiting period, because you didn't mention it during your orientation."

"I didn't mention it because it doesn't exist."

"Then, I suppose that makes us even."

Pale eyebrows lifted slightly. "Does it, Ilene?"

Ilene leaned forward. "Yes, it does. We both made money and I got a little extra in gifts. I'm relocating but you can send my 1099 to the address listed in my file."

She had decided to hold on to her co-op. The apartment was the first thing she'd owned outright, and despite what Amelia had promised her, she was still too insecure to rely on another person to take care of her. Once bitten, twice shy had become her mantra.

"In all sincerity," Ilene continued, "I'd like to thank you for giving me the opportunity to work for Pleasure Seekers."

Enid smiled and inclined her head. "You're quite welcome. However, if you change your mind..." Her words trailed off. She knew Ilene wouldn't call because Claude Wells had informed her that Ilene Fairchild now owned one-quarter of Pine Cay. "Good luck, Ilene. I wish you much success. Maybe we'll meet again in the very near future."

Staring at the woman with the ash-blond hair and cool eyes, Ilene nodded her head. "I'm sure we will."

Enid came to her feet and Ilene followed suit. "You've done well for yourself." She extended her arms, and she wasn't disappointed when the model hugged her. "Be happy, my exotic jewel."

In a gesture of sheer impulsiveness, Ilene kissed the older woman's soft, scented cheek. "Thank you, Enid." Pulling out of the embrace, she turned on her heel and walked away from Enid Richards and P.S., Inc., and all she'd experienced in her brief tenure as a social companion.

CHAPTER 79

Enid waited until Ilene walked out of her office before she sat down again. She still hadn't moved when Marcus walked in three-quarters of an hour later and kissed her cheek.

"You're frowning, beautiful."

Her frown deepened. "It doesn't matter because I have an appointment with my dermatologist next week for a Botox treatment."

Sitting on the edge of the desk, Marcus reached over and took Enid's hands in his. "Who or what has upset you?"

"I've just lost one of my exotic jewels."

"Which one, darling?"

"Ilene Fairchild." She told him about Ilene owning a share of a private island in the Caribbean.

Marcus tightened his grip before releasing her fingers. He'd expected Enid to say Alana Gardner not Ilene. Earlier that morning he'd met with Derrick Warren who'd discussed the possibility of purchasing Alana's Central Park West co-op. He'd attempted to pressure his childhood friend to disclose why Alana had put her co-op on the market, but Derrick refused to tell him.

He lifted an eyebrow as he stared at the bonsai plants

on the table behind Enid's desk, his mind working overtime. Marcus shifted his gaze, staring at Enid as her hand went to the nape of her neck. Whenever she was tense or stressed, she'd massage the back of her neck.

More than aware that Ilene was Pleasure Seekers' most popular companion of color, Marcus knew he was in for a rough time with Enid because whenever she set her sights on something, she was as tenacious as a rabid coon. She'd pledged five million dollars to Habitat for Humanity for the rebuilding of New Orleans, and he knew she would make good on her pledge, even if it meant dipping into her personal resources.

"Do you realize how many clients have been asking for her?" Enid asked Marcus, her frown still in place.

"No. You know I never want to get involved with the scheduling part of the business."

Enid lowered her hand and glared at him. "Well, you need to, Marcus." She hadn't bothered to mask her annoyance when her reprimand took on a waspish quality.

"No, Enid. We're not going to shift responsibility arbitrarily. I monitor the bottom line and you deal with the social companions. And I don't know why you're so upset about losing Ilene when you still have Faye and Alana. Besides, Faye has earned more than Ilene."

Enid fixed him a hostile glare. "And how long do you think it's going to be before I lose her too?"

Moving off the desk, Marcus sat on the chair facing the woman who'd become as essential to him as breathing. What surprised him was that he'd never viewed her as a substitute for his mother. He'd dated and slept with women before meeting Enid, but there was something about the New Orleans native that completed Laurence Marcus Hampton.

"Why do you think you're going to lose Faye?"

"Bartholomew Houghton is obsessed with her."

"A lot of our clients are obsessed with our companions," Marcus countered. "Remember the prince who offered you fifty million to take that giggly redhead back to Bahrain with him?"

Enid smiled. "Don't you remember me telling him that I will not become a party to trafficking in white slavery? The poor child would've become nothing more than a love slave, because there was no way she would've become one of his wives."

"And you think it's different with Bart Houghton?"

Enid nodded. "It's very different, and I've known Bart long enough to know that when he wants something he won't stop until he gets it. Right now he wants Faye Ogden."

"Shouldn't he be content to have her as an exclusive companion?"

Sitting back in her chair, Enid studied Marcus's chiseled face with the strangely colored gold eyes. He was so intelligent in all things intellectual yet naïve when it came to matters of the heart. And one thing she knew about Marcus was that he loved with his heart and not his head. If she'd been any other woman she would've messed over him, but she hadn't and wouldn't because there was something about her lover that frightened Enid. That beneath the polished veneer of impeccable deportment was a hoodlum who would and could hurt anyone who crossed him.

"No, Marcus."

"Why shouldn't he?"

"Because the man's in love with her."

A look of surprise crossed Marcus's face. "You're kidding, aren't you?"

"I wish I was. Bart came in personally to deliver the checks for Faye. He stayed long enough to share lunch with me, and whenever he mentioned Faye's name his face lit up like a neon sign."

"Do you think she knows how he feels about her?"

Enid lifted a shoulder under a blue-gray silk blouse that was an exact match for her eyes. "I don't know, but I'm willing to predict that whenever he makes his feelings known she's going to either run like hell or resign as a companion."

"I don't think she'll resign. Why would she cut off the money?"

Lowering her lids, Enid stared at Marcus through her lashes. "Most black women love with their hearts. Faye signed on with P.S., Inc. as a business venture, but when it stops being business for her she'll quit because she refuses to see herself as a prostitute."

"So you're predicting that if she falls in love with Bart, she won't accept money from him?"

"I know she won't."

Leaning closer, Marcus cupped her chin in his hand. "Now you see why I don't want to get caught up in the minutiae of your clients and companions. What else do you know?"

She smiled. "I know that I love you."

"What else?" he asked teasingly.

"I know that you love me."

"What else do you know, darling?"

"That you want me to marry you."

Marcus's white-tooth smile was dazzling. "Damn. Not only are you beautiful, but you're also brilliant."

A soft laugh escaped Enid's parted lips. "There's an expression that says if you can't baffle them with brilliance then dazzle them with bullshit."

Sobering, Marcus dropped his hand. "Are you bullshitting when you say you love me?"

Her expression matching his, Enid moved from behind her desk to sit on Marcus's lap, surprising him because she'd made it a rule never to display any show of affection in the office. "No, I'm not. You know that I love you, Marcus. And you know that I'm going to marry you."

His inky-black eyebrows shot up. "Do I?"

"Yes, you do. What do you say we change our marital and tax status before the end of the year?"

"Give me a date."

"December twenty-eighth."

He exhaled a long sigh of relief. Enid had chosen her birthday. "You want to make certain I never forget your birthday or our anniversary."

Resting her chin on the top of his head, Enid kissed his

close-cropped hair. "And the first time you forget will be your last."

"Where do you want to get married?"

"I'm partial to Saint Barts."

Wrapping an arm around her waist, Marcus pulled her closer. "Do you want me to make the arrangements?"

"No. I'll take care of everything. The only thing you'll have to do is show up."

Marcus flashed a Cheshire cat grin. "What kind of ring do you want?"

"Surprise me, my darling. Surprise me," Enid repeated as she kissed Marcus with a passion that shocked him.

Enid had asked Marcus to surprise her, and he would. P.S., Inc. may have lost its most celebrated exotic jewel, yet the loss would be a temporary one. He planned to ask Derrick to send him head shots and résumés of dancers the producer hired for his music videos, and before he and Enid exchanged vows he would make certain P.S., Inc. would have a coterie of exotic jewels.

CHAPTER 80

Faye, ambivalent about returning to work after a three-week absence, was oblivious to her coworkers filing into the employee lounge for coffee and bagels. She mumbled a greeting to the receptionist and the copywriter as she neared her office. A note attached to a magnetic board on the door indicated she was scheduled to attend a 9:30 a.m. meeting.

Opening her office door, she looked around for overt changes. Finding none, she sat down behind her desk, stored her handbag in a drawer and turned to stare out the window.

Bart's reference to her being his love had haunted her throughout the weekend. He wasn't the first man who'd confessed to loving her in the throes of passion, and she was certain he wouldn't be the last.

Faye exhaled a long sigh. What had she gotten herself into? The moment she opened her legs to Bart Houghton she'd become a call girl, and if she'd wanted to be vulgar—a whore—or as they said on the street, a ho.

The upside was that she was high-price, top shelf and, for a girl from Queens, she hadn't done too badly: a half-million dollars for eight weeks of work, a wardrobe filled with haute couture and priceless jewels from designers who counted clients among the rich, famous, upwardly mobile and wannabes.

"Welcome back, Faye."

She turned to find John standing in the doorway. His tanned face indicated he'd spent time outdoors, and she wondered who he had spent it with—his wife or Jessica.

She forced a facetious grin. "Thank you, John."

"How was your vacation?"

"Excellent."

"You look rested."

"I am. What's on the agenda for this morning's meeting?"

John crossed his arms over his chest and leaned against the door frame. "We're meeting with an architect from a real estate group looking for a major ad campaign for one of their Harlem construction sites."

Reaching for a legal pad and several pencils, Faye pushed back her chair. "I'm ready." And this time she *was* ready for John and Jessica. Normally she would present her ideas in front of an in-house committee, but that would change today when she'd go over John's head and interact directly with the potential client.

Faye declined the available coffee, bagel and miniature pastries and settled into a chair at the conference table. The usual suspects had gathered for the meeting: John Reynolds, two senior execs, a newly hired African-American copywriter, Jessica and Zachary. John sat down next to her and opened the meeting with introductions.

She listened intently to Geoffrey Morris, a bookish-looking, auburn-haired architect from the Stembridge Management Sales Group, Ltd. make his presentation, jotting down notes as he outlined the details of one of two new residential developments in Harlem with a select number of spacious two- and three-bedroom apartments and four-bedroom penthouses, all with soaring sixteen-foot ceiling heights and floor-to-ceiling windows. The development would offer five-star hotel services, a private ten-thousand-square-foot health club/spa and on-premises parking, along with many other state-of-the-art amenities. Copies of floor plans and a rendering of the landscaped exterior were displayed on an easel for easy viewing.

What surprised Faye was the overall design of the building. It wasn't a modern structure but Art Deco, reminiscent of the celebrated Dakota. And like the luxurious apartment building on Seventy-second Street and Central Park West, it boasted sixty to the Dakota's sixty-five apartments. Overall, the Stembridge architects had designed four apartment buildings for Harlem and upper west side neighborhoods: east and west Harlem, Morningside and Washington Heights. She jotted down buzzwords, filling the legal pad with catchy phrases.

"May I say something, Mr. Morris?" she asked when the architect concluded his presentation.

Geoffrey stared directly at her, then inclined his head. "Please do, Ms. Ogden."

Faye glanced up to find all eyes fixed on her. She put down her pencil. In each of the buildings a number of apartments would be set aside for low-income families. "I like what I see." Her voice was layered with neutral tones. "It's like old greets new, affordability meets luxury."

Geoffrey Morris sat up straighter, his warm brown eyes shimmering with excitement. "That has been Stembridge's mission from the beginning, a blending of the old with the new while allowing longtime residents the opportunity to remain in their neighborhood by offering updated, affordable housing. Ms. Ogden, I believe you've just given us our sales slogan."

There were murmurs of approval around the table. The meeting was unique because it was the first time a client had given an endorsement of their product during an introductory discussion.

Geoffrey looked at John. "I'm ready to discuss the details of our agreement."

John nodded to those around the table. "Thank you for your time."

Faye pushed back her chair and filed out of the conference room with the others. Jessica and Zachary were huddled together as if sharing a top secret. She'd put the others on notice that the slogan had come directly from her. If John gave the Stembridge account to Jessica she planned to pack up her personal items, tell John exactly what she thought of him and his *niece,* then hand in her resignation. John had messed her over once, but it would never happen again.

She returned to her office to find Gina Esposito waiting for her. The petite, Brooklyn-born biracial brunette, the issue of a black mother and an Italian father, reminded Faye of a fragile doll. "How did it go, Faye?"

Faye smiled and angled her head. "I'll find out soon enough. I haven't had time to go through my files, but what else did they take besides the Andino account?"

"They took *Chocolate Living,* but returned it the next day."

"I wonder why," Faye drawled facetiously.

Gina rested a hand on Faye's arm. "Listen, I've got to go and finish some copy for Bobby who's out with strep throat." She headed to the door, then stopped. "What about lunch?"

Faye smiled. "You're on." She waited for Gina to leave to sit and study the notes she'd scribbled during the Stembridge meeting, her mind churning with ideas. She'd wait to see what John was proposing before she followed through with her plan to clean out her desk.

CHAPTER 81

"Bartholomew, Assemblyman Collins is on his way up."

Bart pressed a button on the intercom. "Thank you, Mrs. Urquhart." He stood up, reaching for his suit jacket. Glenwood Collins had changed his demand—yet again. This time he wanted to increase the number of low-income units from fifteen to twenty, and it had taken all of Bart's self-control not to tell the man where he could stick his offer.

He'd had the politician checked out, and the private investigator reported that Collins had gotten into trouble as an adolescent when he'd joined a gang but got out after his best friend was killed in a drive-by shooting. At nineteen, he returned to school, earned a GED, then attended college at night while holding down a day job working in the garment district. Graduating in the top one percentile, he furthered his education when he enrolled in Fordham Law School. Within a year of earning his law degree and passing the bar, he caught the attention of a veteran state legislator who eventually handpicked Collins to succeed him. Glenwood Collins was only twenty-nine when he was elected to represent his Harlem assembly district.

Three minutes later Mrs. Urquhart escorted the nattily

dressed man into Bart's office. Glenwood was short and slender with a receding hairline, yet presented an attractive figure in a tailored tan suit, close-cropped hair and neatly barbered mustache and goatee. A sprinkle of freckles across his nose and cheeks gave his henna-brown face a youthful look.

Forcing a smile he didn't feel, Bart extended his hand. "Good morning, Glen."

Glenwood grasped Bart's hand, squeezing and shaking it harder than necessary. "Good morning, Bartholomew. You've got quite a setup here."

Bart smiled. "It'll do."

Glenwood strolled around the expansive space, taking note of the furnishings. He stopped and stared at a framed black-and-white photograph of a high-rise office building; the year 1961 was engraved on an attached brass plate. He turned and met Bart's gaze. "Is this your building?"

"No. It was my father-in-law's first construction project."

The politician's spare mouth thinned. "So, you married the boss's daughter. Nice move, Houghton."

Ignoring the snide insinuation, Bart said, "If you haven't had breakfast I can have my chef prepare something for you."

Glenwood waved a delicate manicured hand. "No, thank you. I'm scheduled to have brunch with the mayor."

Bart gestured to the white club chair. "Please have a seat." Waiting until the younger man sat down, he took his favored Louis Quinze–style armchair. Looping one leg over the other, he stared at the toe of his polished slip-on.

Bart studied the brash, very ambitious young politician. There was no doubt he was on the fast track to make a name for himself in the New York political arena, and rumors abounded that he had set his sights on a U.S. congressional seat. The investigator had uncovered something else about the assemblyman, something Bart was certain Glenwood wouldn't want to be made public.

Glenwood Collins had gotten a taste of power, and he was intoxicated with it. Each meeting Collins had called the shots—where and when they'd meet; however, this time Bart had taken control of the game when he told Glenwood they'd either meet at DHG's offices or the discussion was moot.

Bart took a quick glance at the timepiece strapped to his wrist. "I'd like to thank you for coming, and because you'll be meeting with the mayor I won't take up too much of your valuable time." He successfully bit back a smile when Glenwood sat up straighter. It was apparent he'd just stroked the pompous man's ego. His investigator had confirmed the rumor that the mayor was throwing his support behind Collins's reelection bid.

"So, I'm going to get to the point. I can't go along with your latest request to up the number of low-income units. It stands at fifteen."

Glenwood Collins jumped as if he'd been impaled with a sharp object, glaring at Bartholomew Houghton with intimidating repudiation. His secret admiration for the slender, silver-haired man who wore hand-tailored suits, imported footwear and a timepiece that cost more than some people earned in six months of backbreaking work dissipated like a drop of water on a heated surface.

Glenwood gritted his teeth. "I thought you were different, Bartholomew."

Pressing his palms together, Bart lifted a dark eyebrow. "How is that, Glen?"

"I thought you were a cut above the greedy white developers who prey on the poor, weak, disadvantaged and, lately, the disenfranchised. You come to my 'hood like a vulture with a beakful of dollars, scavenging and feeding on prime Harlem real estate like carrion. My constituents elected me to stop the foraging, and I intend to make good on my campaign promise."

Bart did not visibly react to the acerbic rant. "I'd like you to answer one question for me, Glen. Is it about my company improving the look of Harlem and the living conditions of those who live there, or is this about race?"

A rush of blood to Glen's face made his freckles more visible. He leaned forward, his hands fisting. "What do you think?" he sneered. "Of course it's about race. There isn't a day when I walk out of my apartment building to see another strange white person greeting me as if they were a friend or relative. And who the fuck do they think they are to speak to me as if they know me like that?"

"They are your constituents, Glen," Bart countered. "They are citizens of this city and state. They pay the taxes that support our schools, fire, police and sanitation departments. They spend money in *their* neighborhood, which also adds to Harlem's tax base. They're the ones who will vote for you to stay in Albany to represent their interests, and if you start alienating them they'll be the ones who'll vote you out of office."

Glen moved to the edge of his chair. "Are you threatening me, *muthafucka?*" Within seconds he'd reverted to the arrogant, fearless gang member who'd do anything to prove his manhood. "Because if you are then you'd better be careful because—"

"Because what?" Bart asked, interrupting him. His voice was cold, filled with contempt for the man who'd believe he would submit to his intimidation. "Do you really think you scare me? You clean up real nice but you're nothing but a project punk all dressed up in a fuckin' fancy suit."

A swift shadow of anger swept across Glenwood's face before it disappeared. "Now, what do we have here? A white boy who's got some thug in him?"

Bart's face and eyes paled as rage singed his lungs. Uncrossing his legs, he placed both feet on the carpeted floor. "Let *me* clear up a few things for you," he said softly. "The year I turned eighteen I became a man. And as for thug, you just don't want to know how much I have. Please don't let *my* fancy suit fool you, because I haven't moved that far from the Liberty Trailer Park. I had relatives who shot people because they didn't like the way they looked at them. I lost count of the uncles who used to write my mother with return addresses from Attica, Elmira and Coxsackie. And Mr. Albany Lawmaker, I don't have to tell you that they're maximum-security prisons.

If you want thug, then I'll show you thug. It'll be just the two of us. It can be public housing versus trailer park. I have about six or seven inches on you, but you have age on your side. What do you say we go downstairs to the gym, put on some gloves and go a few rounds?"

Glenwood couldn't believe that billionaire real estate mogul Bartholomew Houghton had taunted him with a boxing match. He had at least twenty years on the man, but there was no doubt Bartholomew was in excellent shape, because there wasn't an ounce of fat on his tall, lean body.

"I came to talk, not fight."

"No, you didn't, Glen. You came to tell me what I should do with my construction project. You've been leaning on me ever since I got the approval to build in your district, and I've tried to compromise with you. I've gone from five to ten, and now to fifteen units for low-income families." He shook his head. "I will not go one unit higher, and if you start shit with me I'll just have to let it leak out that your secretary, in addition to her secretarial duties, is also performing wifely duties. And don't ask me how I know this because money talks and bullshit walks. You're full of shit, Assemblyman Glenwood Collins, and I'd like you to walk out of here and not come back again unless I invite you."

Bart came to his feet. He almost felt sorry for the younger man when he saw his crestfallen expression. "I want you to remember one thing about me. I'm a businessman, which means I'm in this to make money. And I also want you to remember that I will never compromise my morals by hurting or cheating those who have nothing. I'm not my father-in-law, so forget about what you've heard or read about the Dunn-Houghton Group, because the day I took control I swore an oath to try and do the right thing.

"You and I are more alike than dissimilar, because the projects and trailer parks share the same social stigma. I got out like you got out, and my only regret is, unlike yours, my parents didn't live long enough to see my accomplishments."

Glenwood stood up. "What did your folks do?"

A faraway look softened Bart's gaze. "My mother worked in a factory and on the weekends she waited tables in a diner. My father was what the kids called a mop jockey. They worked themselves into an early grave because they refused to accept a handout from the state. They likened welfare payments to a terminal disease."

"They were proud, Bartholomew," Glen said reverently.

"It was false pride," Bart spat out contemptuously.

Glen angled his head and smiled. "My folks were better off than yours. My dad was a butcher in a supermarket and my mother worked for the public library."

Bart's expression softened considerably. "You've done well, Glen. I'm sure your parents are proud of you."

"They are," he confirmed.

"I'm not going to change my decision to increase the low-income units on this project, but I'm willing to compromise on the others."

Glenwood smiled and offered his hand. "I can live with that."

Bart shook his hand, then pulled him close in a rough embrace. "After trying to put the muscle on me, you could've at least sent me an invitation to your fund-raiser tomorrow tonight."

"You want to come?" There was no mistaking the surprise in Glenwood's query.

Pulling back, Bart smiled down at the assemblyman who hadn't learned to conceal his emotions. His expressive face was an open book. "Of course I do." He'd learned to keep his friends close and his enemies closer. "How much are the tickets?"

"I believe to a man of your means, a thousand dollars a plate shouldn't set you back too far."

"Put me down for two. Where and at what time?"

"It's in a town house on 138th and Striver's Row. Cocktails are at six, speeches at seven, dinner at eight and dancing and bullshitting at nine-thirty."

Bart threw back his head and laughed, Glenwood's laughter joining his. They were still laughing when Bart personally escorted him out of his office to the elevator and down to the street, where a driver waited outside the town house for the assemblyman.

The two men shook hands again. Bart stood on the sidewalk watching the car as it drove away. He hadn't wanted to threaten the elected official, but there was no way he was going to become a party to coercion and intimidation. He'd endured enough of that as a boy.

At fifty years of age he knew who he was, what he wanted, and he was aware of the power he wielded because of his name and wealth. But he would give it all up for a woman with hair and skin the color of burnished gold, a woman whom he loved enough to forfeit his life.

CHAPTER 82

"Hurry and open the card," Gina urged Faye as she plucked the small envelope attached to a profusion of pale blue cellophane off the enormous bouquet of white flowers that had been delivered to her office.

Someone had sent her a vase filled with calla lilies, white violets, magnolias, peonies and roses. Others had gathered in Faye's office by the time she'd taken the card out of the envelope. A delivery of flowers always elicited excitement and curiosity for the employees of Bentley, Pope and Oliviera.

Her eyes widened as she read the message on the vellum: *Congratulations on landing the Stembridge account. BLH.* "How did he know?" she whispered aloud.

"How did who know?" Gina asked, seeing her shocked expression. "Are you pregnant, Faye?"

Faye recovered quickly, staring at the many pairs of eyes staring at her. "No!"

Jessica, pushing past the others, leaned over to sniff the fragrant flowers. "What's the big occasion?"

"That's for me to know and for you to try and find out," she whispered for Jessica's ears only.

Jessica flushed a deep red. "You don't have to be such a bitch," she spat out.

Rising to her feet, Faye dropped the card and moved toward Jessica, who had the sense to back away. "I remember warning you once before about calling me a bitch."

Gina grabbed Jessica's arm and pushed her toward the door, the others stepping back as if they'd choreographed the move beforehand. "I suggest you take your fake ass outta here while you can."

Jessica tried pulling away, but Gina had dug her nails into her skin. "Take your hand off me!"

Gina's dark eyes flashed fire. "Get loud with me and I'll wait for you after work and give you a Brooklyn beatdown that your grandchildren will remember."

Jessica stopped struggling. "How can I have grandchildren when I don't have children?"

A wicked grin curved Gina's generous mouth. "You really are an empty-headed ho."

"I am not a whore."

"Yeah, you are if you shit where you have to eat."

Gina left Jessica pondering her statement and returned to Faye's office where the others were filing out one by one, and mumbling under their breath about Faye. It was apparent she hadn't told them the reason for the flowers.

Faye smiled at Gina. "I got the Stembridge account."

"Dang, Faye. That was fast."

"It was apparent Mr. Morris liked what I presented." What Faye couldn't tell her assistant was that Geoffrey

Morris probably would've approved anything she'd said because Bart had followed through on his promise to "take care of everything," and "if I told you then it wouldn't be a surprise."

He had taken care of everything *and* he'd surprised her by indirectly giving her a DHG account. A smile softened her expression. She would thank him for looking out for her when she saw him later that evening.

Faye was two blocks from the Olympic Towers when her cell phone rang. She glanced at the display. "Yes, Lana."

"Where you at?" she quipped.

"I'm on my way to Bart's. What's up?"

"I just got notification from my bank that a bank check for the sale of my apartment was deposited into my account. I have an appointment to see my boss in about ten minutes. I'm going to tell her that I'm out at the end of August."

Faye bit down on her lower lip. It had become a reality, one which she hadn't wanted to accept. Her best friend was leaving the city to move upstate to care for her mother and await the birth of her own child.

"When are you moving?"

"Not until after Labor Day. It's going to take me that long to decide what I'm going to take and what I plan to give away."

"If you move before I come back from Europe I'm going to hurt you, Alana Elizabeth Gardner."

"Damn! It must be critical when you call me by my full

name. But I ain't scared because you'd never beat up on a pregnant woman."

"You're right about that, Lana."

"Ilene called me this weekend, and she wants to get together before she leaves for her private paradise. I know you're scheduled to go away with Bart the end of the week, but can you spare some time to hang out with your girlfriends?"

"When and where?"

"Don't you have to check in with your man?"

"Don't get funny, Lana."

Alana's distinctive laugh came through the earpiece. "What about Thursday at my place? We can either cook or order in."

"I'm for cooking if you make potato salad."

"You're on," Alana confirmed, "only if you fry the chicken."

"Deal. What time should I come?"

"I'm only working half a day, so after two is okay."

"I'll see you Thursday." That said she rang off.

She had spent Sunday night at Bart's penthouse packing for their European vacation. She'd also left notification with her local post office to hold her mail during that time. After leaving the post office, she stopped at a pharmacy to pick up a three-month supply of the Pill that was touted to give her four periods a year. When she'd called her gynecologist with a message for him to contact her pharmacist to fill a prescription for an oral contraceptive, he'd suggested this new method. She wasn't about to go away with Bart for almost a month and rely solely on him to protect her from an unplanned pregnancy.

Faye turned down the street leading to the building where she spent more time than she did at her own. The doormen were used to seeing her, and a few greeted her by name. Bart had given her the keys to his penthouse the night of Alana's frantic call, and hadn't asked that she return them.

Entering the richly appointed lobby, she smiled and nodded to the doorman on duty, and made her way to the elevator that would take her directly to the penthouse. Inserting her key into the slot for PH2, she turned it to the right and removed it when the door closed, the car rising swiftly and silently upward. It came to a stop, the doors opening with a soft swoosh.

Faye let out a gasp as she looked up to find Bart looming over her. Her heart was racing. He wore a pair of cutoffs but had left his chest and feet bare. And it wasn't the first time she'd admired his body—a swimmer's body with broad shoulders, long, ropey muscular arms, flat belly, slim hips and strong muscled legs. He'd admitted to swimming at the pool in his office building on a daily basis.

"You've got to stop coming up on me like this."

Taking her arm, he led her out of the elevator. "I was just waiting for you."

She rolled her eyes at him. "Did Jacques tell you that I was coming up?"

Bart shook his head. "No. Come with me."

Faye dropped her handbag on a chair, following Bart

to the spacious sitting area that separated her suite of rooms from his. Grasping the frame on a landscape painting, he pulled it back to review a monitor that revealed the empty elevator car.

"Anytime someone places a key in the elevator to this floor it sends a signal, and a bell chimes. I can see you coming up before you get here." He settled the painting against the wall.

Moving closer to Bart, Faye pressed her breasts to his back. "What other secrets do you have?"

He went completely still. "What are you talking about?"

Wrapping her arms around his waist, she placed light kisses over his shoulders. "What's your connection to Geoffrey Morris?"

He went pliant in her embrace. "He works out of my West Coast office."

Shifting until she and Bart were facing each other, she gave him a reproachful look. "What you did wasn't very nice."

"Did it work, darling?"

"It worked, but it was underhanded."

A slight frown appeared between his eyes. "If you plan to go into business for yourself, then you're going to have to stop thinking like an innocent schoolgirl. You've got to step on someone every once in a while to get where you want to go. What John Reynolds did to you was inexcusable and unconscionable. Believe me when I say that the son of a bitch is a lucky man."

Faye's face clouded with uneasiness, becoming more uncomfortable with the man with whom she'd fallen in love.

Gone was the easygoing man and in his place was one she didn't recognize. Which one, she wondered, was the real Bartholomew Houghton? The open, relaxed man who managed to put everyone in his presence at ease? The man who'd so charmed her parents they'd invited him back to their home for a Labor Day gathering? The man who made love to her in ways that made her crave him in and out of bed?

"What would you have done?" she asked in a trembling voice.

"Please don't ask me, Faye."

"Why not?"

"Because it doesn't concern you."

"We're talking about my boss, and you tell me that it doesn't concern me?"

Bart felt like shaking Faye until she was too breathless to speak. And he knew he had to give her a plausible answer or she would shut him out. The one time they'd disagreed on something she'd stopped talking to him, and no amount of coaxing would get her to respond. They'd gone to bed, their backs to each other, and it wasn't until the next morning that she climbed atop him, asking him to make love to her.

"Okay. All I'm going to say is that Mrs. John Reynolds wouldn't be too pleased if she saw photographs of her husband and his *niece* in a rather compromising position."

"Oh, shit!" Faye said before covering her mouth with her hand. Her hand came down. "Don't tell me you were going to blackmail John."

"I was hoping I'd never be faced with that decision. But there is an alternative."

"What?"

"I can buy BP&O and you can run it."

Faye shook her head. "Thanks, but no thanks. I don't want a large company."

Cradling her face between his hands, Bart smiled at her. "Do you want your own company?"

She returned his smile. "You know I do."

"Do you want it *now?*"

"What are you talking about?

"After we come back from Europe I'll have someone check out available office space in midtown. Then—"

Faye placed her fingers over his mouth, stopping his words. "We'll talk about this when we get back." She'd promised to give him the summer, while Bart was talking about her future plans, plans that did not include him.

Grasping her wrist and pulling her hand down, Bart lowered his head, brushing a light kiss over her mouth. "We're invited to a fund-raiser tomorrow night. Can you get off work early, because the cocktail hour begins at six?"

"Yes." She rested her head on his chest, counting off the strong, steady beats of his heart as she kneaded the muscles in his back. "I forgot to thank you for the flowers and the Stembridge account."

"You just did."

"How?"

"Being here with me is thanks enough."

"But you're paying me to be with you."

Bart wanted to ask Faye if that was the reason she'd come to him, the reason she'd opened her legs to him, because he'd paid her. He'd found himself praying that it wasn't the money but something deeper, something more intangible.

He wanted her to love him, and it didn't have to be an all-encompassing love. Just enough to make her want to stay and perhaps consider sharing her life with him.

The summer season would end officially after the Labor Day holiday weekend, and he had less than four weeks to convince Faye Ogden that what they had was no longer a business arrangement; it'd stopped being business the first time she slept under his roof in Southampton.

CHAPTER 83

Faye walked into the Striver's Row town house on Bart's arm, resplendent in a coffee-brown Calvin Klein organza slip dress lined in bronze silk. Gold leather Bruno Frisoni heels, a matching Bottega Veneta lizard Ravenna clutch and gold studs in her pierced lobes pulled together her simple, elegant look.

She smiled at Bart when he rested a hand at the small of her back. Instead of a tux, Bart had chosen to wear a dark blue suit, white shirt with French cuffs and a pearl-gray silk tie.

Unlike the Scarsdale fund-raiser, she recognized the faces of local, state and a few Washington politicians who'd come out to lend their support for the reelection of Assemblyman Glenwood Collins.

Bart caught the assemblyman's eye and nodded. Glen wove his way through the crowd that had spilled out into the spacious backyard.

His eyes dancing with excitement, he offered Bart his hand. "Welcome, Bartholomew. Thank you for coming out."

Bart shook the proffered hand. "I'm glad I could make

it." He turned to Faye. "Faye, this is Assemblyman Glenwood Collins. Glen, Faye Ogden."

With wide eyes, Glen's Adam's apple bobbed up and down his throat until he found his voice. "It's a pleasure to meet you, Faye. I hope Bartholomew won't take offense if I tell you that you're incredibly beautiful."

Bart's arm went around Faye's waist. "No offense taken. In fact, I tell her that every night." His declaration, notwithstanding, he had announced to the world their social relationship: they were a couple.

Faye forced a plastic smile. "Thank you, Assemblyman Collins."

Glen waved a hand. "Please, no titles tonight." He returned his attention to Bart. "Have you met our new governor?"

"I'm afraid I haven't had the honor."

"Come and I'll make the introductions."

Faye lost count of the number of times she was photographed on the arm of Bart, exchanging pleasantries with the governor, the mayor and several U.S. representatives. It appeared as if everyone wanted to know something about the woman who'd come to Harlem with the enigmatic real estate mogul who was rumored to control more land in America than Donald Trump. There was even talk that his holdings equaled Xu Rongmao, chairman of China's Shimao Group.

Bartenders continued to pour and mix drinks as the invited guests settled down to hear their elected officials extol the credentials and dedication of Glenwood Collins to those who'd chosen him to represent them. The governor and mayor filed out with their state and local police bodyguards as a sitdown dinner was being served.

Faye drank one martini that was so potent she found herself leaning against Bart for support. It was even stronger than the one she'd been served the night she met him. She ate, hoping to counter the effects of the alcohol, and when Bart asked if she was ready to leave she practically genuflected.

Faye lay with her head in Bart's lap as Giuseppe maneuvered away from the curb. "How many drinks did you have?" he asked. His voice seemed to come from a long way off.

"One," she replied.

Bart placed a hand over her forehead. "You can't be drunk on one drink."

She sighed but didn't open her eyes. "This is the first time. It could be because I'm taking the Pill."

Bart stared at Faye as if he'd never seen her before. "You're on the Pill?"

"I started taking it Monday."

"Does it usually make you sick?"

"No. I really can't say that about this one because I've never taken it before."

His fingers toyed with her curly hair. "I told you before that I'd protect you."

"I know you did."

"So, why are you on the Pill?"

Her eyes opened, and she stared up at him in the light coming from the high-intensity lamp along the rear windshield. "Just once I'd like to make love with you without a barrier of latex between us. I want to feel you—all of you, Bart." Faye closed her eyes, shutting out his intense stare, unaware how much her erotic confession had shocked him.

Bart eased Faye's head off his lap before she could feel his growing erection. He wanted and needed her so much that he feared he'd take her in the back seat of the car. Cradling her to his side, he counted off the blocks until his driver parked in the underground garage.

"I can walk by myself," Faye said in protest as Bart carried her out of the elevator and in the direction of his bedroom.

"It's okay, baby. You're not heavy." He placed her on the bed, his body following hers down.

Bart took his time undressing Faye; it'd become a ritualistic dance as he kissed every inch of flesh he bared. Once she was completely naked he undressed, then joined her on the bed. He stopped himself as he opened the drawer in the nightstand for a condom.

Faye had taken the first step in cementing their relationship when she'd decided to assume responsibility for contraception. Other than Deidre, he'd never slept with a woman without using a condom, and that had only occurred once she'd become his wife. And he'd slept with Felicia once more since the time he saw Faye at the Waldorf-Astoria because he wanted Faye Ogden to be the last woman in his life.

Faye felt the warmth and press of Bart's body as he moved over her, her legs opening to permit him access to her femininity. She gasped when his hardness filled her, shuddering and moaning when he established a rhythm that made her grip the sheets, her passion rising and spiraling out of the control.

Bart's tongue traced the soft fullness of Faye's soft lips; his mouth moved lower to the pulsing hollow at the base of her throat. She was on fire! He was on fire! Anchoring his hands under her hips, he pulled her up to meet his heavy thrusts. Then, without warning, the dam broke as he spilled his seed into her quivering body. He never knew when he collapsed heavily onto her, or when she clung to him shivering and moaning from ecstasy neither had ever known.

They'd fallen asleep, their bodies joined as they became one with the other.

CHAPTER 84

Reaching for the pitcher on the top shelf in the refrigerator, Ilene made her way to the dining area and filled three goblets with fresh-squeezed lemonade.

"I hate that artificial mess in a can," she said sitting down at the table. "Real lemonade is made from lemons not some powdered crap."

"I hear you," Faye intoned.

Alana waved her hand like she was testifying in church, unable to speak because her mouth was filled with a fluffy biscuit. "If you keep eatin' those biscuits like water you're going to be so *swole* up that you're going to be on bedrest before you're six months along," Ilene warned.

Alana rolled her eyes at Ilene and took another bite. "At least I have someplace for my fat to go. What's going to happen when your skinny ass gets pregnant? You'll end up looking like moon over sticks."

Faye almost choked on a forkful of potato salad. Reaching for her glass of lemonade, she took a deep swallow. "Y'all are going to have to stop with the snaps until I finish eating."

"Easy there, star," Alana drawled, pointing at the plate

in front of Faye. "Are you sure you're going to be able to eat all that?"

Faye gestured with her fork. "Watch me."

The three women had prepared a small feast of fried chicken, biscuits, dirty rice, collard greens, and Alana had baked a sweet-potato pie for dessert.

Ilene picked up a forkful of dirty rice. "Are you sure you don't have a little rye bread in the oven?"

Alana sputtered, bits of biscuit coming from her mouth. "Sorry about that," she said, apologizing.

"Hell, no," Faye mumbled.

"Are you sure, Faye?" Alana asked.

"Of course I'm sure. I'm on the Pill." She stared at her friends when their jaws went slack. "What's up?"

"Nothing," Alana murmured.

"Not a thing," Ilene said, lifting her shoulders in a perfect Gallic shrug.

Faye put down her fork. "I know you're both dying to ask me about Bart, so ask away." Ilene glanced down at her plate, but Alana gave her a direct stare.

"Are you in love with him?"

Faye blinked once. "Yes."

"Is he in love with you?" Ilene asked.

"I think so."

"You think so," Alana repeated. "Is he or isn't he?"

"He hasn't come out and said it, but there was one time he said that I was his love."

Ilene rolled her head on her neck. "Hel-lo, Faye. Translation. The man said that he loved you."

Picking up her fork, Faye pushed the greens away from her potato salad. "Bartholomew Houghton isn't shy about anything. And if he did love me, then he'd just come out and say it."

Alana shook her head. "Maybe he's not saying anything because he's afraid you'll reject him."

Faye stared at her. "Reject him? I'm living with the man."

"Because he's paying you, Faye," Alana argued. "Would you live with him if he stopping paying Enid for you?"

"I'm going to stop after we come back from Europe."

"Stop living with him or stop accepting his money?" Ilene asked.

Faye looked at Ilene, then Alana. It was a question she'd asked herself over and over. "I'm going to continue to see Bart, but I plan to leave P.S., Inc."

"Good for you," Alana said, smiling.

Ilene raised her goblet in a toast. "Enid is going to have a shit hemorrhage when she loses another one of her so-called exotic jewels."

Faye touched her glass to Ilene's then Alana's. "Enid is a survivor."

Ilene's mouth twisted in a sneer. "You've got that right. She's like the cockroach, who scientists predict will be around after a nuclear bomb wipes out mankind."

"Don't be so hard on her, Ilene," Faye said with a smile. "After all, you never would've become part owner of an island if you hadn't met her."

"Word," Alana drawled.

"I guess I am too hard on her," Ilene admitted. "I

know I never would've met Amelia if Enid hadn't sent me to Pine Cay."

Faye and Alana listened as Ilene told them she was subletting her co-op, and that she and her lover had decided Ilene would be artificially inseminated after they celebrated their first anniversary together. She planned to have the procedure in the States; two weeks before her due date she would leave Pine Cay for Puerto Rico because she wanted her child born on American soil.

Alana shocked Faye when she revealed that Derrick Warren had asked to be her baby's godfather, and she was quick to reassure them that Derrick wasn't the father. She kept her promise not to tell them about his sexual predilection.

"I almost felt obligated because he paid me my asking price for this apartment, and he also gave me these." She pushed her hair behind her ears to reveal the diamond studs.

"Dam-m-n-n," Ilene and Faye chorused.

"Those bad boys can choke a horse," Ilene teased.

"I had them appraised because I wanted to add them to my insurance policy and they're worth a small fortune. They appraise for enough to pay full tuition at a small private college."

"I ain't mad at you, girl," Faye said in encouragement.

"That's why..." Her words trailed off when the telephone rang. "Excuse me. I'm expecting a call from my brother about my mother."

Pushing back her chair, Alana walked down the three

steps that led to the living room. She picked up the phone from the coffee table. "Hello."

"Hey, Lanie."

She froze. The voice coming through the earpiece was the last one she'd expected to hear. "Calvin?" Alana saw two pairs of eyes staring at her.

"How many other Calvins do you know? I know you ain't messin' around on me."

A sardonic smile twisted Alana's mouth as she sank onto the leather sofa. "Whatever do you mean, Calvin? Are you asking if I've been fucking another man?"

"Whoa, Lanie. What's up with you?"

"What's up, Calvin McNair, is that either you had amnesia or you were too busy to call home. Even E.T. tried to phone home. Now listen up good so I don't have to repeat myself. Don't bother to call me again, because this number will be disconnected at the end of the month. And you're going to have to find a new place to park your dusty ass because effective September first a new owner will occupy the premises. And by the way, I'm pregnant. And we both know it's not yours. Bye-bye."

Faye and Ilene laughed so hard that they found it difficult to breathe. Ilene fell off her chair and rolled on the floor while Faye blotted the tears rolling down her cheeks. Alana lay across the sofa, trying unsuccessfully to hold back her own laughter. She'd waited more than two months to kick Calvin to the curb, and never had she experienced the inexplicable joy that she felt when she told him that she was having a baby.

Calvin was her past, a past filled with pain, disappointment and broken promises. She had a new life growing inside her that needed the love and protection only a mother could give. Although her baby hadn't been conceived in love, that hadn't stopped her from loving her son or daughter, and she couldn't wait to see it for the first time.

Faye sobered enough to sing the Frankie J hit "Don't Wanna Try." Ilene joined in, then Alana, the three voices blending like those in black church choirs in a Sunday-morning worship service. Their singing gave way to weeping when they realized it would be the last time all three exotic jewels would be together. Ilene had scheduled to fly to Pine Cay Friday morning.

They talked and cried about the men they'd loved and lost as they cleaned up the kitchen. Over dessert, they exchanged addresses and telephone numbers. Faye and Alana made Ilene swear an oath that she would contact them when she came to the States for her in vitro procedure.

Ilene left first, saying she had to go home to finish packing. Faye stayed until after the sun set; she had the doorman hail a taxi to take her to Bart's penthouse.

Her puffy eyes had given her away when he gave her a strange look. He didn't ask and she didn't tell him what had gone on at Alana's. He waited up for her while she showered, and when she finally climbed into bed next to him, he held her until she fell asleep.

CHAPTER 85

Bart walked into the second-floor formal conference room, smiling. He'd called a meeting of the entire staff to apprise them of the changes he'd put into place during his three-week absence. Those who were standing and talking quietly to one another claimed an empty chair.

He tapped Hakim Wheeler on the shoulder, and leaned over the urban planner. "Please sit in the chair at the head of the table."

It took all of three seconds for Hakim to process what he'd been told. Rising to his feet, all eyes in the room following him, he sat in the chair Bartholomew Houghton occupied whenever he chaired a meeting. Gazes shifted to Bart when he took the chair Hakim had vacated.

Bart glanced around the large mahogany table, meeting the curious gazes of the men and women who were responsible for DHG's ongoing success and profitability.

Lacing his fingers together, Bart paused for effect. He knew everyone was curious as to why he'd called the impromptu meeting, but after a restless night tossing and turning he'd gotten out of bed and spent the next two hours in his office-study drafting a number of documents.

His existence had changed dramatically since he'd become involved with Faye, and for the first time in his life he planned to execute a number of legal measures.

"I'd like to thank all of you for being prompt," he began in a quiet tone. "I know you're wondering why I called this meeting." There were nods from everyone. "I could've put this in a memo but thought that would be too impersonal." He paused again for effect as he heard intakes of breaths.

"I'm going to be out of the country for the next three weeks."

"Where are you going?" asked a paralegal whose latest biannual evaluation indicated she had boundary issues. It was apparent her supervisor was right. A secretary on her left punched her softly on the arm. "Oops. Sorry about that."

Bart stared at her as if she'd temporarily lost her mind, then shook his head in amazement. "Hakim Wheeler will stand in for me in my absence." He ignored the loud gasps and the undercurrent of whispers floating around the table. "Anyone wishing contact with Hakim will have to go through Mrs. Urquhart." A rolling of eyes and suppressed moans followed this announcement. Most employees preferred facing a rabid dog than interacting with Geraldine Urquhart.

The chief financial officer raised his hand. "Are there any other changes?"

Bart shook his head. "No. The table of organization remains the same with the exception of Hakim." He looked at Hakim, noting his stunned expression. The seconds ticked off until Bart said, "Thank you for your time." Pushing back his chair, he stood up, the others rising and filing out of the conference room. Only Hakim remained.

Slipping his hands in the pockets of his trousers, he stared at Bart. "You could've given me prior notice," he chided softly.

Shaking his head and crossing his arms over his chest, Bart laughed under his breath. "Why, Hakim? I'd expected you to say something when I made the announcement. You're now in a VP position, which means you'll have to make split-second decisions."

A muscle twitched in the chiseled jaw of the tall, dark and extremely handsome urban planner, but he did not drop his gaze as he stared directly at his boss. "Point taken, Mr. H."

"Do you have any questions?"

"Yes."

"What?"

"Why me?"

"Why not you, Hakim?"

Hakim took his hands out of his pockets and crossed his arms over the front of his stark white shirt. "Why didn't you pick Frank or Curtis?" The urban planners were senior VPs with a staff of ten between them.

"I didn't select them because they're not ambitious enough. Neither of them are risk takers. We never would've ventured into Harlem if not for you. So, I hope that answers your question."

Hakim smiled, nodding. "Yes, it does."

Bart patted Hakim's shoulder. "Come upstairs with me. I'll show you what I've been working on, and it's time you become better acquainted with Mrs. Urquhart. She barks a lot, but she doesn't bite."

"That's not what I heard," Hakim countered.

"She likes you."

Hakim walked with Bart out of the conference room. "How do you know that?"

"When I told her that I was promoting you to VP, she said it was about time I picked someone who didn't have a face for radio."

"She didn't," Hakim said, stopping in midstride as they approached the elevator.

Bart stepped in and held the door. "No shit."

Laughing, Hakim joined Bart in the elevator as it took them to the fourth floor. This was a side of Bartholomew Houghton he'd never seen, a side he liked and could get used to.

The doors opened and he stepped out to a carpeted area where Mrs. Urquhart sat behind a massive oak desk. Her face lit up when she saw Bart with Hakim.

"Good morning, Mr. Wheeler."

"Good morning, Mrs. Urquhart."

She waved a delicate blue-veined hand. "You can call me Geraldine."

Bart's expression mirrored his shock. His executive assistant was flirting with the urban planner.

"I can't do that, Mrs. Urquhart."

"Hakim, please go into my office. I'll be in as soon as I discuss something with Mrs. Urquhart."

Waiting until the younger man was out of earshot, Bart leaned over the desk and glared at the older woman. "Hakim's going to have enough to deal with adjusting to running this place, so I don't want you starting up with him."

Geraldine affected an expression of innocence. "What did I do?"

Bracing his hands on the desk, he leaned closer. "Don't play with me, Geraldine."

The hardness in the gray eyes and the cold, no-nonsense tone told Geraldine Urquhart that her boss was not in a teasing mood. "Okay, Bartholomew."

Straightening, he smiled at her. "Please call A Voce and make luncheon reservations for a party of three."

"What time?"

He glanced at the brass clock on the wall behind the desk. "One o'clock. Call Giuseppe and have him pick us up downstairs at twelve forty-five. I hope whatever it is you're working on will be completed by that time because you'll be joining Hakim and me."

He made his way into his office, leaving Geraldine Urquhart with her mouth gaping. This time she had no comeback.

CHAPTER 86

Enid picked up the head shot of a very pretty Asian woman, studying her stoic expression. Although she wasn't smiling, there was something behind the eyes that spoke to her. She pushed the photograph across the table to Astrid.

"What do you think about her?"

The booker stared at the photograph before she turned it over to read the printed information on the back. The classically trained former ballet dancer spoke English, Mandarin, Cantonese and French.

"She's good."

Enid and Astrid went over the more than a dozen head shots, deciding half would not be suitable for P.S., Inc. They'd selected two African-Americans, three Latinos and one Asian.

"Set up interviews for them," Enid instructed Astrid.

"What do you want me to do with the other photos?"

"File them away. We may need one or two in the future."

Astrid put the photos into separate folders with the corresponding labeled tabs. She opened her large cloth-covered notebook. "I want to give you an update on your fund-raiser. To date we have ninety affirmatives, twenty-two declinations and twelve maybes. All of the declinations sent checks totaling close to two million. Bartholomew Houghton won't be able to make it because he'll be out of the country, but he sent a corporate donation of seven hundred and fifty thousand."

Enid couldn't smile. She'd gotten her Botox treatment the day before, and her face was stiff as dried cement. "Is that figure included in the two million?"

"No. A messenger just delivered his check."

"Do you think we'll get our five million, Astrid?"

"I don't see why not. Senators Bruce and Kent still haven't replied, and there's no doubt they will be generous with their donations." Both men were self-made multimillionaires before they decided on a career in politics. "I'll wait until California wakes up before I start calling your Hollywood contacts." Astrid found the three-hour time difference bothersome at times.

"Thank you, Astrid."

The booker smiled and gathered her files. "The stationer called before you came in to say that your wedding invitations are in. They plan to deliver them this afternoon."

A rush of color darkened Enid's face. Anytime someone made reference to her marrying Marcus she became the proverbial blushing bride and the two-and-a-half-carat emerald ring surrounded by diamonds on her left hand was a constant reminder that she would change her name from Enid Richards to Enid Hampton before the end of the year.

And despite reminding her fiancé of their age difference

and that she would never give him a child, Marcus was insistent that he wanted her as his wife and life partner.

A week following their official engagement she was introduced to Marcus's parents for the first time. If they were surprised to discover that their son was marrying a woman old enough to be his mother or that they would never become grandparents, they didn't show it. Both were happy that their son had found happiness with a woman he loved enough to marry. It had taken Enid less than five minutes to see that the elder Hamptons adored their only child.

She'd planned a simple ceremony at a private villa on Saint Barts with a few close friends and business associates. The first time she'd married it was for financial security; this time she was marrying for love.

CHAPTER 87

Faye sat on a sleeper-sofa in the private jet, staring out the window. They'd been in the air for more than four hours. Bart had arranged to leave New York at 7:00 a.m. in order to arrive in France at night. Within an hour of takeoff they were served a sumptuous breakfast prepared by an onboard chef.

Their travel itinerary included three days in Paris before venturing southward to Saint-Tropez and Monaco. From there they would go to Ibiza, then over to the Italian Riviera before jetting back to the States.

She glanced across the aisle at Bart. He'd reclined his sofa into a bed and was sound asleep. She studied his composed face, feature by feature. His close-cropped silver hair was now flecked with white. He'd disclosed that he had begun graying at twenty-five, and by age forty he was salt-and-pepper.

Faye felt that if it wasn't for his remarkable eyes, Bartholomew Houghton would've been thought of as nondescript. Other than the penetrating gray eyes, eyes that darkened in passion, softened in tenderness and paled in anger, he claimed no distinguishing features.

She'd asked herself over and over why she'd fallen in love with him. Why Bart and not some other man closer to her age and the same race? And each time she asked the question the answer was the same: because he is who he is. Once she extracted the most obvious variables it'd become just the man.

Bart had become her protector, someone she'd learned to trust, and a gentle, passionate and considerate lover. There was never a time when she didn't enjoy making love with him. And when she compared him to Norman she found they were more similar than dissimilar except that Norman had shattered the trust she'd had in him. She believed it was trust and not love that reinforced relationships and marriages.

A cheeky attendant came into the cabin. She glanced at Bart. "Can I get you anything to drink, Ms. Ogden?"

She gave the woman a warm smile. "No, thank you."

"Just ring me if you need anything."

"I will."

Reaching for a cashmere blanket, Faye pressed a button on the armrest, reclining the back. She lowered the window shade, lay down and covered herself with the blanket. The incessant hum of the aircraft's engines and the rising and falling motion all contributed to her relaxing enough to fall asleep.

Bart shook Faye gently. "Baby, wake up."

Her eyelids fluttered. "What?"

"We're landing."

Faye sat up. Her window shade was up and the City of Light sparkled like diamonds on dark blue velvet beneath the descending aircraft. She raised her seat back and fastened her seat belt.

Bart took the seat facing her, buckling his belt. "You slept through dinner."

Faye covered a yawn with her hand. "Did you eat?"

"I had a salad. We'll eat dinner at the hotel."

She stared out the window as the jet came in for a smooth landing on a private airstrip at Orly Airport. The pilot's voice came through the speaker announcing the local time and temperature. It was 9:03 p.m., 27 degrees Celsius.

Faye was wide awake by the time they'd deplaned and cleared Customs. A handler carried their bags out of the terminal to a parking lot where a driver had awaited their arrival. Within thirty minutes of touching down they were motoring toward the Right Bank and the Four Seasons Hotel George V Paris.

Bart assisted Faye out of the spacious sedan and escorted her into a hotel lobby filled with light, space and an impressive collection of objets d'art. Reaching into the breast pocket of his jacket, he withdrew a leather case, placing a credit card on the counter.

The desk clerk glanced up and smiled. *"Accueillir au Quatre George d'Hôtel de Saisons le Cinquième, Monsieur Houghton. Comment long cet a été?"*

Bart returned the clerk's friendly smile. *"A petit plus qu'une année, Pierre."*

Pierre swiped the card, returning it to Bart with a card

key. *"Vous et votre invitée sant au huitième étage. Est-ce que vous aimeriez manger le dîner dans votre suite?"*

Bart looped an arm around Faye's waist. *"Nous mangerons dans notre suite."*

"Quelqu'un vous apportera le bagage en haut momentanément. Encore, le dos d'accueil à Paris."

"Merci, Pierre."

"Will you kindly translate what you just said to the desk clerk," Faye asked as they entered the glass-enclosed elevator. She had no idea Bart spoke fluent French.

He pulled her closer. "The clerk welcomed me back to Paris and asked how long I had been away."

"How long has it been?"

"About fourteen months. He also asked whether we would be dining in our suite, and I said yes."

Tilting her chin, Faye stared up at Bart staring down at her. "Where did you learn to speak French so well?"

The elevator stopped at their floor, and he led her down the hallway to their room. Inserting the card key in the slot, Bart pushed open the door. He bent slightly and swept Faye up into his arms. Lowering his head, he kissed the end of her nose. "Why are you so full of questions?"

"Why are you always so mysterious?" she asked, tightening her grip around his neck.

"You know more about me than most people."

"I'm not most people, Bart. In case you've forgotten, I'm the woman who has been living and sleeping with you."

"And in case you've forgotten, I'm the man who loves you, Faye Anne Ogden."

Faye went completely still, her breath stopping and congealing in her lungs. She closed her eyes and buried her face against his shoulder. She'd admitted to Alana and Ilene that she'd fallen in love with Bartholomew Houghton, but she didn't want to tell him what lay in her heart because it would make her vulnerable, vulnerable to the pain and loss when they'd eventually part.

"You're changing the rules," she said instead.

Bart carried her through the living room and into the bedroom suite with a direct view of the Eiffel Tower. "There are no rules when it comes to matters of the heart," he said, placing her gently on the silk-covered duvet. He lay beside her and pressed his mouth to the side of her neck. "I hadn't planned on falling in love with you, but there was something about you, Faye Ogden, that changed my life."

Shifting slightly, Faye stared directly at Bart. The light from the table lamps flattered the lean contours of his face. "How, Bart?"

His firm mouth softened as he smiled. "You're fun. You make me laugh, and because you're sexy as hell I can't stay away from you."

Her lashes came down, concealing her innermost thoughts. "Is this the part where I tell you that I love you, too?"

"No, Faye. You don't have to say anything."

She glanced up. "You don't mind being in a one-sided relationship?"

"It's not that one-sided, darling. I've been with enough

women to know when they're faking and when they aren't. The first time I made love with you I knew you were for real. You had to feel something to offer that much of yourself."

Her eyebrows lifted. "You would continue to see me even if I never told you that I loved you?"

Bart nodded. "I would because I'd hope and pray that one day you'd come to love me as much as I love you."

Her heart turned over with his passionate entreaty. "I can't love you," she lied.

"You can't or you're afraid, Faye?"

Her eyelids fluttered wildly. "I'm afraid."

"Are you afraid I'll be unfaithful to you?"

"Yes," she said truthfully. Her voice was low, barely a whisper.

"I'd never cheat on you, darling."

"That's what my first boyfriend said, and not only was he sleeping with me but also with the girl who lived next door. I managed to protect my heart until I met Norman, and he told me that same thing when he asked me to marry him. I'm sorry. I can't go through that again." She'd confessed to Alana and Ilene that she'd fallen in love with Bart, but that would remain their secret.

His eyes caught and held hers. "Perhaps you can explain something to me."

"What do you want to know?"

"Where does all of your passion come from?"

For a long moment Faye looked back at him. "I enjoy sleeping with you."

"Why?"

"What do you mean why?"

"Why do you sleep with me?"

"I like you."

"Do you sleep with every man you like?"

She frowned. "No."

"So it goes a little deeper than liking?"

Her temper exploded. "Why are you goading me?"

His temper rose to match hers. "I want to know where I stand with you before we go any further."

"How much further are you talking about?"

"I want you to marry me."

Faye felt as if someone had reached into her chest to squeeze her heart. She moved off the bed as if she'd been struck with a bolt of electricity. She turned on her heel and sprinted out of the bedroom, wanting and needing to escape Bart, but she'd miscalculated his reflexes because he'd sprung off the bed, caught her arm and spun her around to face him.

"Where are you going?"

"Out for a walk. I need to clear my head."

"If you want to leave the hotel, then we'll go together."

She pounded his chest with a fist. "You set me up. You wait until we're six thousand miles from home, then you spill your guts. Why didn't you tell me this last week? Or even last night?"

Bart held her hand to keep her from hitting him again. "Would you have come with me if I'd told you that I loved you?"

"I don't know. Besides, it's not the loving me that bothers me."

He angled his head, his eyes narrowing in suspicion. "It's my wanting to marry you?" His statement had come out like a query.

"Yes."

Even as she'd signed the documents to dissolve her marriage, Faye believed she would marry again and have a child. Bartholomew Houghton was presenting her with the opportunity, but she was unable to accept his proposal because she didn't want to have a child with a man old enough to be her father; a man who might not live long enough to see their child to maturity.

Releasing her wrist, he cradled her face between his hands. "I'm going to ask you one more time, and I want you to be truthful with me. Do you love me?"

Faye compressed her lips as tears filled her eyes. "Yes."

Bart pulled her against his body. "I—" A soft tapping on the door preempted whatever he was going to say. He pressed a kiss to Faye's forehead. "It's probably our luggage."

She was grateful for the intrusion because it would give her time to recover her thoughts. She was thirty-two years old, supposedly a mature woman, but right now she was as gauche as a teenager leaving home for the first time. And for the first time since she'd contracted to be a social companion for Bartholomew Houghton, Faye felt as if she was in over her head.

Enid Richards had hired her to provide companionship to wealthy men. However, it was apparent that she was very good at what she'd been hired to do because not only had she gotten her client to fall in love with her, but he also wanted to marry her.

Anna Nicole Smith had nothing on Faye Anne Ogden.

CHAPTER 88

Faye reached for a small bag the bellman had left in a corner of the living room. "I'm going to take a shower," she said to Bart as he closed the door behind the hotel employee.

His expression was impassive when he turned to look at her. "I'm going to order dinner. What do you want?"

"It doesn't matter, Bart."

She was hungry, but eating wasn't a priority when she had to make sense of the turn her life had taken. Bart knew she loved him; her dilemma wasn't their love for each other, but if she married him did she want to have a child with a man eighteen years her senior.

Retrieving her cell phone from her purse, she went into the bathroom and locked the door behind her. The magnificent marble bathroom was designed for hotel guests to spend hours there. And the full bathroom was designed with a powder room. It was apparent Bart had spared no expense in booking the beautiful suite that was larger than many Manhattan apartments.

She turned on the faucets in the large bathtub, adding a capful of scented bath oil; she sat on a padded vanity bench and dialed her parents' number as she waited for the tub to fill. It was almost ten o'clock in Paris, which meant it was four in the afternoon in the States.

"Hello."

Faye sighed audibly when she heard Shirley's voice. "Hi, Mama. I'm calling to let you know we arrived safely." She'd lowered her voice to just above a whisper.

"That's good to hear. But why aren't you using the hotel phone? The charges to your cell phone are going to be outrageous."

"Mama, I didn't call you to discuss money."

"What's the matter, Faye Anne?"

She told her mother about her conversation with Bart, leaving nothing out.

"I told you to be careful, baby. The first time I saw you and Bartholomew together I knew he was more than a friend. I know you didn't call me to hear 'I told you so.'"

"No, I didn't," Faye countered.

"You love the man and he loves you. What's the problem, Faye Anne? You're both single and consenting adults, so what's stopping you from marrying him?"

"I want a baby."

"Is he sterile?"

"Um—I don't believe he is." Faye assumed Bart was capable of fathering children because he'd always used a condom to protect her before she opted to take the Pill.

"He asked you to marry him yet he hasn't talked about children?"

"He can't talk about children when I haven't accepted his proposal," she said in Bart's defense.

"Why did you really call me, Faye Anne? What's stopping you from marrying the man you love?"

"Bart is eighteen years older than I am, Mama. If we have children, what are the odds that he'll live to see them to adulthood?"

"You didn't talk this way before you married Norman. You married him believing you'd be together for the rest of your life. It didn't happen because no one can predict the future. I don't know what it is about Bartholomew but he's changed you. I realized that the weekend we stayed at his house. You're more relaxed, softer. Even your daddy noticed it.

"Life is hard, baby girl. Life can be ugly, but you're so focused on being a strong black woman that you refuse to see the happiness that's right in front of you. You've met someone who loves you, someone who wants to take care of you. And no matter what women say about being able to take care of themselves, they still need male protection."

Faye swallowed the lump forming in her throat. "I know you're right, but I'm frightened, Mama."

"No, you're not. It's your brother who's frightened, frightened every single day he has to wake up in that concrete cage. So, pull it together and stop acting like a girl. You're a woman, Faye Anne. Act like one!"

"Mama!"

"Goodbye!"

"Mama, don't..." Her mother had hung up on her. "Dammit!" she screamed.

"Faye. Is everything all right in there?"

She groaned. It was apparent Bart had heard her. "Yes."

"Why is the door locked?"

"I'm doing my business," she lied. When, she asked herself, had she become such an accomplished liar? "I'll be out as soon as I finish taking a bath."

There was a beat of silence. "Okay."

Faye opened her eyes to near darkness. The bedroom would've been completely dark but Bart hadn't drawn the drapes. She'd dozed off twice, only to be awakened by his tossing and turning. They'd eaten a sumptuous dinner on the terrace in total silence. Not even the romantic views of the city's most famous monuments could dispel the chill between them. They'd come to one of the most romantic cities in the world yet were reacting to each other like strangers.

She'd wanted to tell him that she loved him, loved him enough to marry him and become the mother of his children, but the words were locked away in the back of her throat.

Turning over, she pressed her chest to his back. "Darling?"

Bart heard the endearment and clenched his jaw. What he'd feared was manifested. He'd bared his soul, confessed his love, offered to share his life, and the woman who had become his obsession continued to view him as her client.

"Yes."

"Do you want children?" Faye felt him suck in his breath before exhaling.

"Where is this coming from, Faye?"

"I need to know if you want to become a father at fifty, because I want children."

Bart turned over to face Faye, his heart pounding a runaway rhythm. "What if we begin with one, and if I'm not too old and broken down to run after the little tyke, then we can have a few more?"

A cry of relief slipped past Faye's parted lips as she moved over Bart like a lithe cat, straddling him. There was enough light coming through the parted drapes to make out his eyes.

"Ask me again," she whispered.

Bart feigned innocence. "Ask you what?"

Her hand moved down his hip, searching between his thighs until her fingers closed around his penis. She stroked him, smiling when he grew hard against her palm.

"I don't think you want to mess with me. Not when I hold your future generation in my hand." She dug her fingernails into the sensitive underside.

Gasping and then shuddering, Bart gritted his teeth against the exquisite erotic torture as Faye alternated stroking him while applying pressure with her nails. It wasn't enough to cause him pain, but he doubted whether he could take much more before ejaculating.

"Will you marry me, Faye Anne Ogden?" he asked in a voice that sounded as if he were being strangled. She released his penis and joined their bodies. Bart's groan matched her long, lingering sigh of pleasure.

Cradling her hips, he closed his eyes and let his senses

take over. It was the first time Faye had assumed the dominant role and position in bed, and he loved it. And if this was what he had to look forward to with her as his wife then he prayed for a long and healthy life.

Bracing her hands on Bart's shoulders, Faye lowered herself until bare chest met bare chest. Love, passion and desire heated the blood throughout her chest and down to the area between her legs. Her body melted against his as she quickened the pace. She moved faster and faster, up and down, and around and around until their bodies were in perfect and exquisite harmony with one another.

She'd fallen in love with Bart when she hadn't wanted to. She trusted him when she'd told herself that she would never trust another man. And her body told him without words that she would marry him and become the mother of the children they hoped to share.

Faye's lips traced a sensuous path from his ear down the column of his strong neck, the hollow of his throat and up to his mouth. Her tongue slipped into his mouth, meeting his tongue in a duel for domination and surrender.

Bart's hands were as busy as his mouth. They traced the indentation where her waist curved inward before flaring out to her hips. His fingers traced the opening separating her buttocks and it'd become flesh against flesh, man against woman.

In that instant he realized he truly loved Faye. He loved everything that made her who she was: her coloring, golden brown eyes, full, lush lips, compact petite body, her soft curly hair and her tiny feet. He loved her strength and the vulnerability that made him want to protect her regardless of the consequences. He loved her passion and her femininity, a delicate, tantalizing femininity that enhanced his maleness.

Faye breathed in deep, shuddering drafts of air as she felt the soft flutters grow stronger until she was mindless with the gusts of desire that made it difficult to know where she began and Bart ended. Passion radiated from her core, and she surrendered to the ecstasy hurtling her beyond herself; he tightened his hold on her hips and met hers in a powerful thrusting that left both groaning and trembling when they yielded to what had become a raw act of possession.

She lay atop Bart, her pounding heart keeping time with his. Talking with her mother had given her a new sense of objectivity. She had the freedom to make choices about her life where her brother didn't. The man in whose arms she lay wanted her and he would have her.

Smiling, she nuzzled his neck. "Yes, Bartholomew Houghton," she said softly. "Yes, I will marry you, but on one condition."

"What's that?"

"I cannot continue to take money from you as a social companion. Once we return to the States, I'm leaving P.S., Inc."

"Don't worry about money, darling. I'll give you whatever you'll need."

"I don't need anything right now."

Bart's fingertips made little circles over her back. "I'll

get you a credit card while we're here, and once we're back in the States I'll set up an account for you. Do you have a favorite department store or boutique?"

"Why are we talking about money?"

"Because it was you who brought up the subject, Faye."

"Can't we talk about something else?"

"Sure. When do you want to get married?"

"Valentine's Day."

"You want to wait that long?"

"It's not long, Bart. By the time we marry we'll have known each other at least nine months."

"I suppose you'd want to wait another nine months before we start a family."

"No. I'll come off the Pill in October. We can start trying then. I assume you're going to want a son so that he can take over your company."

Reversing their positions, Bart withdrew from Faye and settled her over his chest, her legs resting between his. "No. If we have a son, I want him to be whatever he wants to be. It's not about setting up a dynasty so my children can takeover DHG. Personally, I'd rather they become teachers or social workers where they can affect change and touch lives."

"You don't like being a builder?"

"It's not about liking, darling. It's about what I do well, and right now I'm at the top of my game. I much prefer designing buildings."

"Maybe you'll be able to do that again."

I know I will, Bart mused. He'd left Hakim Wheeler

with the responsibility of running DHG until he returned because he was grooming the talented urban planner to take his place when he went into semiretirement.

At sixty he wanted to design homes and office buildings, make love with his wife, travel extensively and protect and love their children. He would do all of the things he should've experienced in his thirties and forties. However, he'd been given a second chance at love, and he planned to make the most of it.

CHAPTER 89

Faye and Bart spent their first full day in Paris at the hotel. Despite sleeping on the transatlantic flight, they hadn't fully recovered from jet lag. They slept late, ate brunch on the terrace with the Arc de Triomphe and Parisian rooftops as a backdrop; dinner was in the hotel's restaurant, Le Cinq. The only competition for the three Michelin-star cuisine and intuitive service were the views of the courtyard.

The next day a courier delivered a package to Bart as they prepared for a walking tour of Paris. He signed for the package, then handed Faye an envelope. She opened it, stunned to find a black-colored American Express card, also known as the Centurion Card.

Bart offered her a pen. "Sign it, darling." He watched as she scrawled her signature over the magnetic strip.

Faye returned the pen. "Are you going to give me a spending limit?"

He frowned. "Do you get a thrill out of pushing my buttons?"

Her frown matched his. "What are you talking about?"

"If I intended to give you a spending limit I would've

said so beforehand. Use the card to buy whatever you want or need." There was a steely edge to his voice.

Faye wanted to push another button and ask him about a prenuptial, but decided not to broach the subject. If Bart wanted her to sign a prenuptial agreement he would've mentioned it. And when she exchanged vows with Bartholomew Houghton she wanted it to be the last time she married.

She slipped the card into a compartment of her shoulder bag and zipped it. "I'm ready."

Reaching for her hand, Bart led her out of the suite toward the elevator. He'd planned a one-day tour that included visiting the Jardin des Tuileries, Musée d'Orsay, Notre Dame de Paris and after dinner riding a *bateau mouche* at Pont Neuf. Tomorrow they would leave Paris for Marseille. He'd reserved a car and driver to take them south, where they would board a yacht for Monaco and Saint-Tropez.

Dressed casually for the warm weather and wearing comfortable footwear, Bart and Faye walked centuries-old streets, stopping and peering into the windows of various shops they passed on their way to the places of interest they'd decided upon beforehand.

"How often do you come to Paris?" Faye asked Bart when he led her to the Metro. He'd disclosed that he learned French at his prep school, and had excelled so much that he'd become president of the French club for three consecutive years. He also admitted to watching French-language films to keep himself fluent.

He shielded her body from the crowd of tourists filing into the car. "I come here once or twice every couple of years."

"Business or personal?" she asked, staring up at his sunglass-shielded eyes.

"It's always for business. This is the first time it's personal." A hint of a smile played at the corners of his mouth.

Bart found himself experiencing things with Faye he hadn't shared with any other woman, and that included Deidre.

His smile vanished, replaced with an expression of uncertainty. He knew he had to tell Faye about Deidre, but he didn't want to spoil his vacation with the revelation he was certain would put their newly formed commitment at risk. However, he'd wait, wait until they returned to the States to tell Faye about his late wife and thereby putting whatever they'd shared to rest—forever.

Faye tightened her hold on Bart's hand when they exited the Metro at Concorde and she spied several of her favorite shops. "I want to buy my mother and friend a little something from Chanel and Hermès."

Bart stopped Faye. She wanted to purchase gifts for family and friends while he'd neglected to give her his own gift. "Hermès and Chanel can wait. I need to buy you something."

Her eyebrows lifted. "What?"

"You'll see," he said cryptically. Her query was answered the moment he escorted her to the entrance to one of the most famous jewelers in the world—Cartier.

Faye sat on a petit-point love seat with Bart as he explained to the sales associate what he wanted to see.

She responded like an automaton when the woman measured the third finger of her left hand.

Leaning closer, Bart pressed his shoulder to hers. "What cut of diamond do you like?"

"I don't know," she whispered. "Why didn't you tell me that you were going to give me a ring?"

Bart removed his sunglasses, giving her a lingering look. "To be honest, I hadn't thought of it until now."

An expression of amusement softened Faye's gaze. "What else are you planning?"

He angled his head and smiled. "Why are you always so curious, my love? Just relax and let me surprise you."

Lowering her gaze, Faye stared at Bart through her lashes. "Okay," she said softly. "You've got a deal. No more questions."

Leaning closer, Bart pressed a kiss to her hair. *"Merci."*

It took more than an hour for Faye to reach her decision as to her engagement ring. She'd chosen a spectacular radiant-cut canary yellow diamond framed with flawless white diamonds set in platinum and eighteen-carat yellow gold. The sales associate complimented Faye on her exquisite taste as she handed Bart his receipt for what had become a very profitable morning for her.

Moving off her chair, Faye looped her arms around Bart's neck and kissed him. "Thank you. I love the ring, I love you."

He returned the kiss with a passion summoned from a

place he didn't know existed, a place so foreign to him that it was frightening. "I love your life," he whispered close to her ear.

Smiling, Faye cradled his face between her hands. "After shopping I'd like to go back to the hotel and celebrate."

Faye's suggestion shocked Bart. He'd thought she wanted to do some sightseeing. "What about touring the city?"

"We can do that during our honeymoon."

"You want to honeymoon in France?"

She nodded. "What did you have in mind?"

"Because we're getting married in February I thought you'd want to go somewhere warm. I've been thinking about Tahiti."

Faye nodded again, wrinkled her nose, then gave him an enchanting smile. "We can always come back here next summer."

"We will, but only if you're not pregnant. I don't want to do anything that will put you or our baby at risk." Anchoring a hand under her elbow, Bart eased Faye from the chair. She felt and smelled so good that he wanted to make love with her right there. "Let's finish shopping, because I'm looking forward to celebrating our engagement."

He escorted his fiancée out of the store and hailed a taxi. It was the first time in a very long time that he experienced a sense of fulfillment, fulfillment as a man.

CHAPTER 90

Enid opened her cloth-covered diary, uncapped her pen and wrote the date: *August 20—Everything is ready for tonight. I can't believe that it's four months to the day when I hosted the soiree introducing my three exotic jewels.*

Although I have lost two—Alana Gardner informed me last week that she was leaving at the end of the month— I am taking the news well because I just added six more jewels to the roster of P.S., Inc. social companions.

The six young women are as intelligent and as exquisite as Faye, Alana and Ilene. They all passed the background check and this time Astrid led the orientation session. I told Marcus that it's time I begin grooming Astrid to take over Pleasure Seekers. The transition will be gradual, probably about five years, but there is no doubt she can run the business as well as I can.

I made my goal of five million. Unfortunately, I had to lean on a few clients and issue gentle reminders to others that they were contributing to a worthy cause. The only holdout was Representative Nolan who had to be reminded of his predilection for having social companions dress up like young boys and crawl on all fours while he masturbated. Once I received his check I told Richard Nolan that I was terminating his membership, and then informed Victor Payton to destroy all evidence of the politician's association with P.S., Inc.

I am looking forward to marrying Marcus, and there are times when I feel like twenty-six instead of fifty-six. I still find it hard to fathom why a thirty-four-year-old man would want to marry a woman more than twenty years his senior, but I have stopped asking myself why because I love the hell out of him. I suppose it helps that he is the only man who has been able to bring me to climax. So, if I am marrying Marcus for sex, then so be it. Women have married for lesser reasons. What helps is that I am in love with him. If I had met Marcus thirty years ago I know I would have adopted several children, children who would have made me a grandmother.

Even though I've never had a child I think of my exotic jewels as my daughters. I want the best for them. Too often women of color are regarded as sex objects who are used and abused before they are tossed aside. I am going to make certain that they are compensated for their beauty and stimulating conversation.

There is no doubt they will do well because I established Pleasure Seekers to empower women; that raison d'être will be in full effect tonight. My only regret is that Ilene will not attend, because I want her to see herself as a role model for the incoming jewels. However, Alana Gardner will make me proud that I, as a woman of color, am also an exotic jewel.

CHAPTER 91

Alana placed her hand on the driver's outstretched palm, permitting him to assist her from the car. "Thank you."

He nodded, successfully averting his gaze from her revealing bodice. "You're welcome, Ms. Gardner."

Glancing around, she silently admired the magnificence of the North Shore Long Island mansion where Enid Richards was hosting what she'd billed as her end-of-the-summer fund-raiser.

Derrick Warren had called and asked if she was attending, and if she was, then he wanted to escort her, but Alana declined his offer; however, she'd agreed to accompany him back to Manhattan.

A smile parted her generously curved lips as she spied Derrick standing at the end of the driveway.

Extending his hands, he closed the distance between them and pulled her into a close embrace. "Damn, you're gorgeous."

Alana kissed his cheek. "Thank you, Derrick." Looping her arm over the sleeve of his suit jacket, she rested her head on his shoulder. "How's the party?"

Derrick gave her a sidelong glance. "Boring as hell until you got here."

The sounds of laughter, the babble of male and female voices, and the music from a live band playing a catchy upbeat Latin rhythm greeted Alana as Derrick led her to an open area covered by an enormous gazebo. Thousands of tiny white bulbs illuminated the space in a soft, flattering glow that reflected off the precious gems shimmering in earlobes, around throats, wrists and fingers.

She caught a glimpse of Enid in an exquisite white wrap dress with a black-and-white-pinstriped obi sash. She held a glass of champagne in her right hand while the other clung to the arm of Marcus Hampton. Alana recalled Faye's reference to his being Enid's boy toy. Boy toy or not, they presented an incredibly attractive couple.

A passing waiter, cradling a tray of glasses filled with a pale bubbly liquid on his fingertips, stopped in front of Derrick and Alana. "Would you like a glass of champagne?" They both declined.

Derrick let go of her hand and wrapped an arm around her waist. "How are you feeling?"

"Very well. So far I haven't experienced any nausea." What she didn't tell Derrick was that her breasts were so sensitive, she couldn't stand to touch them. Having the water from a shower on her nipples was akin to torture of an erotic nature.

He directed her to a portable bar. "What are you drinking?"

"Water."

"Bubbly or flat?"

She smiled at the record mogul. "Flat, please."

Derrick was everything Calvin wasn't or couldn't be. He always offered her a choice. It hadn't mattered whether it was a beverage, food, activity or destination. If only he were straight, she mused, then he would've been perfect for her.

Alana had asked herself over and over how important sex was in a relationship, and the answer always was: very important. In fact, it was the substance that cemented any relationship—at least for her. However, she'd known women who admitted they were lucky if they made love with their husbands or boyfriends once a week, yet they stayed with them out of love.

Alana had fallen in love with Calvin, but look where it'd gotten her. Although he never refused her sexual overtures, their relationship had ended with "out of sight, out of mind." He loved her when she was taking care of all his needs, and quickly forgot her when someone else replaced her as his provider.

Her slow, seething anger had erupted into rage during their separation once she realized that Calvin McNair had pimped the hell out of her. And she couldn't say that Faye hadn't warned her.

Well, the Alana Elizabeth Gardner who Calvin knew had died—never to be resurrected. It had taken her thirty-three years, but she now saw herself as a woman mature enough to take care of herself, a woman who looked forward to becoming a mother—with or without a man.

She'd achieved financial independence, so she could afford to stay home with her child for the first four years of its life; she'd resumed working on her manuscript; and she'd arranged for a certified health-care professional to see to the needs of her mother for around-the-clock care. Once she moved back to New Paltz, she would reassess Melanie Gardner's health-care needs.

"Alana, are you sure you're all right?"

Derrick's voice broke into her reverie. She blinked once. "Yes. I'm sorry, but my mind was elsewhere."

Smiling, Derrick handed her a goblet of water. "I hope I was a part of your thoughts."

She returned his smile. "As a matter of fact you were."

"Good or bad?"

"Good," she admitted. "Very good, Derrick."

He accepted a glass of club soda from the bartender. "Does this mean there is hope for us to become a couple?"

Alana took a sip of her chilled water, staring at Derrick over the rim of the glass. She lowered the glass, her gaze softening with tenderness and compassion.

"I can't, Derrick. You have everything I'd ever want in a man, but..." Her words trailed off.

"But you'd need me to make love to you," he said, finishing her statement. The loose folds in his face shifted as he clenched his teeth. "I don't know why I'm drawn to men now, because it hasn't always been that way. I've slept with women in the past and liked it, yet I enjoy being with a man more. I suppose I'm the perfect example of what folks call a homo-thug. I give off the appearance of being an alpha male, but underneath I'm soft. I've always managed to maintain a low profile with women, so I haven't cultivated a persona that I'm a ladies' man. Most women take one look at my face and keep it moving. But to the ones who recognize my name, it doesn't matter what I look like because all they want is to sleep with Derrick Warren and become his baby mama. All the tit and ass shakin', and even if they put their shit on my face wouldn't get me to sleep with them."

Alana met his direct gaze. "What's so different about me, Derrick? In case you haven't noticed, I have my share of tits and ass."

Lowering his head and his gaze, Derrick stared at the thick carpet of green under his imported footwear. "I don't know what it is, Alana." His head came up. "If there was ever a woman to make me straight, then it's you."

Looping her free arm through his, she shook her head. "I'm flattered, but I can't take you up on your offer. You'll be the godfather to my son or daughter, which means we'll always remain friends. Perhaps one day, when we're both different people, we might hook up. I never thought I'd say this but I don't need a man. What I do need is a good male friend. I need you."

Derrick took a step and kissed her fragrant curly hair. "And I'll always be a friend, Alana."

Turning her head, she kissed his mouth. "Thank you."

Patting the hand tucked into the bend of his elbow, Derrick led her over to where Marcus stood with Enid.

* * *

Enid's eyebrows lifted in surprise when she saw Derrick Warren and Alana Gardner heading in her direction. Although she was pleased to see the two together, it was the presence of the other six exotic jewels that had filled her with indescribable peace. Not only were they exquisite, but intelligent and charming. And for the second time in a matter of three months her blondes and redheads found themselves taking a back seat to their peers of color. One had the audacity to complain to Astrid, who calmly told her to "step up her game."

Removing her arm from Marcus's, Enid extended a hand to Alana. "Welcome. You look wonderful."

Alana shook the slender hand, smiled. "So do you, Enid. I love your dress. Vera Wang?" she asked *sotto voce*.

Enid's pale eyebrows lifted. "Why, yes." She turned to Marcus. "Darling, you do remember Alana Gardner?"

Marcus's catlike gold eyes swept over Alana's full figure. He wanted to ask his fiancée what normal sighted man could forget the drop-dead gorgeous woman with the profusion of curls that made her look as if she'd just been made love to. A black halter dress with an Empire waistline barely skimmed her curvy body while leaving everything *and* nothing to the imagination. It just depended upon who was doing the looking.

"Of course," he said, offering her his hand. "It's nice seeing you again, Alana."

"Same here," Alana returned.

Enid recaptured her fiancé's arm. "Alana, I hope you'll

be available in late December to come to Saint Bart's to witness my wedding to Marcus."

Alana noticed the stunning emerald and diamond on Enid's left hand for the first time. "I'm unable to commit, because I'm with child."

Enid's eyes sparkled. She leaned over and kissed Alana's cheek, surprising everyone, including herself. "So, that accounts for your glow. Congratulations. When's the big day?"

"Late March or early April."

"I can understand your reluctance to travel, but you must let me know what you have because I'd like to send you something for the baby." What Enid was dying to ask Alana was whether Derrick Warren was the father of her baby. Since she'd refused to see him again, but it now appeared that they'd reconciled.

"Why don't you get something to eat," she continued. "I'm told the food is wonderful."

Alana smiled up at Derrick. "Speaking of food, it is time for mama and baby to get their eat on."

He patted her hand. "Come sit down, and I'll serve you."

CHAPTER 92

Within an hour of arriving at the Sands Point, Long Island, mansion Alana was overcome by a wave of fatigue and couldn't keep her eyes open. When Derrick asked how she was feeling she'd said well. As long as she hadn't been plagued with losing the contents of her stomach she was well. Tender breasts, weight gain and fatigue were all preferable to nausea.

She touched Derrick's shoulder. "I'd like to leave now."

He gave her a quizzical look. "Are you all right?"

A lingering sigh escaped her. "I can't keep my eyes open."

Pushing to his feet, Derrick extended a hand, pulling her gently to her feet. He led her to the area set up for parking and found his driver sitting with three other drivers who were engaged in a raucous game of spades. He caught the man's attention. Five minutes later they were in the Bentley as the driver maneuvered onto the expressway toward New York City.

Alana came awake when the car slowed and stopped in front of her apartment building. Running her fingers through her mussed hair, she sat up straighter and smothered a yawn.

"Would you like to come up and see what you've purchased sight unseen?"

Derrick reached for Alana's fingers, squeezing them gently. "Yes." Leaning forward, he opened the panel between the back seat and the chauffeur. "I'm going upstairs with Ms. Gardner. I'll call you when I'm ready to leave."

The doorman approached the car at the same time the locks were disengaged. He opened the rear door, nodding to Derrick as he stepped onto the sidewalk. He offered Alana his hand. "Good evening, Ms. Gardner."

She smiled, nodding. "Good evening."

"Nice building," Derrick whispered in her ear as they walked into the lobby.

"It is. And I don't look forward to moving," Alana admitted as they entered the elevator.

"Why don't you stay?"

Alana closed her eyes for several seconds. When she opened them the elevator had stopped at her floor. "I can't because I'm committed to taking care of my mother." She told Derrick about her mother's medical needs as they walked the length of the hallway. She stopped at the door behind which the most important thing in her life had been represented: independence.

She unlocked the door and pushed it open. "I'm going to give you a set of keys," she said over her shoulder as she walked into the lighted entryway. She'd left on the overhead light and a floor lamp in the living room.

Derrick glanced around at the tasteful furnishings as he moved from the entryway into the living room. The dominant color of a soft apricot pink was the perfect contrast to shades of brown ranging from ecru and fawn, to mahogany. Wall-to-wall drapes were open to reveal spectacular views of Central Park.

His footfalls were muffled in the pile of a chocolate-brown and shrimp-pink area rug as he walked over to the window. Light from the windows of towering apartment buildings on the other side of the park dotted the darkened landscape.

"I would've paid you twice what you asked for a view like this," he said reverently.

Alana, having slipped out of her heels, padded barefoot across the living room to stand beside Derrick. "I wasn't out to cheat you, D. If I'd listed it with a Realtor, I probably wouldn't have gotten my price or sold it so quickly."

He gave her a soulful look. "I don't need another home, but this place is perfect if I want to stay over in the city after a heavy night of partying."

"Do you really party that much?"

Derrick smiled, the expression deepening the folds around his eyes. "More than I actually want to. I suppose it goes along with the business. Work hard and party even harder."

Reaching for his hand, Alana threaded her fingers through his. What surprised her was that his hand was as soft as hers. "How did you get into the music business?"

"Do you want to interview me?"

Alana shook her head. "No. I'm just a little curious about the man who's going to become godfather to my son or daughter."

"Do you have a couple of hours?"

"I have all night."

Derrick stared at Alana. He was only a couple of years older than she was yet felt much older. And despite her lush body and exotic face, Alana Gardner projected an innocence that made him want to take care of her as one would a child. Underneath her sophistication was a woman who loved and trusted with her heart instead of her head.

Releasing her hand, he shrugged out of his suit jacket. "I'll answer all of your questions, but first I'm going to need some coffee." He was still feeling the effects of the champagne and brandy he'd drunk the night before, a night that ended at six in the morning.

"Caffeine, decaffeinated, flavored or plain?"

Derrick stared at Alana, complete surprise on his face. "Damn, woman. I didn't know you had it like that."

"What are you talking about?"

"Most girls I know will break out the instant, and that's it."

Rising on tiptoe, Alana kissed his cheek. "That's because they are *girls,* Derrick. It's time you start dealing with a full-grown woman."

"Sure you right," he drawled.

Alana snapped her fingers. "You better recognize. Make yourself at home while I put up the coffee. Then I'm going to take this makeup off my face before I slip into something more comfortable."

"I prefer the caffeinated," he said as Alana turned on her heel and walked in the direction of her bedroom.

Derrick placed his suit jacket over the back of a tan leather club chair with a matching ottoman, then made his way over to a desk in the corner. Built-in shelves were crowded with books and sleeves packed with magazines. He scanned the titles of the books. It was apparent Alana was blessed with beauty *and* brains. Many of the titles were required reading in high school and college.

His gaze shifted from the books to a large stack of paper sitting next to a computer. He picked up the first page. It was a manuscript. Alana was writing a novel.

Derrick picked up the unbound pages and sat down on the sofa. Reaching over, he turned on the lamp sitting on a massive square of rosewood that doubled as a table and began reading. The aroma of brewing coffee filled the air as he turned page after page. He'd completed the first two chapters when Alana reappeared in a pair of cotton pajama pants and an oversize T-shirt. He glanced up at her and smiled. Her fresh-scrubbed face and the curls she'd brushed off her forehead and secured in an elastic band on top of her head served to enhance her natural beauty.

"What are you doing?" She wasn't able to conceal her annoyance.

Derrick ran a hand over his shaved head before putting the manuscript on the cushion beside him. He stood up. "I was reading your masterpiece. Is it completed?"

Some of the fight went out of Alana. She didn't know whether Derrick had referred to her novel as a masterpiece to placate her or if she truly liked what she'd written.

"You like it?"

"I love what I've read so far. Have you finished it?" he asked again.

Alana nodded slowly. "It's done. But I still have to go over it and do some line editing and probably some tightening here and there."

"From what I read I don't think you should change anything."

"That's because I rewrote the first hundred pages three times before I felt comfortable with it."

"Do you mind if I read it?"

"When?"

"Now."

"You want to read the book tonight?"

Derrick smiled. "Yes, I do."

Alana's body stiffened in shock. "I can't let you take the manuscript with you. It's my only copy."

Derrick met her gaze. "Then I'll stay here and read it."

"It will take you all night to read more than seven hundred pages."

Shrugging a shoulder under his custom-made white shirt, Derrick moved closer to Alana. Cradling her face between his hands, he dropped a kiss on the top of her head. "I have all night."

Wrapping her arms around his trim waist, Alana leaned into his warmth and strength. "I'll sit up with you for a while. Then I'm going to bed." Pulling back, she stared up at the man who unknowingly had become her friend and knight in shining armor. "The coffee's finished brewing." Hand in hand, they walked out of the living room and into the kitchen.

Derrick called his driver and informed him that he would call him the following day to let him know when to pick him up. He sat in the large eat-in kitchen with Alana, drinking coffee and telling her of his childhood. Alana cleaned up the kitchen and went to bed, while he returned to the living room to read. The hands on his watch moved slowly as he found himself pulled into a world of power, glamour and fame with larger-than-life characters that leaped off the page.

Alana had written a bestseller. And he knew a movie producer who'd been looking for something for the small screen. He'd wait until Monday before making the telephone call, a call he was certain would change her life—forever.

CHAPTER 93

Faye lay on a deck chair, her face and eyes shielded from the strong Mediterranean sun with a wide-brimmed straw hat and sunglasses. She sat on the sundeck of Bart's mega yacht that had been their floating hotel for the past two and a half weeks.

The gleaming sailing vessel, custom-built by the Burger Boat Company with steel hulls and fiberglass for speed was considered the Rolls-Royce of yachts; a crew of ten had catered to their every request. The captain, two chefs, steward, first officer, engineer, his assistant and three other crew members moved about the two-hundred-foot-long, thirty-five-foot-wide boat with a top speed of twenty knots almost sight unseen.

She felt movement and opened her eyes. Bart had come on deck, sitting down on the chair next to hers. She'd gotten up early to watch the sun come up, leaving him sleeping soundly in bed. It was to be their last full day at sea before the *Kay-Ann* docked at Marseille, where they would board a jet for the return flight to the States.

Faye offered Bart a warm smile. *"Bonjour, mon chéri."*
Bart returned her smile. He'd been tutoring Faye in

French, and he found her a quick study. *"Bonjour, mon amour. Est-ce que tu as mangé le petit-déjeuner?"*

She sat up. "Slow it down, big daddy. You know I—"

"Is that how you see me, Faye, as a father figure?" he asked, scowling and interrupting her.

Faye moved off her chair, straddled Bart's lap and looped her arms around his neck. She kissed his forehead. "No, I don't. Even though I initially had issues about your age, I've never thought of you that way."

His frown vanished. "And I've never thought of you as a daughter."

"Are you into younger women?"

"No. I've always dated women within my age group."

"What about your wife?"

Bart's expression did not change with her query. "What about her?"

"How old was she when she passed away?"

"Forty."

"How long were you married?"

"We'd just celebrated our eleventh anniversary."

"What happened, Bart?"

He'd wanted to wait to return to the States before telling Faye about Deidre but knew what he'd had with his wife had to be resolved with his fiancée's query.

"The short story is I married the boss's daughter."

Easing back, Faye gave him a long, penetrating stare. "What's the long story?"

"One of my professors at Yale got me an apprentice position with a Boston-based architectural firm. I was there for less than year before I sent my résumé to Dunn Management Sales Group because I felt stymied."

Faye moved off his lap and stretched out on her chair. "Had you given them a chance? After all, you weren't there a year."

Bart shook his head slowly. "The firm was very small and I felt at that time there wasn't much room for growth. They liked my designs but weren't so enthused that they used them. Most times I assisted on projects with other more experienced architects.

"Whenever I read architectural or design magazines, the name Edmund Dunn captured my attention. Believing I had nothing to lose, I forwarded my résumé and one of my drawings to his company. A week later I got a phone call from the boss himself. He sent his personal driver from New York to pick me up, and as they say, the rest is history.

"I was hired on the spot, given an outrageous salary, and three weeks after I'd come face-to-face with the infamous Edmund Dunn I moved into an apartment in one of his buildings. He'd asked me what I wanted and I told him that I wanted to go to Columbia's School of Business. He made it happen with one telephone call.

"I worked hard, Faye, attending classes and working long hours for Edmund Dunn. It didn't take me long to realize the man was a tyrant and somewhat of a Svengali. Once he did anything for you he owned you body and soul. If he set aside an apartment in one of his buildings for a judge's son or the police commissioner's daughter, then they owed him. And whenever he called in a favor they acquiesced. It wasn't until after I'd married his daughter that I became privy to his under-the-table deals.

"He thought nothing of sending his goons after the elderly to frighten them so much that they were afraid to stay in their rent-controlled apartments. Once the building was vacant, he razed it and put up high-rise co-ops."

Bart was unable to ignore what he thought was a reproachful look from Faye. He'd seen the look and overheard the whispered insinuations whenever he'd disclosed that he'd married the boss's daughter.

"You'd become family, so why would he not trust you? How did you meet his daughter?"

"Edmund hosted a party for me at his summer place along the Jersey shore when I graduated from Columbia, and I met Deidre for the first time. She'd been raised by her maternal grandmother who'd become her guardian the year Deidre celebrated her eighth birthday."

"What happened to her mother?"

"She died in an automobile accident. To say Deidre was spoiled was an understatement. Whatever she wanted she got."

"And she wanted you."

Bart stared up at the cloudless sky. "Yes."

Faye's gaze narrowed as she removed her sunglasses. "Did you want her?"

He lowered his head, meeting her quizzical stare. "At first I tried to stay as far away from Deidre Dunn as I could because she was the daughter of the man who not only signed my paycheck, but at that time held my future within his grasp. A few of my designs had won several awards and I later discovered Edmund had been a major player in those final decisions.

"My relationship with Deidre began with invitations to dinner and segued to spending time at her family's summer home. Once I let down my guard I found out that she wasn't a snob. She had a wicked sense of humor that I found charming and refreshing. Once we began dating seriously I discovered that she was a frightened, insecure young woman who was always seeking approval. If it wasn't from her father, then it was from her peers. A week after her grandmother passed away I proposed marriage because she'd cried nonstop about not wanting to be alone. Edmund wasn't what one would call a hands-on father. There were times when I believe he even forgot that he had a child."

"Were you in love with her, Bart?"

There was a beat of silence before he said, "Not when I married her. But within the first six months of our marriage I couldn't remember when I hadn't. We decided not to wait to start a family and the day Deidre told me she was pregnant was the happiest day of my life. Three months later, she'd miscarried.

"We waited two years and tried again. This time she made it past the first trimester before she lost our second child. The doctor cautioned Deidre about trying again, but she refused to listen.

"She begged me to try one more time, promising to stay

in bed for the duration of her pregnancy. I gave in and it happened again. She'd suffered three miscarriages in nine years, and with each one she'd become more mentally unstable. I thought about a vasectomy, but before I could schedule the procedure, Deidre told me she was pregnant again. She'd waited until she was three months along before telling me."

Bart closed his eyes. "I lost it, Faye. I went off on my wife for the first time in eleven years. I told her that she was thoughtless and selfish because she'd been willing to risk her life and our future together to bring a child into the world when there were thousands of children waiting for adoption." He opened his eyes. "I told her that I'd planned to have a vasectomy and she threw a tantrum. She told me that she hated me and ordered me to get out."

"Did you?"

He nodded. "Whenever Deidre became hysterical it was impossible to reason with her."

Faye lifted her eyebrows. "It wasn't her first tantrum?"

A wry smiled parted Bart's lips. "No. I packed a bag and checked in to a hotel."

"What did your father-in-law say?"

"I never involved Edmund in my marriage. He'd made me an equal partner and Dunn Management Sales Group became the Dunn-Houghton Group. I'd been out of the apartment two days when the housekeeper called to tell me that she'd found Deidre in the bathroom, hemorrhaging. I got to the hospital minutes after she'd been taken into surgery. Her doctor informed me that she'd undergone a hysterectomy because they couldn't stop the bleeding.

"She lapsed into a deep depression when she realized she would never have children, and I took her to Oahu because we'd honeymooned there. Two days after we returned to the mainland, Deidre swallowed a bottle of painkillers. By the time I found her, her heart had stopped. The EMTs were able to revive her, and she was placed on a respirator.

"I had her examined by one of the country's leading neurosurgeons and his prognosis was that she'd suffered irreversible brain damage. Legally she was brain dead."

Leaning over, Faye rested her hand on Bart's fisted one. "How long was she on the respirator before she died?"

His fist tightened as he exhaled a long sigh. "She's still on the respirator."

Faye placed a hand over her mouth. Eyes wild, she stared at him, unable to believe he'd planned to marry her when he still had a wife. A wife who was alive!

"You lying bastard! How can you ask me to marry you when you're still married?" She jumped up as if propelled by a powerful force.

Bart stood up, seemingly in slow motion, and caught her upper arm. "Come with me, Faye."

She tried pulling away, but he'd tightened his hold. "Where? In case you haven't noticed we're in the middle of the ocean."

Lowering his head and his voice, he said quietly, "I don't want to fight with you. Not here."

"Why?" she spat out. "You don't want your crew to think ill of their boss?"

The blood darkened Bart's face under his deep tan, making his eyes appear lighter than they actually were. "I really don't give a *fuck* what they think of me," he ground out between his teeth.

Faye was stunned. The curse had slipped off his tongue as naturally as taking a breath. She'd forgotten that under the tailored clothes and acquired refinement Bartholomew Houghton had clawed and scratched his way out of poverty to change his life. And that he could revert to his humble beginnings in the blink of an eye.

"Okay," she conceded. "Downstairs." It was her turn to talk between her teeth.

CHAPTER 94

Faye followed Bart down the narrow staircase to their stateroom. The door stood open and a crew member busied herself making the bed. The woman glanced up, meeting Bart's thunderous gaze.

"Out!" She put down the pillow and rushed out of the stateroom, closing the door behind her.

Resting her hands on her hips, Faye glared at the man to whom she'd pledged her future. "Not only are you duplicitous but you're also a bully."

Bart threw up a hand. "Don't start, Faye. Please don't start a war you have no chance of winning."

Her temper exploded. "Is this how it's going to be once we're married? You give the orders and I lockstep and salute you!"

He took two long steps, reaching out and pulling her to his chest. "No! That's not the way it's going to be," he countered, his voice considerably softer, almost conciliatory. "All I want is for you to hear me out. Please, baby."

Faye bit down on her lower lip to still its trembling. She wanted to hate Bart but she couldn't. Not when she'd fought her feelings the moment she turned to face the man who'd arrogantly ordered a drink for her. Not when he'd provided her with the means to appeal her brother's conviction. Not when he'd intervened to protect her position with BP&O. And not when his gentleness, generosity, patience, passion and humility helped her overcome her biases about his race.

"Do you have any idea what you've done to me? You used me, Bart. You made me fall in love with you when I didn't want to, and you made me trust you when I swore never to trust another man."

Bart steered her over to the bed, sitting, and pulling her down with him. "Please don't give up on me. Not until you hear what I have to say."

She heard the pain in his voice, saw it in his eyes. The seconds ticked off as they regarded each other warily. "Okay, Bart. I'll listen."

Bart sucked in a lungful of breath before releasing it slowly. "It was my fault, Faye. My fault that she got pregnant so many times, my fault that I didn't listen to her doctor when he told me that Deidre would never carry a baby to term, and it was my fault that I delayed going through with the vasectomy. I could've had the procedure, not told her and pretended that she couldn't get pregnant again because she'd lost too many babies. I could've and would've lied to her if it meant saving her life.

"I should've seen the signs that she was losing her grip on reality, but I was too wrapped up in my own egotistical shit to make the Dunn-Houghton Group number one. Day in and day out I told myself that one false slip and I'd be back at the trailer park, son of the mop jockey and a factory worker, the nephew of uncles who preferred three hots and a cot in a six-by-eight cell to getting a real job.

"So if I've kept a woman hooked up to a machine because I'm too much of a coward to let her go, then blame me. And if I'm going against her written wishes not to resuscitate if anything ever happened to her, then blame me for that, too. Blame me, Faye! Blame me for falling in love with you, for asking you to trust me when I don't deserve your trust."

Faye felt a fist of pity squeeze her heart when she saw the tears in his eyes. Collapsing against his chest, her arms went around his neck. "Bart." His name was torn from the back of her throat.

"Forgive me, forgive me, baby," he chanted over and over.

"There's nothing to forgive. Nothing," she whispered. "I love you, Bart. I fell in love with you when I didn't want to. I fell in love with you even though I knew it wasn't the best thing for me to do. I kept asking myself how could something that was so wrong feel so right?"

"I wanted to tell you, Faye. I swear I wanted to tell you."

She placed her fingers over his mouth. "Don't swear."

Grasping her wrist, Bart pulled her hand down. "The moment I knew I wanted to marry you I realized I had to let Deidre go. It's time I honor her wish not to keep her alive with tubes and machines." Tears streamed down his face.

Faye closed her eyes, unable to watch him cry. "Where is she, Bart?"

"I had her transferred to a small private facility not far from where I grew up. Once we get back I'll sign the order to disconnect her feeding tube. But I'm going to need your help. I can't do this alone."

Faye realized Bart would have to grieve twice—once when Deidre Houghton was declared brain dead and a second time when he disconnected the machine that had kept her heart beating.

She buried her face against the side of his neck. "I'll wait for you."

Bart nodded. He needed to hear that Faye would be there for him. He'd asked himself many times why he hadn't given the order to take Deidre off the respirator and disconnect the feeding tube but knew it was because of guilt, guilt that he hadn't listened to the doctor, that he hadn't followed through on the sterilization procedure, and guilt because he knew if he hadn't married Deidre Dunn he would've never become CEO of the Dunn-Houghton Group.

"Thank you."

They held each other, offering comfort, understanding, then as if on cue they left their stateroom to go back up on deck.

CHAPTER 95

Alana waited in the doorway, watching Faye as she made her way down the hall. With her approach she had to admit that she'd never seen her friend look better. Vacationing with Bartholomew Houghton definitely had a positive effect on her friend. She wore a stylish three-quarter swing raincoat over a white blouse and dark tailored slacks. It'd been raining continuously for five days, but meteorologists were predicting the weather would be warm and sunny for the upcoming Labor Day holiday weekend.

Faye had left a voice-mail message the day before informing her that she was back in the States and wanted to meet her for dinner. She'd offered to cook because her bouts of fatigue had increased and there were times when she'd nodded off at the most inopportune times.

"Hey, girlfriend, welcome home," she crooned, wrapping an arm around Faye's neck.

Faye kissed her cheek. "It's good to be home." She handed Alana a small shopping bag emblazoned with the Louis Vuitton logo. "Here's a little something for you." Walking into the entryway, she left her umbrella in a large wastebasket and hung her raincoat on a coat tree.

Alana's jaw dropped slightly. "Oh, damn! You bought me something from Louis. What is it?"

"Open it, Lana."

"Let's sit in the living room."

The two women navigated the maze of boxes lined up against the walls and those stacked in corners. Seeing the boxes had become a reality check for Faye. Her friend was really leaving the Big Apple for upstate New York.

She sat down on the sofa while Alana took an armchair with a footstool. It'd only been three weeks, but her friend had changed. Her face was fuller and she was gaining weight. The overall effect was an incredible lushness that only served to enhance Alana Gardner's exotic beauty.

Alana removed a small mini-monogrammed canvas trunk from the bag and opened it to reveal a yellow-gold charm bracelet with a red-gold Big Apple charm. Her lashes fluttered as she attempted to blink back tears. The bracelet was designed with a gold LV padlock accompanied by two little keys.

"Oh, Faye..." She couldn't get the words out to thank her friend for the extravagant gift.

"Between you and Derrick I've become a bling-and-Louis diva."

Smiling, Faye lifted her right hand and pulled a matching bracelet with an Eiffel Tower charm from under the cuff of her blouse. The charm dazzled with the light of nineteen diamonds that represented the illuminations for the new millennium.

"Compliments of Bartholomew Houghton," she said proudly.

Alana noticed the sparkle of diamonds on Faye's left hand for the first time. Moving off the chair, she sat down on her friend's left and picked up her hand. "Is this what I think it is?"

Grinning like a Cheshire cat, Faye nodded. "Yes." Alana hugged her so tight that she found it hard to breathe. "You're crushing my ribs, Lana."

"Sorry about that." Alana angled her head, shaking it slowly. "When's the big day?"

"Valentine's Day."

"Are you having a big wedding?"

"No. We decided just family and close friends."

"Where are you getting married?"

"Bart said he wanted the Cloisters. He's on the board of the Met."

"What do you want?"

"City hall."

Alana waved a hand. "You're full of shit. You can't marry a man like Bartholomew Houghton at city hall."

"Why not, Lana? When I married Norman I had the whole nine yards and it was over before I got used to signing my signature with my married name. This time I want something very simple."

Alana stared at Faye, unable to believe she was actually that naive. "Once you become Mrs. Bartholomew Houghton nothing in your life will ever be simple again. Doors will open for you sight unseen. You can't go back to being Faye Anne Ogden from Springfield Gardens, Queens. Girls from around the way don't give friends souvenirs that cost ten grand."

Faye frowned. "I hope I'm not going to have to get into it with you when I buy my godson or goddaughter a gift."

"No," Alana said honestly, "because then I'd have to get into it with Derrick Warren." She smiled as she rested her hand over her belly. "With you and Derrick as godparents, this child probably won't want for anything."

"I'm sure of that."

"Speaking of babies," Alana continued, "do you plan to have any with Bart?"

"Yes. I told him I wanted at least one."

"You can't have just one."

"Why not?"

Alana rolled her eyes at Faye. "Get real, girlfriend. A rich only child is not the way to go. Have at least two. But on the other hand, if I were you I'd have a baseball team."

"Do you realize how old Bart is?"

"If Michael Douglas and Donald Trump can father children when they're breathing hard on senior-citizen status, Bart can. Shit, Faye, the man's only fifty."

"My father's in his fifties."

"And so was my dumb-ass father when he married a woman less than half his age."

"Speaking of babies, how are you feeling?"

"Except for feeling tired all the time, I'm good."

"Good enough to be my maid of honor?"

Alana stared, complete surprise freezing her expression. "Do you realize I'll be about eight months pregnant in February?"

"I know."

"And you want me there looking like a beached whale?"

"You're my girl, my sister, Lana. Of course I want you, belly and all. I'll have a doctor in attendance in case you decide to upstage my wedding and go into labor."

Alana scowled. "Bite your tongue."

Faye glanced around the number of boxes. Alana had emptied the bookcases, packed away her computer and stereo equipment. "When are you moving?"

"Wednesday. I couldn't get anyone this week because of the holiday."

She told Faye that Derrick had paid her to leave most of the furniture because he planned to use the apartment for out-of-town clients instead of covering the cost of putting them up in hotels. So the arrangement had worked out amicably for both.

"We've come a long way since the night Enid Richards slipped her business card in with our check," Alana said reflectively. "You're going to marry your Prince Charming, Ilene has the financial security she's been searching for and I'm solvent enough to take care of myself, my child and my mother for many years to come and..."

"And what?" Faye asked when Alana didn't finish her statement.

She ran a hand through the profusion of curls falling over her forehead. "I didn't want to say anything until it was official, but Derrick gave my manuscript to a movie director with his own production company and he's seriously considering optioning it for a made-for-television movie. He said it's a cross between Danielle Steel, Sidney Sheldon and Jackie Collins. I believe it's the Ilene-type supermodel character that did it."

Faye pressed her palms to her chest. "I can't believe it! You were working on this novel even before I met you."

"And I thought about it for six years before I started it two years ago."

Reaching over, she hugged Alana, mindful of her condition. "You are truly blessed, girlfriend."

Alana hugged her back. "You're right about that. Meanwhile, I thought I needed a man to make my life complete."

"Your Prince Charming is out there, Lana. He's only waiting for you to make your appearance."

"If you don't stop, you're going to have me soupin' snot." Sniffling, she pulled back and touched her fingers to the corners of her eyes. "I hope you don't mind that I ordered in. I'm trying not to buy too much food because I don't want to throw it away when I leave."

"Of course I don't mind. Speaking of food, will you come with me Sunday to my folks' for a cookout?"

"Girl, please. If your uncle's cooking, then I'll be there." The phone in the entryway rang. "That's dinner." Alana pushed to her feet and went to answer the call.

She hadn't lied to Faye when she told her that she didn't need a man to make her feel complete. It had taken her thirty-three years but she had come to like and accept who she'd become. And she felt sorry for the next man who decided he could take advantage of Alana Elizabeth Gardner, because he would be in for the fight of his life.

CHAPTER 96

Enid rose to her feet when Astrid escorted Faye Ogden into her office, taking in everything about her in one sweeping glance. From her deeply tanned face and the gold in her hair toned down to a tawny brown and the ring on her left hand. A knowing smile parted her lips. She was about to lose the last of her first trio of exotic jewels. First it was Ilene, then Alana and now Faye.

"Hello, Faye."

Faye returned her smile. "Thank you for making time for me."

Enid gestured to a love seat. "Please sit down. Can I have Astrid bring you something to drink?"

Shaking her head, Faye sat down. "No, thank you. I won't be staying long."

Enid stared at the young woman who had enchanted Bartholomew Houghton the moment he saw her. She claimed an understated sophistication women twenty years her senior couldn't perfect. And there was never a time when she hadn't met her gaze, which meant she wasn't easily intimidated.

"You're resigning," Enid stated simply.

Faye's eyebrows lifted slightly. "You know?"

"Yes. Bartholomew called to inform me that he would no longer be a client."

Faye smiled. "We're getting married in February."

Enid returned her smile. "Congratulations. May I see your ring?" Faye extended her hand. "Exquisite. You're deserving of it and so much more."

Pinpoints of heat stabbed Faye's cheeks with the unexpected compliment. "Thank you. I wanted to see you instead of calling because I want to apologize."

"What on earth for?"

"For being presumptuous when you asked me to work for P.S., Inc. When you told me it was an escort service I'd assumed you wanted me to become a prostitute."

Enid tented her fingers and the overhead caught the brilliance of the emerald and diamonds on her hand. She focused her gaze on the profusion of flowers in a crystal vase on a low table. "You weren't that far off, Faye." She ignored the younger woman's gasp. "As women we all become prostitutes at different times in our lives. And despite my rule that social companions are not to sleep with their clients, there's no way I can enforce it because everyone is a consenting adult.

"I know what prostitution is firsthand because my grandmother ran a sporting house in Storyville. She tried to shield my mother from the life that had afforded her a grand lifestyle, but in the end she failed. My mother was fourteen when she found herself pregnant with me, and had just turned fifteen when she died in childbirth.

"Grand-mère swore it would never happen to me and shipped me off to a convent where the nuns beat all salacious thoughts out of my head. It wasn't until I became a woman and had my first sexual encounter that I realized as women we prostitute ourselves, not in the traditional sense, but every time we sleep with a man because he puts out money to feed us, buy us little baubles or take us away with him. We service him because he's offered the goods."

She held up a hand when Faye opened her mouth to refute her. "I'm quite proud of how you, Alana and Ilene turned out because I've permitted you entrée into a world wherein if you do opt to sleep with a man it will be worth your time *and* effort. There's no doubt you love Bartholomew as much as he loves you, but you could've as easily fallen in love with someone where if you decide to have a baby you'd have to take a short maternity leave then put your child in day care because you wouldn't be able to make ends meet on one income.

"Too many times *our* women end up with the short end of the stick because whenever *our* men make a lot of money they seek out women outside their race. I learned this firsthand when I went to college. The brothers flocked to me because of my color not because of my brains or because I was nice. And I'm here to tell you that I've never been *that* nice, Faye."

Faye was caught off guard by the harshness in Enid's voice. "Why are you telling me this?"

"I want you to be aware of who you are and the power you wield. You had Bartholomew Houghton even before he introduced himself to you. You've done what not one of my social companions has been able to do, and that is commit to a future together. You will marry Bartholomew and give him children," she predicted quietly. "I'm proud of you, Faye. I couldn't be more proud if you were my daughter."

Faye felt a warm glow flow through her as she and Enid shared the moment. It was the first time she felt something for the older woman other than respect.

"Thank you, Enid. I'd be honored if you would attend my wedding."

"I'm afraid Bartholomew beat you to it. He asked me and I said yes. However, the two of you will receive an invitation to come to Saint Barts at the end of the year."

"What's happening there?"

"Marcus Hampton and I are tying the knot."

"No!"

"Yes," Enid confirmed as a smile light up her beautiful face and eyes.

"I saw the ring, but I didn't want to be presumptuous and ask," Faye countered. "It's magnificent."

An attractive blush suffused Enid's face. "*He's* magnificent."

"Congratulations."

"Thank you, sweetheart." Rising to her feet, she extended her arms to Faye. "Be happy."

Faye stood up and hugged Enid. "Thank you. I'll see you in Saint Barts at the end of the year."

Enid did something she'd never done before. She kissed Faye's cheek. "Good luck until we meet again."

Faye nodded, turned and walked out of the Soho loft, her face split into a smile when she realized that Enid Richards was going to marry her boy toy.

Damn, she mused. Some women have all the luck!

However, she wasn't about to sell herself short, because she'd managed to snag one of the world's richest men. And even if he hadn't had *goo-goobs* of money she would still marry him because she'd fallen in love with the man and not the real estate mogul.

Raising her hand, she hailed an oncoming taxi. She got in, gave him the address to the penthouse, then settled back to enjoy the ride uptown.

She'd waited for her family's Labor Day get-together to inform her parents that she was marrying Bartholomew Houghton. Craig Ogden, her uncle and male cousins had taken Bart somewhere in her uncle's SUV while she passed around the pictures she'd taken in Europe.

The women were more interested in the clothes she wore than the images of Venice, a city built on water, or the opulence of the Grand Casino in Monte Carlo where Bart taught her to play blackjack. She'd lost all of her money while he'd made several thousand.

She'd bought back Hermès scarves for each of her aunts, and had given her mother a Louis Vuitton treasure box that was a smaller version of their famed steamer trunk, where she could store her letters or jewelry. She'd also given Shirley a pair of diamond and sapphire earrings she'd been unable to resist when she saw them in a jewelry store in the Piazza San Marco.

When the men returned two hours later, all of them except for the designated driver were so drunk they couldn't stand upright. Faye wanted to scream at her father for getting her fiancé pissy drunk, but Alana's "let it go" and Shirley's warning look quickly doused her tirade. It had become an Ogden male tradition to get the affianced drunk so they would get him to do or say anything, but somehow Bart had successfully run the gauntlet, because he'd matched them shot for shot.

Faye drove back to Manhattan, and with Alana's help managed to get Bart into the elevator without a mishap and into bed. Alana stayed over, sleeping in the guest bedroom.

Faye couldn't stop thinking about children, and because she'd never been pregnant, she did not know whether she could get pregnant. And, unlike Deidre Houghton, if she was unable to conceive she would be content to adopt. After all, there were too many children languishing in foster care waiting for someone to love them enough to give them a permanent home.

Her eyes shimmered with a strange light when she thought about adopting a child. The idea was something she would discuss with Bart when she saw him later that night.

CHAPTER 97

For the second time in a month Bartholomew Houghton transferred the responsibility of running DHG to Hakim Wheeler. "I'm not certain how long I'll be gone," he told the urban planner.

"Are you going to be in the States, Mr. H.?"

"Yes. I doubt you'll need me, but if you do, send me a text message or e-mail my BlackBerry."

Hakim's dark eyes were serious when he stared at his boss. Bart had returned from his trip abroad tanned and relaxed, but there was an underlying tension that was evident whenever he thought he wasn't being observed. And Hakim had worked closely enough with the man to have learned something about him. There were rumors floating around the Big Apple that Bart was involved with a young black woman, and it hadn't taken the IQ of a nuclear physicist to identify that woman as Faye Ogden.

At first Hakim was somewhat put out because he'd wanted to get to know Faye better, but if Bartholomew Houghton was more to her liking then who was he to judge her? There was something about Faye he liked from the onset because she seemed different from the other women he met who seemed more interested in the gross earnings in the box of his W–2 than his character.

"Don't let Mrs. Urquhart get to you," Bart warned as he walked out of his office.

"I won't," Hakim said, chuckling under his breath.

Geraldine Urquhart wasn't at her usual position behind the massive desk when Bart entered the elevator that would take him to the first floor. For the first time in a very long time he felt the weight of his guilt for ignoring Deidre's wish not to be kept alive by artificial devices. At eight years of age she'd remembered the tubes and machines that worked around the clock to keep her mother alive, and swore she didn't want the same if something were to happen to her. Little did she know when she'd made that request that it would be a respirator and a feeding tube that would regulate her breathing and keep her alive although she'd been declared brain dead.

Giuseppe, leaning against the bumper to the Maybach, straightened and opened the rear door when he stepped out onto the sidewalk.

Bart managed a tight smile. "Thank you." He ducked his head, got into the rear of the car and closed his eyes. It would take about two hours to reach the private facility that had been home to Deidre Dunn-Houghton for the past nine years—nine long years during which he'd been too much of a coward to let go of his past.

And he had to let go of the past if he hoped to have a future with Faye. The night before, she'd mentioned adopting a child, and at first he thought she'd changed her mind about having his children. But when she talked about adopting an older child he told her he would think about it, and she warned him not to take too long because the entire process could possibly take more than a year. What his soon-to-be-wife would learn was that as Mrs. Bartholomew Houghton she wouldn't have to wait in line like those taking numbers in a deli. If you had enough money you could get people to do whatever you wanted them to do. That was something his father-in-law had taught him: everyone has a price.

For the past three weeks Faye had sat up in bed reading every night until sleep and exhaustion claimed her. But tonight was different. She wasn't going to spend another night in the penthouse.

She'd lost count of the number of times she'd picked up the telephone to call Bart but changed her mind. Now she knew how Alana felt when she'd waited for Calvin to her call from Europe. It was now day number twenty-four and she still hadn't heard from Bart.

She couldn't understand how Bart professed to love her but hadn't bothered to call her. After the first two days she thought perhaps something had happened to him but quickly dismissed that notion when she overheard Giuseppe telling Mrs. Llewellyn that Mr. Houghton would be away for some time.

Well, she fumed, whenever he came back he wouldn't find her waiting. She'd grown up hearing her aunt Faye say, 'It's a sorry-ass rat that only has one hole.' Thankfully she had someplace to go—home.

Gathering her purse, she headed for the elevator. The door opened on the first level and Giuseppe stood in front of her. "Are you going somewhere, Miss Ogden?"

She blinked once as he stepped into the elevator. "Yes. I'm going home."

"Do you wish that I drive you?"

"That won't be necessary. I can get a taxi."

"I cannot permit you to take a taxi when I can drive you."

Faye looked at Giuseppe for the first time, really looked at him, because most times she saw only the back of his head. She estimated he was somewhere in his forties. He was handsome and his body language was wholly European in nature. He wore no wedding band, so she assumed he was single. She wanted to ask the man what he did when he wasn't driving for Bart, but didn't want to cross the line. After all, he was her fiancé's employee, and when she married Bart he would also be in her employ.

"Okay, Giuseppe. You can drive me."

They took the elevator to the underground garage, where the chauffeur maneuvered the car out of its assigned space and into the warm autumn night.

Faye felt strange walking into her apartment. Since she'd had her mail forwarded to Bart's address, she only came by to wipe away the dust that collected on the tables and countertops. Unlike Alana, she hadn't planned on selling her co-op. She would, like Ilene, sublet it.

It took ten minutes to go through her closet to decide

on something to wear to work the next day. Twenty minutes later she crawled into bed, after a quick shower, and fell asleep as soon as her head touched the pillow.

CHAPTER 98

"Faye. There's someone here to see you."

Her head came up and she stared at Gina standing in the doorway to her office. "Who is it?" Gina stepped aside and Bart stood in the space where she'd been.

Faye closed her eyes and when she opened them he was still there, which meant he wasn't an apparition. When she'd returned from Europe wearing an engagement ring, everyone wanted to know who he was. But she refused to tell them that she was engaged to Bartholomew Houghton because once she married, it would be impossible to keep their union a secret.

Rising slowly to her feet, she walked from behind her desk. If it hadn't been for his silver hair and eyes she wouldn't have recognized the man with whom she'd fallen in love. He had lost weight—he could ill afford to lose. And there was no doubt he'd grieved and was still grieving.

She closed the distance between them and looped her arms under his shoulders, holding him fast. "When did you get back?" She felt his heart beating wildly in his chest.

His arms went around her waist. "Last night."

"You came back and I wasn't there to be with you. I went home."

Pressing his mouth to her forehead, Bart smiled. "I thought home was the Olympic Towers."

"It is, Bart, but only if you're there."

Faye heard someone clear his throat and she pulled back. John Reynolds stood outside her office.

"John, I'd like to introduce my fiancé, Bartholomew Houghton. Bart, this is John Reynolds."

Faye thought John was going to faint on the spot. His Adam's apple bobbed up and down in his throat and his hand was shaking when he offered it to Bart. "I'm honored to meet you, Mr. Houghton."

Bart gave him a cold stare, extending his hand. "Mr. Reynolds. I wonder if I can ask a favor of you."

"Sure. What is it?"

"Is it possible to give Faye the rest of the day off?"

"Of c-course," John stammered nervously. "She can take all the time she needs."

Leaning down, Bart brushed a kiss over Faye's mouth. "Get your things, baby."

She returned to her desk to put away several files before retrieving her handbag. She and Bart had barely walked out of BP&O when the office grapevine hummed with the news that Faye Ogden's fiancé was none other than billionaire Bartholomew Houghton.

Gina Esposito pumped her fist and shouted, "Yeah!"

Faye lay in bed with Bart, her face pressed against his shoulder. She listened, not interrupting once, when he told her that it had taken twenty-two days for Deirdre's heart to stop beating. He had stayed at her bedside around the clock, leaving only to shower and change his clothes. He hadn't remembered eating because there were days when he hadn't been able to keep food down or swallow more than a few morsels. He had her cremated, then he'd flown her remains to Oahu and scattered her ashes in the Pacific.

The tears filling Faye's eyes overflowed. "I promised you that I'd be there for you, but when I didn't hear from you I thought…"

"Stop it, Faye," Bart chided softly. "I should've called you, but I couldn't because if I'd heard your voice I wouldn't have stayed. And I stayed because I needed closure." He let out a heavy sigh. "It's done. It's over and now I can move forward. I want to marry you and have a house filled with children. I don't care where they come from as long as you're their mama."

"You know I'm going to spoil them."

"Not if I spoil them first."

She sat up. "How is that going to work when I threaten them with 'Wait until your father gets home'?"

Reaching out, Bart pulled Faye down to the pillow. "That's something you're going to have to figure out."

"I've been thinking," she said after a comfortable silence.

"What about, baby?"

"It's time I give BP&O notice that I'm leaving. Then I need to move all my personal things out of my apartment and have them moved here. Then I want to hire a real estate agent to interview folks who might want to sublet my condo. I'm also going to have to hire a wedding planner for our wedding. But before I do all that I'm going to have to take over the cooking duties from Mrs. Llewellyn and fatten up my man. What you need is some down-home country cooking to put some meat back on your bones."

Tightening his hold on her body, Bart shifted her until she lay under him. "I love your plans."

"You do?"

"Don't you know by now that I love everything about you?"

Faye felt the movement of Bart's breathing keeping rhythm with her own. "Yes," she whispered.

It was the last word she uttered because Bart showed her wordlessly how much he had come to love her. And when she rose to meet him in a moment of uncontrolled passion, she, too, told him without words how much she in turn, loved him.

CHAPTER 99

Faye and Bart spent Christmas Day with the Ogdens. Later that night they flew to Fort Lauderdale where they boarded the *Kay-Ann,* planning to spend two days at sea before docking in Gustavia Harbor on the tiny island of Saint Barts.

It was winter, the height of the tourist season, and Bart decided to use the yacht as their hotel. He'd regained most of the weight he'd lost and had unofficially shared the responsibility of running DHG with Hakim Wheeler. Most days Hakim could be found in an office created for him on the fourth floor of the town house.

As promised, Faye had given her notice and was genuinely surprised when the employees at BP&O hosted a gathering at a restaurant that served to double as an engagement party. The employees had given her gift cards for her favorite stores: Bloomingdale's, Barneys and Takashimaya. John Reynolds appeared sincere when he spoke of losing one of the best ad executives in the agency's half-century history.

She'd gotten a young couple, both doctors, to sublet her apartment, and begun working with a wedding planner for her Valentine's Day nuptials.

She had also stopped taking the Pill, and she and Bart had begun trying for a baby. Each day she didn't see her period he noted it in his day planner with a smiley face.

Bart waited on deck for Faye. The card accompanying Enid's invitation indicated casual tropical attire and in lieu of gifts donations were to be sent to Habitat for Humanity in the name of Marcus and Enid Richards-Hampton. He had to admire Enid for her tenacity, because she'd become the consummate fund-raiser.

Faye emerged, resplendent in a ruffled chiffon poet blouse in a shocking fuchsia with a flowing inky-black chiffon skirt and matching silk-covered high-heeled sandals. Her hair, now long enough to touch the tops of her ears and graze the nape of her neck, was styled to frame her flawless face. He walked forward to meet her.

"You look so incredibly beautiful."

Faye pressed her cheek to Bart's clean-shaven one. "You're biased."

"No shit," he confirmed.

She patted his shoulder. "Once we have children you're going to have to watch your language."

"No shit," he repeated.

"Bartholomew!"

"Okay, baby." He reached for her hand. "Are you ready?"

"Yes."

They left the yacht and walked a short distance where a driver waited to take them to Shell Beach, where Enid and Marcus were waiting to exchange vows.

The sun had dipped lower in the horizon by the time

they joined the other guests who'd gathered for the beach-front ceremony. It was the second time in three months that Faye had stood with Bart on a beach in the Caribbean as a wedding guest.

She and Ilene saw each other at the same time. Grinning, she beckoned to her. Lifting the hem of her dress, Ilene came over to greet her.

"I wondered whether you'd be here," Ilene said, pressing her cheek to Faye's as she gave her an air kiss.

"You look wonderful, Ilene." Her hair was braided in a single plait and festooned with tiny orchids.

Ilene held her at arm's length. "You're the one who's glowing. Are you sure you're not pregnant?" she asked *sotto voce.*

"I'm not sure," she whispered. And she wasn't. She'd stopped taking the Pill in October, had a menstrual flow in mid-November, but so far nothing in December. She'd decided to wait until after the beginning of the year before taking a pregnancy test. The possibility that she was carrying Bart's baby was frightening, but she had nine months to get used to it.

Ilene spied Faye's ring. "Hot damn, you got engaged!" Several people turned in their direction with her outburst. She ignored the curious stares. "Let me get back to my partner before the ceremony begins. We'll talk later, girlfriend."

Faye watched Ilene's departing figure as she stood next to a petite woman with a full figure and curly hair that reminded her of Alana. Enid had invited Alana to her wedding but her former exotic jewel had declined because of her advancing pregnancy.

A hush fell over the assembly as the sun sank lower on the horizon at the same time as a lone trumpeter played the distinctive chords of the wedding march.

Bart moved over to Faye, threading his fingers through hers as a barefoot Marcus Hampton in a white shirt and slacks made his way down to the beach. Minutes later, Enid, in a filmy pale pink gown, strolled down to the beach to join her fiancé and a local minister who waited to perform the ceremony.

A warm breeze filled with the scent of flowers wafted in the air as movie stars, politicians, CEOs, European royalty and two of P.S., Inc.'s three original exotic jewels watched and listened to Riva Enid Richards pledge her troth to her business partner and now her husband.

Bartholomew Houghton lowered his head to kiss Faye Ogden at the same time Laurence Marcus Hampton leaned over to his wife.

"Six weeks," Faye whispered. In another six weeks she and Bart would become husband and wife.

Bart deepened the kiss, molding her length to his. "It can't come soon enough."

They broke the kiss long enough to join the others in applauding and congratulating the new couple. Neither could have imagined when they'd walked into the Soho loft in May that their lives would inexorably change—for the better.

EPILOGUE

Two Years Later…

Enid uncapped her pen and opened her journal to a blank page. *December 28th—Today Marcus and I will celebrate our second anniversary. It has been an incredible two years filled with love, laughter and lots of passion. My husband still complains about me being controlling in bed, but he wouldn't have me any other way.*

Business is wonderful. I now have more than a dozen exotic jewels, much to the delight of my clients. Next year I will focus more on fund-raising for my favorite charities and leave much of the day-to-day operation of P.S., Inc. to Marcus and Astrid.

I got a telephone call this morning from a former client, now an appellate state judge, who is asking for my assistance. He has received word that he may be disbarred because as a former Queens County prosecutor he deliberately withheld evidence in a high-profile rape case. Evidence from the rape kit revealed DNA from not one but two men. Parker McCain suppressed this evidence, and when independent investigators questioned the victim she finally admitted she hadn't been raped but had had sex with her boyfriend and estranged husband. When her husband found out that she had been sleeping with another man he raped then beat her. She subsequently perjured herself, and an innocent man went to jail. This case would not have been of interest to me except that the innocent victim is Faye Ogden-Houghton's brother, Craig Ogden. I told Parker that I am unable to help him because Craig Odgen's attorney, Rooney "the Barracuda" Turner, has filed lawsuits against McCain and the state of New York. As a nonpracticing attorney, I know when to bow out.

I have kept up with my first three exotic jewels: Ilene Fairchild gave birth to a daughter this past summer, and when Marcus and I went to Pine Cay for vacation we found Ilene changed. She was more relaxed and appears to be enjoying motherhood.

Alana Gardner sent me an updated photograph of her son with her letter. I find him a little too beautiful for a boy. All I can say is Alana is going to have trouble in another ten years when the girls come looking for her son. She's doing very well with a bestselling novel that has been optioned by a cable network for a made-for-television movie. She said she's dating an elementary-school principal. They'd attended the same high school but were dating others at the time.

I get to see Bartholomew and Faye Houghton several times a year at social functions. Their family is growing by leaps and bounds. Their son had just celebrated his first birthday when Faye made Bart a father again at fifty-

three. He was ecstatic because he had a son and a daughter. They have also adopted two school-age boys who are brothers and are the mirror image of the male supermodel Tyson Beckford.

The Houghtons invited Marcus and me for dinner, but I believe I will wait until their daughter is out of diapers. I've never been very good around babies. The last time I held a baby on my lap he ruined my Chanel suit.

Marcus and I decided to celebrate New Year's Eve with his parents. I invited them to our place for dinner. Dining on the rooftop terrace should add a festive touch. Afterward we will open a bottle of champagne and watch the ball drop on television.

The year has been good to me because I find myself more in love with my husband. The older I get the more I realize life is about choices and chances. That is the way it has been with Pleasure Seekers.

I took a chance, made my choice and won!

A special Collector's Edition from
Essence bestselling author

KAYLA PERRIN

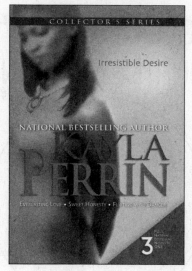

Three full-length novels

From one of the most popular authors for the Arabesque series comes this trade paperback volume containing three classic romances. Enjoy warmth, drama and mystery with EVERLASTING LOVE, SWEET HONESTY and FLIRTING WITH DANGER.

"The more [Kayla Perrin] writes, the better she gets."
—*Rawsistaz Reviewers* on *Gimme an O!*

Available the first week of January wherever books are sold.

**What if you met your future soul mate…
but were too busy living in the here and now
to give them the time of day?**

friends: a love story

ANGELA BASSETT &
COURTNEY B. VANCE

An inspiring true story told by the celebrities themselves—
Hollywood and Broadway's classiest power couple.
Living a real-life love story, these friends-who-became-lovers
share the secret of how they make it work with love,
faith and determination.

Available the first week of January wherever books are sold.

KIMANI PRESS™
www.kimanipress.com

KPABCV0580107TR